IKON
RAVIN TIJA
MAURICE

To Carolyn
Thank you for the support.
I hope you enjoy it!

Ikon Copyright 2017 by Ravin Tija Maurice

Second Edition

All rights reserved. This book or any portion thereof
may not be reproduced or used in any manner whatsoever
without the express written permission of the Author
except for the use of brief quotations in a book review.

Cover by RMGraphX

Edited by Fox Chapman

RAVIN TIJA MAURICE
IKON

ALSO BY RAVIN TIJA MAURICE

THE AFFLICTED SERIES
R EBIRTH

P ROPHECY G IRL

For Michael - with love.

"The promise given was a necessity of the past,
the word broken is a necessity of the present."
-NICCOLO MACHIAVELLI

"I am terrified by this dark thing that sleeps in me;
All day I feel its soft, feathery turnings, its malignity.
Clouds pass and disperse. Are those the faces of love,
those pale irretrievables?
Is it for such I agitate my heart?
I am incapable of more knowledge.
What is this, this face
So murderous in its strangle of branches?"

- ELM BY SYLVIA PLATH

Anastasia.

RUN

Her mother had told her many times that death was not always the end. That even when you prayed for death, it did not always come. Only when life was finished with you could you receive death.

The look in her daughter's eyes, the words she had screamed when they stood face to face, Anastasia knew that in all this death her daughter had found life. A life that was better than anything she could have dreamed.

Pain shot through her body as she ran, the wound in her hind leg burned and pulsated every time she moved. She was lucky, the shot had gone straight through and did not cause extensive damage.

She hid in the woods outside Paris for some time before moving on, sleeping all she could and hunting only when she needed. The new body healed quickly, and as soon as she felt strong enough she moved on, running back the way she came. Although she was almost at full strength it still hurt. But she needed answers.

As she ran the smell of the forest enveloped her like a glove, growing stronger as she headed for home. She had always felt connected to the forest, her mother had said it was because of magic. But that woman was not really her mother, and in this body Anastasia could not help but wonder about all of the other things that had been hidden from her.

This body, the fur, the legs, the teeth, they all felt right somehow. As though this was her true form all along.

Anastasia ran until she reached the forest that surrounded the Countess's town. Only then did she rest, giving her body the time it needed to fully heal.

The other animals in the forest kept their distance, as if they had encountered her kind before. She caught the faint tingle of others like her on the far edges of her senses, as if they were watching her from afar. What she had seen in Paris had proven the existence of others with these bizarre afflictions, but she doubted they all behaved as those had.

She found the small path her daughter had followed to a clear view of the castle. Katrine's scent was still there even after so much time had passed and seasons changing. That smell may have been different to others, but to Anastasia it only brought back images of her newborn daughter, the perfect babe she used to watch sleep.

Not the thing she had become.

Csejthe castle looked deserted, as if it were only a neatly arranged pile of stones and not a grand home. The home of a Countess and her family.

Anastasia knew, somehow, about the crimes Countess Bathory was accused of. She had strange, vague memories clouded with a haze of conversations with Katrine but they did not fit. She was in the wrong body, and they had been the only survivors. If they had been truth she would not have had to go back for the old witch.

But there was something about them that seemed so real they could not be ignored.

She sat and watched as a group on horseback came to the main gate. One dismounted to open the gate for the others and they gathered in the courtyard. The smallest rider was helped down from their mount, the hood of her cloak falling back to reveal shiny, dark elaborately styled hair. She turned her head and Anastasia caught a glimpse of a beautiful young woman with sharp dark eyes that darted around. Her companions handed her a small basket and she headed off alone towards the main doors.

Anastasia's eyes began to sting as she ran through the possibilities of who this young woman could be in her mind, and they all came to a similar conclusion.

So Anastasia quickly ran down to the castle to try to get a better look.

The woman and her company left a short time later and the closer proximity did no good, so Anastasia went with her instincts.

That young woman was her sister. Half-sister, but sister nonetheless. She could not help but wonder about her other siblings, if she had any.

And a visit from the daughter meant the mother would still be inside.

Anastasia did a quick search around the castle and found an old wooden servant's door open, and there was a basket of laundry discarded as if someone had to leave in a hurry. She found a dark corner of the main kitchens to return to her other form, she struggled at first but was soon able to clothe herself.

She walked quietly out of the kitchens and into the main part of the castle. The rooms were empty and cold; there was no sign of any servants, or anyone else for that matter. Even though she knew something had happened to the Countess she was still shocked by the state of the castle.

Her bare feet were cold on the stone floor as she explored the hallways and rooms that were completely bare. What it would have been like to grow up here! The splendour of this house and a version of her childhood self running through it appeared fully formed in her mind as if it were a memory.

She wondered if that young woman felt the same way when she came inside this place.

She walked up the stone staircase, her feet making no noise. She tried to sense if there was anyone around but the upper level appeared just as empty as the lower.

She came to a doorway which had been sealed up with stones, she could hear a soft voice from beyond. She crept closer, kneeling down beside a small opening close to the floor so she could listen.

A woman sang, her voice soft and clear with the passion some had when no one could hear them. Anastasia got down on her hands and knees and inhaled deeply.

The smells of a well lived in room were what hit her first, along with the food the young woman had just brought. The aroma of an unwashed body and personal waste was not as bad as one would expect from the situation.

It took some time but Anastasia was able to get beyond all the barriers and reach the person's underlying scent; she jumped back, startled.

The Countess was beyond this wall.

How could this have happened?

Anastasia stood quickly and looked around the hallway, trying to find something to use to break through the stones. Her foot tapped a small pile of metal plates which clattered to the ground, bits of half eaten food spilling about.

"Hello?" a female voice called out, rushing to the opening. "Kata? Kata, my child, is that you?"

So my sister is called Kata, Anastasia thought to herself as she stood paralysed with shock.

"Hello? Is someone there?" the voice asked.

"Yes, but I am not Kata, Madam," Anastasia said, surprised at her own voice.

"Then who are you?" the woman asked, her voice getting a sharp tone. "Have you come to laugh at my fate? Mock me in my prison?"

"No, Madam. I just wanted to see you for myself."

There was a pause, then the woman said, "Katrine, if that is you, why would you not..."

"How do you know my daughter's name?"

"Your daughter?" the panicked voice said, and Anastasia immediately regretted the comment. She wasn't sure she was ready to have this particular conversation but now she did not have a choice.

"Your daughter came to see me. She is beautiful," the voice began. "Truly a blessing. You should be proud."

"Who are you?" Anastasia asked, her vision cloudy with tears from thoughts of her daughter.

"I am what is left of Countess Erzsebet Bathory, the Lady Widow Nadasdy. Who are you?"

"I am Anastasia. Katrine's mother."

The two women fell silent, lost in thoughts of what to say to each other, *why* the lingering question floating between them.

"I am so pleased to finally meet you," the Countess said, and she was crying. "I am so sorry for what happened to you. Please know that I had nothing to do with it. Those witches acted on their own, I was not involved in any way."

"I know, Madam. But I am quite alright, I can assure you. Katrine has found a home with others like her in Paris."

"Did Kata see you?"

Anastasia paused, then simply said, "No."

"Kata....I am sorry, I should explain. That was Katalin, my youngest daughter. She is so kind, she comes to visit me and brings me some fresh food. She is the middle child, with an older sister called Anna and a younger brother called Pal."

"Do they come to see you often, Madam?"

"No. Only priests come on a regular basis, trying to encourage me to repent for crimes I did not commit. You may call me..."

"I will call you Madam, Madam," Anastasia said with some force.

"Well, at the very least I insist you take the name Bathory, as your daughter has done. It may not be much but it is all I have to give in this state," the Countess replied. "I am truly and deeply sorry for what has happened to you. I wanted to keep you, but my mother..."

"It appears that all the women of your line have some difficulty in regards to the actions of their mothers."

The Countess began to cry harder. "I only have myself to blame for what my children have suffered and will continue to suffer. I hope that when I leave this earth that my family will have some peace."

Anastasia stood perfectly still, considering what course of action to take next. In this form she felt emotions she did not have in the other, and she was glad to be free on them. Pain, hurt, and sadness felt useless to her now.

"I cannot free you, so I should go," Anastasia said, her voice flat and empty.

"I understand," the Countess said. Two slender delicate fingers came out of the hole, the nails were short and cracked. Anastasia stared at them for several moments before softly touching the skin with the tips of her fingers.

"Goodbye Madam," Anastasia spoke in a voice completely void of emotion. She heard the Countess's sobs, a sound that echoed in her mind as she returned to her true form and ran back to the woods.

Anastasia did not leave, did not turn and disappear into the sunset as many others would've. Instead she stayed, patrolling Csejthe castle like an armed sentry, watching the comings and goings.

Visiting the once great Castle Csejthe was now, to the few who came and went, more like visiting a cemetery.

It was not a huge shock, Anastasia thought, since the place had essentially become the Countess's tomb.

The one called Kata came again, always with a guard. Anastasia did not see any others who she believed to be her siblings. She just watched. She did not need to go back inside the castle. She did not feel the need to speak to the Countess again, or somehow speak to her sister.

But she felt compelled to stay, watch for the chance that she may be able to free the Countess, or for some explanation as to why this had happened to her and her family.

KATRINE

PASSING

PARIS, FRANCE – JANUARY 1614.

"It is a fitting tribute, I assure you," Vincenzo said as he handed me the stone. It was another brick in a new wall, a tribute to the fallen.

One of the underground rooms of the Theatre des Danse Macabre was entirely devoted to the wall; each stone that was laid etched with a few words of tribute for those who had fallen, I ran my fingers over the marks on the stone in my hand.

'*Kardoska. All Hallow's Eve. 1613*' was all it said. I did not know what else to include, I did not know her birthday, her age, her family name, or even her birthplace.

No one except us knew about this memorial, or her final resting place on the grounds of Notre Dame. She had told me once that her children wanted nothing to do with her so perhaps it was better this way.

"It doesn't feel like enough. I feel like I should do more," my quiet voice seemed to echo off the walls.

Vincenzo placed a hand on my shoulder after I lay the stone on the wall. I was surprised by how many others there were, the wall reached up to my waist.

"She's in good company," Vincenzo said as if she lay at our feet.

"Will you tell me one day? Of them, I mean?" I asked.

"Of those I know I would happily." he replied. "And I suppose there will be time on the way to Russia. Perhaps you could tell me more of your journeys with Kardoska."

"Perhaps," my voice almost a whisper. As my best friend and a person who valued Kardoska, Roza to her friends, I'd asked Vincenzo to come and stand by me while I did this. I had not been to her actual grave yet, but I would ask him to come along when the time came. He was the only person I felt comfortable truly breaking down in front of.

"I do not mean to rush you, Katrine, but if we are here too long she will send someone. And we left her with Charles," he reminded me.

I smiled at him. "Do not fret, mon ami. I have not forgotten."

My mentor Grisela Delphine, often referred to as Gigi, was upstairs waiting until we were finished or she grew impatient, whichever came first. It was best not to keep her waiting, but I did not mind her moods. She and Vincenzo were my family now and I valued them immensely, and she cared for me so I would cater to her.

I touched my fingers to the stone, running my fingertips along the letters of her name. Before the tears could start I followed Vincenzo back upstairs.

"And who do you expect to stay behind to watch the girl?" Gigi snapped, Vincenzo stopped me in the stairwell so we could listen to the argument.

"We cannot take everyone to Russia, Gigi, you must be realistic," Charles, Lord Westwick, the founder of the Danse Macabre, replied. I could hear the frustration in his voice.

"The Baroness is stalling, Charles. She seems to think if she avoids the subject of her daughter and sends more money it will sidestep the inevitable," Gigi continued. "But the truth must be faced. She tried to kill Katrine and I will not allow that deed to go on unpunished any longer. You must make up your mind before we leave for Russia."

His face wrinkled in frustration. "What if I decide to leave you both behind?"

She began to laugh, a soft, pretty sound.

"That is ridiculous! I am your lead dancer and my protégée comes with me. You could not survive at a court of any kind without me, you would get everyone imprisoned or worse!" she exclaimed.

"Your ego is becoming unattractive, Grisela. I could replace you if need be," he said with more force then necessary. Vincenzo and I stepped out of the stairwell at that point, my friend adjusting his collar as we walked across the stage. He looked just as dignified in his suit as the day he found me in Vienna two years before and had not seemed to have aged a bit, he appeared to be in his 35th year. Lord Westwick's trip to Russia had given him cause to plan some trade opportunities along the way and I was looking forward to learning about his profession and watching him work.

"Are you going to tell Petite her attacker will continue to remain unpunished or should I?" Gigi asked to Charles as she stormed off the stage. Charles looked to me, his face a bright scarlet.

"Please do not speak to me of this now," I said before he could reply. His last bid for my affection had consisted of him purchasing my maternal Grandmother's cousin, a newly turned vampire, from a slave market in Germany.

My Grandmother being Countess Erzsebet Bathory, her cousin Gabor Bathory, once Prince of Transylvania. We called him Gabriel now.

"After what I just did, I do not need to hear any of your bizarre actions at this moment," I said, following Gigi off the stage. I lifted the edge of my white mourning dress as I walked down the steps, Gigi waited for me at the bottom.

"Come now, ma petite. That man is trying my patience," she gestured sharply at him as we headed up the aisle and out into the main lobby.

"Should we not wait for Vincenzo?" I asked.

"No," she said. "They are working on the carriages for transport to Russia. Charles is putting a large sum of money into this; it appears it will actually happen."

"And what shall we do?" I asked.

Her beautiful face lit up. "We shall go and try to learn more about Russia, of course. As we have been doing. But today we shall have tea with a friend who has travelled there, hopefully it will give us some insight."

"Who is this person?" I asked as we walked out into the freshly fallen snow to our waiting carriage. We both pulled up the hoods of our winter cloaks at the same time, pulling them back again as the carriage began to move.

"Petite, I do no use the word 'friend' very often so do not take it mildly. I expect your best behaviour," she told me.

"You will not prepare me for what you are about to introduce me to? How unlike you," I joked. "How am I to know how to gauge my behaviour?"

She sighed loudly, rolling her eyes. "Her name is Charlotte, and she is regular woman. You will address her as Madame Charlotte. She and I were at court together. She has since retired and done much travelling in her lifetime."

"Retired?"

"She was a courtesan, like myself," she said and she sighed again. "Are you trying to be difficult? I understand you are scarred, ma petite, but an attitude is not becoming for a lady."

"My apologies. I will work on it."

She smiled. "Do not lose it, just know when to properly use it."

We arrived at a house closer to the centre of Paris, it was small and compact compared to the chateau we lived in and not what I expected from a friend of Gigi's. Her eyes looked clouded and heavy as we stepped out into the afternoon sunshine, as if she was trying to make her gaze appear more guarded.

She looked up at the sky, her blue eyes had turned to cold stone. "Looks to be a storm coming. We must keep that in mind."

The front door opened as we reached the top, a small man in a black valet's uniform appeared in that doorway.

He greeted us in French, calling Gigi by name as if he had known her for some time. He brought us inside and took our cloaks, disappearing back into the house.

I could hear the laughter of a child from somewhere inside the house, it reminded me of my brother and my heart began to feel hard in my chest.

"Grisela! A pleasure, as always," a female voice said from the top of the flight of stairs in front of us.

A woman appeared, her long chestnut locks cascading down her shoulders almost to her waist. Her gray satin gown was cut so low in the front her entire bosom was almost visible. As she came down the stairs I could see the signs of age around her eyes and mouth, how hard her life had been showed on her face.

"Charlotte, thank you so much for receiving us. I am pleased to introduce to you my protégée, Katrine," Gigi replied. I smiled and curtsied, Charlotte appeared quite shocked.

Before I could say anything, Charlotte said, "So the rumors are true? It seems much has changed since the last time we saw each other. Please come in and sit so I may have a chance to see why you have chosen this young woman, I cannot imagine it is for her beauty alone."

We followed Charlotte into the sitting room and I had to stop myself from staring, the strange and interesting decorations that lined the room overwhelming my eyes with stimulation.

"So, Gigi, what has happened to you? The last time we spoke you were running away with an Englishman and carrying a child, and now you are a dancer with a beautiful young protégée," Charlotte began, I had to fight to hide my shock. "Clearly much has changed!"

"Yes, well, you know how men are. And all can be answered very simply," Gigi said. "The Englishman and I are no longer romantically involved but are still good friends, we dance for his company, and what I thought was a child was really a health problem. But that is not why we came."

"I hope you recovered well and were not too disappointed."

Gigi smiled. "I am quite well. Our company will be travelling to Russia, and I am having some difficulty learning about the culture and its people, and since you have travelled there I thought we could discuss it."

"I envy you, mon ami. More than you could ever imagine," Charlotte said with a smile.

"What on earth for?"

"Because you have found a place in this world beyond court life. You did not get stuck or chained. But you had the most incredible mother."

"I have my own difficulties, Charlotte. You know that," Grisela replied.

"Yes, Grisela, but you will forever be known as Mademoiselle Delphine, instead of la mére des bâtards," Charlotte proclaimed. Gigi's expression remained blank.

"My mother was a bastard," I blurted out without thinking.

Charlotte grinned like a devious cat. "Well then, we have something in common. Perhaps we are fated for this life, no?"

"Perhaps we are fated to be more than just a label, mon ami," Gigi said coldly. "At least you have those bâtards."

"And you have a beautiful young protégée. Your time is not up yet, you may get your own bâtards after all," Charlotte replied.

Gigi laughed. "None with blood such as yours."

"Oui, they do come from good stock," Charlotte continued, when she smiled this time I noticed the large quantity of cosmetics she had on her face. "An important thing to keep in mind about the Russians. They are quite serious and deeply passionate about their religion. If you understand their practices and follow them while in their presence, regardless of your own faith, you will benefit greatly."

"What is their religion called?" I asked.

"It is part of the Orthodox, my dear," Charlotte said.

"I know of it. There were many of that faith in the village where I was raised," I replied.

"And where is that?" she asked.

I smiled. "Wallachia."

"Really? A lovely country. I do not think I have ever seen so many trees. I had the pleasure of passing through on my latest trip to the Orient," Charlotte said. "So it must be quite hard for you to work alongside a man you loved so deeply. You were giving up everything for him."

"My mother was furious," Gigi chuckled.

"But I am getting side-tracked. When I was at the Russian court it was a different time, and they've had years of troubles since, so it could be radically different. Women lived rather sequestered lives and did not participate much in court life. Even their ruler's wife....nothing like our French queens!"

"Our court is a very different place than anywhere in the world. Even the

Papal court is not as glorious as that of our beloved France," Gigi replied.

"You are so right!" Charlotte exclaimed. "And perhaps you will be treated differently than I was. Not that I was treated poorly, not by any means. But you are aware of the perils of our profession. There are not many like us in Russia."

"Really? I thought women like us were common," Gigi said.

Charlotte giggled. "We are a dying breed, mon ami. If you are having gowns made you should err on the side of modesty, just as a precaution. The Russian's are not particularly fashion forward, you will be very surprised by what you see."

I took a small sip of tea, using the cup to conceal my face, just as Gigi had taught me. I had so many questions, but I could not help but wonder why Gigi had brought me along.

If she did not want me to know details about her relationship with Charles this was a very strange situation to put me in. But perhaps she wanted me to know and just could not tell me herself.

"Have you heard the latest gossip? This strange practice called alchemy has become all the rage," Charlotte began. "There is this new group who says they can turn coal into diamonds and congregate with demons! Can you believe it? Demons! And the court is all a flutter. Someone who could simply make things like diamonds and gold could rule the world!"

"I have been so focused on preparations for Russia I have not heard about the latest court craze," Gigi replied.

"You must prepare for winter. It is dreadfully cold in Russia and if you get stuck there, which you will if it snows, you will regret it. It is colder than anything you could ever imagine," Charlotte told us, shivering at the mention of cold. "But your protégée would understand. Wallachia winters are also unpleasant."

A few moments of awkward silence passed and the situation became uncomfortable. I took it as a cue to do what Gigi taught me during this type of situation; I drank my tea in two sips, making sure it was not noticeable to others and prepared for our exit.

"Well, Charlotte, as always it has been a pleasure," Gigi said, putting down her empty tea cup shortly after I did. "But, I fear we must be going.

A storm is coming and we must return to the theatre before heading home."

"Of course. You must come back before you leave, or perhaps I shall come to the famous Danse Macabre salon?" Charlotte's tone felt condescending as she walked us back out to the front entry, the valet returned with our cloaks so quickly I wondered if he had been standing in the shadows waiting.

"Au revoir, Grisela," Charlotte said, smiling at me. "It was nice to meet you, young lady."

We turned and left without another word, our carriage was waiting outside.

"That was an enormous waste of time," Gigi huffed.

"I am a little confused," I began. "Was there a reason why I needed to hear what she had to say? Because certain things she mentioned...."

"We will discuss it another time," Gigi snapped. "Now we will go home and you shall get the peace you so crave."

She stared intently at me, as if she was taunting me to probe her.

Now might not be the time but I would certainly be asking questions.

Katrine

SPARKS

"It is all part of being nobility, especially in the eastern parts of Europe," Gabriel said. "There is so much fighting your position is never quite secure. Your grandmother would have faired much better if she had not been a woman."

He had come to my rooms at sunset, a habit he had picked up after Roza's death, sitting and talking to me while my hair was being styled for the evening. Sometimes I listened quite closely and asked questions, but on evenings like this I allowed him to speak and said rather little.

"I am unsure what life would have been like if Istvan had not become King of Poland. We had held the Transylvanian seat many times but it is not the same, partially because of its location within Europe and the constant battles with the Turks and between the nobles. Did you know King Istvan was Somlyo as well? So am I, for that matter," he said with a huff. "That may have been another of your grandmother's difficulties, her mother was of the Somlyo branch and her father the Ecsed. They expected much of her because she had only Bathory blood in her veins. One day I can take you to Ecsed castle in Nyìrbátor, it is quite tremendous, being the family estate. But we must wait till I am forgotten."

He silently stared out into nothing for several moments, then I said, "What are you thinking?"

"It is quite odd, this life. Don't you think?" he asked. "You get to survive but with nothing you have ever known, and you must hide away until people forget you or die. It is a bit odd."

"I had not thought of it that way," I replied.

"Mathilde says it will pass, and that its best not to grow too attached to those who will perish at a normal rate," Gabriel said. I looked at Hannah in the mirror behind me as she braided ribbons in my hair.

He did not understand that pain like I did, and I hoped he never would. I tried not to cry, pulling it back into my body and down into an ache in the pit of my stomach.

"So will this be our life, Cousin? Parties and salons, the French social scene?" He asked.

"I will be dancing, perhaps you could as well."

He chuckled. "From Prince to a dancer who sleeps in a dirty cage in the basement."

"I told you they will make you a room in the underground at the theatre," I said.

"I do not wish you to be here alone, Child."

"Please, Cousin. Grisela takes fine care of me, same with Vincenzo and my lovely maid Hannah. We would not be separated for long and see each other quite often and you would have a proper room of your own and a decent bed to sleep in." I replied.

"I am honoured you have such faith in me, Mademoiselle," Hannah said. She finished tying the last white ribbon and stepped away to examine her handiwork.

"Perhaps I should speak to Charles in regards to my living arrangements," Gabriel said, standing from the stool he was sitting on.

I paused. "Perhaps, since he is the one who makes these sorts of decisions."

"I will see you in the salon, Child," he took my hand and kissed it, then quickly left.

"Perhaps he should work with Signor Amori, or involve himself with the preparations for travelling to Russia. He needs to do something to occupy his thoughts, I am concerned he will give in to melancholy and get consumed by it," Hannah said. I did not reply, playing mindlessly with the hem of my dress of such a pale blue it was almost white. It was the beginning of my transition out of mourning clothes, it had passed the customary 40 days and I wasn't quite ready to leave them behind so I figured heavily whitened, not quite colours was a decent compromise.

"Mmm," I said quietly. I was having trouble with my own thoughts.

"She would have wanted you to move on, Katrine," Hannah said. "To live the life you were born to have. That is why they came for you, is it not?"

I nodded, another quiet sound coming from my lips. I wanted to try to spend one evening not thinking about Roza, so I shook off my thoughts and began to make my way downstairs.

The Danse Macabre salon was crowded, as usual. The dancing had already commenced so my entrance was not noticed. I was happy for it, I was not particularly interested in sitting and chatting with the women and hoped I could find a way to avoid it.

I stuck close to the far wall and my body eased as I felt a hand touch mine.

"May I ask you something, William?" I said, my face staying turned out to the room.

"Anything, il mio amore," William replied.

"Do you think we could leave this place? Find a small farm, live a simple life without...all of this?"

He squeezed my hand tightly in his, then said, "Anytime. Say the word and we'll be gone."

"Thank you," I smiled at him. "I do not know what I would do without you."

"You may have to find out. Charles has asked if I would stay behind to take care of things while you all are in Russia," he said quietly.

"You can't be serious!" I exclaimed. "Vincenzo would not allow it, he has many things planned for the route....besides, *I* will not allow it. He cannot expect you to stay behind."

"He said someone needs to watch Klara," he said, and he tried to grab my arm as I stormed across the room in Charles's direction.

I got as close to his face as I could without touching him, burrowing holes into him with my gaze.

"You will not punish other people because of your mistakes," I growled at him. He smiled at me, a strange glint in his eyes.

"Whatever do you mean, my dear?" he asked coyly.

"William will not be staying behind to take care of your problem," I began. "How dare you even say such a thing! The decision will be made about what to do with Klara before we leave for Russia, if you do not I will be staying behind. Perhaps finding another place to live."

"I asked what you wanted me to do and you would not answer me!" he snapped.

"It is not my place to direct! I am in your care, living under your roof! Or are you concerned the Baroness will stop giving you money?"

He watched me angrily for a moment. I had overstepped myself and I knew it, and then he said, "It shall be dealt with before we are scheduled to depart, you have my word."

"And William?"

"He can come if he likes," he cooed. "I am sure he and Vincenzo have much to do on the journey."

I smiled, bowing low as I could before walking away.

"In common situations you would be beaten for such behaviour," Gigi said quietly to me, coming up beside me from across the room.

"What a relief that this is an uncommon situation," I growled.

Gigi grabbed my wrist. "Such behaviour in a public setting is inappropriate, ma petite."

"I will be sure not to do it again, Mademoiselle." I replied, bowing to her and continuing across the room before she could say more.

"Charles looks like his head is going to explode." William said when I got back to him.

"Good. He needs someone to tell him the truth on occasion," I told him.

"You could have got in a lot of trouble. He could have hurt you. Grisela could have hurt you, for that matter. She may still."

I looked him in the eyes and smiled. "I will not leave you behind."

He took my hand and led me away, quietly weaving through the crowd and trying not to be noticed. He pulled me through a door near the back of the room, into the dark dining room and through to the other side and out another door, into the sitting room that wasn't often used.

"What are you doing?" I asked.

He pulled me into his embrace. "Something I should have done a very long time ago."

He gently took my face in his hands and kissed my lips; a warm, deep, passionate kiss that sent energy out through my body. I pulled him closer to me and wrapped my arms around his neck, easing into the kiss and trying to pour all my emotion out through my mouth.

I felt the sparks, wondering if they were in my head or actually flashing around us.

We broke the kiss but I would not let him pull away.

"I was wondering when you would do that." I said.

He laughed. "You could have done it first, il mio amore."

"I was too afraid."

"Afraid of what?" he asked, hugging me tightly to his body. I could feel his heart quickly beating.

"That I would be so terrible at it you would laugh. I don't have much experience."

"Then perhaps we should practice." he kissed me again, this time softly and slowly.

"They will start to wonder," I said between kisses.

"Let them."

"It would be improper." I said, but did not stop him.

"Then marry me," he said, cradling my face in his hands.

"I am too young, and besides, I am not quite sure you are serious."

"Technically you are getting quite old for marriage, and I am completely serious. Whether now is the proper time for an engagement could be questioned but, my love, I do very much wish to marry you. And only you." he confessed, kissing me one last time before leaving the room. I tried my best to straighten myself out, waiting as long as I could so we would not be suspected.

The dancing had not stopped and I took my first opportunity to enter into it when I stepped back into the doorway; I could use dancing as an explanation if Gigi had not been able to find me.

But I was not concerned. I was floating, my heart fluttering so fast I could barely breathe.

I never thought a man would want to marry me. Especially for love.

KATRINE

CONFRONTATION

Morgana sat quite still, so still I wondered if she was, in fact, still breathing.

"Morgana," I said. She jumped, startled, shaking the tea cups on the tray in front of us.

She looked at me, her pale eyes nervous. I had not seen her at all last night.

"Morgana, this has been going on for much too long. I have told you repeatedly I am not angry," I began. "Now, please, you do not need to be so tense."

"I am sorry, I am trying. But you must understand people have reacted quite badly to my predictions in the past, and what I saw for you was dreadful." she replied.

"I should have listened to you, perhaps things would have been different."

"Please don't say such things, Katrine. My guilt is already too much to bear."

"There is one thing you told me that I will not allow. Gigi will not be the one to kill Klara."

"May I tell you something wonderful?" she asked, and I nodded in agreement. "You are the love of the blue eyed demon's life. He will marry no other in his lifetime."

"That is a heavy weight," I said. "Will we marry?"

"I am not sure of that, but I do know he will not marry unless it's you. He loves you like he has never loved another person," she continued, her face lighting up. "Do you love him?"

I felt the colour rising to my face. "I do. I truly do."

"So why not marry him and leave this place?"

"Not yet. I could not leave here yet, I have so much to learn. I am in a good position and I am happy. I am not ready to leave. I enjoy the dancing."

"I am hoping to work with Josephine, I think that was a wise suggestion. We have spent some time together and I think we might work well," Morgana replied.

"I must be honest, if I was not dancing I would be working with her also. I am quite interested in costumes," I said. Morgana closed her eyes and breathed deeply, I wondered if she was having visions when she did this.

"I see two Mademoiselle Delphine's with us in Russia," Morgana said quite suddenly as I sipped my tea.

"Two? What does that mean?" I asked, trying to seem unshaken.

"I see two Mademoiselle Delphine's in Russia, that's all it means," Morgana replied, opening her eyes slowly.

"Two of me?" Gigi's voice said from behind me. "Perhaps it is a representation of me stretching myself too thin, trying to put myself into two places at once."

She came swishing into the conservatory, her full, cream coloured skirt seemed to be growing wider by the day, giving her the illusion of very exaggerated hips. She sat on one of the chairs across from us, pushing a stray blonde curl off her face.

"I am sorry, I cannot see the exact circumstances," Morgana replied, her voice quieting.

"That is alright, child. Now, I have come to collect you both. It is time we did some reading, perhaps practice some dancing," Gigi said. "We cannot spend the day drinking tea, we must be prepared for our Russian adventure."

"But we know so little of their culture," I said.

"Yes, but that does not mean we cannot be proficient in manners, conversations and the other behaviours that make us proper women," Gigi replied. "Even you, Morgana."

"Can we not dance? My feet are sore from last night," I said, my thoughts wandering back to William and last night.

"You shall have to pay more attention to such things, ma petite. I cannot have you ducking out of your responsibilities," Gigi said, rising and clapping her hands. "Come now, girls. We don't have all day."

I stood, suddenly feeling quite light headed. I had to sit back down.

"When was the last time you had any blood, petite?" Gigi asked.

"I am not sure. Several weeks, maybe more....," I began.

"Are you mad? You *cannot* go so long between feedings, you could become quite dangerous," Gigi snapped. She headed to the door and said something to a maid, then came back and sat down.

"So you feed, then we work," Gigi said. "While you're occupied Morgana and I can discuss the contents of this new vision."

A maid shuffled quietly into the room and placed a silver canister on the tea tray, then disappeared. I poured the blood into my cup as if it were tea and sipped it casually. Morgana watched me in shock for several minutes before saying, "I'm not quite sure I will ever get used to that."

"I am not used to it myself," I replied.

"Morgana, do you think you could try again?" Gigi asked. Morgana nodded and closed her eyes, Gigi looked as if she might pull her hair out in anticipation.

"Do you have a sister?" Morgana asked, keeping her eyes closed. The blood began to run through my body, a warm heat that made me feel as if I had awoken from a deep sleep.

"Yes, I have several. You have said something about my family before. Could the second me be my sister?" Gigi asked.

Morgana stayed silent for several moments, as if she was studying what she was seeing of her eyelids. When she opened them again her gaze seemed clouded, her eyes unfocused.

"I....I cannot tell for certain. I am sorry," Morgana replied, trying to shake off her thoughts. I sat and drank, unable to process completely what was happening.

Gigi began to vibrate nervous energy, wringing her hands together. "If you see anything else, you will come to me immediately."

"Yes, of course," Morgana said. Gigi got up and left without saying another word, the swish of rustling silk following her out.

"Perhaps I should not speak of my visions," Morgana said, snapping me out of my daze.

"Nonsense," I said, refilling my empty cup with more blood. "She would not have asked if she did not want to know."

"And now she is in her room writing letters to half the Continent trying to find out if there's any truth to it," Vincenzo said, entering the room and sitting in the seat Gigi had just vacated. "She left me in charge of you two, she said you could not sit around and drink tea all day. I suppose I shall bring you to the yard where the carriages are being built."

"Sounds better than dancing and conversation," Morgana said happily.

"Don't we have carriages?" I asked.

"No, my dear. For those of us who cannot be exposed to sunlight we needed something appropriate for them to travel in that did not look particularly off putting," Vincenzo began. "Charles has been working on the design for some time and we've not had the means to build until now, or the money."

"How much of this is the Von Dores's money? I suppose I should take pity on Klara so Charles can pay for his adventures," I said. I put my cup down, it appeared that I had finished the entire canister without even realising.

Vincenzo chuckled. "I thought you might think that way, so I wanted to let you know that your inappropriate outburst last night lit a fire under Charles and he is spending most of his time trying to decide how to best deal with Klara."

"What are his solutions?" I asked.

"Lifetime imprisonment, death, or being sold into slavery. I believe he is in talks with the man who had your cousin....there was a word he used, I think it was your native tongue. Hajuke? Haduke?" Vincenzo said.

"Hajdukes?" I asked.

"Yes, yes. That's the one," Vincenzo replied.

"*They* had Gabriel? I thought they were freedom fighters," I replied.

"Perhaps they are, and having him guaranteed their freedom," Vincenzo said. "Now, let's get on with our day. It would do you both good to get some fresh air."

The yard was in close proximity to Vincenzo's office, so not only were there carriages being built but ships and other modes of transportation. He showed us which was ours, massive wood wagons without any windows. One was fully assembled and several others were still in progress.

"How many do you suppose we'll need?" I asked him.

He shrugged. "Many. Not just of this sort, but others. If you think, the entire company, households, costumes, some set pieces; all of that and more, plus our personal belongings."

"Good Heaven's, we'll look like a travelling city!" I exclaimed. Morgana was turned away from us, staring out at the river.

"Do you miss your home?" I asked her.

"Do you?" she snapped. "One cannot spend too much time in their painful past. One must look forward, but can never forget what they left behind. Do you understand that, Katrine?"

"Of course," I said, and I knew that was her comment about my state since Roza's death. She would not speak of it outright because of the blame she lay on herself for her visions, but she would tip toe around it. I preferred it that way. I only needed one person giving me directions on how to behave and Gigi was quite enough.

"Charles is having rather luxurious carriages built for the rest of us," Vincenzo said. "Not that the covered ones won't be, but they will be rather simple outside, the others will be much more dramatic. I believe he is fashioning them after the Royal carriages."

He examined our faces for several moments then said, "I thought you'd be excited. The other women were."

"I have never seen a royal carriage," I said.

"Of course you haven't. Silly me, I apologise," Vincenzo replied. "But I am sure you can imagine they will be quite opulent. Since it will take several months to get there Charles feels it's a necessity."

"We cannot travel through Russia in the cold from what I've learned.

While I appreciate his attention to detail I am not sure Royal quality is necessary, the money could probably be spent better elsewhere," I said.

I heard some commotion, men yelling in heavily accented voices. Morgana was watching them, and they were watching her.

Vincenzo noticed it also, we stayed silent as they approached.

"They are speaking her native tongue, aren't they?" I asked him, and he nodded in agreement. There was more yelling then they all turned and saw Morgana.

It happened so quickly it confused me. The men were on her, yelling something about a curse and sinking ships and throttling the little witch till her eyes popped out.

I took a deep breath and stepped towards them, trying my best to think of what Gigi would do in this situation.

I extended a white gloved hand to them and tried to push back my fear. "I am sorry, I do not believe we have had the pleasure of meeting."

The larger one looked down at me and snorted, then continued on his tirade.

"Sir, I cannot allow you to harass my employee in such a manner." I said sharply. They paid me no mind and continued.

When one of them reached out to grab her throat I latched on to his wrist and twisted it into the most unnatural position I could manage.

He started to keel over and I said quite flatly. "It is quite disrespectful of you to ignore me. Now, will you and your men leave my employee alone or shall I break your arm?"

"You best be careful, woman. With this witch around you'll lose everything. She cursed me!" He screamed. "You'll face the fires one day, I swear on the graves of my dead men! You'll burn, I'll make sure of it!"

I turned his wrist a little farther and pushed him away as I felt Vincenzo stand close behind me. I had not thought of who could be watching. My boldness could destroy me.

"I think that's quite enough, my dear," Vincenzo said. "I am sure that now that the gentlemen have voiced their opinion they shall be on their way."

One of the other gentlemen was about to say something when Vincenzo raised his hand to silence him. "We do not want any trouble. Can you prove the girl has done the things you accuse her of?"

The group of men stared at Vincenzo as if he had sprouted a second head.

"You cannot believe that we would even entertain listening to the allegations without proof, do you?" Vincenzo said flatly. "I have to ask you to leave our presence, you are upsetting my fiancee."

They looked at me then, but this time it was an appraisal, an attempt to see if they could figure out how someone as young as myself would end up with Vincenzo.

Perhaps it was not common for a husband to be chosen in Scotland. I would have to ask Morgana.

We walked away before the men did and went back to our carriage.

"Do you think we should be concerned about them damaging our property?" I asked Vincenzo. He put Morgana and I in the carriage then went to say something to one of the workers.

"No, they would not want to add to the Scots barbarian stereotype. They are, after all, attempting to do business." Morgana replied.

I smiled at her. "Did you curse them?"

"Because they are dumb enough to believe I would I did not tell them any different. That is not my fault, they originally agreed to take me along because they believed I was one of the fairy folk," she said.

"Do you think they're real? Fairies, I mean?" I asked.

She chuckled. "I have never encountered one, if that's what you're wondering. But if my grandmother is to be believed then yes, they do exist."

Vincenzo returned, climbing in and tapping on the roof of the carriage, which lurched forward when the door closed.

"My apologies," Vincenzo said. "Now I must take you somewhere I really don't want to. I thought I could avoid it...."

"What is it? What is so terrible?" I asked.

He sighed, and before he could reply Morgana said. "He's taking us to speak with Klara."

"Why?" I exclaimed. "I thought Charles was supposed to be dealing with it? Why do I have to see her?"

"It is all part of his plan to figure out what to do with her. Gigi had planned to take you but with this morning's events she asked that I do it and she'd meet us there," he said. "I am sorry. I wanted to tell you earlier but Gigi thought it best if you were not given a choice."

"What did you know of this?" I snapped at Morgana.

"Nothing, except that nothing could possibly make him look more uncomfortable," Morgana replied, "than Klara."

"There is nothing I can do to avoid this, is there?" I asked. He shook his head, trying his best to smile at me as if it was reassurance that he wasn't leading me blindly into a fire.

"She is in a cell, you have nothing to worry about." Vincenzo said.

"Where is William?" I asked.

He smiled and nodded. "He will be there, I am sure of it."

"I will not see her without him and Morgana. There is no negotiation, if I have to do this I demand they both be present." I said.

"I would expect nothing less." he replied.

"Take no offence, I am sure you and Gigi could protect me adequately but...."

"No need to explain. If I was in your situation I would insist on his presence also," he said.

I leaned back in my seat as the carriage rattled on. My stomach was creeping its way up into my throat, I was hoping I would not panic or pass out from lack of oxygen.

"It will be alright, Katrine," Vincenzo said, patting me on the knee. I was glad he was so sure.

Anastasia

OLD GHOSTS

The smell of fresh bread woke Anastasia from sleep. The fortnight she'd spent in her new form in the forest around Csejthe had been difficult, she'd had trouble finding food and the aromas from the village were becoming too tempting.

She had no money, no ability to get food unless she stole it, and that wasn't in her nature. Since she could hunt she could not justify having to steal. But the aroma of bread felt as if it were in her veins.

After rising from the bed she had made for herself in the hollow of a tree she ran slowly to the castle and began surveying the area. Nothing had changed, and she walked with ease and no worry of being seen. She still had to be cautious however, as a large wolf would frighten people.

The town was active and lively, Anastasia could see people going about their business as if the castle did not even exist. She could not help but think of the woman who was still in there, all alone.

The priests came through the gate at about midday. Anastasia found an ideal place so she could watch them, creeping in the back kitchen door and moving deeper into the castle. A door sat slightly ajar at the top of the staircase and Anastasia quietly crept inside so she could listen to their conversation.

"I do not understand why we continue to come here," one priest said flatly.

"We come because it is our duty," another priest snapped. The three walked quietly down the hall.

"But the woman is not interested...."

"What she is interested in at this point, does not matter. God wants us to come and try to speak to her, I am sure she will see the error in her ways."

"How long do you suppose she shall survive like this?"

"It all depends who is on her side, the Lord or Satan," a third voice said, he sounded older. Anastasia could smell something strange under the heavy aroma of church incense that seemed to stain their bodies.

Anastasia thought long and hard about killing the three priests and dragging their bodies into the forest, mainly because of their foolish notion that God or Satan played a role in what happened to the Countess. *This was the work of men*, she knew that in her heart. But she could not kill the priests for doing what they know.

She sat down on the cold stone floor and listened to the priest's feet as they shuffled along towards the Countess's chamber. She heard the men call to her Ladyship through the stones and get no response.

She listened intently and could faintly hear a woman's voice, it seemed she was too far away to hear her clearly.

After listening to their prayers and words of encouragement to try to sway her in their direction, Anastasia crept back down to the kitchens to wait for the priests to leave.

Once they were gone she returned to her other form and began to forage through the kitchen for food. She cleared the room of all that was rotten and put it in a pile out in the garden; she was lucky to find a few vegetables and some stale bread. Someone had cleaned out all of the preserved foods, herbs, and anything else like oils and vinegars that had any value.

But what was there was enough to fulfil the emptiness she'd felt from only eating as a wolf would.

A cold, bitter wind came bursting in the wood door, sending Anastasia cowering down behind a wood cupboard, her naked body not used to such frigid temperature. She decided, as the wind continued, that she would spend the night inside then move on to somewhere else. Answers would not stop her from freezing to death, and she'd spent enough time in Csejthe. Where she would go was another issue entirely, she needed to get through the night.

She decided to stay in her other form, believing it would be easier to explain a naked woman than a large wolf. She knew she was taking a risk, but after walking the main level of the castle she found a small corner that was oddly warm with no fire, and a pile of discarded and torn curtains that she used to cover herself.

In the night she heard wailing, the cries of a tormented woman. She felt something, a pain in her heart that made her truly uncomfortable. She did not want to feel anything for the woman who gave her up. For the mother she never knew.

That was one reason why she preferred animal form, what she felt to be her true form, because all human emotions fell away. Animals did not feel guilt or shame or sadness, they only felt suffering when one of their own was close to death, and even then it was not the same.

The cries seemed to echo off the walls. She sat up in her corner and she could see white shapes moving around the empty hallways. She watched them and tried to use her sense of smell, she was suddenly bombarded with the smell of blood.

The shapes became figures, the pale images of girls walking the halls and making their way upstairs.

They did not notice Anastasia stand and approach them, and when she reached out to one of them her fingers passed through like the girl was made of smoke.

Anastasia's mouth fell open in shock. She had seen and heard many incredible things in her lifetime, growing up in a witch's household, but she had never seen a ghost. The woman who raised her had said only certain special people got to see ghosts; Anastasia had asked many times if she would ever see the father she had never known, it had only recently occurred to her that the man who had played such a role in her childhood fantasies was a lie.

But these ghosts who walked the halls of her birth mother's prison she could see, clear as day, as if they were real people.

She stumbled back, quickly returning to her corner and pulling the curtains around her. Had others seen this? She wondered. Did the ghosts go into the Countess's chamber and torment her? Was that why she was wailing like that?

Anastasia buried herself under the pile of curtains and tried to block out the sounds and images that surrounded her.

She would leave Csejthe tomorrow for good.

Katrine

LITTLE RAT

She was dressed in a plain, colourless servant's dress with her orange hair plaited down her back. Her face looked gaunt, her eyes sunken and hollow. She was a shadow of her former self.

"Have you all come to kill me?" Klara asked.

I had not anticipated so many people. Vincenzo, Morgana and I, as well as Charles, William, Gigi, Victorie and Mathilde were surrounding Klara's cell staring in at her.

"Not necessarily, Klara. You have committed a heinous offence to another member of this company and we are still trying to decide on your punishment," Charles said flatly.

"My parents…" Klara began.

"Your parents are paying to keep your alive, or did you forget you have been banished from Vienna?" Charles said angrily.

She rolled her eyes, her face turning into a ghoulish smile. "I do not believe they have banished me."

Charles pulled a letter from his coat and handed it through the bars.

"If you don't mind. I have no need to lie, and this proves I am not," Charles continued. "I took you in as a favour to your parents and you dishonoured them as well as me. I should kill you, I should have killed you when it happened but unfortunately I pity you. So it is under some debate as to what to do with you."

"Do I have a say in what happens to my person?" she asked.

William took my one hand, and a smaller hand took the other. I was surprised it was Morgana.

"You forfeit that when you attacked Katrine!" Gigi's angry voice was like a lashing whip, the hands had to pull me back so I wouldn't go to her. Klara didn't reply, but she did turn her eyes to me for the first time. I saw Charles back away, dropping the letter into the cell out of the corner of my eye but I did not break my gaze from Klara. I would not back away in fear.

"And how are you feeling, little rat? Did you let our good Lord Westwick deflower you yet?" Klara said.

"How *dare* you say such things to my cousin!" Gabriel yelled, appearing beside Mathilde. "I should kill you myself!"

Klara looked away from me and at him, anger started flowing through me.

Charles said from between clenched teeth, "Because of your actions you deserve severe punishment. You will be banished from the Continent from the remainder of your days, you will be taken to the holy land to live as a slave. If you try to escape you will be killed...."

"Why not just kill me now? Because I will escape," Klara retorted.

"That would be far too simple," Charles said, his smile caused me to step back. "You will be sold into slavery. In my opinion that is what you deserve."

"I am my parents heir. I am a noble," Klara said with as much confidence as she could muster but her voice sounded shaky.

"You have been disinherited, disowned, and banished. You are no longer a noble. It is all in that letter I tried to give you," Charles told her.

Klara pointed at me. "I have lost everything because of *her*?!"

"No! You have lost everything because you have violated the rules! You enchanted men! That is wrong and against all we stand for! We work as a group! That is how we survive!" Charles yelled. "Our safety will not be jeopardised because of what you think you are entitled to!"

I wanted to say something, felt I should say something, but I could not find the words. Klara turned her angry eyes to me, this time I stepped back. I wanted to turn away but I knew I would appear weak, so I stared at her with every inch of anger I had inside me. All I had felt about Roza's death, my mother's condition and my grandmother's imprisonment I projected into my eyes, I was surprised when Klara stepped back.

"The arrangements are being made," Charles said. "You shall leave before the month is out."

I wondered how that corresponded with our trip to Russia, I would prefer it if she was long gone before we left. I wondered if she remembered our plans, or realised she was funding it.

Charles nodded and we each started to leave.

"Don't ever forget what I told you, little rat! You will never be anything! You're a waste of skin!" she screamed at me. "You don't deserve to live!"

I felt Morgana's body tense, then she let go of my hand and walked towards the bars. She said something and the air grew thick around us. William pulled me from the room, leaving Morgana alone with Klara.

"Are you sure that's wise?" I asked him.

He chuckled, then said, "She'll be fine. I just hope she doesn't kill her."

"She wouldn't…" I began, then I turned to find Morgana coming to us.

"What did you do?" I asked her as she started walking past.

"Just a little curse, nothing to concern yourself with," she replied, dismissing me with a hand motion she learned from Gigi and following the others out through the underground.

The cells were farther down into the ground, the sun was just beginning to set so the other vampires were up and around. It was important we appeared a united front to deal with Klara, because of the way Charles had decided to deal with the situation. I was a bit curious to explore all this space but wasn't sure where to begin, and I'd need to escort so I didn't get lost.

"Are you pleased with my resolution Katrine?" Charles asked when we reached the main level in the underground. It was really more of a statement than a question, and something he was clearly doing out of courtesy then necessity.

"If it is what's appropriate and best for us all, then yes I am," I replied. He smiled coyly at me and I tried my best to be polite.

"I believe it is appropriate," Vincenzo said.

"It is unfortunate we will not get to watch her suffer, but I suppose it is best," Gigi added.

Mathilde laughed loudly. "Be careful, Grisela. Anger is very aging."

"I have faith that Lord Westwick has dealt with this appropriately," Gigi said, her eyes lowering as Charles glared at her.

"If it's not too much trouble, Gigi, we have a show to prepare for tonight. Do you think you'll be able to work past your anger?" Charles called back as he walked on ahead of us.

I had forgotten about the show; since Roza's death we had only done two a month and this would be our first of the New Year.

Gigi rolled her eyes. "Come now, ma petite. We need to prepare."

I squeezed William's hand, then turned and followed her up and out of the underground.

Katrine

THE NEED TO EXPLAIN

Gigi and I returned to the theatre several hours later, pulling up our hoods as we ascended the stairs. I was amazed at the amount of people coming to see the show on such a cold, blustery day, the type of day best spent in front of a fire.

I lost Gigi in the crowd when we got inside, trying to push my way through the people and towards one of the doors to the underground. I wasn't as worried about getting noticed as Gigi was, she liked being the star of the show but she found the idea of being stopped on the theatre grounds rather unsettling.

I finally got through the crowd and had my eye on the door, before I could reach the knob a hand reached out and grabbed my arm, pulling me into a dark corner.

I wanted to scream but my body felt paralysed with fear. Could another of Klara's men have found me?

"Don't be afraid, Katrine," a female voice said. "If I wanted to kill you then you would already be dead."

I looked into the face of the figure but could only see startling amber eyes under a dark hood. She had me against the wall but not pinned, her reassurance was not eliminating my fear.

"It has taken us some time to find you. We lost you in Vienna, the Danse Macabre is good at covering their tracks," she began. "But I am happy we did. Your blood could help you achieve great things, if you only understand."

"Who are you? What do you want?" I asked.

"We are the Order of the Dragon. A group of special individuals brought together to help rid this world of evil. We're made up of people like you, Katrine, people of extraordinary means who are meant for more than this life," she continued.

"I don't understand."

"We have been watching you your whole life, you as well as your mother. Your mother's magic has done something unexpected to you both. You are so much more than they will ever understand."

"I don't believe you."

"That is expected. When your mother scratched you you should have become a shapeshifter but you did not, because you were already dhampir when this happened."

I stood and stared at her, completely startled. Something inside my mind told me to strike out, to attack somehow, but I had flashes of what had happened with Klara and realised I was not capable of defending myself against those who are afflicted. That thought was more frightening then anything this person could tell me of a family I knew so little about.

"I know what a dhampir is. Are you implying that my father is not my..." I asked in a very quiet voice. I did not want my suspicions confirmed; Nikoli would always be my father. Even if proven otherwise.

"No. Anastasia was attacked by a vampire because of her Bathory blood, her birth father is vampire," she said, a slight accent starting to show through. "But, you are dhampir, Katrine. By nature dhampir are the only things strong enough and skilled enough to hunt the evil that walks this earth. Because they are part of such darkness they are better equipped to destroy it."

"I still do not understand. What do you want? How am I supposed to believe you?" I managed to say, there were so many thoughts swimming in my head I was impressed I could form a sentence. My biological grandfather, a blood drinker? Could it be true?

"You don't have to, just know we are here. In time you will understand and we'll be waiting," she said, turning to walk away then added. "Ask Gabor Bathory about the Order. He will understand."

Before I could think further, or even get a closer look at this person, she had faded off into the crowd.

"Petite, what on earth happened?" Gigi exclaimed when I finally got to the costume room. I sighed, going behind the screen to change.

"Is Charles on you again?" she asked. "Dégénérer. He should be lynched."

"And you are concerned about my attitude?" I said. "No, it was not Charles, but just as unimportant."

When we finished dressing Gabriel was waiting outside the room for us.

"I shall wait with you in the wings, cousin," he said, turning to marvel at Gigi's costume. "You look incredible, Grisela. An absolute vision."

Her face turned scarlet. "Merci. I hope you enjoy the show."

"I find something new every time I see it. Especially when I see you," he replied. Gigi flushed again, then bowed to us as she headed into the stairwell.

He escorted me up the stairs, to the same place I had gone when Klara's minion attacked me.

"I was approached earlier," I began.

He chuckled. "By one of your many admirers? I would expect nothing less."

"No," I said as we stepped out into the off side of the stage. "By a woman who said she was from the Order of the Dragon."

He paused, his body going very still.

"She said some strange things, then said you'd know what she was talking about. Actually, she said rather plainly, 'ask Gabor Bathory about the Order. He'll understand'. So I will need you to explain," I said as calmly as I could. He stood as if he was paralysed with fright.

Before I could say more the curtain was up and the stage lights were on, I had only moments before I had to go.

I turned and looked back at him, standing as if he was a statue as I stepped out onto the stage to join the dance.

When it was finished Gabriel was gone. I had tried to banish all thoughts from my mind except the task at hand but as soon as I stepped off the stage it all came rushing back.

I changed in silence, everything was so hectic no one seemed to notice I wasn't talking. I went back upstairs when I was done to try to look for Gabriel, it appeared he had headed up to one of the private boxes after escorting me onstage.

I pulled my cloak over my head and moved into the crowd, trying my best to remain unnoticed. Out of the corner of my eye I saw a dark figure as I ascended the stairs, I moved over to the stone railing and tried to make my turn to look out at the room seem graceful.

But when I saw Gabriel deep in conversation with a dark clad figure I almost fell over. There was always a chance it was not the same person who had stopped me but that would be an awfully big coincidence, so I stood and watched the pair until the figure left and Gabriel finally noticed I was watching.

He paused, as if he was considering walking in a different direction. We had spent lots of time together since he arrived several months ago but I did not believe we really knew each other, and his having to consider whether or not to approach me really showed that fact.

Perhaps he'd thought he would have time to prepare, a chance to explain exactly what he had pulled us into. Perhaps he thought I would tell Charles, and he would be punished and cast out into the world on his own.

He took a deep breath and came towards me, smiling brightly.

"Hello cousin," he said, taking my arm in his. "You were fantastic tonight."

"Thank you, cousin. Are you in some kind of trouble?" I asked.

He chuckled uncomfortably. "Whatever do you mean?"

"We will not discuss this now, Gabriel, but we will at some point, you can trust in that. I will give you the chance to come to me before I begin to ask questions."

"Will you keep this private?"

"Are my friends and I in any kind of danger?"

"No! No, not at all!"

"As long as there is no danger this will remain our secret. But if I get even the slightest notion of any...."

"That won't happen. I assure you," he said sharply. "Let me prepare myself, so I can remember all the details you should be aware of."

"Until then," I said, bowing to him when we reached the top of the stairs. He did the same and I watched as he went back down the stairs, weaved through the crowd and passed through the door, disappearing into the underground.

Anastasia

MY CURSE

Clattering of hooves and the sound of voices woke Anastasia the next day, scaring her so deeply she tried to bury herself deeper in her covers.

She thought maybe she could wait it out in her spot until they were gone, then she heard the woman's voice.

"My Lady, please! Your husband…" a young man's voice called. Anastasia carefully poked her head out and found a young squire following a well-dressed woman who was carrying a basket.

"I am going to visit my mother, so unless you care to join me I suggest you wait outside," the woman said, and the hair on the back of Anastasia's neck stood up.

Kata. This was the one Countess Bathory had called Kata.

Her sister.

Anastasia had to fight the urge to step out of the pile of curtains and introduce herself. As she watched Kata and her squire continue to argue, she was shocked by how much her sister reminded her of her daughter. Her smile, her tone of voice, the way she moved her hands; the vision brought tears to Anastasia's eyes.

She missed Katrine so much it physically hurt, like someone had taken one of her limbs.

Kata continued up the stairs to see her mother, Anastasia thought to follow but the squire kept guard at the bottom so she dared not move. She so wished she could hear what they were saying, if the Countess was going to tell Kata about her.

As quickly as she came, Kata left. It looked almost as if she ran out the door.

Anastasia waited until all she could hear was the wind, then crept up the stone staircase for one last time.

She stopped before she entered the corridor to the Countess's chamber and listened. She crouched down so she could listen for footsteps, using her senses as she would have in her true form.

The Countess was walking around her room, Anastasia could not quite tell if she was crying or singing. She could not help but wonder if Kata had been told about the ghosts of the girls that came in the night, if Kata would believe anything her mother said at this point.

Anastasia crept quietly along the floor until she was sitting beside the walled in door, close to a slot near the floor.

"Madam?" she called close to the hole, the walking stopped then the Countess hurried to the small space.

"Anastasia? Is that you?" the Countess asked.

"Yes, Madam. I have returned because there is something I wanted to say."

The Countess's voice grew louder as she got closer to the ground. "And what is that, my dear?"

"Last night I took shelter in your great hall, the wind was bitterly cold."

"It is quite alright, I am sorry you did not get to see my home when it was glorious."

Anastasia paused. "In the night I saw something."

"What did you see?"

"I...I saw girls, Madam. The... the spirits of young girls wandering the halls. I was unsure if you told anyone, or if you'd even seen them yourself."

"I've seen them. I see them almost every night. They are my curse."

"I wanted you to know that I saw them, and that if no one believes you it least you know that I saw them, too."

She could hear the Countess's shallow breathing, as if she was trying to calm herself. She suddenly wished she could see the woman's face.

"If you stand by the air hole at the right angle I may be able to see your face," the Countess began. "Could we try?"

"Only if we may do something similar so I may see yours," Anastasia replied. She stood and tried to position herself so the light shone on her face but her naked body was not visible.

"Your daughter is the spitting image of you, Anastasia," the Countess told her proudly. "Now, come closer. I apologise for my dishevelled appearance but I am sure you understand, considering the circumstances."

Anastasia peered through the small air hole, the Countess had stepped back so the small bit of light from the other air hole by the window gave a clear view of her face.

"I believe, Madam, a more accurate observation is that my daughter is the spitting image of her grandmother. To be as beautiful as you would be a gift," Anastasia told her.

"I can tell you quite confidently that you look more like me than any of my other children," the Countess proclaimed. "Thank you for coming back, Anastasia."

She stepped back from the wall. "This time I must leave for good, Madam. Goodbye and God bless you."

"And God bless you, my oldest daughter. May your life be filled with untold joys and may you be free of my curse."

All she could think about was running. She did not consider who may see her, or what people would think of the naked woman running from Castle Csejthe. But when her feet touched grass she began to shift, and faster than she ever had before. Soon enough she was back in the forest in her true form and running north.

It was like the wind was pulling her forward, and she did not notice the world go by. Distance was what she needed, between her and someone else's ghosts.

The mountains were closer than she had expected. She had no memory of ever seeing them but somehow they were familiar, as if she had come home.

Snow began to fall, lightly at first but with large flakes. As she began making her way up the mountain her mind began to clear and the world of men fell away around her.

All she thought about was finding food and shelter, the wilderness seemed new with a lush feeling that she'd never experienced before.

The snow grew heavy very quickly with a bitter wind and it made moving along very difficult so Anastasia took shelter in a cave. It wasn't particularly warm but it kept out the wind the farther away she went from the entrance. She did a quick check of the cave to make sure it was empty then sat and watched the snow fall, concealing herself enough so if anything came in she could take it by surprise.

As the sun began to get low in the sky, Anastasia considered changing so she could try to light a fire.

Human thoughts still invaded her psyche time after time. She could not help but wonder if they would ever leave her, if she would always try to problem solve as a person.

Living was a wolf, in the company of other wolves, would be difficult if she could not assimilate.

But her soul felt torn apart, scattered in many directions like fallen ash. She thought endlessly of the Countess, and of her slender fingers poking through the small holes in her prison. How delicate they were as digits, encompassing what she was sure was an exquisite hand. Smooth skin with a touch of cold underneath, Anastasia wondered if she was gentle.

And although she thought of her often she never dreamed of the Countess, or anything else for that matter. She felt guilty for not thinking more of her daughter, but Katrine had told her quite clearly to leave and move on so that was what she would try to do.

Anastasia spent the better part of seven days in that cave, waiting until the snow became mud and puddles and she could see the ground again before moving on.

She continued on through the forests that surrounded the mountains, savouring the beauty around her. She found it quite amusing that she would never have gotten to experience this in her other form; how limited people were by each other and the ways of the world was a thought that never fully left her mind.

And, of course, the Countess's fingers.

She passed the outskirts of a small village, stopping to sit in the undergrowth to watch the back of a farm. It was the first time she had really thought of her husband. She sat and watched a man go back and forth to his workshop, a small building set quite a ways away from the main house.

She could not help but wonder if she would ever find love, honest and pure love that came when two people were not 'forced' or 'expected'.

Not that she hadn't grown to enjoy Nikoli's company, but the truth of the matter was that she did not love him in the manner that a wife should love her husband. He may have love for her but not that she had ever been aware of.

A small boy, no more than ten years old, came out of the main house with a tray of food and walked slowly to the workshop, being careful not to stumble.

Anastasia's throat felt tight. Her poor son, her poor, sweet little boy; she had almost forgot about him. His father would take care of him, and she prayed he had not developed the same affliction as his sister; an affliction she had passed on to her daughter, maybe both of her children.

Treading lightly, an animal touched the edge of her senses. When she realised that whatever it was was trying to get her attention she slowly rose and turned back to the forest, a haze cast spots of light on the ground where the sun came through the trees. Something moved in the distance, it was close to the ground and on four legs.

Anastasia began to move closer, being careful of where her feet touched as not to make unnecessary noise. She understood the idea of stalking prey but she was still learning, and she felt clumsy and awkward.

Then a snout pushed out from the brush, along with a pair of bright yellow eyes. Anastasia moved closer then caught its scent, standing in shock as their eyes met. She wasn't sure what to do with the shifter who stood a few feet away from her, so they just stared.

Katrine

DISCRETION

I was already awake when Hannah came in the next morning with my breakfast.

"William wants to see you in the parlour when you're up and about," she said. She seemed annoyed.

"What is the matter?" I asked. I sat up in bed and took some bread and cheese.

"Does he have no thought of your virtue?" she said. "Meeting alone is rather improper."

"I can assure you, Hannah, my virtue is well intact. And William has no concern since he wishes to marry me, and the people whose opinion matters are well aware that there is nothing immoral going on."

She squealed in glee. "You did not tell me he proposed!"

"He has not officially, but he has made his intentions known and when the time comes I will accept," I said.

"Thank Heaven, I thought I had missed it," she replied, sighing loudly.

"Are you mad? You would be one of the very first to know!" I said. "Was there anything from my cousin?"

"No. Why? Are you expecting?"

"Yes, but I have no idea when so it is not of great concern. But if it does come please let me know immediately," I replied. "I think one of my gray dresses would be appropriate for today, don't you?"

William was pacing back and forth across the parlour when I arrived, looking frustrated. He stopped when he noticed me, his face lighting up.

"Good, you're here," he said, kissing my hand.

"What is going on?" I asked.

"What do you know of magic?"

I examined his expression, looking for signs of intent. "Very little. Roza taught me a few small things."

"Forest magic and what I speak of are very different," he replied.

"Alright, so I know nothing. Will you explain what this is about?"

"I was hoping you would tell me."

"William!"

"Something approached you at the theatre last night. Something very powerful. I want to teach you to protect yourself."

"You saw it and you did nothing?" I did not want to admit that I could use the help, and how thankful I was that I didn't need to come to him with this first.

"I could not without attracting attention and I could not get there fast enough. By the time I did it was over. What was it?"

"I am not sure. I am waiting for a complete explanation from Gabriel."

"You will tell me when you find out," he said, and it was not a question.

"Of course," I replied.

"Good, good. Now, today we will start with something basic," he began. "And I am not saying to forget what Roza taught you but you *cannot* get the two mixed or confused in any way or it could cause serious harm."

"I do not remember much of it anyway and it was primarily based on herbs."

"If at any point you have any doubt *don't* do it, do you understand?" he said angrily.

"Yes, of course."

His expression softened. "I am not trying to be harsh, but this is very important. It can cause...."

"Disastrous effects? I know, or did you forget what happened to my mother? Believe me, I know better than anyone what can happen if magic is used incorrectly."

He frowned. "I am so sorry, il mio amore. I am terribly insensitive."

"Think nothing of it," I replied, trying my best to smile at him. I could not expect him to remember something I rarely spoke of.

"Let us begin with something simple. The magic I will be teaching you is casting spells, which will draw from your own internal powers," he began. "There are no potions or herbal mixtures, just the proper words and the energy flowing through your body."

"How do you know I have such energy?" I asked.

"Because I can feel it," he told me. "Now, the candlestick on the mantle, we are going to move it. There is a spell to move objects and a spell to move people which is much more complex. Now, eyes on the candlestick and repeat after me."

We both turned and focused on the large silver candlestick on the left hand side of the fireplace mantle, he said the words first and it moved slightly to the right.

I took a deep breath, then said the spell, "Permoveo is," the candlestick shot quickly to the left, clattering loudly to the floor. William laughed loudly.

"Why is that so amusing?" I asked.

"Because I continually underestimate you," he explained. "Now, do it again, this time use your hands to put it back into place."

I did as he asked, the candlestick shook quite violently as I used my right hand as if I was picking it up and putting it back on the mantle.

"That one is tricky and will take some practice, but you got it back in its place without dropping it so that's quite positive," William said.

"Where did you learn to do this?" I asked.

"My father trained us since birth," he told me.

"Us?"

"My siblings and I. But I was not the heir so I was not quite as relevant, even though I was more powerful."

"Why did you leave Naples?"

His eyes lowered. "What are you getting at?" he asked with a note of anger in his voice.

"Nothing, I was just curious. You never speak of your family."

"With good reason."

"William, if you intend on marrying me you will have to tell me something of your family. I would not want any surprises."

"But you will never see or meet them."

"You will never see or meet my father or brother but I will still tell you about them, if you wish. I want to know all about you, including your family. I have no desire to meet them unless you want it."

He sighed. "I will tell you everything when the time is right."

I broke a vase, pulled down tapestries and three paintings, tipped over a chair and knocked over every candlestick in the room before William was satisfied, and I moved it all back into place except the broken bits which I put into a neat little pile in front of the fireplace.

"Shall we move on to something else?" he asked.

I sat and slumped down in the closest chair I could find. "Not right now, I am exhausted."

He summoned a maid and sent for some food and a canister of blood for me.

"I have fed recently, I should be alright," I said as he sat in the chair across from me.

"Grisela said you are not feeding enough and ordered me to make sure you take more blood at every opportunity," he replied. "She said it is not good for your health, and the longer you go between feedings the more ravenous you could become."

"Why did she not mention this to me directly?" I asked.

"She probably did but you did not listen, you have not been particularly receptive since Kardoska's death," he replied, his expression then full of concern. "I am not trying to offend you, il mio amore. I am just trying to be honest."

I touched my hand to his arm. "I appreciate your honesty, darling, and I know I have been difficult. I am working on it."

The maid came in with a tray of food on a rolling cart, sweeping up the vase on her way out.

"I hope it wasn't valuable," I said.

William smiled. "You could blow up the chateau and Charles would think it was cute. I highly doubt he will miss one little vase."

I poured us both a cup of tea, adding blood to mine before I handed the other cup to William.

"Hannah was quite angry at the idea you may have proposed and she had no knowledge of it," I said.

"But I did not propose," he replied.

"That is what I told her, and when it happens she will be one of the first to know."

"Should I do that now?"

"What now?"

"Propose. I should propose now," he said. It was a statement not a question.

"No. Not now, I am not prepared for married life just yet."

"That is what I thought. I thought I should enquire in case something has changed."

"Have you seen these wagons Charles and Vincenzo are building? They are quite fantastic," I began. "I am actually getting excited for the journey."

"It is going to be long," he said.

"Have you forgotten how far I have come? Wallachia borders the Ottoman Empire...."

"We shall stop for some time in several cities along the way so it will take much longer than one might expect. Vincenzo and I have some work to do in Frankfurt."

"I hope you will allow me to come along. I would like to learn."

"Women are not always taken seriously...."

I smiled at him. "We shall have to change that then, won't we?"

He laughed as I sipped my tea, his entire face lightening up. "I doubt I could convince you otherwise."

At the salon that evening I actively searched out Vincenzo. I had too many questions, I could not keep to myself any longer and he was the only person I could trust to maintain a level head.

I bowed to him when I found him, quickly grabbing his arm and pulling him aside.

"I need your ear, mon ami," I said, talking quietly to him.

"What seems to be the trouble?" he asked.

I sighed. "I was approached last night at the theatre, someone claiming to be from the Order of the Dragon. Said they were an organization who had come together to rid the world of evil, and I am specially equipped to do so."

"Oh? And how so?"

"They were watching my mother originally, then began watching me. The person said I am dhampir, and since they are half evil they are perfect for such a task."

"Do you believe them?" he asked.

"I find it odd that they would know about my life, how I got here. That they would think the man I know as father is, in fact, not. And that they would say to ask Gabriel to explain it all," I began. "In one of the dreams I used to have about my mother, she said I was *her* daughter and implied I had a different father. What is a dhampir?"

Vincenzo sighed. "When a vampire begets a child by a human woman the child is called a dhampir. In many cultures it is believed that dhampir's are always male, but our Gigi is proof that myth is quite false."

"How would I know if I am one?"

"I do not know, but I will find out if it's possible," he said, looking at the expression on my face. "You are frightened. This scared you."

"They said I will join them, and in time I will understand. I do not, and I am unsure I even want to. I am happy here, in this life. I have no intentions on leaving it."

"Until you are married," he replied.

"Why would I leave if I am married? This is where we both belong. The idea of something simpler is appealing but I think if I was destined for such a life I would have stayed in Wallachia," I said. "Perhaps I will retire someday but that is far into the future."

He pat my hand. "We will figure it out, Katrine. You can trust me to be discreet."

"Thank you," I said, breathing a sigh of relief.

Katrine

FOR PROTECTION

The salon ended, and as people were leaving Gigi grabbed my arm and pulled me aside.

"I need you to accompany me on a quick errand, ma petite," she said quietly to me.

"Now? It's quite late. Where could you possibly need to go at this time of night?" I asked.

She took my arm in hers. "Is there ever a time when you will just do what I ask and not question it?"

I looked at her face. Something was different, I could see it in her eyes.

"Of course. When would you like to leave?" I said.

"Now," she replied, pulling me through the people to a maid holding our cloaks. We quietly slipped past as everyone was saying their goodbyes into a waiting carriage.

The carriage stopped at the mouth of a dark alley, the cold seeming to swallow us as we stepped out into the Paris night.

She grabbed my arm and pulled me along beside her. "You say nothing, do you understand? Not a word! You keep your eyes low as if you are my servant."

I said nothing, I just followed along beside her doing exactly what she wanted.

We stopped at a large wood door and she knocked twice, a tiny old crone holding a large candle opened the door a crack.

She held the light up to Gigi's face the motioned for us both to come inside.

Herbs hung in bundles from the ceiling like leaves dangling from a tree. The stench of incense and filth was overwhelming and I had to hold myself back from covering my mouth, watching the crone as she moved around the room collecting things she was bundling together. Her body made a strange sound like the creaking of old wood, like she would crumble into dust at any moment.

"Do you have payment?" the crone asked Gigi, her voice was hoarse and raspy. The French she spoke sounded different, as if with an accent I couldn't place.

"Do you have what I requested?" Gigi asked in a plain, flat voice.

"You had such specific instructions I wondered why you did not make the talisman yourself."

"But then you would be out of a job, Madame."

The crone chuckled. "Better I burn and not you, eh? You courtiers are all alike, you want the power and not the responsibility."

Gigi crossed the room and growled. "My kind don't burn so easily, crone."

The old woman's eyes grew wide with fear, and she hurried around to finish the package.

She handed Gigi a piece of metal wrapped around a stone and a small bundle of other things wrapped in cloth.

"Tell no one I was here, or our next meeting won't be so civilised," Gigi said calmly, and I followed her back out the door and into the dark alley.

"I know what you are thinking, petite, but you do not understand," Gigi began as our carriage got moving, her hands raised in protest. "I cannot risk being unprotected. She said she saw *two* of me in Russia, and if it happens to be one of my....my....oh, for Heaven's sake I cannot even say the words out loud! I *need* this, petite, to protect me from *them*."

I took one of her gloved hands in mine and squeezed in gently, then asked in a soft voice. "Who do you need protecting from?"

"My family!" she said, and she burst into tears. "I have to protect *us* from them, I cannot risk going to Russia unprepared."

I put an arm around her shoulder and pulled her to me as she sobbed. I wanted to know more, press her for answers to the questions that were burning the tip of my tongue but I knew better. She had taught me better manners, I would wait until she was ready.

We returned to the chateau and I took her to her room, she sent the servants away and I helped her undress. She would not look at me as she stood and quietly sobbed, her shame was heartbreaking.

She lay in her bed in her plain white chemise, her face bare and her hair undone; I had never seen her look so beautiful.

I bent down beside her bed and said quietly in French. "Please don't forget that I love you. You are my family now, nothing will ever change that."

I slipped out of the room in silence and continued on to mine, Hannah was dozing in a chair when I stepped inside.

"Is everything alright?" Hannah asked as she started to undress me. "You were gone and no one knew why."

"Mademoiselle Delphine had an errand, nothing of any concern. Can you please tell Signor Amori in the morning that I need to speak with him?" I asked her. She unlaced my corset and put it away for the night as I slipped into bed, my chemise getting twisted in the covers.

"Of course," Hannah said. She headed to the door, turning back to me before she left.

"If something was wrong you would tell me, would you not?" she asked, a bit of distress in her tone.

"Of course. Bonsoir Hannah," I replied.

"Bonsoir, Katrine," she said, closing the door behind her.

ANASTASIA

INTO THE FOREST

The wolf began to slowly creep out of the bushes, pulling forward inch by inch. Every hair on Anastasia's body stood at attention and she physically began to react. The wolf in her went from curious to nervous to frightened very quickly. She considered engaging the other wolf, standing her ground and behaving as a wolf should.

Before she knew it, when the wolf's front paw came into view, she was running, tearing her way through the forest without a thought in her mind except 'get away'.

The wolf followed but made no attempt to overtake or attack her, just ran along like two children playing a game. Anastasia was a little confused, this behaviour seemed totally out of character for a common wolf. As that thought permeated her system and she really focused on it, she could not help but wonder if her pursuer was no common wolf.

Anastasia slowed as she approached a clearing, circling around until she and the wolf were once again face to face. She watched its eyes, how its body moved, the tilt of its head as it stared back at her, looking for any signs of who or what this being may be.

The first crack was loud like a tree splitting. Anastasia watched in shock and awe as the wolf before her rather quickly became a woman, similar in age to herself.

As the woman stood and stretched Anastasia could not help but think of her daughter, and how traumatised she must have been when she witnessed this.

"Do not be afraid," the woman said. "I mean you no harm. But I would like to speak with you. May I see your other face?"

Anastasia considered what she had said; changing in front of another was very revealing and intimate experience and she wasn't sure how she felt about doing so with a complete stranger.

But this woman had the same affliction. Perhaps, at the very least, she could answer some questions.

So she began her change. She tried not to scream in agony as the bones and skin pulled and reformed. It felt to her as if the process took hours.

Finally, she closed her eyes, and when she opened them again she was lying in a pile of leaves, panting loudly.

"What are you running from?" the woman asked as Anastasia pulled herself to her feet.

"Everything and nothing," Anastasia's voice was hoarse and she began to cough.

"I was like you once," she continued. "Lost, confused, running all the time. Not sure which world I fit into. Not quite wolf, but not quite human either. It seemed as if I was alone for years."

Anastasia did not respond, leaning her body against a tree for support as she tried to compose herself.

"But there are others like you. We live together in the forest and have built a life that none of us had dreamed possible. We are not monsters, as the world would have us believe. And sometimes we go out into the forest looking for others. We do not often find any, in fact we have found several dead from attack by other animals, or starvation because they could not handle this life. I want to offer you help. What is your name?" she asked.

"Anastasia," she replied.

"Do you have a family name?"

Anastasia paused, then said, "No."

"Alright. My name is Lynde, Anastasia. If you want to return to wolf form and follow me I will guide you to our camp. I believe we should move quickly before the snow begins again."

The two returned to wolf form and Lynde lead the way, moving quite smoothly through the forest as Anastasia stumbled along behind her. She felt clumsy and foolish as she kept up behind Lynde, who had clearly been doing this for some time. Smell would be the only clear identifier.

Anastasia's thoughts went to those who had been killed by animals. Had they tried to assimilate? Had they tried to challenge them, only to be torn apart because of human thoughts?

On one hand she was grateful, relieved almost, that Lynde had found her, but on the other this all seemed too good to be true.

She needed to tread carefully. She tried to take stock of her surroundings and plan her escape, if it became necessary. But Lynde knew the forest so well she did not know if it would work, but she could try her best to slow her down.

She had to be on guard at all times.

KATRINE

SENSING

"I am worried, Vincenzo," I said.

He raised an eyebrow, his green eyes fixed on me. "She was crying, you say?"

"You must never tell her I told you, but she slipped out in the night to get a talisman from *a crone*," I continued. "She's petrified Morgana's premonition of two means her family is in Russia. I don't understand what this all means, why she is so afraid of her family. I do not know what to do."

"All you can do at this point is quietly listen and stay by her side. I agree this is most distressing but since we have little knowledge of parts of her family we do not know what would be the best action to take."

"Do you have any contacts in Russia?"

"Why?"

"Perhaps we should send our own letters, try to find out for ourselves. I know she sent letters but I cannot imagine they would end up with same people....what do you think?"

He was silent for a moment, then said. "I am unsure what to ask, but I suppose it's worth trying. I'll see what I can do. Thank you for coming to me with this, Katrine. It is wise not to keep this to yourself."

"I could not see her in such a state and not try to help. That seems wrong somehow."

He smiled, pouring some blood into my tea, the morning sun streamed heavily through the windows of the conservatory.

"Now, today Charles and I wanted to try some dhampir tests with you. Firstly I must ask, how bothered are you by the sun?"

"I am not anymore. I was in the early days after being scratched but that stopped. I thought it had something to do with whatever was in the canister other than blood."

His expression brightened. "Can you smell anything else in the canister?"

I picked it up off the tea tray and brought it to my nose, closing my eyes and taking a deep breath before I breathed the scent in as deeply as I could.

The blood was most definitely human, but that was all. I told that to Vincenzo and he chuckled.

"Have you always had a very strong sense of smell?" he asked.

"Not that I remember."

"When you think of your childhood what do you remember?"

I closed my eyes again and tried to think clearly. "The scent of my mother's hair, and of my father's workshop. Also my mother's cooking, the way the aromas would invade the entire house until the middle of the next day. My little brother reeking of dirt since he learned to walk on his own..."

"Did you notice these memories are all tied to smell?"

I paused for a moment, rethinking what I had told him. "No, I didn't. What does that mean?"

"What about your travels with Roza? Are any of those memories tied to smell?"

It didn't take me long to remember, and realise that there were many; from Roza's own smell to the river, the chicken blood in that one inn, and bread. I would never forget the smell of the fires at the executions in Bytca.

"Yes, they all are. But they are fresh. I can taste the fire in the back of my throat, like I'm still standing in Bytca…" I began.

"What happened in Bytca?" he asked.

"My grandmother's supposed accomplices were executed in Bytca," I replied.

"Oh," he said quietly, watching my face. "Have some tea, it should help with the taste."

I did as I was told, trying my best to remove the thoughts from my mind. I suddenly felt very lonely, since that experience was now mine alone.

"I must warn you now I am not entirely sure what Charles has planned in regards to these tests. This is something he has been doing for many years before he brought me into the equation. I am almost positive it will not hurt, mostly because you are not a shapeshifter. He has a very curious mind and wants to become an expert of sorts on our...conditions," he said.

"Why would it matter? And how can you be so sure I am not a shifter? My mother is and I bare her mark," I replied.

"We will begin testing from what we already know. You drink blood, so we'll start with tests related to that," he continued.

"I shall not hurt you, my sweet. You have my word," Charles told me as he came in in a flurry of excitement and energy. "And the shifter tests are painful because they test if one will...well...shift. That is kind of the point. Are you two ready? When you are we shall go to the basement, Vincenzo. I am sorry but you will have to be more involved than you might like. You are the only other blood drinker around the chateau today."

"That is quite alright. I will do what I can to assist Katrine in this matter," Vincenzo replied. "But I insist she must finish her tea first."

*

When Charles opened the basement door I was hit with the strong smell of blood. I followed him and Vincenzo down the stairs, Vincenzo looked visibly shaken.

I saw the man when we got to the bottom of the stairs, his body limp as he lay slumped in the chair with huge gashes up his bare arms.

"What on *earth* is this?" I asked, feeling a bit unnerved.

"Did you ever wonder where that lovely canister of blood came from?" Charles replied.

"I did not realise it involved butchering someone!"

"It is not like that," Charles snapped. "The man is a vagrant, is very well paid and remembers nothing. So reserve your judgments for something else."

"I do not understand how this is supposed to prove anything," I began, then turned to Vincenzo. "Are you alright, mon ami?"

Vincenzo's eyes were glowing, the green so bright it looked like sun rays, his pupils tiny black dots. His lips were twitching, he looked as if he was having difficulty holding his composure.

"I do not understand," I said, looking from him back to Charles.

"It is my belief that a dhampir has the power to resist an open vein, other blood drinkers do not," Charles replied. "Now, let us go back upstairs and test your senses. I do not want our Italian friend losing control."

Charles came to take my arm, before he could I grabbed Vincenzo and started to pull him away.

It took some strain but I finally got him up the stairs and back onto the main level.

His green eyes turned to me, now calm and back to normal. He appeared embarrassed.

"Je suis désolé, Katrine," Vincenzo said. "I never wanted you to see me in such a state."

"Please, you have no need to apologise. It is not your fault it is part of your instincts," I replied as we followed Charles through the chateau and up to the second floor.

I had not gone to the opposite end of the hallway from where my bedroom was so I was genuinely surprised when Charles opened a door into a library.

Bookshelves surrounded the room, filled from floor to ceiling. It smelled of dust and wood and was surprisingly warm and inviting. A few chairs surrounded a large stone fireplace, which was cold and dark.

"Come, come! Sit!" Charles said, motioning us to the chairs. They were made of soft, plush leather, and as I sunk in I felt like I was sitting on a cloud.

"Katrine, I want you to close your eyes and tell me how many people you can sense in the building, first the humans then the non," Charles continued, easing into the chair.

I closed my eyes and took a calming breath, the silence pulling things out in my mind I wasn't aware were even there.

Quite suddenly I could hear every breath, every heartbeat within the walls of the chateau. There were small trickles of emotions and a strong wave of fear coming directly from Gigi.

"Katrine?" Charles's voice broke the silence and I remembered my task.

"Twelve humans," I began. "Tolone and Hannah are not here. Seven non-humans, including us. And there is something strange outside."

I felt a hand on my knee. "What is it?" Charles asked.

"Well, it gives the impression of Klara but it's male," I replied.

"Is it her family?" he asked.

"No, it is something else entirely," I said. I opened my eyes just as one of the male servants came in the room.

"My Lord," the man began. "There is a gentleman outside looking for Mademoiselle Von Dores."

"Tell him she no longer lives here," Charles said.

"Begging your pardon, sir, but I already did. He refuses to leave until he speaks to her."

Charles stood and went to the window, I heard his frustrated sigh from across the room.

"The man is sitting in the road!" Charles yelled. "Cross legged like some child *in the road*! It's January in Paris! He is most certainly insane."

"Non, mon ami, he is most certainly enchanted. We will have to find a way to break the connection," Vincenzo replied.

"And if we cannot?" Charles said.

"Then I fear we will have a camp outside our door," Vincenzo continued.

"She has officially become more trouble than she's worth. We cannot have this kind of attention," Charles said with some force, sounding like a true leader.

"Perhaps we should have William and Morgana scare them away," I said. The two men turned and looked at me, sparks behind their eyes.

"That is actually not a bad idea. I shall go see what I can do," Vincenzo stood and left, I watched him in a panic but he ignored me. I did not want to be alone with Charles, his pleased expression when my friend was gone unnerved me.

"At last we are alone," Charles said. He returned to the seat he had vacated, watching me intently.

"We shall work on the testing, nothing more," my tone had a sharp bite.

"Why do you continue to reject my gifts and push me aside?" he asked.

"I have said this multiple times, your intentions are not noble and you should turn them elsewhere."

"I have tried to prove you wrong but you will not allow it. You are so influenced by others...."

"*You bought me a human being!*"

"He is your family. I thought you would be pleased."

"You did not buy him out of the kindness of your heart. I wonder what he would say if he discovered he was saved as a way to try to deflower a young woman," I began. "Since it appears I have not made it clear I will say it plainly so there is no confusion. I am in love with someone else, Charles. I would most gladly take your friendship and nothing more."

He stood, moving back to the window. "I do not believe you. You have been coached by Grisela...."

"Am I so transparent?" I yelled. I stood and gathered myself, then began towards the door.

"But the testing," he said when I got to the doorway, that earlier command gone from his tone.

I stopped, turning my head but keeping my back to him, and said, "Suddenly I am not concerned with such details."

I watched the commotion from the top of the stairs, I considered going down but thought better of it. One of Klara's enchanted men had tried to kill me just before she did, I didn't know how another of these men would react to seeing me.

For all I knew, he could be here looking for me.

I could hear William's angry voice followed by Morgana's, I hoped they were working together to try to fix the problem. We could not have such attention brought to us, I wondered if we could not repair the problem if we would have to eliminate it.

I decided to go back to my room until things had calmed. I'd had enough for one day.

KATRINE

A TASTE OF BEAUTY AND MAGIC

"Katrine, may I ask you something?" Hannah asked as she was helping me dress for the evening. I had spent the rest of my day reading and trying not to think about what had happened with Charles or what was going on outside.

"Of course," I said. She pulled another dress that was such a pale blue it was almost white over my head and began to lace it up the back.

"May I sit in on the events tonight? I have never seen fabrics from Venice and Spain before," she said carefully with a cautious tone.

"When will that happen? Of course you can but I am not sure exactly what you are talking about," I said.

"All the women are gathering in the sitting room tonight to choose fabric for their new gowns for Russia. No one told you?"

"No, but Gigi has been stressed lately. I cannot blame her for being forgetful. Do you know the time of when this shall happen?"

"At sunset, I believe. So we should be done just in time," she said, turning to look out the window.

I sighed. "I suppose I should be more excited than I am, I feel it inside my head but something else is there also, making me sad. I am unsure what it could be."

I twisted my ring around on my finger, thoughts of my grandmother made my heart sink.

"I am still working on something to wear your father's cross with, if that has anything to do with it," Hannah replied.

"Did you know I wrote my grandmother a letter? She never replied," I began. "Gabriel said they walled her up in her bedchamber. Could you imagine, Hannah? There were bricks filling the doors and windows, with only tiny slits for air and to pass food through."

Hannah began combing through my hair and said quietly. "I am so sorry."

There was a knock at the door and Gabriel came in, taking his usual spot on a stool close by.

"Will you tell me about my grandmother, cousin?" I mused, my eyes staring off into space.

"What would you like to know?" he asked.

I turned my eyes to him and said, "Everything."

"Okay," he said, taking a deep breath in and out. "She is the smartest woman I have ever met. She spoke several languages at an early age and excelled at her studies, she is also one of the most highly educated women in all of Hungary. A brute like Ferenc was lucky to have such a wife, I liked him just fine but he was not even remotely as remarkable as Erzsebet. But he was aware he had married the most beautiful woman in the country, her intelligence was a fantastic asset, because she was more capable of managing the estates while he went to war."

His eyes lowered and he continued. "She did not have a child for the first ten years of their marriage, that is an awfully long time. There were some serious concerns that she was barren, but I suppose your mother's conception and birth may have added to the circumstances. I don't believe Ferenc knew of your mother, if he did he did not care. I think he genuinely loved Erzsebet, an uncommon thing for noble marriages. From what I was told her parents loved each other also, they were both Bathory but from different family branches. That made their children, Erzsebet and her sisters and older brother Istvan, that made them purely Bathory. I believe, and that may have changed now, that they are the only pure Bathory in existence."

"Is that a positive thing?"

He stared down at his hands. "That depends on who you ask. The family is slowly dying out, there are not many of us left."

"But we are, cousin," I took his hand and squeezed it. "And through us the Bathory will continue to live."

He looked into my eyes and smiled, the action not transferring to his pain filled gaze. I wished I knew what so troubled his thoughts.

I thought to ask if the Order of the Dragon was somehow tied to our family, but I would not press him. He would tell me when he was ready.

"There are so many things you should know about the family, but I am unsure I can tell you all that you seek. I know some but not all," he said, examining my face.

"You know nothing of my mother's conception or birth?" I asked. I thought I knew what he would say, but considering what that person from the Order had told me I wasn't taking any chances.

"No, only my suspicions regarding how long she had until she birth of another. And I fear all those who may know have passed from this earth," he replied.

"Except that woman who approached me in the theatre. She claimed to know things," I snapped, gasping at my own boldness. "I am so sorry. I do not mean to be rude."

"You are not, but I am not sure they know the truth. I thought we may ask one of your Grandmother's sisters but I am unsure how, they believe I am dead. They could also be dead for all I know," he said. "I shall explain all I know of that woman you spoke with soon, I have not forgotten."

I lowered my eyes to him in respect. "And I thank you for that, cousin."

Hannah began work on my hair, the styles were beginning to get more and more elaborate. Today she bundled it in a finely woven silver net, leaving small pieces falling around my face as if by accident.

"Your maidservant has true talent, my dear," he said, pulling back to examine me. "And you look so much like Erzsebet. More and more every day. I wish I could have met your mother."

I chuckled. "You may get your chance yet. I am not sure if she is dead."

He looked slightly confused; he had witnessed the wolf who we believed was my mother, and the injury it had received but we did not know if it had survived. I knew in my heart she had but I did not have any proof.

"What shall the men do tonight while we shop for fabrics?" I asked.

He shrugged his shoulders. "I am not sure, all I know is that we men shall be leaving for the evening. Charles has something planned, I gather."

"Hopefully the debauchers behaviour will not disrupt any fun you may have," I said and he laughed.

"Do not fret, Katrine. I shall guard your William well."

I snorted. "Thank you for the gesture but I trust him completely."

"Of course," he replied. The look in his eyes was unsettling, as if he knew something I did not.

Hannah stepped away from me to admire her work. "You are ready, Mademoiselle."

"Thank you, Hannah. I shall escort my cousin downstairs, you will join us shortly I hope?" I said, taking Gabriel's arm in mine.

"Yes, Mademoiselle, I will help the merchants prepare then join you afterwards," she replied, bowing to us as we left the room.

"It is kind of you to include Hannah on such an endeavour," Gabriel said as we walked down the stairs.

"Of course I would. I trust her judgment and value her opinion, she is in charge of dressing me after all," I replied. The men were gathered at the bottom of the stairs preparing to leave, William's face brightened when he saw me.

"I trust you shall be on your best behaviour, gentlemen," I said to the group.

Charles's devious smile sent a cold shiver down my spine. "Would you expect anything less?"

The front door opened and the men began to leave, Gabriel and I bowed to each other as he left and William came over and kissed my hand.

"Please enjoy your evening," I said calmly. I did not want him to think I was concerned.

"And you as well, my love," he replied, pulling on his cloak and stepping out into the night.

The women were all getting seated, I took my place on the couch beside Gigi who seemed to be at the centre of it all. Victorie sat on her other side, with Mathilde, Josephine, Morgana and two other women I did not know well were seated around the room. Morgana sat in a chair so close to me she was almost in my lap.

Gigi looked pale and slightly nervous, her eyes were red and she looked as if she had not slept through the night. She sat with her back completely straight as if preparing for something to happen.

"I did not mention this to you, ma petite. I apologise. I am not myself," Gigi said, her voice without emotion and inflection.

"Did you see anything more?" I whispered to Morgana.

"No, and I have tried. I am so sorry," she whispered back.

I went back to watching my mentor, I wondered if the others could sense her fear.

The dressmaker who had made all of my gowns came in with several other men carrying many different fabrics, each individually wound around long wood sticks. I immediately gravitated towards forms of white but I knew I could not, I had to remove all visual signs I was in mourning long before we left for Russia.

My excitement grew as colours and textures appeared before me, it took all of the strength I had to keep my composure. Gigi and Victorie remained stoic, I noticed Josephine's eyes light up when certain colours appeared, our costumer had quite the eye for colour.

I noticed Hannah come into the room out of the corner of my eye and stand against the wall with three of the other maidservants, I wondered if they were personal to the other women and I was not aware.

"Petite," Gigi said sharply. "Are you paying attention?"

"Yes, of course," I replied.

"Good, because you will need some very grand gowns made and they *cannot* be white. Or red, for that matter, which reminds me," she began, then turned to the rest of the room, "Ladies, we can have nothing in red. Please, Monsieur, only red accents. Red is for royalty only in Russia."

Mathilde let out a huge huff, smoothing down the front of her red skirt. "Shall I switch to pink or wine?"

Mathilde had taken to wearing red quite often these past months, I had begun to wonder if it was at the suggestion of my cousin.

Before Gigi could respond the man who had made my gowns pulled out a length of fabric and placed it in front of Mathilde.

"A mix of red and purple, we have been calling it 'plum'. I think it's quite fantastic, don't you?" the dressmaker said.

Mathilde giggled in delight. "It's perfect!"

He turned his eyes to me and said. "I have something quite magical for you, Mademoiselle, if you'd allow me to show you."

I nodded in agreement and watched as he put a length of black silk in front of me that shone great shades of purple, red and pink when it caught the light. I smiled happily as he placed a similar piece in front of Gigi that shone in blues and greens.

For the first time in what seemed like an eternity Gigi smiled.

"You have a keen eye, Monsieur. Perhaps you should show us your personal selections for each of us," Gigi said.

The dressmaker sprang to life, his face alive with delight as he placed fabrics in front of each of us, his joy rising from our pleased expressions. By the time it was done I had six colours and the shining black; rose, deep sea blue, charcoal grey, green, silvery white, and another black that shone like polished stone. Gigi had brilliant shades of blue with silver and gold thread and one cloth of highly polished silver that looked like it was taken from the stars themselves.

Each woman had equally stunning pieces specifically for them, even Morgana had something beyond her plain undyed linen.

I looked at Hannah, who winked at me with a big happy smile on her face, and I knew that meant she approved of what was picked for me.

"So," Mathilde said while the room was being cleared. "The men are gone, what shall we do?"

"You know they went to a brothel," Victorie said and I gasped.

"Do not worry the girl, Victorie," Mathilde said, then she turned to me. "No need to concern yourself, Katrine. Even if they did go to a brothel William would *never* fornicate with whores."

I looked to Gigi, who rolled her eyes and said. "We don't know if they did in fact go, ma petite. You could not expect men to control themselves in such a manner anyhow. Even if they are married."

"*Especially* if they are married," Victorie added.

I wanted to yell that my William would never do such a thing, but I only had my faith in him. I had no proof.

And the absolute truth was that he may not have been as much mine as I perceived him to be, and I was a foolish, inexperienced child who did not understand the ways of the world.

But he had said he wanted no one but me. That meant something.

"If Charles had his way he would have his own harem," Victorie said. "He sure tried to turn us into one."

"You cannot be serious!" I exclaimed.

"Quite," Mathilde replied. "We have a little wager on when he will try with your Scots friend."

I turned to Gigi, my eyes wide with shock.

"Relax, petite. Morgana will remove one of his hands first," Gigi said, then asked Morgana, "He has not tried, has he?"

"No. I was unsure if I should be insulted," Morgana replied as she played with the end of her long blonde plait.

The other women began to laugh and for a moment Gigi looked relaxed. Before they could say more one of the maids came in, looking rather distressed.

"Pardon me, Mademoiselle Delphine, but there is a small problem and Lord Westwick said specifically to come to you should the need arise," the maid said.

Gigi sighed. "What is it?"

"That man who was here this morning looking for Mlle. Von Dores? He has returned and this time he is not alone," the maid said quickly then rushed away, fearing Gigi's wrath. Gigi got angry and began to hurl obscenities under her breath in rapid French.

"What is this about?" Mathilde leaned over and asked me.

"It appears that Klara's enchanted men are more of a problem than we had believed," I told her. "I thought William had taken care of it."

"It appeared that way," Morgana said, sounding extremely frustrated. "I will go and deal with the problem. Katrine, I believe it wise for you to remain inside."

"Why?" I asked, wondering if she had the same thought I'd had earlier.

"Because they tried to kill you once, I cannot guarantee they will not do it again," she turned and left the room before any more could be said.

"Perhaps I should assist her," Mathilde said, standing and leaving. "Been some time since I'd been in a good scuffle."

The other women rose and followed her out, all except Gigi.

"We shall watch from the window. He may have left me in charge but that does not mean I have to be involved," Gigi said. I followed her over to the window where she had a maid bring us two chairs so we could watch comfortably.

A small group of men had gathered in the street, they turned when the women stepped out into the night. They seemed to be focused on one in particular, I wondered if they were looking at Victorie thinking she was me.

Morgana approached, looking rather small and unassuming. I hoped she knew she could not kill them and cursed myself for not reminding her.

"You seem tense. Is something troubling you?" I asked Gigi.

"I am unfortunately troubled, ma petite. I cannot seem to shake it. I wish the girl could tell me more," she said casually.

"If she sees more she will say so, I am sure."

"And that is the most troubling thought of all."

I watched my mentor's cold, beautiful face and my heart sank.

I took her hand tightly in mine, and said, "Whatever it is, we shall get through it together. You took me in, you gave me a chance, and I will do whatever I can to show you it was worth it."

The scuffle outside escalated into something aggressive, the men looking angry and shuffling around as if they were about to fight. The women seemed almost amused by this behaviour, and one of the men began to advance, Mathilde grabbed his throat so fast I did not see her move until he was dangling.

"Mon dieu," Gigi said. "She best not kill him out on the street like a common animal."

Mathilde tossed the man away from her like a dirty rag, his body fell limply to the ground and he scrambled away in fear. I had no idea she was that strong. Morgana said something and a pulse erupted from her body, like the earth had shook and the movement knocked the men to the ground.

"Qu'est-ce que?" Gigi said, her voice barely a whisper.

"A taste of Morgana's *other* powers," I said, gripping her hand tighter.

Katrine

TRUTH AND CONSEQUENCES

After the other women left and went to bed I snuck into William's room and waited. I needed to know and I would not rest until I saw his face.

The knob did not turn until almost dawn, my candle burned down to a nub. He looked startled when he noticed me sitting in the chair by his writing table.

"Katrine, you…" he began.

I raised my hand to stop him. "Did you go to a brothel tonight?"

He paused, before he could speak I crossed the room and took one good sniff of him. I closed my eyes and cleared my mind, trying to figure out exactly what I was smelling.

"Katrine, if I had known I would not have gone. I did nothing wrong," he said quietly.

"In who's eyes, William? Men behaving in such a way is accepted by some, but not me," I replied, backing slowly away. "I do not have it in me. I am not built that way."

"I did not have relations with those women, Katrine. I swear."

"Whores, William. You mean those whores, because that is what they were."

He reached out to me and I pulled away, his expression looked heartbroken.

"Katrine, please," he said. "I would never do anything to hurt you. You are my world."

My eyes welled up with tears, I looked away and said. "I am very tired. We shall speak more of this tomorrow."

I turned then and ran, out the door and down the hall to the other end, to my own room and closed the door behind me. Tears streamed down my face as I undressed myself and crawled into bed.

A thin, pale hand slid up his clothed thigh, I fought with everything I had to run away but I could not.

Then there were two hands, fumbling with his pants to release his swollen member. William's face eased, his eyes rolling back in his head as the hands grabbed for dear life.

I tried to scream, I could feel myself crying but could not move. I watched the hands as they pleasured William, my chest hurting as if my heart was being torn in half.

He turned his eyes to me, startling me out of my sleep.

I sat up in bed, covered in a cold sweat and breathing heavily. Every time I closed my eyes I saw it again, my stomach lurching as if I was about to vomit.

I lay in my bed and tried to fall back asleep but there was no use. I lit the candle beside my bed and picked up one of my books, a novel in French that Gigi insisted I read, and decided I would read until I fell back to sleep or it was time to wake up. Whichever came first.

KATRINE

WORRY

Hannah came in early as I lay in silence, book discarded on the floor. I had not slept but had been desperately trying for hours by lying in bed with my eyes closed.

She noticed my pile of clothes lying in a heap by the bed, she said nothing as she picked them up and began to straighten up while she waited for me to wake.

I opened my eyes and watched her until she noticed me.

"I do not want to leave my bed today," I said flatly.

She raised an eyebrow at me. "Are you ill?"

"Not exactly."

"Have your monthly courses arrived?" she asked.

"No," I replied.

"Then there is no reason why you should not leave your bed."

I sighed. "The men went to a brothel last night."

She snorted at me, looking at me as if I was a stupid child.

"You are quite naive, child. They are men, that is what they do. You should not expect anything more from them," she replied.

"I expect more from William," I said. She laughed, the sound like a knife in my back.

"You can leave now, Hannah," I said sharply. "I'll not have such condescending behaviour in my presence."

She stared blankly at me and before I could start yelling she left. I rolled on my side and stared at the wall, praying silently to myself for sleep.

It never came. And as the sun got lower in the afternoon I knew if I spent much longer in bed it would raise eyebrows. I did not want the other woman thinking I was bothered by what they had said. The idea they might think I was some naive child did not sit well with me.

I dressed myself and plaited my hair, deciding to go to the kitchen to find something to eat. I thought maybe I should apologise to Hannah then decided against it, I would not go back on my feelings.

I went quietly downstairs and tried to attract as little attention to myself as humanly possible, not making eye contact with anyone as I walked through the salon and into the kitchen.

One of the younger maids was hunched over the oven, the familiar whiff of Roza's baking overtaking my senses. My heart sank and I bit back my sadness. Another of the maids noticed me standing there and began fixing me a plate of bread, cheese and preserves.

I pulled up a stool and sat in the corner and ate, watching the bustling had a calming effect on me.

"Madmoiselle Bathory," a maid came over to me and spoke quietly. "Signor Amori and Madmoiselle Delphine have been looking for you."

"Where are they?" I asked.

"In her room, I believe," she replied.

"I will take my food with me," I said, before she could say more I took my plate and headed for Gigi's room.

"Petite, where on earth have you been?" Gigi asked when I got in her room and sat down.

"It seems our little girl was rather disturbed by William being at a brothel," Vincenzo said from his seat by the window across from Gigi. I sat by her writing desk.

She gasped, giggling a little. "Mon dieu, what did you do?"

"Nothing," I said, quietly eating my food.

"Whatever this 'nothing' was William is rather distressed about it," Vincenzo continued, both their eyes turning to me.

"I told him I did not approve of brothel visits or of men having relations with women other than their intended or wife," I replied quite flatly.

"So you disapprove of me?" Gigi asked.

I snorted. "To the best of my knowledge you are not a trollop. You are a former courtesan, not a common whore. You've told me that often."

"She's right, Grisela," Vincenzo replied.

"I know," she said, sighing. "I have taught her too well."

"William did nothing questionable Katrine, you have my word," Vincenzo said. I winced as he said it, they continued to watch me in confusion. I continued with my meal, feeling inappropriate speaking while having my meal. We said nothing, the two of them continued to watch as I cleared my plate, the tension in the room growing thicker.

I finally said. "Something doesn't feel right."

"What do you mean?" he asked.

"Vincenzo, I could smell it," I said sharply. "Something is not right."

He sighed. "So not only do you not believe him that nothing happened you do not believe me."

I looked into his eyes, his eyes that were greener than spring grass, and tried to find something to ease my anxiety.

"You don't trust him," Vincenzo said.

"I don't understand why. He has never given me a reason not to," I replied.

"You are smart not to," Gigi said.

"Grisela, please! You are not helping," Vincenzo said angrily.

"Why should any woman trust men when they consider us pieces of property?" Gigi snapped.

"If you wish to argue I shall return to my room," I began.

"No, no! We are not arguing. You have no reason not to have faith in William. Please trust me," he said.

"And what of you, mon ami? Or my dear cousin Gabriel? What is the purpose of going to a brothel if not to fornicate with whores?"

"You would have to ask Charles, since it was his idea," he replied.

"He is starting to test my nerves with his constant advances," I said.

"Do you think he did it on purpose, to drive a wedge between you and William?" he asked.

Gigi snorted. "It is awfully calculated, even for Charles."

"You are right," Vincenzo said, sighing. "Perhaps he is becoming sloppy."

Gigi laughed this time, I remained completely still as I watched them.

"Ma petite doux has driven her first man completely mad. I am so proud," Gigi said happily. "Hopefully Charles will regain his composure before we leave for Russia, I cannot imagine the state we will be in if our leader is not in top form."

"I have told him repeatedly to leave me be, it is not my fault if he chooses not to listen," I replied.

"But poor William, ma petite, you cannot punish him if he truly did nothing dishonest. And our dear Vincenzo would not lie to you," Gigi continued, her voice a low purr. "You are wise to be suspicious but perhaps in this case it is quite extreme."

"I know what I felt. Something isn't right," I replied.

"Your senses are part of what make you dhampir, Katrine. You should not ignore them. Investigate further," Vincenzo said, his expression gone blank.

I smiled at him and said. "I believe you, Vincenzo. I trust you and Gigi completely, though sometimes it may not appear that way."

"What about William, then?" he asked.

I sighed, lowering my eyes and examining the rug as if it held all the answers.

"Whatever you decide, petite, you must do it soon. Charles has said we shall leave for Russia after Easter," Gigi said.

I felt my eyebrows raise. "That is sooner than I expected."

"He has spent much time and money preparing, it should all be ready by then," Vincenzo said.

I smiled at them. "It appears we are going to Russia."

Gigi's eyes began to sparkle, the smile of a mischievous child blossoming across her face. She began to laugh and I could not help but smile wider.

"I hope they are prepared for us, for we shall take the country by storm!"

she said, her smile lighting up the entire room. "I hope they are preparing for our arrival!"

Anastasia

CAMP

They went deeper into the forest, the trees were so tall they appeared similar in height to the mountains. Nothing else was around for what seemed like miles, then after passing through a barrier of sorts they were surrounded.

Lynde slowed her pace to keep close to Anastasia as they approached the camp. They slowed to a walk, and after passing an enormous oak tree the great fire appeared in a clearing down a small slope.

People stood as they approached. Anastasia wondered what position Lynde held among them. Anastasia watched as Lynde quickly returned to human form and stepped into the circle.

"Good people! This is Anastasia," Lynde proclaimed. "She is new. Please show her the kindness you were shown when you were in the same situation."

Anastasia began her change in the shadows, and it seemed to take longer than it ever had before.

When she was finally done several hands were extended to her, bringing her up and giving her a place to sit within the circle. A small clay bowl of stew and some bread were placed in front of her then they continued on with their business.

Anastasia sat and enjoyed the warmth of the fire for some time before picking up the food. That first bite of bread was so wonderful she thought her mouth was watering.

"How is it?" Lynde asked.

"Wonderful," she said between bites.

"Good. There is plenty more if you need. Then, if you wish, you may sleep before I introduce you formally to the others."

Anastasia considered her food for a moment, then said, "That sounds too good to be true."

"What do you mean?"

"Good things such as this do not just happen to people like me, I would be foolish not to question it."

"You have quite the story, I imagine?" a tall, silver blonde haired man who stood beside Lynde said. He was broad shouldered and stood a full head taller than everyone else.

Anastasia made eye contact with him. "You will be shocked, if you believe me at all."

"Give us some time," another woman said, "and we will prove ourselves. And if not you are free to go. You can come and go as you please, you are a guest not a prisoner."

"Is this all of you?" Anastasia asked.

"No. The young are asleep," the woman continued.

"You've found children?"

The woman laughed. "Heaven's no! While I suppose it is not impossible these particular children were born to us."

"I did not know it was possible."

The woman bent down and Anastasia could clearly see her face, she had small delicate features and large green eyes. She held out her tiny hand to Anastasia, who put her food down and was surprised by how soft the other woman's skin was when their hands finally touched.

The woman smelt the inside of her wrist. "You were born with your affliction."

"From what I was told. But my first full change came...," she paused, "because of magic."

"Do you have children?"

"Yes. My daughter is afflicted with something but it is not a change in her shape."

"Perhaps another time you will share your story with me, I know some things about magic. My name is Saskia."

Anastasia nodded at her then went back to her food. "Pleased to meet you all."

Lynde took Anastasia to a tent and a small bed made of straw with pillows and furs and woven blankets.

"Come out when you are ready, you will not be disturbed," Lynde said.

"Thank you," Anastasia called to her as she turned to leave.

"Thank me when you decide to stay," she replied, closing the tent behind her.

Anastasia fell asleep quickly, the warmth of a proper bed giving her a comfort she had greatly missed.

She dreamed of Katrine, only not the Katrine that she knew, but a woman dressed in a stunning gown at what looked like a court function. She wondered, at first, if it was in fact the Countess but it did not seem to fit, and she would recognise her seed anywhere.

And how beautiful she was indeed! She kept close to a very attractive blonde woman but Katrine was clearly the most beautiful woman in the room. She moved with such grace and such style, it was as if she was destined for this life.

Anastasia felt a warmth spread through her body, a comfort that her daughter was in her proper place. That in all the horrific things that had happened she had still given her daughter the best, what the girl truly deserved.

She had known as soon as the screaming infant was placed in her arms that she was to be so much more than anything she could give her.

Soon the dream faded into darkness and Anastasia fell into a heavy sleep.

When she opened her eyes again two little girls stood watching her. She had heard of the concept of twins before but had never seen them, and the two girl's identical, perfectly matched faces were fascinating as well as a little understanding.

"Hello," Anastasia said as she sat up.

"Good morning," the girl's said in unison.

"Can I help you with something?"

They smiled. "No."

"So you just came to watch me as if I was a caged animal?"

The girl on the left frowned. "No. We only wanted to see you for ourselves. A new wolf has not joined us in our lifetime."

"And how old are you?"

"Five," they said together. Their little faces reminded her of Bodi, she hoped he was doing well on his own.

"I am Astrid," the girl on the left said. "This is Amalie. We are the daughters of Lynde and Lief, the Erôs. What is your name?"

"Anastasia," she swung her feet over the side of the bed. "Am I everything you thought a new wolf would be?"

The girls exchanged glances, then Astrid said, "Not exactly. I thought you would be more frightening, or perhaps a bit menacing."

"Sorry to disappoint you," Anastasia replied. "Could you take me to where I can find some food?"

"Of course," they said, each girl taking a hand and leading her outside.

Anastasia was shocked when she stepped out into the morning sunshine to find a settlement she had not seen in the darkness.

Everything seemed to surround the fire pit, which was the main gathering place and centre of what was really a small village. Tents were erected under the trees and coloured in a way that blended them in with the forest, some even had entrance coverings made out of leaves.

The twins lead Anastasia across the fire pit to a large tent close to the edge of the clearing.

"Girls!" Lynde yelled sharply at her children as they all passed through the doorway. "I told you to let her be!"

"It is quite alright," Anastasia told her. "I was coming to get something to eat anyhow."

"We will get you something," the girls said, leading Anastasia to a seat.

She glanced around only briefly, not wanting to bring any more attention to herself.

A large man watched her from across the tent, where he sat surrounded by others. He was head and shoulders taller than those around him, even when they were seated, and had a body thick with muscles.

His eyes were so dark they appeared to be black, and he stared with a force and confidence normal men did not often possess.

He must be their leader, Anastasia thought to herself. He looks like a King.

The two little girls appeared beside her, one with a clay bowl of food and the other with a mug of liquid.

"Thank you, girls," Anastasia said happily. She took the bowl and dug in, the gruel was well seasoned and had pieces of salty meat and vegetables.

"Your cook is fantastic," she spoke to no one in particular. There was a soft chuckle from across the room and words of gratitude.

"So are you going to stay with us?" Astrid asked. Her mother quickly pulled both girls away before she could reply.

"Things cannot be decided so quickly, young one," the large man said with a chuckle. "We should find out what use she could have yet."

"Use?" Anastasia looked into his eyes as she continued. "I was under the impression all who...shifted were welcome."

"So they can come and sit around while the rest of us work?"

"And who are you to judge?"

The man laughed loudly at that, a thunderous roar. "I am Gavril, and I am Király Farkas of this tribe. So I am, in fact, in my right to judge."

"Király Farkas means King, I am assuming?"

He laughed again. "At least you seem to have a brain...and what is your name, woman?"

She put down her bowl of food, took a large sip out of the mug and said, "My name is Anastasia."

"Wonderful. Well, Anastasia, after we eat we will take you on a tour of our camp, and show you the work that is done..."

"It will be cooking or cleaning or mending, I suppose? Women's work, some might say?"

He smiled, a wide grin of perfectly straight white teeth. "Women are equals to men here, some even hold high ranking positions, like Lynde. You can choose to do whatever you feel you can contribute, no more no less."

"That sounds fine. Perhaps I shall find my true calling, Király Farkas."

"I should hope so," he nodded in recognition, then turned his attention back to his other subjects.

Anastasia smiled to herself and continued to eat. Perhaps this was more of a blessing than she had originally thought.

Katrine

A TIME TO LEAVE

That evening we went to the theatre, we did not have a performance that evening but another group did and we decided to attend. When we arrived a large caravan was parked at the steps leading to the theatre.

"It appears Klara's escort has arrived," Vincenzo said as we stepped out of the carriage. Gigi looked quite pleased to see them, I wondered what had happened to change her mood so dramatically.

"They will just walk her out the front door like a common criminal? In front of all these people?" I asked. "Would that not attract unwanted attention?"

"Good. That is better than she deserves," Vincenzo mumbled. I looked at him in shock, I was used to such a comment from Gigi but not him.

"I am sure it will not be such a spectacle, petite," Gigi said, and we started up the stairs. When we got to the front doors Tolone and Hannah were waiting to take us to the underground.

Klara had on wrist and ankle shackles, heavy iron I was surprised she could move with. All that she'd had in her cell was being packed around her into a trunk; only her most personal belongings were being taken, all bits of her once extravagant life left behind and divided up. Gigi had said Klara's jewels were being sent back to her parents, and her more extravagant gowns given away or Josephine was reconstructing them for costumes.

She seemed smaller and less flashy when being weighed down by heavy chains. I felt almost sorry for her, I knew what it was like to be brought up but not torn down.

She looked up at me, an evil spark in her eyes. A large man who appeared to be dressed in curtains was talking to Charles, I assumed he was Klara's new owner. His skin was brown from sun and dirt, his small eyes darting around the room as if he was nervous, his stance like he was expecting something to pop out and startle him.

"Are you alright il mio amore?" William said, he came up behind and stood close to my body. I sighed, his presence always made me feel safe.

"I am. Just tired. I did not sleep well," I replied.

"I am sorry if I was the cause," he said.

I turned my head, looking at his face out of the corner of my eye. "Can we not speak of this here and now?"

"As you wish," he replied. I felt him step back, my nerves suddenly more on edge. I was not sure I could handle torments of the heart, perhaps I should never fall in love.

Two servants pulled Klara to her feet and followed Charles and the large man towards the door. We walked up the stairs and out a door that lead out the side of the theatre where the caravan was now parked. She was covered in a dark cloak and put in the back of the covered wagon with the other luggage, and in a matter of moments Klara Von Dores was out of our lives, hopefully for good.

"Madmoiselle Bathory," a small voice said behind me as we headed up the stairs to a private box. I turned around to find a boy standing behind me, he looked similar in age to Bodi.

He handed me a letter, it was sealed with red wax and a dragon emblem.

"Boy, who gave you this?" I asked.

"A woman in a dark cloak, I didn't see her face. She gave me a gold Louis to deliver it to you," he said proudly, smiling widely despite his rotten teeth. "Can I go?"

I nodded, giving him a silver coin before he took off.

"What was that?" William asked. I showed him the unopened letter and the seal, he nodded slowly like he understood. We continued on to the box with Vincenzo and Gigi, she and I close to the front so we could be seen by the crowd and the men behind us.

I used my finger to carefully open the letter without disturbing the wax, quickly scanning the writing on the page. It was my native language and I could understand most of it but not all. My mother had taught me very little, but in my lessons with Gigi I had learned some more. I found it odd that the author of the note assumed I could read the form spoken in my village as different versions were spoken all over the countryside. How did they know which was mine?

The note said something like 'Be careful in your travels. Your powers are blooming, do not ignore your instincts. Prepare for danger beyond your understanding, your world will be turned upside down again and you can do nothing to stop it'.

I sighed, folded the letter up and put it in my sleeve.

"Everything alright?" William asked.

I smiled and nodded. "Fine. Fine. Everything is just fine."

Katrine

OUT OF THE DARKNESS

When I went looking for Morgana the next day I couldn't find her. I had a strange feeling she was hiding, not ready to tell what she had seen, a new vision making her anxious.

I ran into Gabriel as I went to check the basement, he was coming up the stairs.

"Where are you off to, cousin?" I asked. "You will not get far in the sunshine."

"I was coming to find a servant to fetch you," he said. "Please come down so we may speak."

I followed him down the stairs and to his makeshift room in the back, there were no signs of Morgana.

"Were you approached again last night at the theatre?" he asked.

I considered the question for a moment, then said, "Yes."

"What did they say?" he continued, his voice sounding panicked.

"Nothing of importance. Perhaps it is time for you to explain why I'm of such interest to these people," I said flatly.

He sighed, examining my face like he was trying to read a map. He looked pained, stressed.

"Why is this so hard for you? Why are you so afraid?" I asked.

"Because once I was sure they were part of what is right and good in this world, and now I am not so sure. Being here, knowing you all, everything has changed."

"I don't understand," I replied.

"What the Order does, I always thought they were ridding the world of evil," he said, sighing loudly. "But it isn't so. You and the others, you are not evil!"

I stood, backing slowly away from him, the weight of the situation heavy on my shoulders.

"They would kill us all," I said, my voice barely a whisper.

"Don't you see? That is what they do! They rid the world of people like you, and I, and everyone else in this house because they say we are evil," he began. "And at one time I agreed. How could vampires, shapeshifters, and witches not be? Since we were children we were led to believe that, if they even existed, they were evil and must be destroyed. Under the guise of Christian crusaders they hunt and slaughter all of our kind. For some reason they are deeply interested in the Bathory, many of our blood have joined, it was natural that I joined after my father and uncles before me."

He smiled, looking up at the ceiling and stretching out his hands. "But, then all of *this* happened. And you, my beautiful Katrine, my heart and soul. Erzsebet can live on through you....she does every time you speak. And I can protect you, I could not protect her."

"Why do they want me?" I asked. He pulled me back down so I was seated.

"I don't entirely understand why they want you. I know little of your mother or your circumstances, but they seem to think you are quite exceptional," he smiled proudly at me. "You are, my dear, but their ideas are much different. They believe you are destined to be a great hunter."

"I....I....I would hunt my own people? My friends? My family? Why would I do such a thing?" I said. I made eye contact with him, and we watched each other for several moments in silence.

"I suppose they believe they will hurt you, that something will go wrong and you'll come running to them," he replied, his eyes never leaving mine.

"What would she do?" I asked. I held back my tears, my voice cracking.

"Who, child?" he said softly.

"My grandmother. Erzsebet. What would she do when faced with something so monumental?" I asked. He smiled at that, the idea of her bringing a glow to his face.

"She would hold her head high, be strong, and fight for what she needed and wanted, tooth and nail like no other woman on this earth. Because she knew she was a Bathory and deserved respect," he said proudly.

"Then that is exactly what I will do," I replied, twisting my ring around my finger. "Because I am a Bathory."

Klara

THE FALL

A large blister had formed on the inside of her right wrist, it seemed to be from the friction of the top of her wrist iron rubbing against where the base of her palm began.

She wasn't entirely sure when it had happened, she only noticed it when she was thrown in the back of the caravan and her forearms had slammed into the filthy wood floorboards.

The iron rubbed sharply against the blister as she pulled herself into the sitting position. It took some manoeuvring to pull her legs up, the chain that connected the ankle shackles was quite short.

Charles had not needed to be so excessive, she thought to herself as she leaned her back on one of the walls. The doors to the caravan had slammed shut behind her, all she could see through the small window with tiny bars was the dark, empty Paris street.

She could not help but smile to herself, chuckling softly.

"It is nice to know someone finds this amusing," a man's low voice cut through the darkness, making her jump, "because I certainly do not."

"Do not be afraid. I am harmless...now," the man continued. "Who are you?"

She thought for a moment, thinking about the blister, and the letter from her mother she had shoved in her sleeve. It may have been meant for Charles but it was important to her to keep it.

"My name is Klara," she said. She would hold the letter over her mother's head when she choked the life from her body.

"And what did you do to receive this fate, Klara?" the man asked.

"I was not very good at following someone else's rules and orders."

"Your father?"

She smiled. "And others."

"And what exactly are you?" he asked. She still had not seen him, all that sat around her was boxes and rags.

"Whatever do you mean? My family name is...."

"Who you *were* does not matter any longer, so you should just forget about your life before because it is gone. *What* you *are* is crucial."

"I am a blood drinker, borne of two blood drinkers."

"Ah! A true daughter of the dark," the man exclaimed. "You are a rare find and will fetch a decent sum. I hope you know how to protect yourself."

"Thank you for the advice, anonymous voice with no body, I will surely keep that in mind," Klara snapped. She used her left hand to try to move the shackle off the blister when the boxes and rags began to unfold into a man. He used his soft, unshackled hands to move the iron off her blister.

"Blending in would be a good art for you to learn, but with hair like that you must shine in pure darkness," he said, pulling a rag up over her hair as if it were a hood.

"You must have done more than simply been disobedient to carry such chains," he continued.

"Who said it was simple?" she replied. She pushed the rags away from his face then leaned in to gently lick away the dried blood from the corners of his mouth. She stared deeply into his eyes and she felt something inside him warm to her.

She had just done what she had been driven from her home for doing, the very thing that blood drinkers despised about themselves. Now she could do it without even trying, with just a simple touch.

"I see now," he said flatly. "You are no mere blood drinker and you have been shunned for the pleasure others have found in your touch. You are a misunderstood soul, Klara. But I must be clear on something."

"Whatever do you mean?" she asked, her voice soft and airy. He pulled hard on her wrist chains, yanking her up and forward, she yelped in pain.

"I am not so easily enchanted. Do not assume that all who cross your path will be," he whispered sharply, releasing his grip so she fell back hard against the wall.

"As long as we understand each other," his voice returned to its earlier tone as he recovered his face.

"You still haven't told me who or what you are," she said. She tried to pull back the anger and annoyance from her tone.

"Call me Balcor," he replied. He folded back into the rags and disappeared, as if he had never been there in the first place.

The caravan was freezing and went on for days without stopping. Klara had devised a way to relieve herself thought a hole in the floorboards without soiling her clothes. She had moved very little since her conversation with Balcor, the small taste of blood she'd got from his mouth had thrown her into a bit of a frenzy and she thought she may tear apart the next thing she saw with a pulse.

She began to watch the door and wait. The man Charles had given her to would open it eventually. If she could rip him apart she would be free.

Klara thought briefly of the Little Rat, the look on that wretched girl's face when she returned to Paris and killed her would keep her going. Killing the Little Rat and all the others who had been so horrible to her would be a beautiful thing.

Klara counted a full seven days of travel before the carriage finally stopped. They could be anywhere by now. She had a brief worry that she would never find her way back, that she would be doomed to wander, but those thoughts quickly fell away when she realised that people in any town or city would know what country their home sat in.

The door finally opened just after sunset and a girl tied with ropes was thrown into the caravan, just as Klara had been. She fell close to Klara's feet, scurrying back into a corner when their eyes met. She crawled into the pile of rags that Balcor had come from, causing Klara to wonder about the strange encounter.

The girl began to cry, big fat tears with snot bubbling out of her nostrils, wailing loudly. Klara rested her forehead on her knees. Silence, anything, being alone in a pit was better than listening to this *thing* blubber on, she thought.

The heavy scent of blood under the girl's skin invaded Klara's system. She leapt across the caravan and grabbed the girl's face, the chain of her wrist shackles under the girl's chin.

"Stop crying or I'll kill you," she growled.

"Please," the girl's pleas began. "Please kill me. I do not want to know what is coming. I do not want to step out of this carriage again. The horrors beyond that door....you must know what I speak of if you are here."

"Perhaps you should remind me."

The girl's eyes widened. "If you thought you were living in hell before you will pray to return to it once you see where we are going. I hope, whatever you are, you have enough power to protect yourself."

She sniffed, then said loudly. "Because I do not!"

Klara pulled up on the chain, choking the sob out of the girl. She thought to grant the girl her wish, but there were too many ways that would work against her.

"Stop. I don't care what you must do to make yourself, but for the love of God *stop crying*! All you are doing is making a lot of noise," Klara growled, pulling away and moving back to her corner. Being ravenous could be useful.

The girl tried for some time to stop crying, and after a while she finally succeeded. It looked as if the crying had taken a lot of energy and the girl quickly fell asleep. Klara was happy for the silence.

The caravan jolted to a stop, knocking most of the contents over, including Klara. She pushed herself up, the blister on her wrist seemed to have been rubbing in her sleep.

The back door opened and the yelling began, the man Charles had sold her to was moving things out of the way so he could get to where the girl lay in the back. Klara decided it was time to call him what he was, a trader.

The trader grabbed the girl by her ankles and began pulling her towards the door; she did not fight, or kick, or scream, and when the huge piece of wood shoved in the girl's throat like a dagger came into view it all seemed to make sense.

Blood was everywhere and had begun leaking out of the floorboards, the girl's neck and chest were crusted with it. The trader pulled the girl's body out, picked it up like a sack of potatoes then went out of sight.

Klara tried to pull herself up so she would be in an optimal position to attack, but the door was slammed shut before she saw anyone else. She eased herself back down, the smell of blood putting her on edge. She hoped the feeling she now had would help her when the time finally came to free herself, and she silently thanked the girl for giving her what she needed to do so.

Everything went back to silence and Klara smiled to herself. She much preferred the silence.

Katrine

FINAL PREPARATIONS

PARIS, FRANCE – MARCH 1614.

Gigi paced back and forth across her room, I was convinced she was making an imprint on the floor she had been doing this so much. The household was being packed for Russia, we were leaving within days, and she had received no reply to any of the letters she had sent trying to solve the mystery of the two Gigi's in Morgana's vision.

"What could possibly be the problem?" she asked me for the fifth time. "Could they not just say they don't know? That would ease my nerves a bit, better than no answer at all."

"Perhaps they though the opposite, that it was wise to say nothing if they did not know," I replied.

"Has the Scots girl said anything more?" she asked.

"Other than her continued apologies? No. She is quite distressed about the whole matter, to be honest," I said. "She has seen nothing at all for weeks."

She sighed. "I have done all I can."

"William has taught me some spells that I can use to protect us, and he says he will be teaching me more. We will be safe," I replied. She smiled at me, crossing the room and kissing the top of my head.

"I would be quite lost without you, petite," she said softly.

"And I you," I replied, and she went back to her pacing.

"We had a travelling cloak made for you, oui? And you have gloves?" she asked.

"Yes, three cloaks for any change in the weather and more gloves then I can remember. I am totally prepared to leave."

"And William?"

"He will ride with Charles and Vincenzo, who said he will join us when he tires of them."

She chuckled. "And Vincenzo cannot discuss all his plans along the route with us, we are not as acquainted with trade as the men. If we were he would ride the whole way with us."

I was pleased William did not ask about riding with us. I was still not comfortable with everything, even though I was constantly reassured nothing had happened at the brothel.

"I am pleased to finally be leaving. I was beginning to wonder if it would never happen," Gigi said, then there was a quick knock at the door.

Mathilde came in, wearing one of her red dresses with her hair a tangled mess.

"Excusez-moi, I wanted to make sure I spoke to you before we departed," Mathilde said, turning her eyes to me. "I wanted to tell you, Katrine, that I will take good care of your cousin while we travel. He will be in one of the covered wagons with me and I wanted to reassure you that he will be alright."

I smiled at her, pleased with the glow in her eyes when she spoke of my cousin. I liked her, I hoped he did not break her heart.

"Thank you, Mathilde. I sincerely appreciate that," I said, bowing my head in respect.

"Good! I am glad," she replied, blushing. "Now, I must return to the theatre. Always a pleasure, ladies."

She left as quickly as she came, Gigi was grinning ear to ear. It was the end of the evening and we were all exhausted.

"Why are you so happy?" I asked.

"Because she came to you, that is a sign of respect. She acknowledged your position and status, petite, that is an important step in your progression to becoming a proper lady," she said, clapping her hands together. "That is fantastic!"

"Why is she riding in a covered wagon? She does not need to avoid the sun."

"That is just her way. Some of us choose to live a more reclusive life, and clearly she would rather spend her time with Gabriel than watching the world go by as we ride."

I smiled. "And if she wishes to be with Gabriel, public life is not an option. At least in places he may be recognised."

"Would they know him in the Russian court?"

"Maybe his name, but not his face. At least not that I am aware of, he never said anything about it."

Gigi smiled to herself, sighing as she stared at nothing. She seemed to have forgotten her troubles while she was distracted by the idea of the foreign court. The smile quickly faded, her eyes lowering.

"Who could it be?" I asked.

"What?" she replied.

"Of your family, who could it be?"

She cringed, her eyes closing slightly. "Speaking their names only makes it real. I will not say it out loud, even my mother's name. It could be her also, you know."

"I did not think of that," I replied. "But please, do not worry. We will protect you, Vincenzo and I especially. You need not be so afraid."

She half smiled at me with empty eyes. "Of course you will, child."

Anastasia

TEACHINGS

Along with the job, Anastasia received a small place in a tent for new wolves, which was essentially all her own. In such a short time they had given her so many things she could not believe it, her luck had finally changed.

She had joined the group who make things, whether it be building or sewing or some other form of creating like making the clay bowls they ate from, and she really enjoyed it. She felt a sense of fulfilment when she went to bed every night that she had not felt since her daughter was born.

"When you can build your own tent we shall find you a space," Lynde came up behind her one night after she had finished work and was heading to the food tent. It had been several weeks since she had arrived and she was happy in her new routine.

"That would be wonderful, not that I have any complaints about the way things are," Anastasia replied.

"Good. I also wanted to speak to you about something," Lynde continued. "I think it would be wise if you learned some fighting techniques...but I suppose it would be wise to ask if you feel you can defend yourself, especially against another wolf?"

Anastasia was silent for a few moments before quietly admitting, "No, I do not believe I could."

"Well, we must do something about that then, mustn't we?" Lynde said happily, clapping a hand on Anastasia's shoulder. She could feel the strength in her grip; after several dinners with the group she had learned that Lynde was part of what made up the muscle of the group, they enforced the laws and were the defenders. There were several others, including females, but Lynde appeared to be one of the strongest. She would be the best person to teach her how to fight.

"So when do we start?" Anastasia asked.

Lynde smiled, her teeth were also perfectly straight. "We can begin now, if you wish. I am teaching some of the others if you would like to sit and listen."

Anastasia nodded, and the two women walked together to the main sitting area where several others were gathered. She was relieved to see it was not only children.

The group lowered their heads in respect as Lynde entered the circle, she directed Anastasia to a seat before she fully stepped in.

"Good day to you all, and thank you for coming," Lynde began. Anastasia recognised a few faces, one from her work duty.

"Some things we can do by instinct, and would come naturally to us as predators. But, depending on how we came to this life, it is not always true. We spend our time divided so things do not always pass one way or the other," Lynde said. "I will not only teach you to attack, but I will also teach you the equally important art of defence."

Anastasia adjusted her hair so it covered her breasts. She was still not entirely comfortable with being so exposed all the time and often used her hair as cover, which now touched the small of her back and resembled a dark sheet of silk. When she was alone it didn't matter, but with eyes looking at her she became very self-conscious.

Lynde motioned for one of the others to stand and they both began their change. Soon two wolves stood facing each other and began circling, their eyes locked in concentration. Lynde kicked her front paw in the sand,

Anastasia thought it was a sign to begin.

The other wolf came at Lynde head on, its lips turned up in a growl. Using the other wolf's momentum, Lynde easily knocked it onto its back with what seemed like no effort at all.

This went on for several more tries, Lynde using the kick to signal to attack and tossing the other wolf aside with great ease. She was quite skilled in using each half of her body separately when fighting someone off.

When the tables were turned and the other wolf kicked its foot in the sand, Lynde leapt across the circle and face first into her prey, pinning it to the ground with all four paws, one pressed firmly on its throat.

Anastasia stood with the others and went to examine the pose.

She smiled to herself, saying quietly, "A simple shift in body weight leads to swift results."

Lynde looked up at her and nodded her head in recognition. Anastasia did not think anyone would have heard her, she kept forgetting about the wolf's fantastic hearing.

Everyone went back to their places as they prepared for another demonstration. This time Lynde circled around the back, swiping the other wolf's hind legs out from under it before using her body weight to knock it a few feet away.

When the other wolf did not bounce back so quickly Lynde shifted and called for some food and water.

"In both offensive and defensive situations having control of your body weight is essential. Even if the other wolf is much stronger a good, hard knock to the side will give you enough time to run," Lynde stood in the centre and spoke to the crowd. "For next time I want you to practice shifting your body weight around, and using it in different fashions. Prepare yourself to demonstrate what you have learned. Thank you again."

The circle bowed, and Lynde motioned for Anastasia to follow her.

"You seem to grasp the concept rather quickly, I am pleased," Lynde told her. "You would be surprised at how many of the others have trouble with the principles of fighting."

"Perhaps it is in my blood," Anastasia said.

"There are stories of those born with wolf blood, more legends, really.

Hungary seems to be full of tales of every sort of creature you could imagine, the truth of them is always up for discussion. You will hear much of it when the storyteller speaks."

Anastasia smiled. "Storyteller?"

"Yes. And I will ask, because you are new to us, that she speak of the White Wolf."

"Why?"

"Because we worship the White Wolf as the humans worship God, or Jesus Christ. These are things you must learn. Do you still believe in the human's God, Anastasia?"

"I am not sure I ever did. There were too many unanswered questions, too many reasons to doubt," she admitted.

"Well, we do not demand worship here, but you can decide. I am sure you will enjoy the stories, though. The storyteller is quite masterful."

"Then I look forward to it," Anastasia replied. Lynde left her at the entrance to the newcomer's tent where Anastasia went inside and continued work on her new home.

Katrine

TIME TO DEPART

When everything was finally together we were a caravan of twenty, including three covered wagons that housed those who could not tolerate the sun. I was in awe at the sheer size of the group as I stood and watched as the final loading was going on outside the chateau.

"We look like a royal party," Gigi said proudly. "Charles has really spared no expense."

"Do you find this slightly unnerving? It is a bit frightening," Morgana whispered to me.

"It is definitely overwhelming," I replied quietly to her. "But I am not frightened yet."

"We three shall ride together then?" Gigi asked. "It will give us the chance to work on our lessons. I believe you should learn some languages, Morgana. Especially French."

Morgana smiled and nodded, they had done some but nothing extensive, especially since she could tell Gigi nothing else of her vision. She seemed afraid, they both were for very different reasons.

"You look beautiful, Katrine," William said. He came up beside me, the other women quietly moved away.

I smoothed down the front of my heavy travelling cloak, the sun was going down and the temperature was dropping.

"Thank you, William. Are you excited for our impending departure?" I asked. He took my hand and I tried not to pull away. I knew he cared for me but I was having difficulty accepting he was true. Why was he different then every other man on earth?

"As can be expected, I wish I was riding with you," he said quietly.

"That would be highly inappropriate, William," I said. I am not your wife, or even your intended."

He sighed. "That could be easily remedied if you wish it so."

"Don't be foolish," I snapped. "You have no wish to marry. Now if you'll excuse me, I must go."

I started after Gigi, who was heading with Morgana to one of the decorated carriages.

"Bon. Fantastique. Charles has outdone himself," Gigi said after poking her head in the carriage door to examine the interior. "Are you two ready? We must go to the theatre to collect the others then we shall be on our way."

"I am as ready as I will ever be," Morgana said, and she climbed into the carriage.

"I forgot to mention, I finally learned to speak some Russian. So we have much to discuss, petite," Gigi said before she got in the carriage.

I took one last look at the chateau, hoping this would not be the last time I saw my home. I thought of Vienna, and my sadness when we had left. I constantly wondered if I should have left Roza behind then, when I had a choice.

The inside of the carriage was decorated in lush velvets with a few pelts lying about, I wondered if there were more stored under the seats. When I sat down my body was cushioned like I was sitting on a cloud.

"Is this what a royal carriage is like?" I asked as we got rolling.

Gigi smiled. "Some of them, yes. It very much depends on the tastes of the family, for both royal and those used by the nobility."

Morgana smiled. "I could grow quite accustomed to this."

"Not so frightening after all?" I said, smiling.

She laughed, a sound I did not hear often. "I must warn you, mes filles, after months of travel the inside of this carriage will not seem so pleasant," Gigi replied.

It seemed as if we arrived at the theatre moments later, the carriage coming to a stop and one door opening, a cold breeze rushing in.

"I must speak to my cousin before we start on our journey," I said, crawling out into the cold winter night.

He was standing waiting for me, wrapped in a heavy man's wool cloak, fresh snowflakes beginning to fall from the sky.

"Bonsoir," I said to him, embracing him casually. He took me in his arms and hugged me tightly to him.

"And what a glorious evening it is!" Gabriel exclaimed. "Are you ready for a fantastic adventure?"

I smiled at him, before I could say anything he continued, "You have too many worries, child. Put them aside and take in the whole idea of this. We are embarking on a journey that most people have never even dreamed on making, that people of greater means than us wouldn't even make! You will see most of Europe, my cousin."

"I had not thought of it that way," I said. "I will be sure to think of that when my worries begin to overwhelm me."

He smiled so proudly at me, holding my face in his gloves hands.

"Do that, my dear girl," he replied. "For I fear you will miss out greatly if you do not."

I went with Gabriel to the covered wagon to help him get settled. Windows and doors were open so air could get in as they rode through the night, trying desperately to make it look less like a rolling wood cage, or a massive trunk used to carry people.

To the best of my knowledge the dead were carried in open wagons, but it did bring to mind the box that one was buried in.

Regardless, he seemed quite pleased. Mathilde winked at me as she was getting inside, I trusted she cared enough for him to keep him safe and secure, regardless of her feelings towards me. I was pleased Gigi saw coming to me as a sign of respect but all that concerned me was that he was taken care of.

I bowed to the group and headed back to my carriage. It seemed by the looks of my surroundings that we were ready to go.

When I got back in my carriage Gigi and Morgana were sitting in uncomfortable silence.

"What is the matter?" I asked.

Gigi tried to smile but the look seemed strained. "Nothing, petite."

Before I could say more the carriage lurched to life, and the entire Danse Macabre was on the move.

In most cases, a group of our size would be safest travelling during the day, but because of our circumstances daylight was one of our biggest hinderances.

Because while the sun shone we were transporting essentially wagons full of bodies.

But we set out into the dead of night, I tried not to think of all the things that could go wrong, or the trials we may face before we even reached our destination. I was determined to do what Gabriel had said and focus on this grand adventure before me.

I watched Gigi finger something on a string around her neck, I assumed it was the talisman from the crone.

After everything that had happened from Morgana's visions I could not put it aside, but I was determined to try to enjoy some of this journey.

Katrine

THE SLAVE MARKET

FRANKFURT, GERMANY.

After several days we arrived at our first stop, where I was told we would stay for it least a fortnight, maybe longer.

We stopped at a large inn on the edges of the city, its thatched roof and wood fence reminded me of home. It belonged to one of Charles's contacts, a local sorcerer and his family, and I was informed early on that we would be here for such a long time partially because of all the local creatures that would be paying respect to Charles and his people while we made a scheduled stop, something that would probably happen at each city we stayed in.

William came to me on the second night, a mischievous glitter in his eyes.

"Good evening, William," I said, I was sitting in the great room watching the stars out the window.

He handed me my heavy cloak. "Vincenzo and I are going on an outing. Care to come with?"

"How did you know I would say yes?" I asked.

He smiled. "Just a hunch."

Vincenzo, William, Tolone and I piled into a carriage and sped out into the night, I could not contain my excitement.

"Where are we going?" I asked no one in particular.

"Slave market," Vincenzo said flatly.

My eyes widened. "The same....Gabriel...."

"The same," Vincenzo replied. "I thought you would want to see it, and since we were going anyhow I thought it best you came along before Grisela had the opportunity to disapprove."

"That is much appreciated," I said, smiling at William. "Do you think it's safe?"

"Not for most women, my sweet. But you are not like most women," William answered. "But, I must warn you, this is not for the faint of heart."

"I cannot even imagine," I said.

Vincenzo's face remained blank. "I am not sure you would want to."

Dark figures moved around the narrow road with wood booths bordering all sides, almost as if they were piled one a top of another. It smelled like church incense, filth, and another thing I could not identify.

Eyes turned to us as we exited the carriage, some glowing red in the reflection of the moonlight.

William took my arm and we strolled into the market like a couple walking through a garden in the springtime, Vincenzo and Tolone directly behind us.

Everything I could imagine was being sold here; herbs, fruits, stones, talismans, religious symbols, thread, fabric, books, pots, and a man at the end sitting on a chair off by himself.

We approached the bookseller while Vincenzo and Tolone went to the crone selling stones; William asked the bookseller for something in French, the man answered in a heavy German dialect. I tried to listen but all my attention was focused on the lone man in his chair.

I heard a child's laughter and a woman appeared with three young through the market. The lone man stood and approached her and they started talking, one of the children turned their eyes to me and they shone bright red for a short moment.

"William, who is that man?" I asked him quietly.

He did not even turn his head. "That's the slave trader."

"Where they found Gabor? I mean Gabriel?"

"I believe so."

"That woman is giving him those children," I said, my grip tightening on his arm.

"I can assure you, Katrine, they are no ordinary children."

"What on earth do you mean? Look at them."

"They would not be here if they were mere children," he said sharply, taking a package wrapped in paper from the bookseller.

"What are they, then?" I asked.

He turned his head to briefly glance at them as we continued on our way.

"For lack of a better term, my darling, they are demon spawn," William said quietly. "Best to think of them that way, they are very dangerous."

"But that man," I said, studying the man's face, "he is the one who had my cousin?"

"I know what you're thinking and you need to stop."

"Whatever do you mean?"

"You cannot kill that man. It is too much trouble. The repercussions would be horrendous."

My eyes widened. "Why would I do such a thing? You are talking of cold blooded murder, William. I have been taught not to kill."

"You have been taught not to kill when you feed, il mio amore, and I know how angry you are about what happened with your cousin. But, I can assure you that particular man had nothing to do with turning your cousin."

"But he bought him! He was a slave because of this man!"

"Which may also be the reason he survived," William snapped. "Some are not so lucky. I promise if we find the one who turned Gabriel you can tear him apart, alright?"

I tried my best not to look sad. He was a bad man who deserved to die but William was right, I could not kill as I pleased.

"What gives anyone the right to enslave another? Who decides which are lesser beings and what gives them the right?" I said angrily.

He sighed loudly. "I cannot answer that question for you, I am not sure anyone can. It is quite the debate, perhaps if you meet God or the Pope, or a King you can ask them. Maybe they would have an answer."

"Maybe I should stop waiting for answers and start making my own," I grumbled. He did not look at me, but pulled me along towards Vincenzo and Tolone.

One of the children ran past us, giggling wildly as it turned its red glowing eyes to us and faded into the darkness.

"We are ready to go, if you are finished," Vicenzo said. He examined my expression, I tried to hide my feelings but he would not look away from me.

"Yes, I think I have seen enough," I said, and the four of us returned to the carriage.

I snuck into Charles's room later that night, moving slowly to give my eyes time to adjust to the darkness.

I crouched down beside his bed and said his name, he jumped about a foot in the air startled from his sleep.

"Katrine? What's happening? Is something the matter?" he asked.

"Nothing is the matter, but I need you to do something for me and I need you to keep it a secret," I began. "Your discretion is most important, and I will forgive you for purchasing my cousin if you do this for me."

Charles sighed, rubbing his face. "What is it?"

"I need you to take me to the slave trader you bought Gabor from, then turn a blind eye to anything that happens afterwards."

"Katrine, I cannot...."

"I do not need a story, a simple yes or no shall suffice," I snapped.

He was silent for several moments. He sat up and tried to straighten himself and, I assumed, to check if he was dreaming. I stood and went and sat on a chair. He lit the candle beside his bed, casting a warm glow over the room and giving him the opportunity to see my face.

He sighed, lowering his eyes for a moment before looking up at me and saying, "Allow me to dress and ready myself."

Klara

THE PIT

The door to the caravan did not open again, and they went on for some time without stopping. All sense of time and place was gone, the movement no longer noticeable.

Klara could not help but wonder if this was what being in prison was like.

What was noticeable was the weather change. Cold winds were becoming less and less and the occasional blast of sweltering heat took all the moisture from the air.

When the caravan finally did stop, Klara tried to pull herself together and prepare for her escape. She needed all her strength, it was a struggle to even lift the shackles she was so weak. She winced in pain as she opened her mouth, splitting her lips so she could taste blood, hoping it would invigorate her.

But there was none, the door opened and the trader's big arms grabbed her chains and yanked her forward, sending shooting sparks of pain up through her limbs. The blister finally tore open, causing her to scream out as the pain burned.

She was thrown on the ground, a cloud of dust rising up as she made impact. A quick glance around and she mostly saw sand, a small building that looked as if it was made of mud and stones loomed in front of them.

The trader grabbed the chain that connected her wrists and pulled her forward, dragging her into the building. He left her on the ground as he took a small piece of metal off the wall and used it to take off both sets of her shackles.

Before she had a chance to do anything the trader punched her in the face, knocking her out.

The building was like a stable but for slaves, others were brought in as Klara lay in the corner. Some had been there before, their anger and defiance clear on their faces, others were new and scared into complete silence.

Eyes watched Klara's body as they examined their surroundings, some even dared step closer to smell her. The blood drinkers twitched uncomfortably, being improperly fed was a way the traders and masters controlled them. Shifters had some difficulty identifying her and kept their distance, two spellcasters remained huddled together in one of the other corners.

Klara started to stir, and the drinkers began to form a protective circle around her as she got her bearings. A hand reached out to help pull her to her feet, she swayed as the world spun.

The young woman smiled and nodded at Klara, releasing her hand then returning to watching the door.

Everyone is watching the door, Klara thought. If they all joined together they could surely overpower the traders, she continued on in her mind, but no one seemed to be thinking that. They all seemed to be standing in fear.

Klara held her head in her hands, a dull ache spreading through her body. She wondered, only for a moment, if all these other people had been here before and that was why they were reacting in such a fashion, but the pain in her head was too much for her to think much further. The fear on all of their faces made Klara a bit nervous.

Quite suddenly a large man appeared in the doorway with a length of rope coiled in his hand. The others all lined up in the middle of the room and held out one arm. Klara watched in wonderment as the large man walked down the line and tied all their arms with the rope, he turned and growled when he noticed one out of line.

He was shirtless and completely hairless, his skin darkly tanned, with a pair of brown leather pants that blended seamlessly into his enormous boots.

Another growl came from his lips and he spat out a string of obscenities, they sounded like French but a different dialect than what was spoken in Paris. He pulled the rope, pulling the line of people across the room as he grabbed Klara, being sure to smack her across the face before tying the rope tightly around her blister.

She tried not to scream as the rope rubbed and burned her wrist while the big man dragged the line along. They stopped at the opening to another building, the loud chatter of a large group of people sounded like the thunder of a coming storm.

Once entering the building it transformed from something simple into an arena, the large man dragged the slaves into the middle then turned and left.

Torchlight put out a strange glow, turning the faces in the seats into bizarre caricatures that leered out at the slaves. Klara thought that some looked like they were wearing white masks, turning them into moving stone statues. She tried to move the rope off the blister, he wrist now caked with blood, the strands of the binding sticking in her torn flesh and make it impossible to move.

The trader appeared and he began giving a speech to the crowd. Klara watched him, trying to decipher what she believed to be his strange French dialect, picking up any hints or clues she could from the situation.

The trader cut the first slave off the line, keeping a bit of rope so the wrist tether remained intact and began parading the man around in a circle like a prized horse. Bidding began, and there seemed to be great interest in him, Klara caught his scent strongly as he walked by. The man was a shifter, and appeared very strong and had some power by the way he projected his scent.

Powerful enough, she believed, to slaughter his way to freedom if he so wished. Someone came forward and handed the trader a purse, taking the shifter out by the rope. Klara watched it all happen, totally shocked at what she was witnessing. She could not understand why all these strong and powerful creatures just sat back and allowed themselves to be sold.

One by one those in the line were sold off, until they reached the spellcasters. They clung together, it wasn't clear if they were male or female, and screamed and hollered when someone tried to pull them apart. The trader just shrugged his shoulders and sold them together, they quieted down and oddly enough went happily off hand and hand.

Klara and the young woman who had helped her in the other building were last, and it seemed as if the trader intended on keeping them both because no one stepped forward when the bidding was done.
He said something to the crowd and hoots and hollers followed. He pulled the two young women back out the way they came and out into the night.

KATRINE

THE DECISIONS OF MERE MEN

We rode swiftly and quietly in the dark, giving Charles no opportunity to examine my expression as we rode. I had no interest in debating the situation or my decision.

"What manner of creature is this slave trader?" I asked, my voice cutting through the silence.

He took a deep breath and said, "I am not sure. He could be human, but that would seem odd. Ones of our nature are not often afraid of humans, and most who have met this man are quite afraid of him."

"So it may be quite complicated to kill him."

"I do not know, Katrine," he replied flatly.

"Well, any advice you have would be appreciated. And don't try to talk me out of it, my mind's made up."

I could hear him breathing, I could not tell if it was frustration or irritation coming though with each pass of air.

"You would need the element of surprise," he began. "For he would be prepared for just about anything one could throw at him. I assume he is attacked quite frequently."

"And no one has succeeded in killing him?"

"They probably do not have the advantages you do, my dear."

I couldn't help but giggle. "What would that be?"

"You are dhampir, you are naturally born to hunt and kill more effectively than other creatures."

"Even shifters?"

"Shifters are animals, and have many animal instincts that cause them to be less.... efficient is the best word I can think of. They are hunters of a different sort."

"So you do not believe I am incapable? I thought you did not want to discuss this?"

"I do not, but if you do not think I can kill him I would like to know."

"If you are truly dhampir the actual act will be no problem," he replied, suddenly sounding quite frustrated.

"Good," I said, and we returned to silence. I was glad for it, I needed time to think.

We stepped out onto the same road, surprisingly enough it was busier than it had been earlier I could hear children's laughter somewhere in the distance, a cold shiver ran down my spine.

I held out my arm to Charles and he reluctantly took it, guiding me in the direction of where the slave trader had been sitting.

But, he was not there. I was about to panic when Charles continued on until we reached a dark house with a battered wood door. All I could smell was burning wood, a common one I had found in Germany.

I looked to Charles, who was trying very hard to avoid looking directly at me, to see where to go from here.

"Do we knock?" I asked, finally getting agitated.

He said nothing, just continued through the door and up the stairs into the house.

The house was a very strange place. It was extremely dark and smelt like nothing, which seemed exceptionally odd. There was no evidence that anyone, human or not, had been there ever, it was as if the house was freshly built. Charles began to lead me towards the back of the house, my eyes finally adjusting to the inky darkness. I wondered if it was some magic protecting this place.

Low light of a glowing candle guided us to a room; the slave trader stood with his back turned to us, his eyes glued to something outside the window.

"Guten Abend Herr Westwick," the man said, keeping his back turned to us. "I trust your latest purchase is to your satisfaction."

I let go of Charles's arm and advanced, leaving no one the time to react or begin to engage. I grabbed the slave trader by the head, exposing his neck to my mouth.

"Did you know who that purchase was, sir? Do you even know his name?" I growled in his ear. "What you do is wrong. What gives you the right to say how much someone would cost? What makes you so superior, so close to God?"

The man said nothing, but I could feel a well of power stirring inside him like a growing fire inside his body.

"His name was Gabor, and he was one name in a line of Bathory Princes. It would have been wise for you to learn his name, since the sale of such a man, my cousin, would bring your downfall," I said sharply. I bit down hard into his neck, the blood began to flow along with the pool of energy into my body, seemingly all the way through to my edges. The burning began in my feet, I tried to ignore it as I felt the life begin to slip from his body.

I pushed everything I had into him through my mouth; energy, strength, anger, hate, and power. All that I had in me, as a female and as a dhampir. I knew now that's what I was, even though I didn't know exactly what it meant.

But I was two half's of something and that's what made me whole.

He was trying to fight me without actually moving, using his magic to invade my body, spreading the burn though me. I wanted to scream but if I wavered even for a moment I knew he would kill me. I tried to pull more of his blood into my mouth while pushing my power into him, focusing on trying to stop his heart and end his life. I had doubts about my own powers, but would not allow the thought to stay long.

Nothing could distract me, and I could not stop now. He had to die.

After what seemed like an eternity the slave trader's body began to weaken, the power inside him dwindling as his life force slipped away. My body still burned with whatever he had pushed inside me, which did not end when I finally felt his life slip away and the blood stopped flowing.

I tossed his body to the ground and breathed deeply, Charles was examining the titles of books on the bookshelf with his back turned to me.

"Are you finished?" he asked. His voice was calm and steady as if I was doing some mundane task like washing my face.

He pulled a handkerchief from his pocket and handed it out to me without looking at my face. I used it to wipe the blood from my mouth, luckily I did not make a mess of myself.

"Is he dead?" Charles asked.

"Yes," I replied, passing the bloody rag back to him. He held it between his two fingers as he crossed the room and threw it into the fire.

"You are quite sure?" he said.

"Of course. You cannot tell?" I asked. "But we must be on our way, I believe he gave me something and it is burning me inside."

He sighed. "I did not think of that. If you want to keep this secret it may be difficult to find someone to treat you if you are ill."

I smiled and held out my arm for him. "Do not worry. I know a Scottish witch who is quite good at keeping a secret."

KATRINE

RECOVERY

The burning spread quickly throughout my body. When we returned to the inn I had been screaming for what felt like days, Charles left me to go get Morgana after much arguing. If he returned with William, who he believed would be the only person who could fix it, I told him I would pull out his tongue with my bare hands.

What I had done would remain a secret, no matter what the cost.

"You should have brought me with you," Morgana said when she got in the carriage, turning up the light on the lantern hanging near the window. "It would have prevented this completely."

I writhed around in pain, she placed one hand on my head and the other on my heart, closing her eyes.

"He was powerful, gave you something quite nasty," she mumbled. "Yes, yes. Very nasty indeed."

"Can you fix it?" Charles' panicked voice was loud, I could not see where he was.

"Of course I can, if you'll get off my back and let me work," Morgana snapped, her Scottish accent thicker from anger. A cold chill spread slowly from her hands, then shot through my body like a bullet, sucking the fire out into two glowing orbs she pulled from my body.

I gasped for air in relief, my eyes focused on the orbs as Morgana said a few words, her eyes glowing red as she crushed both the orbs in her hands.

"Next time come get me," she said again.

"I did not know it was at all necessary," I replied, my voice hoarse from screaming.

"You decide to kill something you know little about? It is necessary to protect yourself in any way you can."

I coughed. "What did he tell you?"

"Only that you were ill from some magic," she began. "I saw the rest. I believe you were right, doing what you did."

"Thank you. I did not think to ask, I assumed there would be lots of arguments so I did not bother."

She smiled. "Do not feel that way about me. You and I think the same, and I am always willing to help you."

She pulled me up and helped me out of the carriage, Charles was pacing back and forth, tugging on his sleeves.

He saw me and sighed loudly. "Oh thank Heavens!"

"I told you I could do it," Morgana said angrily. I was feeling quite weak and she used her small body to support me.

"Can we go inside please? I do not want to make a scene," I replied. I pulled Morgana forward, Charles eventually helping us inside.

The inn was quiet, the sun about to rise, I was happy to be returning to my bed in the room I shared with Gigi. I listened to her steady breathing before sneaking in, careful not to wake her.

I fell into my small bed and quickly fell asleep, my body had had enough for one night.

The next day at our afternoon meal Charles would not look directly at me, his eyes darting around the room nervously. If I had known that killing someone in front of him would turn him away from me I would have done it some time ago.

"Petite," Gigi said quietly to me. "What did you do? Charles seems quite unnerved by you."

"Perhaps returning to the scene of the crime has made him realise the wrong he committed," I replied.

Gigi snorted. "That is quite impossible. He is not capable of processing his own wrongs. You must have frightened him somehow."

"I cannot imagine how," I said, trying to hide my smile.

"And I was going to mention it to you earlier but I thought I would wait until you had bathed to see if it dissipated," she began. "But it has not so I must tell you. You have this smell that I cannot explain."

I said nothing, continuing to eat as she watched me.

"What have you done?" she asked quietly.

I did not look up at her, and said very quietly, "Nothing."

I could feel her eyes burrowing into me as if she was digging through my brain for the answers she wanted. I did not look at her, I would not involve her in this mess by any means.

Vincenzo and William seemed rather undaunted by Charles' behaviour, I was quite surprised they had not noticed.

I heard a soft whisper in my mind, as if someone was calling my name from a far off distance. I tried my best to ignore it, hoping it was nothing other than my conscience being penetrated by Gigi's probing stares.

Morgana shifted uncomfortably in her seat next to mine, I suddenly wondered if she had heard the call as well.

"Have you seen my cousin, Gigi? It has been some time since I have heard anything of him," I asked. "I wonder how their journey is going."

"You could ask our Hannah when she appears. She is in charge of caring for the others," she replied.

"I was wondering where she had got to. I have not seen her since we left Paris, I feel quite silly that I had not thought to check."

She smiled. "That is quite odd, petite, being that she is your personal maid. Are you sure you are well?"

"Perhaps I am not," I said, and I sighed. "I am used to people looking out for me, not the other way around. I have only ever travelled with you and with Roza. We were only with my mother and the witches for three days."

"You still cannot see that not only was Roza a witch but perhaps your mother as well?" Gigi replied.

I still kept my eyes away from her, saying quite flatly, "No, and I don't believe I ever will. I will not do anything to alter my memories of either of them."

"You are a stubborn child. I hope you won't let it cloud your judgment," she said. "Now, let's finish here so we can work on our lessons. I refuse to even pretend like I want to socialise in this place. I am too cold!"

The voice continued calling to me as we did our lessons, causing it to become quite hard to concentrate. I tried to hide it from Gigi, she was already too suspicious, and had some difficulty. Luckily Morgana was just as distracted as I was so I was not worried about her questioning me.

When I was able to lie in my bed and close my eyes the voice got louder, a figure came out of the darkness that now consumed my vision. I heard the rustling of silk and slight tap of a heal that, to me, identified the figure as a woman.

"Katrine," the voice said, clearer now as the woman approached. "Katrine, can you hear me?"

My voice spoke out in my mind, without me saying a word. "Yes, I can. Who are you?"

The woman giggled and I caught a glimpse of her profile.

"Grandmother?" I said, my voice barely a whisper.

"I am not sure how this is possible, you seem to have got some powers. I hope not dangerously," she began. "By the way, I received your letter. I am very pleased to hear you are doing well and being properly educated. Please send my best wishes and eternal gratitude to Mlle. Delphine for taking such great care of you. We have met several times, she is a remarkable woman and I could ask for no one better to care for you outside the family. I would have sent you to live with my cousin, who was Voivode of Transylvania, but I am sad to say he was murdered recently."

"Do you mean Gabor?" I asked.

She paused, then said, "Yes, I do. What do you know of him?"

"You do not need to worry, he suffered some but now he is with us. He is safe, he has taken the name Gabriel."

"I do not understand. Are you sure it is him? How has this happened?" she asked.

"He was not killed, he was turned. The leader of our group rescued him from slavery and now he lives comfortably with me and mine, being called Gabriel, but everyone knows who he is and he is treated with the respect he deserves, along with taking his place as my cousin."

She began to cry, it started quietly then she began to sob. I wanted desperately to comfort her, tried to reach out to touch her but I could not.

"Please don't cry," I said.

"Tears of joy, my dear sweet child. You are the one joy I have left in this world. And now that I know my favourite cousin is with you I am happier than I have been in some time, since before Ferenc died. The Bathory family will live on through you both. But, how did you identify each other?" she asked.

"He recognised the ring you gave me. He was unsure at first, he thought I had stolen the ring somehow. He is trying to tell me stories of the family," I replied. "I am lucky to have him. He is truly a gift from God."

She smiled. "I am surprised you still believe after the hell you have lived though. I had a vision. I know the truth of what happened to your mother Katrine. Please know that those women acted on their own, I had no part in it."

"I have known that all along, but I did not want to trouble you. You have suffered enough. And I have faith because I am a good person. I can do nothing more, I have to believe he has helped me survive."

"I am so proud of you, Katrine. You are every inch a Bathory," she said proudly. "I am not sure when I will see you again, child, so I must tell you that you are my very soul, and the news that my favourite cousin is with you gives me some peace. I think of you always."

"And I you, Grandmother," I said, and the darkness closed around us.

Almost as quickly as she appeared, she was gone.

Katrine

A NEW VIEW

"Something has happened to you," Morgana said quietly to me. "I can see it in your eyes. How are you feeling?"

"I had a vision," I said. I quickly turned my eyes away from her.

"What sort of being was this man you killed?" she asked.

"I do not know. Charles did not know either," I replied.

She sighed. "Perhaps he gave you something to remember him by."

"Is that possible? You make it sound like some sort of infection."

"Yes, I believe it is," she said. She sipped her tea, turning her eyes to look out the great room window at the light dusting of snow that had covered the landscape last night.

"So what do I do? How do I fix this?" I asked.

"Fix what? What has happened to you Katrine?" Charles came over to us, buzzing around like an annoying insect.

"Will you sit down please," I snapped. "I cannot have you attracting unwanted attention."

"I am sorry, but if something is wrong I need to know so I can hire someone to fix it," he said sharply, giving Morgana an evil look when she laughed.

"If you knew what sort of being he was that would help," I began, "because it seems I have developed some new powers."

"What? I will find someone to fix this," he said, pointing at Morgana. "I knew the girl couldn't help you...."

"Calm down, my Lord," I replied between clenched teeth. "Everything is fine and I do not need 'fixing'. I would advise you to be more careful with your words. I will not tolerate such behaviour, and if my secret is discovered because of something you have done I will hurt you."

William and Vincenzo came in, William's eyes shone brightly as he met my gaze. He smiled his warm and inviting smile that was reserved specifically for me, and something inside me melted.

But I now had a secret that could destroy what we had.

"Good day to you both," William said happily. "Would you care to come on a short outing with us, ladies? We thought you may enjoy seeing more of the country. What say you?"

"An outing?" I asked.

"Purchasing another item for trade," Vincenzo said, examining my face. "You are welcome to refuse if otherwise engaged."

"Don't be silly, we would be quite pleased," I replied, standing up and starting for the door. "Come now, Morgana. We won't be a moment, gentlemen."

Vincenzo continued to watch me as we rode along in the carriage, studying my face and movements.

"Something wrong, mon ami?" I asked.

"I was about to ask you the same question," he replied. "There is something different about you."

"Perhaps the German air has done me some good," I said.

He was silent for several moments, then said, "Have you done something?"

"Nothing at all. But I appreciate your concern," I replied, and I smiled. William began his appraisal then, my stomach began to feel like it was sinking out of my body. He said nothing, I was unsure of what he could sense with his own powers but I tried my best not to seem nervous or bothered.

"So where are we going?" Morgana asked and I was pleased she broke the silence.

"To collect some silver plate. I must admit it is much less exciting than the slave market," Vincenzo said. "My apologies, Morgana. Next time I will remember to include you on the more stimulating parts of our excursions."

She bowed her head to him. "Thank you, my Lord. I am most grateful."

"Now, we must ask the both of you quite seriously to mind your tempers," William began. "The man we are about to visit is very old and quite temperamental."

"What manner of being is he?" I asked.

"A wolf," he replied. "Born with the blood in his veins, to the best of our knowledge. And very traditional, so women are to be seen and not heard."

"What manner of tradition is that? Because I have never heard of such things," I said. Morgana chuckled, and the two men shot her a look that silenced her immediately.

"That is exactly the type of behaviour I was speaking of. Now, either you both keep quiet or you can wait in the carriage," William said with a touch of anger in his tone.

"As you wish, my Lord," I replied, and we rode the rest of the way in silence.

The old wolf lived in a small wood cottage with a thatched roof and clouds of smoke billowing out of the chimney; it reminded me so much of my village it brought me to tears.

And because the old wolf only spoke German, Morgana and I were left standing on the side-lines as the men did their business. He only looked at us once, a quick observation through his beady little eyes before he lifted his massive bear-like body to gather up the silver.

At one point he said something to the men that caused them to pause, and I somehow knew that news of the slave trader's death had got around. I wondered if Charles had heard and was making plans to move on.

When we got back in the carriage and were on our way, William turned to me and said, "It seems you have got your wish."

"In regards to what?" I asked.

"The slave trader was murdered two days past," he said. "Rumour is by a vampire."

I tried my best to look startled. "Was not my wish, was what he deserved."

"What do you know of this?" he said.

"Nothing. Why? What are you implying?"

"Perhaps you told Gabriel...."

"You specifically told me to leave it alone, William. Do you honestly think I would go behind your back and do this?" I said angrily. "If I told Gabriel the truth he would surely kill Charles. I am not that desperate for him to leave me alone."

"There would be no need since you have clearly frightened him into submission. Bravo, by the way. Another of your wishes granted," he replied, his voice sharp and full of venom.

"What have I done that has angered you so?" I asked, biting back tears. I turned to Vincenzo, who was making a serious attempt to appear as if he wasn't paying attention.

"Are we back yet?" I asked, and before he could reply the carriage slowed and came to a stop. As soon as the door opened I flew out and stormed back to the inn.

Gigi was pacing back and forth in our room, when I entered she stopped and stared blankly at me.

I could not help rolling my eyes. "Good Lord, not you too!"

"Enforcing vigilante justice is no job for a woman, especially one under my care," she snapped.

"You honestly believe I killed him, Gigi? That I would jeopardise my existence for it?"

"For something you felt strongly about? I would expect nothing less," she said, raising her hands in defeat. "I do not want to know, because on one hand I agree with your decision on the other I am angry you would put us in danger. Perhaps you should discuss such matters with me next time before you act on them, if you, in fact, did this."

I sat down on the bed and held my face in my hands.

"Do not fret, petite. Whatever happened to this....he deserved it. No man has the right to sell another living being, regardless of their circumstances.

This is for the greater good, I can assure you," she said, and I was oddly comforted. She seemed willing to accept me, regardless of my less than womanly behaviours, and I cherished her greatly for that.

"Merci, Gigi," I replied. I tried to smile proudly, hoping I did not look too much like a small child gazing up at its mother.

"Soon we shall leave this wretched place and go to Prague, the only city in Europe I have found that could be comparable to Paris in its beauty. I am counting the days."

Anastasia

FIRESIDE

Night fell, and a rhythmic thump began from within the camp. It was as if a vibration was coming up from within the earth, and when Anastasia stepped out of the tent she was hit by a pulse of energy and with the heavy smell of excitement.

She had been with the camp for almost two months; her personal tent was built, she had fulfilling work and her lessons with Lynde and the others were coming along beautifully. She really felt like she was part of something, and it was bigger and more amazing than anything she could imagine.

As she walked through the camp towards the fire pit she could hear chanting, and the smell of a large flame. She had not been informed of any celebration and she was quite confused as to what was going on.

Then a woman stepped in her path. She was draped in crimson cloth, more adornment then she had seen on any other in the camp, and carried a large staff with brightly coloured objects dangling from it.

"You are the new one," the woman said. "I am Racquel, the Storyteller."

"My name is Anastasia," she replied.

Racquel sniffed the air. "Your story is very complex. With many layers.

You will be spoken of for some time and not even be aware of it."

"How?"

Racquel smiled. "Because you are only a small part of an enormous legacy, Anastasia."

"And how to you know this?"

"You are not the first to doubt my words, and most certainly will not be the last," she turned and began to walk away. "But you will learn that I speak the truth, with time."

Anastasia went to go after her but people began to get in her way and soon she could not see her, she was stuck in the crowd headed for the fire pit.

There was dancing and some sort of ritual going on around the fire that was preparing for Racquel, a path cleared for her as she made her way to the centre. She went and sat beside a statue of a wolf carved from white stone, the Király Farkas sat on the other side.

His eyes carefully scanned the crowd, observing his people with a watchful eye. He seemed to be looking for someone and when his eyes locked with Anastasia he smiled and motioned for her to come forward.

"You summoned me, Farkas?" Anastasia addressed him, bowing.

"Come and sit near the front," he said, pointing to a stump close to him for her to sit on. "You have not heard our storyteller before, you should have a good seat."

Anastasia nodded and sat, wrapping her arms around her body as eyes turned to her. She wished she had something more than her hair to cover her body, she quickly pushed the thoughts from her mind because she did not want to appear uncomfortable.

Racquel began to walk around the fire, following the rhythm and doing her own chant. A flash of another fire appeared in Anastasia's mind, with two naked women dancing around it. Katrine's frightened pleas began to echo in her ears, although she had no memory of hearing them during that fateful night.

"Are you alright?" Lynde asked as she slid in the seat beside her.

"Just remembering something," she mumbled back. She was able to shake the thoughts from her mind but not her daughter's voice.

"Do you think of it all, Mother?" Katrine's voice asked. "Do you think of what I have become at all? Did you know that something like this would happen?"

Anastasia began to massage her temples and tried to push the words from her mind. A mug of warm liquid was handed to her and she happily drank. When she was able to set her eyes on Racquel her mind seemed to clear, the storyteller's presence invading her body and pulling her in.

All those who were circling the fire stopped, paying their respects to Racquel before they took a seat around the fire. She raised her hands to the Heavens, and the fire seemed to stretch up with her. Anastasia watched carefully for any other magic coming through her fingers, if she wove anything other than words.

Racquel pounded the bottom of her staff on the ground three times and a wave of silence fell over the group.

"We have someone new sitting among us!" Racquel exclaimed. "That has not happened for many moons! But it is a lovely thing to be able to share our tales with someone who can learn from them as we all have! So tonight I will speak again of the White Wolf, and although you have all probably heard this tale many times before, think of it as our new wolf would. As if you were hearing it with fresh ears. As if you were sitting around this fire for the very first time and remember the excitement! And the curiosity!

"Because I am sure there will be many questions, and it is not shameful to ask questions. It is a sign of the open minded and a valued asset. If we did not allow a wolf to question we would be no better than the Christ worshippers. And we are stronger, we are wolves!"

A howl went out among the crowd and everyone else joined.

"Yes! Yes, good people! And when I look into the face of this female wolf, beautiful face of an angel, I see something pure and innocent. She has the qualities of the White Wolf, truly admirable in any female, not unlike our Királyno Farkas who models herself in the White Wolf's image," Racquel began to walk around the fire. A woman with glistening blonde hair that hung past her waist smiled proudly from her place behind the Király Farkas, she stood proud with her naked body on display as only someone called Queen could do.

"But the White Wolf started, as all great women do, as a young girl," the storyteller began. "Born of light she came into a world that did not understand her, and to a family that treated her badly. She suffered more cruelty in her earliest years then most do in a lifetime! But she was very smart, you see, even without the cherished mother's love. For her mother cared nothing for her because she was not a boy! When she was just five years on this earth she escaped the cruelty of her family by running into the forest; she ran until she was exhausted, curling up and falling asleep under a large cherry tree. She awoke in the darkness and began to cry, because she was smart enough to realise a young child alone would not last long in such a place.

"A mother wolf was walking through the forest, looking for some food for her pups, when she heard the child's cries. She watched from afar for some time and when she saw the child was alone she felt sad. Who would send such a beautiful girl away, she wondered. She slowly approached the child, who stopped crying and reached out to touch the mother wolf's fur, which she immediately nuzzled up to. The mother wolf urged the girl to her feet, and from that day on raised the girl along with her cubs."

Racquel lifted her hands again and the fire spit and crackled. "This child thrives with the wolves, and finally the Gods decide to smile on her. As a gift, the Gods give her the ability to live in perfect harmony with her new family, the ability to change shape into a white wolf. Her colour was a symbol not only of the child's innocence but of the purity of love from her mother wolf. She had found her true destiny and place in this world."

"And this is where our worship begins, does it not? Because without such purity and kindness from the mother wolf, the White Wolf would not exist!" Racquel exclaimed. "And that we, as wolves, are capable of great things! We are not just mere predators!"

Anastasia leaned her chin on her hands with her elbows firmly placed on her knees, listening intently to her story. It was much more interesting, and far less depressing, than the stories she had heard about Jesus Christ.

But she had always wondered if she had only been told the bad stories.

"As the White Wolf grew she blossomed and fell in love, finding her mate. They had many pups, including a female white wolf. And so began a long line of shifting wolves, a white female born into every generation,"

Racquel's pace slowed as she said, "But the first, the White Wolf from our very story, is said to walk the earth still, blessed with immortality."

Anastasia watched the crowd, it appeared as if they did not take the idea of the

White Wolf's immortality seriously.

This was baffling, how could these fantastic creatures not believe in something like immortality? Did they also not believe in other creatures of myth similar to themselves?

"I am sure you all must wonder what this new wolf's story is!" Racquel exclaimed, making a sweeping gesture towards Anastasia while regaining the group's attention. "This female carries wolf blood deep in her veins, a true born with an amazing family legacy to rival any royal line. She is an honourable addition to our tribe."

Anastasia's face flushed, she leaned her head forward to try to hide behind her hair. Perhaps she would be able to tell such things once she had spent more time with others like her; her shifts were smoother and less painful and she could now sense others when she could not see them. She was learning to be both wolf and woman.

"Now what story should I tell next?" Racquel asked. "Perhaps the story of how the great Gavril came to be our Király Farkas?"

Anastasia watched the crowd as the howling began, examining Gavril out of the corner of her eye. He seemed to enjoy basking in the attention. His beautiful wife placed a hand on his shoulder and smiled with pride.

"The great Gavril became our Király Farkas by proving his might and strength in the Great Tournaments," Racquel began, throwing something into the flames so it sparked and danced as she walked, "a competition put forth by the elders, when they saw it was time for us to have *one* ruler. The eldest sons were brought forth to battle, and our great Gavril was not expected to win! Because even though he was brave and cunning and wise beyond his years, he was not the best fighter or the strongest.

"But he had more of an advantage then anyone could expect! Using his great mind he was always three steps ahead of his competitors, and won many battles by tiring others out. Soon, Gavril found himself in the last battle with the legendary Tuoa, the one the whole tribe, including the elders, believed would be our Király Farkas," Racquel smiled. "But they were very wrong. Great Gavril beat Tuoa, and according to the rules of the Great Tournaments it was a fight to the death so he took his competitor's life and his rightful place as Király Farkas! And he was accepted and welcomed with open arms, wasn't he?"

The howls began again, Racquel and Gavril laughed in unison and Anastasia saw some similarities in their faces as well as mannerisms. She was surprised the tribe had been around long enough to warrant such things.

"When the elders left this world many took it as a good time to challenge Gavril's authority. But he took them all on, didn't he?" she exclaimed, and the crowd howled, "And he killed every single one of them, didn't he?" the howls got louder. "He is our Király Farkas by blood and right, and may his rule be long and prosperous!"

A cheer went out among the group and the thumping began again, Racquel returned to her seat and the celebration continued. Anastasia quickly grew uncomfortable as she sat alone trying not to stare at the groups that gathered to converse around her.

No one seemed to notice her, but before she could slip away a large hand clamped down on her shoulder.

"So did you enjoy our stories?" Gavril's booming voice drew a few stares.

"Yes, very much," Anastasia said quietly.

"Were you going somewhere?" he asked.

"Well, you see, I...I do not really know anyone and I thought..."

"Don't be silly!" he exclaimed. "How will you meet anyone if you do not introduce yourself? Come! You shall sit with my family. Perhaps that shall improve your social status."

Anastasia glanced around briefly, Lynde had been sitting with her earlier but was now gone. She reluctantly followed Gavril to where his family was seated, his Queen rose to greet them.

"I apologise for not introducing myself sooner," his Queen came forward, brushing her hair behind her shoulder. "I am Iren, and I am Királynó Farkas. Welcome."

Anastasia extended her hand and Iren sniffed the inside of her wrist. She closed her eyes, as if remembering something, and smiled to herself.

"I can see what my sister was speaking of," Iren began. "You are of pure blood, and from an old family. What is your family name?"

"My name is Anastasia," she paused. "I have my mother's Bathory blood and I know nothing of my father."

Iren let go of her hand, and when they made eye contact a shiver ran through Anastasia's body.

The Queen smiled. "I would be honoured if you would dine with our family tonight."

"Thank you, Királynó Farkas. I appreciate your kindness," Anastasia said.

"You have done well for yourself, Mother," Katrine's voice rang though Anastasia's mind as she was seated. "Do not take it for granted."

KATRINE

SEE WHAT I SEE

It came rushing at me as if I had run into the room, the lights and sounds of a grand ballroom full of people. I could see splashes of red and guilding, smell beeswax candles and the fur that some were wearing.

I lay back on my bed and let the vision come, my body vibrating as I tried to take in my new environment. Gigi was two steps ahead of me, as she would be when we entered a function, and I could feel her anxiety.

A woman dressed entirely in red came out of the crowd and started towards us, turning eyes and heads as she moved. I felt the hair on the back of my neck stand up as we focused on her, Gigi's heart rate sped up so much I thought she may faint. As the woman got closer I could see that she was the second Gigi that Morgana had spoken of.

Only the angles of her face were sharper, her dark blue eyes full of anger, and her blonde hair more of a shimmering white.

When she and Gigi stood face to face I could see she was the younger, but she was by no means as beautiful. She was stunning, but she was not Gigi; I wondered if this had been a problem their entire lives.

They did not bow to each other, only stood and stared at each other as the tension grew like a storm cloud.

Gigi's initial fear turned to something else, it seemed almost like impatience.

As the woman opened her mouth to speak everything went dark, my eyes focusing on the ceiling above my bed.

I could hear Gigi's soft breathing as she slept, I thought about getting up and finding Morgana but decided against it.

I couldn't change anything. It could wait till morning.

Morgana came to my room early the next morning when Gigi was gone, sneaking in quietly and sitting at the edge of my bed.

"You had another vision," Morgana said, a statement instead of a question.

"I saw the second Gigi in a grand hall, it seemed like a court function," I said. "I think I know who she is."

"There are occasions where it is unwise to share your visions," Morgana replied.

I sighed. "But she has been so worried. She bought a talisman from a crone in Paris...."

"Do you know for sure that telling her would ease her concern or would it only complicate things further?"

I studied her face for several moments before asking, "Did you see more?"

"If you believe it would help her then tell her, if not I strongly suggest you don't bother," she replied. "You already have enough worries with the blue eyed demon."

"How do you live with the visions, Morgana?" I asked.

She stared out at nothing as if there was something there I could not see.

"It is a heavy burden," she said coldly. "You can only hope that on some occasions you help people."

I sat up in bed and wiped the sleep from my eyes.

"The sun has just set, I was told your cousin wishes to speak to you," she said.

"Heaven's sake, I hope he has not heard of this mess, I did not want him involved," I replied. She stood, helping me out of bed and handing me one of my plain gray dresses. I pulled it over my head and she helped tie me in as I washed my face.

"Have you seen Hannah at all? I have not seen her since before we left Paris," I said.

"Only for a moment, she has been spending her time attending to those in the covered wagons," she replied.

I grabbed my cloak and folded it over my arm, I did not know if I would need it later.

"Take me to him."

I found Gabriel standing out behind the inn, staring out at the open countryside.

"Cousin, what are you doing? It's very cold!" I said as I approached him, putting on my cloak.

"I do not like this place, my cousin, but I do not remember ever being here," he said.

"This is where Charles found you. I am surprised you do not remember," I replied.

"Perhaps with time I will. Or maybe it is better I should not. What do you know of this dead slave trader?"

I sighed. "It seems that I am the prime suspect in his murder."

"I felt relieved when I heard of his death but I am unsure why. Why do they blame you if you did not kill him?" Gabriel began. "I must say, now that I have spoken of his place I have this strange feeling, like I know this place well. Staring out at the land, makes it all seem familiar. I don't like this country, Katrine."

I put my arm in his. "Neither do I, Cousin."

He continued to stare, searching the darkness for something. I was curious about his thoughts but said nothing, I would wait until he felt like talking.

Eventually I was able to bring a shivering Gabriel inside and sit him by the fire. Our entire company had gathered in the great room for a meal.

"We need to talk about the slave trader," William said sharply to me.

"If you say *anything* that may upset him, you and I will have a problem," I snapped.

"Do you have any idea the problems you have caused for us?"

"Why do you keep blaming me? I said I did not kill him!"

"Do you think I am a fool?"

"Are you calling me a liar?"

His brows lowered, I couldn't stop the anger from pouring out of me. Others in the room turned, Gigi paused her conversation with Victorie.

"They think it was one of us," he began. "Do you know what that means? Now they can come after us. Now all eyes are going to turn to whatever we do."

Gabriel turned on William. "I believe my cousin said she did not commit this crime. Back away, my friend."

"Yes William, back away," I said flatly. "You cannot claim to want to marry me than accuse me of murder. It doesn't work that way."

His face turned bright red and he began to back away, every step he took away my heart split deeper in two. I wanted to cry and scream and beat him into submission but I didn't, I only watched as he walked away from me and my heart felt as if it was being pulled from my chest and smashed into pieces. The agony made my whole body ache.

"He is undeserving of your love, my dear," Gabriel said quietly to me. I looked at Charles, who smiled at me from the other side of the room, as if he had known this secret would tear William and I apart.

I had misjudged him. I would not make that mistake again.

"It is better this way, ma petite, I promise," Gigi said to me later that night in our room. "It will be better for you if you are not emotionally tethered to anyone."

I sighed but did not reply, just continued to copy out my letters and phrases in French.

"I know you believe you are in love and you are hurting but it will pass. It is better now that you have seen William's true nature instead of when you are married and trapped with him forever," she continued. "I admit he had changed since his time with you but it was bound to come back. I am proud that you stood up for yourself and Gabriel, you did so with grace and dignity. You are every inch my girl, and your Grandmother would be proud."

I smiled to myself, thinking of what my Grandmother had said in my vision. "Thank you, that means a lot."

She smiled at me and continued on with her reading, I thought about telling her about what I had seen. About the woman, the 'other' her, who I was assuming was one of her sisters and that I was quite sure she was somewhere in Russia.

But in my heart I knew Morgana was right, telling her would not help anything. That did not mean I could not prepare for it myself.

KATRINE

UNDESERVING

PRAGUE, BOHEMIA.

Gigi opened the window of the carriage and took a deep breath.

"Bon! Finally some clean air!" she exclaimed. "I am so relieved to be in Prague! You will love this place, girls, I promise."

I looked out the window at the winter landscape as we rode by, happy to be moving again. The last four weeks in Frankfurt had been like hell, from the murder of the slave trader to all the stress I had suffered afterwards I was overjoyed when the maids began packing us up to go. My secret remained a secret and William and I were no longer speaking.

Vincenzo smiled, placing a hand on my knee. "We shall put it all behind us, mon ami. I have some little trips for us to go on once we are settled in Prague, unless Gigi has plans to keep you busy."

"You can borrow her as long as you promise to return her in the same state you found her," Gigi replied. "I will not have that wretched boy terrorising her anymore."

I looked at Morgana, who sat silently staring, as if she were watching something play out in her mind.

I wondered how many visions she had that she never told anyone about.

Instead of the inn outside the city like in Frankfurt we stayed at a manor house in the city. As soon as we stepped out of the carriage I immediately liked Prague; the house was large and reminded me of our home in Paris.

"Katrine!" a voice called out and Hannah came out from one of the other carriages. I rushed to her and was about to hug her but stopped myself.

"I am so happy to see you. I was worried you had not come," I said. "I am sorry for the way I acted in Paris. You were right, please forgive me."

She smiled and I immediately felt at ease. "Think nothing of it, child. All is forgiven. How are you fairing?"

"Better now that I have seen you," I replied.

"Hannah," Vincenzo said, approaching from behind me. "Are you very busy? Katrine needs to be dressed for an outing with me tonight."

"Of course, my Lord," Hannah replied, bowing to him.

"Bon. I will come and collect you when it is time to go," he said, turning and walking away.

"Come, child. We shall find your room," she said, and I followed her inside.

"Katrine?" Hannah began as she was brushing out my hair. "May I say something?"

I smiled at her in the mirror. "Of course."

"In my opinion, if you are to choose a husband Signor Amori is the best choice," she replied.

"I suppose you have heard," I said. I had my own room and we were alone so I felt we could speak freely, something I relied on Hannah for.

She sighed. "I did. I am proud you protected your cousin, and if I may be so bold if that man really loved you it would not matter if you killed someone."

"Can I tell you something in confidence, Hannah?" I asked, and she nodded. "The man who was killed is the man Lord Westwick bought my cousin from."

I watched her face as she processed the information, then continued brushing.

"Men like that are undeserving of life of any kind. It is unfortunate that no one killed him sooner," I began, Hannah said nothing, "and you may not agree with my motives but what's done is done. I could not allow him to continue."

Hannah smiled. "You are a good girl, Katrine. It is a loss to those who cannot see it."

She plaited my hair, wrapped it around itself until it made a sort of knot. It suited the simplicity of my dark blue dress.

"Is it wrong that I am deeply hurt by William?" I asked her.

"Of course not! As I said, he should love you regardless. He can speculate all he likes, he will hear nothing from me," she said. "He is rotten to his core, and there is nothing you can do."

I sighed loudly but said nothing. She was right and there was no question about it, but I did not want her to know how truly heartbroken I was.

There was a slight rap at the door and she became all a flutter with excitement. I motioned for her to go answer it and Vincenzo came in, the black wool of his suit was crisp and slick as if it had never been worn.

"You are a vision, mon ami," I said happily.

He blushed. "You flatter me, my dear. I wanted to let you know it will only be you, Tolone, and I on this excursion tonight. But when we go to give the book he must come, being his contact."

"Of course. I cannot expect to avoid him, especially when we live in such close quarters," I said, standing up. "So, am I presentable? I was unsure of what to wear on such an adventure."

"You are wonderful, as always. Thank you, Hannah," he replied.

"Yes, thank you, Hannah," I said, and I hugged her tightly. "I do not know what I would do without you. Please stay close as we continue on, I have missed you."

I took Vincenzo's arm and we headed out, my cloak was waiting for me at the bottom of the stairs.

As we sped out into the late afternoon I stared at Prague out the window and was amazed at its beauty. Not a young city, but pretty, with a vast array of people in all shapes and colours like I had never seen before.

"Tis the capital of the Holy Roman Empire," Vincenzo said to me as he saw the expression on my face.

"Really? Does that mean he is here?" I asked.

"Quite possibly. Why do you ask?"

"Because I would like to catch a glimpse of the man who was trying to have my Grandmother beheaded," I replied.

He smiled. "I have such respect for your determination. You are almost alarmingly loyal."

"Thank you. I will do whatever I can to right the wrongs against those I love."

"You cannot kill the Emperor."

I chuckled. "I am aware of that, mon ami. I would not even try. The Lord will deal with him in the end for what he has done."

"You still believe in the existence of God?" he asked.

"Of course. I must," I began. "Because we are not damned, as one may think, as the result of our condition. If you are a good person you will be rewarded in Heaven, as I know my Grandmother will be. The truth about her will be known and remembered for centuries."

"I see you have warmed to Gabriel," he said.

"I would not allow William to attack him over some foolish notion that has no basis," I snapped.

"Katrine...."

"No! No Vincenzo! What William did was wrong and you know it, even if I had killed that man," I said. "Gabriel does not remember much and I would like it to stay that way. I will not have him provoked in such a manner, he does not need to be pushed into reliving whatever hell he's been through."

"You are right, my dear. Gabriel does not deserve such treatment," he replied, I could tell he wanted to say more but he didn't. I was glad, I felt terrible lying to him.

The carriage came to a stop and the door opened, Tolone was standing outside holding it open. It appeared that he had driven.

"Afternoon, Madmoiselle," he said as I stepped out.

"Good afternoon to you Tolone," I replied. Vincenzo handed him a small chest before getting out himself. He took my arm in his and led me through an open doorway to a small wood house on a street where if you stood in the middle and stretched out your arms you would be able to touch front doors on both sides.

The house smelled of ash and something I couldn't place, a large contraption sat in one corner of the room near the fire.

A well-groomed older man came in, he was all smiles as he and Vincenzo chatted in quick Italian. I caught a few things, but nothing of note. There was one word that kept being said, so quickly I was not sure I could even repeat it to ask what it meant.

Vincenzo gave the man a small velvet bag, which I assumed contained the stones we had bought in Frankfurt, and Tolone brought forth the chest that he opened to show the silver plate.

The older man clapped his hands in excitement, handing Vincenzo back another velvet bag, his payment I assumed. He took my arm and we left, the older man wishing Vincenzo a good journey and hoping to see him again.

"What did that word mean?" I asked him when we got moving in the carriage. "You kept saying this word, 'alchimia', what does it mean?"

Vincenzo sighed. "It loosely translates to the word 'alchemy' in english."

"What is alchemy?"

"It is a form of science, my dear. Involving turning nothing into something. I do not quite understand it myself so I am afraid I cannot explain clearly."

I smiled. "Not a problem, mon ami. I am sure if I am meant to know I will find out."

"You continue to amaze me," he said. "You are, in so many ways, the most even tempered woman I have ever met. I cannot figure out how you are this way when you are in such closed quarters with Grisela and Morgana. I wonder if all Scots are so hot headed."

"I find that once you get to know her she is quite agreeable," I replied. "Even Gigi is beginning to enjoy Morgana's company."

"You are very good at seeing past obvious character flaws. I think you are the best woman I know."

"Thank you. That means a lot coming from you," I said, I felt the colour rising to my face.

The carriage stopped and I heard a woman's voice yelling, the door flew open and Gigi's face appeared.

"Where on earth have you two been?" she exclaimed. "We are going on an outing, would you care to join us, Vincenzo?"

He chuckled. "No thank you, my dear. Good luck, Katrine."

He got out of the carriage and Gigi and Morgana got in, the Scots girl looked rather flustered. The carriage started moving again.

"Where are we going?" I asked.

Morgana grumbled. "Some bloody church for some crazy reason."

"As I explained to you, petite sorciére, it is one of the finest examples of construction still standing in Europe," Gigi began, "and I intend on trying to expose you both to some culture on this trip, whether you like it or not."

"It cannot possibly be more beautiful then Notre Dame," I said.

"A church is a church is a bloody church," Morgana added impatiently.

"Things cannot ever be compared to Paris, but there are certain sights that should be seen when you are staying in a city. Unfortunately many of them are churches or housed inside churches," Gigi began, "or are kept behind closed doors by greedy royalty. So when the opportunity arises you should take it, and later it can be used when having a conversation. Women with opinions on such things is always an asset."

She looked over at Morgana, whose eyes were lowered. "That is, if you choose to speak to anyone. And it may do you some good to communicate with others."

"I am not a fan of others," Morgana said flatly.

Gigi sighed and rolled her eyes, I couldn't help but giggle.

When we finally got to our destination I could do nothing but stare up at the two massive spires. In style it looked quite similar to the cathedrals in Paris but something about it seemed older and full of strange spirits.

"Beautiful, isn't it?" Gigi said. "I find it quite captivating."

"I think it has ghosts," I replied.

"All churches do," Morgana added quietly from her place beside me.

I heard the clatter of hooves, I turned in enough time to see a grand litter ride past with an emblem on its door that had two large black eagles included in it. The carriage itself had guilding and heavy red curtains over the windows, with two stunning white chargers pulling them through the streets. They reminded me of the horses from my Grandmother's carriage that had pulled me into this life, a place I never thought I'd be.

"What was that?" I asked Gigi.

"That is the badge of the Holy Roman Emperor. Now, if you two will follow me....," she began, but I stopped hearing her. I watched as the carriage rode away, wondering if *that* man had just gone past me. If I had really come so close to him, if he was staying somewhere nearby. If he was sleeping in a grand bed in soft, clean sheets while my grandmother lived in a sealed up room. The man who had a hand in destroying her life had been a stone's throw away from me and all I could do it watch.

"Petite? Petite, what's going on?" Gigi asked.

"Where....where....would he be staying?" I said.

"The palace, of course," she replied, then smacked my arm. "Whatever you are thinking, stop it right now! Are you listening, Katrine? If I get even a hint that you might try something so unbelievably stupid you will be locked in a cage until we reach Moscow, do you understand?"

"Yes, yes, of course. Now, can we see this church? I am suddenly not feeling well," I said, walking ahead of them and heading for the door.

Klara

FIRST DAY

The young woman yanked hard on Klara's arm, trying to pull her out of her heavy sleep as the trader came storming into the small hut where the slaves were kept. All she could do was jump out of the way as the man punched Klara in the side of the head.

The hit woke Klara up but was too hard, it rattled her brain and make her disoriented as she tried to pull herself to her feet. The young woman rushed forward to help her, putting her body between the two to stop the assault from continuing. The trader yelled at them and she nodded, Klara watched as he seemed satisfied and walked out.

"You understand him?" Klara asked the woman, who nodded. "What did he say?"

The young woman stared blankly at Klara.

"Well?" Klara continued, the young woman shook her head quickly. "What's wrong with you?"

The young woman opened her mouth and Klara gasped.

"Did *that* man cut out your tongue?" Klara gestured in the direction of where the slave trader had been, the young woman shook her head no.

"Well, what am I supposed to call you if you cannot tell me your name?"

Klara continued angrily. Her companion smiled then began to write in the dirt floor with the tip of her finger.

Klara nodded. "Lovely. I'll feel much better calling you by your name than something like 'girl with no tongue'. So it's Olivia, am I correct?"

She tapped on the word and smiled to show Klara yes, that was correct. Olivia then took Klara's hand and led her out of the hut and off to their duties.

The trader had a group of slaves who were there for the specific purpose of mixing and bottling herbal remedies and poultices. Whether they were magical or not was irrelevant, because such things only happened when they were in the proper hands.

Olivia fell in line quite easily, instructing Klara with a series of hand gestures and sharply pinching her arm just before she made a mistake.

Soon the picking and grinding of herbs became easy and mind numbing, and the hunger for blood became overwhelming.

Klara watched Olivia flick the inside of her wrist as she moved through her work. She could not understand why she would do that, and asking her to explain could be very complicated.

Finally she got frustrated, "Why are you doing that?"

Olivia nodded, making the sign for drink then extending her fangs like she would bite herself.

"I understand, but what does...," Klara continued. Then Olivia flicked her wrist again, pointed at her head then signed stop.

"It really helps you stop thinking about it?" Klara asked. Olivia nodded happily, and the two seemed quite pleased that they could understand each other so simply. Klara was even beginning to enjoy Olivia's company, and was more pleased then she had anticipated at the other's woman's lack of speech.

Work went on into the night, and when they were finally released from their duties they found a rat in a cage waiting where they slept. The other slaves seemed not to notice except a young boy, who watched them carefully from across the room. Olivia reached into the cage and twisted the rat's body, finally biting down and drinking its blood.

But she stopped rather quickly and handed it off to Klara, pushing it closer when Klara cringed. Reluctantly she took it and the rat's blood was the finest thing she had ever tasted. She silently thanked the rat for its help as she placed its body back in the cage; this was the most time she had spent thinking about something she had taken blood from.

Olivia gave her a pat on the back, trying to give her a look of encouragement.

"I am not used to being so...so...feral," Klara said. Olivia pinched her hard, giving her a warning look that said she better get used to it, *quickly*. Klara apologised without thinking, then stared down at the greenish bubbled scab on her wrist and wanted to cry.

Then Olivia took Klara's hand, took a small bundle from in her sleeve and began applying it to her wrist.

"You...you did this..." Klara began. Olivia held Klara's lips closed and shook her head no. They both knew what would happen if they got caught and they couldn't risk that, even hiding it from the other slaves.

"Thank you," Klara said. They made eye contact, Olivia's rich green eyes radiated with pride. She pushed a loose strand of flaxen hair from her brow, using the back of her hand to wipe the sweat from her brow.

Klara moved closer to Olivia and whispered in her ear. "This will not be our fate. One way or another, we will be free."

Olivia's expression remained blank as Klara pulled away, laying down on the ground and trying to get comfortable. Olivia did the same and the two quickly fell asleep.

In the corner of the room the young boy continued to stare, smiling to himself as he wiped the blood from the corner of his mouth.

KATRINE

FAMILY BUSINESS

"I must speak with you privately," I said quietly to Charles at dinner that evening. It was our first night in Prague and proving to be a grand affair, with many visitors coming to pay their respects.

"Another errand you need my assistance with?" He asked.

"I've had a vision," I replied.

"I told you I would find someone...."

"That is not important," I snapped. "Morgana had a vision in Paris, of a second Gigi in Russia. I have had a similar vision and I believe the woman to be from Gigi's family. I am thinking a sister."

He then said the name for the first time, and once I heard it it never left me, haunting my thoughts like an evil spirit.

"Beatrix? I cannot imagine what she would be doing in Russia, she hates the cold. What does Gigi think?"

I sighed. "I have not the heart to tell her. That is why I came to you, to get an idea of what we are dealing with."

"I am not sure what to tell you, Katrine. You cannot prepare yourself for one such as Beatrix. She is unpredictable, ruthless, barbaric, and incredibly manipulative. She is one of the most dangerous women I have ever met," he said, someone came and handed him a sealed message. "You should tell Gigi, for if it is, in fact, Beatrix, she should prepare herself. She may know how best to deal with her younger sister."

I tried to continue but he stopped me so he could read his message, his eyes grew wide as he refolded the pages.

He tapped gently on the side of his glass, all eyes turning to him. "Good people, I want to inform you that you should not get too comfortable for we shall be quickly moving on."

The whispers began, and I quietly asked the question on everyone's lips. "Is this about the skinwalker, Charles?"

"Yes, as a matter of fact, it is," Charles replied, smiling deviously at me. "And I think, because you are so grateful for my help in Frankfurt, you are going to help me catch it. My sources say it's running around Moscow, and Lappish Witches are after it so we have no time to waste."

"I would have helped you, regardless," I said.

"Why?"

"My mind has changed about you in many ways, Charles. I am beginning to trust your judgment, hopefully you have learned from your mistakes."

He sighed. "I have learned more from you than any other woman in my life, save my mother."

"I am not sure if that is a huge compliment or an insult," I replied. He laughed loudly, turning some heads, including William's angry stare.

"You are a pleasure, my dear," he said, squeezing my hand where it sat on the table. I felt William's eyes grow cold as he watched me, my stomach turned. I could not bring myself to look at him.

I was at the door to my room when the vision hit me. The world went blurry then faded to black, colours and objects returning as if someone opened the door to the dark room I was in.

The furnishings were plain and simple, nothing I recognised. I could hear a strange gurgling noise from somewhere in the room. I felt myself gripping the wall in reality as I began to walk through the room in my mind, the noise got louder as I moved farther in.

I saw the pool of blood first as it began to flow out from the opposite side of the bed, a large wood framed thing meant for a grand person. I could feel my heart beating faster as the possibilities of who it could be ran through my mind.

I thought of something Charles has said, about my powers as a dhampir, and I tried to smell who it was without being overpowered by the blood.

But something was clouding my judgment, so I did the only thing I could do and stepped around the bed.

William's body writhed on the floor as the blood poured from his neck. The wound was rough, a deep tear that had taken a large amount of flesh. I could hear my screams as they vibrated through my mind, it took all my strength not to scream out loud. He reached out for me and I got down on the ground and pulled him to my body, cradling him in my arms as I sobbed uncontrollably. He had someone else's scent all over him that I did not recognise immediately, but it was familiar.

I felt William's life leaving his body and could hear my desperate pleas to him, and God to not take him away from me. The scent suddenly hit me, it was vampire. I could not figure out who, and I could think of little past William dying in my arms.

Then, suddenly, I was back in my doorway and shaking in fear. I heard someone call my name but I did not listen, I pushed my way into my room and quickly shut the door behind me.

Katrine

TRUTH AND SECRETS

I watched Tolone as he shaved Vincenzo's face, sitting on edge in one of the small chairs in his room. I did not sleep much after the vision I had of William, so when I was told the next afternoon that we would be going to drop off the book I was ready so quickly I spent most of the day following Vincenzo around as he prepared.

"What is going on with you, Katrine?" Vincenzo asked.

I changed the subject to the other thing plaguing my thoughts. "What do you know of Beatrix Delphine?"

"Where did that come from?" he asked. Tolone even paused, but only for a moment.

"Morgana had a vision of two Gigi's in Russia, do you remember?" I began. "Well, I said something to Charles and he mentioned that name. What can you tell me?"

"Does Grisela know you think it is Beatrix?"

"I have not said, but I cannot imagine she has not thought it so."

"That would explain her fear," he said. "I am sure Charles told you all the important things. I cannot say much more other than Grisela should be told. And there is more, I can sense it. You can tell me, I am quite sure she will be asking for further details."

He sat up as Tolone wiped his face clean and began combing his hair back.

"I have also seen something, I have seen the woman's face. I know she is one of Gigi's family, I just do not know which. Charles said he does not believe Beatrix would be in Russia for she does not like the cold."

Vincenzo chuckled. "He would know better than I. But, she must be warned. When we return I insist you speak with her immediately."

I sighed but said nothing, I was not convinced telling her would help anyone.

Once we were ready we headed out, I had insisted Morgana come along to act as an extra buffer between William and I. Vincenzo had said it was William's contact so he had to come.

The carriage ride was short and silent, the tension heavy. I kept my eyes focused on looking out the dark window, I could not bring myself to look at William directly.

Before long we were walking into a small old house, heat blasting at us as we entered. A huge fire roared in the fireplace, being carefully tended by a young woman in a plain linen dress, her big blue eyes sparkled when she saw William.

"I did not think she would remember you, my boy," a small older man said to him as he came towards us from the back of the house. William handed him a small package, the man smiled happily.

"Thank you for this, I would not have found it without you. Your mother sends her love," the man continued, moving over to us and examining our faces. My arm suddenly became very itchy.

He smiled at Morgana and said, "Your troubles are over, little witch. Be at ease."

He turned to me, then, watching me scratch my arm.

"You have been marked," he said, taking my arm and pulling up my sleeve. "And you believe this mark did this to you, but it did not. This mark is only useful to the beast who gave it to you, as a way of tracking you.

That beast can find you anywhere in the world because of it. Whatever has happened to you has nothing to do with this."

I stared at him, down at my arm, then back up at him again. I had so many questions, everything started swimming in my head.

"Perhaps one day you shall have the answers you seek, young lady. They all lie within the roots of your family," he said, then he smiled proudly. "Only the Bathory know the truth."

I pulled away from him and held my scratched arm to my chest. It was obvious that this man had some sort of powers.

"You did not tell her this, Will? She seems quite surprised. I assumed you would have told her," he said.

William's face turned bright red, and he said, "You are much stronger than I am, I did not sense anything of that sort."

The old man laughed loudly. "Or did you think it would hurt your chances? A Bathory would be a suitable match, and it would please your mother...."

"Thank you for your time. I will be in touch," William said, pushing us towards the door. When he thought we were out of earshot he said a proper goodbye in Italian, and asked the man not to mention me to his mother.

I could not help but smile to myself, William admitting openly to someone being more powerful was totally out of character. Which either meant he was lying or we had been in the presence of one of the most powerful beings on the planet.

My gut feeling was it was a bit of both.

William started intently at the bottom of the carriage, as if his eyes may burn a hole in the bottom. I could not help but smile at his discomfort. He deserved it after what he had put me through in Frankfurt; what I had or had not done mattered not, if he loved me truly it would not matter.

"So," I said, finally breaking the silence. "Do you think this could be true? That I would have been turned even without the scratch?"

"If you are truly dhampir then I suppose it could, but I have not heard of someone being unaffected by a scratch from a shapeshifter," Vincenzo said, turning to William. "What do you think, mon ami?"

"I suppose, I suppose," he mumbled. I had to pinch Morgana to stop her from laughing, I wondered with all her powers if this was something she could have sensed also.

"It is an interesting theory, and I will speak to Charles. But before we can continue I insist you speak to Gigi," Vincenzo said sharply. "Perhaps both of you should speak to her."

Morgana grabbed my arm as we walked back into the manor. "And why do we need to speak to Gigi?"

"I spoke of my vision to Charles and he mentioned Gigi's sister. Supposedly she should be warned," I replied.

"This is not going to go well," she said as she followed me up to Gigi's room.

"Petite, I am so pleased to see you," Gigi said as she ushered us both inside.

"You may not be for long," I replied, closing the door behind me. "Please sit and allow me to speak."

She quickly sat, staring intently at me as I paced the room.

"Because of circumstances beyond my control, I now have visions," I said quickly, trying to avoid the opportunity for her to speak. "And I had a vision of a second you in Russia. When I described the other you to Charles he mentioned the name Beatrix, and he and Vincenzo were in agreement that I should tell you immediately."

She sighed, then said. "I am assuming these circumstances are why Charles is so afraid of you?"

I nodded, and she raised her hand to stop Morgana or I from saying more.

We stayed like this for several moments, until I finally asked Gigi. "Should I be concerned?"

Her blue eyes were cold and hard as she turned to me, her face gone pale.

"I am not going to lie to you, petite," she began, standing and pacing herself. "Yes. We should be deeply concerned."

Anastasia

INTRUSIONS

Dreams of her children changing into wolves woke her from her sleep, she had drunk far too much with the Király and Királyno after Racquel had told her stories and her stomach was queasy.

Anastasia sat up and put a hand on her aching belly, becoming very still when she heard someone outside her tent.

Lynde crept quietly into her tent at a low crawl, whispering to Anastasia that the camp had intruders and they must prepare.

Anastasia immediately regretted saying the Countess's name to Iren. Perhaps someone had come looking for her, the Countess's angry children coming to permanently erase their mother's mistake from the earth.

Or Katrine's new friends have come to finish what they started.

She shifted as quickly as she could, the transitions were getting easier, and went outside. She immediately found Lynde and sat and waited with the others, a small group of her students had gathered to await orders. The Király and Királyno were nowhere to be seen, but Dragan and Saskia, the Második or second, were clearly in charge, with the strong ones pacing around like generals leading the charge into war.

Anastasia immediately got nervous. She did not want anyone to sacrifice themselves for her. Some of the others had very young children.

Lynde appeared and began to pace in front of them, the others all lined up alongside her. Anastasia stayed seated in her place at one end of the line and waited for some more movement. She wished someone was still in human form so they could explain to her what to do.

Lynde scraped her front paw in the dirt and the others fell in line behind her, Anastasia in last. They walked along ahead of them into the forest; the less experienced fighters were being kept back so if they had to fight it would be on equal ground.

Anastasia concentrated very hard and tried to use all her senses to try to figure out what or who it was.

She thought long and hard about Katrine and the situation in Paris to see if she got any of the same feelings, anything that may identify them as who was in the forest. She wanted to believe she would be able to smell another Bathory but she was not quite sure she would, only Katrine. She was sure she would know if her own daughter was in the woods.

But what about Bodi? What if her son had changed and run off into the forest, scared and alone?

Guilt began to overwhelm her, she had not thought enough of her young son. But his father would take good care of him, she knew that. His sacred son would be fine, her daughter may not have been had she been left behind.

All they could do now was sit and wait for whatever it was to show itself.

They waited, watched as groups went into the forest and returned empty handed. This continued on until the sun was full in the sky and the heat beat down on their heads. Anastasia's thoughts went to water, and when all the patrols returned the leaders changed and gathered everyone together.

"We found clear sings of multiple intruders," Lynde said loudly. "They all appear human but we found lingering traces of magic. We must prepare for the chance that they will come back."

Everyone began to disperse, and Anastasia stood and started back for her tent. Her thoughts were swimming with ideas of what she could do to help. She knew some magic, she had previously believed that was how she had come to her current situation but when she saw Katrine her mind had changed.

Because Katrine had become something, but it was not a wolf.

She had not thought of the woman who raised her since she left the castle. All of this began with her, she had learned so much from her.

She had not even thought about Darvulia, the shock of seeing her again in those moments when they first came to her husband's house. Darvulia and her mother's friends had made that cure for her thirst and...she paused in the middle of the tent and remembered.

Perhaps she should talk to Lynde. About her life. About all that had happened.

Katrine

THE KING'S LEGACY

WARSAW, POLAND.

Time began to slip away as days turned into weeks, we rolled through cities and towns without consequence. I had wanted to remember each country as much as possible but by the time we reached Poland I was exhausted and my memories became fuzzy.

I questioned myself as I watched Gigi sitting across from me in the carriage. Her distress began to show on her face since I mentioned Beatrix and I had trouble containing my guilt. So I decided to no longer speak of my visions, no matter how disturbing. William and I were still not speaking, but I felt better after the encounter with the shaman. If he had been keeping something so serious from me since the beginning he was, in no way, the man I thought he was.

Although it was now May, in most places a warmer month, when we stepped out of our carriage in Warsaw I was hit by a cold wind that caused my body to quake.

I looked up at the sun, which was beginning to set. "I thought the summer was upon us. Why on earth is it so cold?"

Gigi pulled her cloak around her and looked out at the landscape with angry eyes.

"Jamaiz l'esprit, petite," Gigi said, and I silently followed her inside the inn.

After changing our clothes we went downstairs for mulled wine and to sit by the fire, where I was pleased to find Gabriel.

He smiled when he saw me. "Do you feel it, child? We once ruled this country. It was before I was born but Istvan, the Polish called him Stefan Batory, was a good king and much loved, especially after the fiasco with Henry of Valois."

"Tell me more, Cousin," I said, sitting down with my mug of wine between my hands.

"Some also called him Stephen, as I am Gabriel and Erzsebet is Elizabeth; English translation of our proper Hungarian names. Sigsmund of Poland died with no heirs, so the crown went to his sister, Anna. The Sejm, their parliament, agreed to Anna's pleas to elect Henry of Valois, a match that would benefit Poland mostly. But the Valois had many problems, some believe curses because of their Medici mother, and when his brother Charles IX died Henry could not get back to France fast enough to take his crown. It is said he ran out in the night with some of Poland's crown jewels stuffed in his saddle bags!

"Luckily Anna never married the Valois so it was uncomplicated to remove him as monarch. Stephen was presented to Anna as an option, and they married, becoming co-rulers of the Polish – Lithuanian commonwealth, the second to hold this title."

"Why did Henry of Valois not try to keep both crowns?" I asked.

"I am not entirely sure but I believe he did not happily go to Poland. He was the favourite son and I cannot imagine the King did not want his brother out of his hair. Their mother, the Medici, tried to control everything through her sons and was quite pleased when her favourite took the throne, she had lost control of the King after the Massacre on Saint Bartholomew Day. Some say that event brought on the downfall of the Valois. Erzsebet's mother was King Stephen's sister, I am sure you already knew that," he said.

"No, I did not," I replied, smiling proudly. "But I am happy to. I believe it may have been mentioned in some format but not so specific."

"I wish we could go out and explore the city, I have always wanted to see it and I am sad I cannot in the daylight," he said sadly. "This is an important place for our family. I wish we could have seen it together."

"We still can. It shall just be in the dark," I said, trying to show my happiness. He did not seem too excited by the prospect of exploring the city at night.

"I suspect we shall not be here long," I continued. "Charles is anxious to reach Russia. So you should decide if you would like to go out as soon as possible. And I must ask you, does the family have any connection to blood drinkers?"

His dark eyes studied my face, clearly looking for intent. "Not that I am aware of. Why do you ask?"

"Curiosity," I replied. Somewhere in the branch of the family that lead to my birth there was a blood drinker, I knew that much about being a dhampir.

But it was probably an answer I would never get, since I had no one to ask the questions to.

"Are you ready to tell me more of the Order of the Dragon?" I asked.

His face turned bright red, and he said quietly, "I thought you had forgotten."

"No, I have not Cousin. But I will give you time," I replied. He nodded, silently staring into the fire as if lost in his own thoughts.

"Prominent Bathory men, for some time, have been members of the Order. Often high ranking," Gabriel said flatly. "It was almost expected of us men, to be involved. Under the guise of Holy Crusaders for the Catholic Church."

"But your mind has changed about their intentions," I replied.

He looked in my eyes, a small smile on his face. "Like you I am conflicted. The wrong should pay for their crimes."

"You know what I have done?" I said quietly.

He smiled truly at me then, and said, "I would have done the same."

"There was another," I continued. "In Csejthe. A priest. He helped with the case against my grandmother."

"That was you?" he asked, and I nodded. "Good show, Child. You did us a favour. I must say, doing such a thing for the family makes you every inch a Bathory."

"He was no man of God and was undeserving of such things befitting that station," I said sharply.

"You have no need to justify your actions to me, Cousin. Your loyalty is admirable, and I can say whole heartily that Erzsebet appreciated it," he replied. "Being a voice of God does not make you a good person. Corruption is rife within the church, one of the reasons people could attach themselves to the religious reformation."

"Why do so many people believe the Bathory to be evil?" I asked.

"With the invention of the printing press viscous rumours could be spread with the simple passing out of a leaflet," he said. "You know, it was once believed that the Bathory Nadasdy marriage would create a family as powerful as the Hapsburgs? We were a formidable force at one time, and the powerful are always picked at."

I smiled at him. "We should go out and explore, cousin. Even if it is at night. This place is part of our heritage."

"I am not sure I have the heart, but I shall think more on it," he replied.

"Of course. Whatever you decide."

We all sat for a very late meal, Polish fare was heavier than what we'd eaten recently. It reminded me very much of home and my father's heavy handed cooking, a rare delicacy from my childhood.

Tolone came and placed a mug of hot ale in front of me, I could smell the blood before he set it down. I wondered if the other people in the inn, and there were some, could smell it too; if the regular people around us were curious about the strange smelling liquid.

I tried to sip slowly, even though I felt like guzzling it in two mouthfuls. I had not had blood since the slave trader and my body immediately reacted to it, I felt renewed and full of warmth.

I should not go so long between feedings. I may not like this but it was part of my life now and I had to accept it.

Katrine

PRAYER FOR HER SOUL

I could sense William's discomfort from across the room that night as we socialised. We entertained as we normally did in Paris, and had done in Prague, with another string of colourful visitors come to pay their respects.

I watched him as he shuffled around, his eyes staring at nothing in particular but something only he could see. I wanted to know what he was thinking, if he was stringing together bits of guilt in an attempt to comfort himself.

The idea that he had known all along about the scratch was burning inside my mind, even more than the idea that I would have become what I am regardless of the ritual. I wondered if my mother had known somehow.

Gigi smiled and dazzled the guests as she often did, but she was lacking her usual sparkle. She seemed distant and sad.

I leaned over to Morgana and whispered to her. "Are your visions ever wrong?"

She turned slightly at her place on my right so she could see my face.

"Not often," she replied after watching me for a few moments. "But yours could be, considering we are not sure of what they are."

"I should not have told Gigi. I hate seeing her in such a state," I said.

"It is not entirely your fault, Katrine," she began. "Vincenzo said you should tell her and you thought it good advice. Perhaps it is better if she is concerned and nothing comes of it than for her to be ill prepared."

"I suppose," I replied, and I went back to watching the room.

There was much dancing and merriment, my cousin danced quite happily with Mathilde, who could not keep her eyes off him.

Gabriel was glowing, radiating happiness as he kept his eyes locked on her. He seemed blissfully happy in her arms, and she a vision of warmth and laughter in his presence.

"It appears you may have an Aunt soon, ma petite," Gigi said quietly.

I could not help but smile. "Is that a problem? They seem quite enamoured with each other."

"Not at all. I just did not take Mathilde as the enamouring type," she replied.

"Could she be leading him on under false pretences?"

"No, no. She is never false, that I know for sure," Gigi said.

I sighed as I saw a maid come in and hand Charles a sealed message.

"I assume it is more stories of the skinwalker," Gigi continued. "He seems to be receiving dispatches several times a day. I wonder what is so urgent he needs to know constantly."

"He mentioned Lappish Witches to me. Perhaps it is about them," I said. Charles read the note, then handed it to Vincenzo, who crossed the room and handed it to me.

"Charles thought you may wish to see this," Vicenzo said. I took it from him, reading the first three lines of elegant script written in perfect French.

"This is about Klara?" I asked. He smiled and nodded as I continued to read down the page. The letter described in great detail how, during a failed escape attempt, Klara was shot, her feet cut off for trying to run, then her throat slit after she attacked her captor.

"So she's dead?" I asked, Gigi snatched the letter from my hand to read then Morgana took it from hers.

"It seems so," he replied, smiling.

"Thank you, mon ami. Perhaps we should pray for her soul," I said.

He chuckled, then said. "Perhaps, but I doubt it would do her any good. She sealed her own fate long be
fore you came along."

"Please show this to William. He will be pleased," I replied. I watched as he took the note to him, and those blue eyes looked at me with the sparkle and adoration they'd once had.

My heart ached and I desperately wanted to cry but I did not, I only smiled back at him as if my heart were not completely broken.

Gigi moved into the room as if she was floating, drifting like a rolling mist into our shared room. I dismissed the servants after they had helped me change and began to undress Gigi myself, her body slumped in exhaustion as I undid her corset.

"Perhaps I was wrong," I said as I helped take off her stockings. "I am not known to have visions."

"But la petite sorcérie is, and she has been correct in our experience with her," she replied.

I sighed. "But that does not mean the woman is...."

"Describe the woman you saw to me, ma petite," she said sharply, keeping her eyes lowered.

"While she did resemble you, her features were sharper and more angular than yours. And where your hair is more golden hers was pale, closer to white," I began. "I do not remember much more than that."

She kept her eyes down, a quiet 'hmm' escaping her lips. I sat on the floor in front of her, she was sitting on the stool used for her toilette, and watched her as she seemed deep in thought.

"Charles said he thinks Russia is too cold for her," I said without thinking, hoping she would not be offended.

She chuckled. "He is right. That was why she decided on Constantinople. And she had developed a taste for Turkish blood."

"So there is a chance she is not there?"

"After Constantinople fell, Russia became the centre of the Orthodox

Church. I doubt that would be a motivator, Beatrix was never interested in religion. She could only really be tempted by luxury," she said, finally looking up at me. "I should not be so concerned. She is my sister, after all. I think I would know better than anyone where she would go."

"I believe so. I'd like to think I would know what my brother would do in most situations," I replied.

"You have a brother?" she asked, smiling. "You never mentioned him."

"I do, I believe he would be sixteen years old now," I began. "I wonder if he is preparing to marry. A wife could fill the space my mother and I left. My father could have remarried, for that matter."

She cupped my cheek with her hand, smiling warmly at me, her eyes full of sympathy and love.

"I hope you do not mourn too greatly for your old life, ma petite," she said. "Because I could not imagine my life without you in it. I value you immensely."

"And I you, Gigi. I have come to believe it was my destiny to be with you, and I do not mourn for what I left behind because it led me to where I currently sit."

She smiled again, stroking a finger along my cheek. "We shall face whatever happens together."

Katrine

MAGICAL ASSISTANCE

Gigi's mood improved along with the warming temperatures as we moved into the summer months. She turned her attention to the dances we were to perform in Russia and started speaking to Josephine about the preparations.

Soon, it was time to move on to our next stop, and there had been no talk of what may possibly reach us in the end.

Just before sunrise the day we were to leave I found Gabriel as he prepared to get into one of the covered wagons.

"How are you feeling, cousin? Are you sad we did not see more of Poland?" I asked.

He came and embraced me warmly. "No, my dear. I am quite alright. I realised that my want to explore was as Gabor, last in a long line of Bathory rulers of Transylvania. But I am no longer that man, so perhaps I should rethink my motivations. Maybe another time when I can look with fresh eyes."

I took his hand and kissed it. "I swear we shall return one day together and see the city as the last of the Bathory, and as cousin and cousin. The past is the past, and we have our future together."

"Thank you, my darling," he said, cupping my face in his hands.

"Are you well riding this way, cousin?"

"Quite," he replied, kissing my cheek. "Now, I shall see you in Minsk."

Our carriage had been well cleaned and sprinkled with lavender, giving it a fresh scent.

Hannah was waiting for us as we approached with a wide, happy smile.

"Will you ride with us?" I asked her.

"No, but I have come to wish you a good trip and I will see you when you step back out into the world," she said, before she could react I embraced her. She was stiff at first than held me to her for a few moments, we both seemed to breathe a bit easier for that short time.

"And a good trip to you, Hannah, and may it be as stress free as possible," I said, lifting my skirt with one hand and holding her with the other as she helped me into the carriage.

"Morgana I must ask you something but I need your word that our conversation will be kept private," Gigi said sharply.

Morgana looked briefly at me, than said. "Of course, Grisela."

"Perfect. Now, as you know, there is a possibility that my sister is at the end of the road in Russia. You may not be aware but she is a very dangerous woman, and I wish to protect us in any way possible," she began. "I would like to know if there is anything you can do magically to assist us."

"I am flattered you would ask for my help. I assumed you would ask the more powerful....," she began.

"I would not ask him for anything unless near death," Gigi answered roughly. "The humiliation he has put my protégée through, I can barely stand to look at him. Besides, I can sense you have more power than you care to admit."

"If we are being brutally honest, Madam, I sense you carry an object that is supposed to have some magical property, but it is useless and you should discard it immediately," Morgana began, gesturing at the talisman the crone had made as Gigi took it out from her sleeve and threw it out the window. "Much better. Whoever made that does not have the kind of power needed to truly protect you. I must begin by explaining that my magic involves chants and charms, a practice that began with the Celts and the Old Ones in Scotland. It takes time and patience and is not as immediate as some other magic, if I have access to herbs I can make some tinctures for protection against poisons and other things that can be used against a person's body."

"William had much to say against the herbal magic Roza had taught me," I said.

"That is because he's a fool," Morgana snapped. "Spellcasters can see no magic but their own. I hope you have not entirely forgotten what she taught you. I trust you are smart enough not to mix any of it together, which would be quite difficult considering it is two completely different languages. But, I need to spend some time thinking in regards to how exactly to go about this."

"Of course. Thank you," Gigi said.

"It is an honour to be able to help you at this time. You continually help me so much I am so pleased to finally have the chance to help you," Morgana replied, and for the first time since we had met she looked genuinely happy.

"Let us pray that it never need be used," Gigi replied, leaning to the side so she could stare out the window.

Klara

EASIER THAN EXPECTED.

A few weeks later as the day became night the trader came into the workroom, smelling of drink with his face a strange flush pink. He grabbed the young boy, pulling his shoulder from its socket as he threw him onto his stomach, the pop of bone on bone a sickening sound.

With one hand he held the boy down and with the other he pull his pants away, not bothering to muffle the tortured screams. The trader lifted the boy up as he entered him and continued to pound his body on the small table as he thrust into him.

Klara had to turn away to stop herself from screaming but Olivia just stared, as if such horror and brutality were a common sight to her.

Then, as it appeared the trader was going to climax he pulled a dagger from his belt and slit the boy's throat, spilling blood all over the table and out in to the workroom.

Klara bit down on her cheek and kept her eyes on the ground as the trader righted himself and left with a terrible grin on his face.

Several of the other slaves began cleaning up the mess, trying to straighten the poor boy out and give him some dignity. Olivia began trying to clear some of the blood off the floor and remove anything that was destroyed.

She seemed to ignore the body as it was wrapped up and carried out. Klara quietly followed along as the young boy's body was tossed into a hole at the far end of the property.

She leaned over and looked in the hole at the other bundles that were rolled up in a similar fashion, well bound compared to the other body that had just been added and was still leaking blood.

She hurried away without looking back, the hunger starting to stir deep inside her. She was accustomed to having what she wanted, whenever she wanted, and she did not like this new life.

Charles had probably taken them to Russia at her parent's expense, she thought to herself. She had only done what had felt natural and, somehow, that was wrong.

Klara decided in that moment she was going to take it back, all that she had lost, and bring the world to its knees.

And under no circumstances would what just happened happen to her.

The days went on so long they began to blend together. The slaves stopped speaking almost entirely, as if they were listening, waiting for the trader to return and someone else to die.

This gave Klara time to plot and stew in her anger. Visions of the shocked expressions of her parents, of Charles, when she tore their throats out kept her going, kept her strong.

But they were distracting, and she did not see the trader until it was too late.

He grabbed her hair and slammed her face into the table. Her head begun to spin and she felt blood coming from her nose, she heard the fabric of her skirts tearing as he tried to get to her skin. He pinned her on her stomach, as he had done with the boy, and she began kicking out with her legs. Her heel connected with his knee cap and he stumbled, giving her the chance to try to wiggle out of his grasp.

He was going to kill her.

She refused to die this way.

Flat on her stomach, she kicked out behind her with both legs. The trader eased his grip enough, giving Klara the chance to pull away. She grabbed one of his large arms and used her other fist to slam up on his elbow, snapping his arm and popping the bone out of the skin. He screamed and Klara punched him in the jaw, hearing another bone snap.

She thought she should make him suffer, break as many of his bones as she could before she killed him. But then she remembered *Her*; if she had killed the Little Rat instead of toying with her she would not be here.

Klara grabbed the trader's adam's apple, squeezing her fingertips around it, and pulled as hard as she could.

It was easier then she had expected. Flesh and tendons just pulled away, blood spraying like a warm rain shower. Leaning in for a taste was satisfying, it took tremendous will power to pull away and offer his throat to Olivia.

The other girl stood and stared at Klara and all the blood, her expression flat and unreadable.

"Come and drink before it all goes to waste," Klara said, pulling Olivia out of her daze. As she drank Klara turned to the others.

"Do not fret, you will all have a turn if you wish. Then you are free," Klara proclaimed.

"Free?" one of the older women said, and Klara realised they may not understand, that perhaps this was all they knew.

"Yes. You can leave and go wherever you please, and no one will come after you. Your life belongs to you now," Klara replied.

With that, the air in the room changed. All those who wished to take some of the trader's blood did so, biting down on his arms and legs like they were ravenous.

Klara stepped into the doorway to assess her surroundings. She would need fresh clothes, some rations and a horse. She did not know which way to ride, only that as far away as she could get from this place was the best.

She would find a village and make her way to Vienna. Then after she killed her parents she would go to Paris.

And one by one she would kill all the members of the Danse Macabre, starting with the Little Rat.

Klara went quickly through the other small buildings, some more like shacks than anything else, until she found the trader's living quarters. She picked up several sets of clothes then headed to where the cooking was done, which was a blackened hole in the ground with a smell that made her nauseous. She grabbed a cloak off a hook that hung by one of the many doors, figuring she would use it to bundle supplies if she could not find saddlebags.

Then, Olivia was there, putting things in a woven satchel.

Olivia smiled a big toothy grin at Klara, pointing at the two satchels she had already filled that were waiting by the door.

Klara continued to watch her as she went back to gathering things.

"Did you grab some things from the workroom?" Klara asked, Olivia shot her a look that said of course you foolish thing.

"And you wish to come with me?" Klara continued, that question causing Olivia to pause. She and Klara made eye contact, pieces of her flaxen hair stained with blood.

"I'm not objecting, was simply a question," Klara replied. "I am going back to the continent, if we have in fact left it, to deal with some unfinished business. You many come if you wish."

Olivia smiled and nodded, then the two of them went back to gathering what they could from the trader's lodgings.

There was only one horse left when it was time for them to go. It was full dark now, and luckily the horse's rigging came with two large saddlebags.

Before they got on Olivia ran back into the building, walking through each of the small set of structures until they were all ablaze.

Klara kept the horse calm until Olivia came back. The two pulled up the hoods of their cloaks and climbed on, following the path away from the building until it lead to a road. Olivia pointed in a direction, not bothering to look back as the trader's buildings burned to ash.

Katrine

DANCING AROUND

MINSK, LITHUANIA.

Warm weather greeted us when we arrived in Minsk, I was pleased to see the sunshine and the smell of the coming summer.

Gigi seemed guarded but her spirits lifted after speaking at great length with Morgana and learning her ways to keep us safe. I hoped beyond all things that all that awaited us in Russia was a grand adventure.

We stayed at an inn in the city, which was bustling with people. It reminded me of Vienna in its beauty and overall warmth.

William seemed to dance around me while we were taken to our rooms, as if he desperately wanted to speak to me but was too nervous to do so. I tried to smile at him, encouraging him to try approaching me but it did not work. I missed him terribly but refused to go to him first.

Gabriel came to me as I was sitting at my toilette, smiling like a mischievous child.

"Hello cousin," I said as he pulled up a stool beside me.

"I have something to tell you," he began. "I am remembering things, about my life and family, and I wanted to tell you about Anna."

"Who is Anna, Cousin?" I asked.

"Now she would be called Countess Zrinyi, but Anna is Erzsebet and Ferenc's oldest child," he said. "She was four years older than me, and we spent much time together as young children. She was beautiful, Erzsebet said she looked like her mother, the girl's namesake. She was born 10 years into the marriage, quite late but Ferenc was gone. She seemed so distant from the world, Anna, and from Erzsebet especially. It was almost as if she was too perfect for this world. I am ashamed that I had forgotten, she was an important part of my young life."

"Do you know why she was so distant?"

"Perhaps she knew about your mother, I can't be sure. But I know she was quite attached to her nurse," he replied. "She left Sarvar when she was 14 to go to the Zrinyi's, Erzsebet and Countess Zrinyi were dear friends. I was only ten."

"How old are you now?"

"I was 24 when I died, I am unsure if we still count birthdays."

"Thank you for telling me. I am happy to know more of the family, especially of my Grandmother's children," I replied.

"Do you remember asking me about blood drinkers in the family?" he asked, and I nodded yes. "For some time the people on her lands called Erzsebet 'the Beast of Csejthe'."

I gasped. "What on earth for?"

"Because the common folk thought she was werewolf, some a vampire. But she could walk in the sun, so a vampire is unlikely."

"Is it true? Is there any truth to it?"

"No, no! None at all. Just rumours to slander Erzsebet. But, after you asked I thought I should share it with you," he said. "It seems my memory is coming back, so I will have more to tell you soon I am sure."

He kissed my hand and left the room as quickly as he came in.

"That was interesting," Hannah said as she finished putting my hair in a gold net.

"He seems like an eager child. I am quite pleased that such things bring him so much joy," I replied. She mumbled and nodded in agreement, stepping away to admire her handiwork.

"I will be quite pleased when we are done travelling," I said, sighing. "I am tiring of all of this."

"We do have to travel *back* to Paris, Katrine," Hannah replied.

"I know. Perhaps I should have stayed behind."

"You do not mean that. Now go," Hannah said, pushing me towards the door.

Another night in a salon, smiling and speaking to people I would most likely never see again. I had begun to grow tired of socialising and making conversation, I envied Gigi's stamina and patience.

I excused myself from Gigi's presence and crossed the room to the window.

I felt William come up behind me, standing at a distance where I could feel him but not be swarmed.

"Do you think we could leave this place? Go somewhere and live a quiet life?" I said quietly to him.

"Just say the word, il mio amore," he replied.

"But you believe the worst of me. Why run off with someone you think is some sort of deviant?" I asked.

"If you told me the truth this would all be behind us," he replied.

I sighed loudly. "This is where our problems lie, my love, for I already told you the truth."

I examined the sky as I stared out the window, it was covered in tiny little specks of light, I had never seen so many stars. In an odd way I was happy to see this with William.

"I have never seen so many stars. It is as if God is smiling down on this place," I said.

"We should speak further, resolve our issues," he said. I turned and our eyes met, I could see something in his eyes that frightened me.

"Of course. But now is not the time, and this is not the place," I said softly. His face turned slightly, like he may smile but he did not. Then he bowed, leaving the salon when he walked away.

"I am unsure I should allow him to even speak to me," I said to Hannah as she helped me undress that evening.

"I do not quite understand what he has to explain or speak of. He has done nothing but tell you how he feels or thinks. I don't know what is left, Katrine," Hannah replied.

I sighed. "That is exactly what I was thinking. But somehow I think I should allow him a moment, even though he could not extend me that courtesy. I am not one who believes in tit for tat."

"Things will right themselves soon enough, Katrine," Hannah said as she turned down my bed. "With or without your help. I think you should let things lie until they do."

I smiled. "You are wise, my friend."

"Thank you, child. Now, you should sleep some," Hannah replied, crawling into a trundle bed set at the end of mine.

"I am very happy you are with me, Hannah," I said. I got into bed and pulled the blanket up to my chin.

"Thank you, dear girl. That means so much," she said, and I quickly fell asleep.

Katrine

SIMPLE INDISCRETION

By midday the weather was beautiful so I decided I would like to walk. I was pleased to see the inn had a tremendous garden and decided to spend some time exploring.

The sun beating down felt good on my face, the air was crisp and fresh but warm and quite soothing. The colours of the garden were quite vivid, a reminder of how beautiful nature could be.

I loved the smell of the trees freshly sprouting for the summer, it reminded me of my village. I had always felt a close connection to the trees because of how they had consumed the buildings and seemed to protect us from the outside world.

I walked quietly along the path, dirt and gravel crunching under my feet, smiling at the just blooming flower buds. I was feeling peaceful and relaxed.

I was interrupted by William, whose presence I sensed before he approached.

"Is now a better time?" he asked.

I kept my back turned to him, saying over my shoulder as I continued to walk. "I am unsure I should allow you to speak at all, William."

"That is what I deserve, I admit that," he said, his breathing pattern changing as he became agitated.

"So tell me why I should listen?"

He paused for several moments, walking quietly behind me as he tried to think of the words.

"Because you felt for me once, and I am hoping you would allow me a simple indiscretion....," he began.

I laughed loudly. "Simple? William, you accused me of murder!"

"Katrine, please. Do you not see how my thoughts would go that way?"

"That is not the point! You were mean and angry and came at me like a common criminal. If you had spoken to me as the woman you supposedly love perhaps I would not have angered so," I said. He reached out to me, maybe to put his hand on my shoulder, but before he had the chance I recited the spell he had taught me to move a man.

I heard him stumble, and chuckle at me as a teacher often does when the student uses their teachings against them.

"Point made, il mio amore, point made," he began. "So what becomes of us, then? Are we no longer, just like that?"

I sighed. "You cannot expect it to return to as it was, William. You accused me, and my cousin for that matter, of murder. You cannot think that I could possibly just forget it all happened."

"Of course that is my wish but I understand I was wrong and that such a thought is unrealistic. I hope that in time we can work past all of this," he replied.

"It will take time, but I am not unwilling to try," I said. "But it will be on my terms, you understand that?"

"Yes I do. You never asked if I changed my mind."

"In regards to?"

"As to whether or not you killed the slave trader. You never asked if I changed my mind about it."

I stopped walking, turning my head to the side so I could see him out of the corner of my eye.

"I do not care either way. I know what I did and did not do, and any who truly love and care for me do just that. I've made peace with myself and know what happened was God's will," I said, then continued walking. He turned and went the opposite way and I continued on my peaceful walk, the smell of lavender stimulating my senses as it carried on the edge of a soft breeze.

When the sun went down I went back to my room to read, I felt the need for some quiet time to myself.

As I sat in a comfortable chair and opened a book I could hear the sound of a woman crying. Before I could question it my vision blurred then went black, and I sat back and waited for the vision to run its course.

I was standing on the edge of a mountain, a small walking path behind me leading up to this point. Snow flurries flew wildly around me so I could see very little of the landscape clearly, but I somehow knew where I was. I felt like I was close to home.

The crying came from behind me, inside a cave on the mountainside. As I entered the mouth of the cave, I could see a small figure near the back, hunched over a fire that I could not imagine was giving any warmth. I slowly approached, the sounds becoming distinctly female. She was wearing clothes that were in tatters, her long dark hair in mats.

I gasped as my mother's eyes turned up and looked but did not actually see me, her face red from cold and her eyes from crying. I tried to reach out to her but could not, I was caught in the vision and there was nothing I could do but watch.

She looked feral, more wild animal than human, the sobbing all that identified her as human.

My heart ached for her. I had not realised how much I missed her until I saw her real face, I wondered if what I was seeing was real. If my mother was really in some cave, freezing and crying all alone, and how I might be able to find her. I had to help her, if I could.

Then, just like that, it was gone. I was back in my quiet room in Minsk, a book lying open in my lap.

The first thought I had was of the Order. They seemed to know so much about my mother and I, things about my life I did not quite understand. Perhaps they could find her now, with such a huge interest I wondered if they would rescue her, if they could even fix what had happened to her.

I closed the book and put it away, then set out to find Gabriel.

Anastasia

BRAVERY

Gavril lowered his eyes, a low growl rumbling from his throat.

"Speak up, woman. Your silence makes you appear guilty," he said angrily.

"She has done nothing wrong," Lynde snapped. "She is only coming to us with useful information."

"Then why does she not speak?" he exclaimed.

Lynde gestured to the circle of others who sat around them.

"You treat willingness to share like a criminal trial," Lynde told him, then she turned to Anastasia. "Go on. No harm will come to you. I will protect you."

Anastasia smiled at her friend, she was happy she had come to her first. It had taken several days after the intruders for her to say something, and tensions were already high.

"I...I...I know some magic," Anastasia finally said. Gavril chuckled but said nothing.

"The woman who raised me was a witch," Anastasia continued.

"Your mother...," Gavril tried to cut in.

"No. The woman who raised me was not my birth mother," Anastasia said quickly. "She taught me some things. I may be able to help."

"And your birth mother?" Gavril asked.

"Bathory," Iren told him.

"Will wolf blood cause my children to shift?" Anastasia blurted out.

"Not necessarily. Your oldest...," Iren continued.

"My oldest is a blood drinker," Anastasia blurted again. All eyes turned to her.

"I do not understand," Iren said to Lynde.

"The magic, Anastasia," Lynde whispered sharply.

"I could set up wards. I could set traps," Anastasia told the room.

"We can set traps," Gavril countered.

"I can use my powers and the forest to protect us."

"You are new. Why should we trust you? This is not how our tribe works."

Anger began to bubble up through her body. "So your tribe will not accept help when something is hunting them? Because if they want it bad enough they will return."

"And how do we know they are not looking for you? The Bathory would not let one of their own go easily, and your daughter..."

"My daughter left me for dead, and I am not exactly the favourite daughter where the Bathory are concerned. If you do not want my help that is fine. I can do my work and keep my mouth shut and fight when I am needed," Anastasia turned and marched out of the tent, anger causing her muscles to tense as she walked.

The refusal wasn't what bothered her, she had exposed herself and her past to a room of people and now she felt vulnerable. She did not know what she had expected from them, but she would not speak so freely again.

She would quietly keep to the side lines. And if she needed to she would go it alone. She would leave and feel no guilt about it.

Iren came with food and drink to her tent some time later.

"You shouldn't have come," Anastasia said flatly.

"I need to apologise for the behaviour of my mate and the others. You took quite a chance exposing your past in such a fashion. I could not have done what you did," Iren replied while making herself comfortable.

"Tis an easy thing to say when you have nothing to hide."

Iren laughed. "You are quick to assume, Anastasia. When your past is not useful there is no need to expose it. What you shared, even though Gavril may deny it, is useful."

"May I ask what you are getting at, Királyno?"

Iren sighed loudly, staring up at the ceiling in frustration. Anastasia ignored it; she would not assume that she knew what she meant, and would only take direction if it was specific.

"I want you to do whatever you can to protect us, Anastasia," Iren said. "If that involves using your magic then so be it. Something is coming, I can feel it in my bones, and I will not tip toe quietly through life to arrive safely at death. Do you understand?"

Anastasia smiled. "Yes, Királyno Farkas. Is that an order?"

Iren stood, her casualness being taken over by her duty. She was a Queen.

"Yes. And I trust that you will keep this discreet? But if we are caught I will take the full blame, you have my word," Iren continued. "I have informed Lynde of my wishes."

"And what about the Király, my lady?" Anastasia asked.

"He will see reason," Iren said as she turned and walked out of the tent. Anastasia watched the space the other woman had occupied, lost deep in thought.

She would do what Iren asked, but carefully. Because although she had the Queen's word she did not entirely trust it.

Katrine

AN UNWISE DEBT

"You're mad," Gabriel said as I paced back and forth in front of him. I had brought him to my room and sat him in the comfy chair.

"Why? They know so much about us I think they'd have no trouble finding her again," I said flatly.

"If they did you a favour you would owe them. I do not think it wise to be in their debt," he replied.

"I would not care if they help her," I said,

He chuckled. "You've gone totally mad. "

"She was human, cousin. She was huddled over a fire, wearing rags in some hole in the side of a mountain somewhere. I cannot see that and, in good conscience, do nothing about it," I continued.

"But Katrine, you are no seer," he began. "Perhaps you were dreaming or your guilt over what happened to her is beginning to consume you. It is not worth being in debt to the Order for something you are not entirely sure of."

"I am sure. I have never been so sure of anything in my entire life. I have been given this gift for a reason and I cannot ignore it," I said angrily. My emotions were surging hot through my veins and I began to feel light headed. I sat on the edge of the bed and tried to regain my composure.

"I wish there was something I could do for you, cousin," Gabriel said.

I sighed. "I will find a way to ask them for help without owing them a single thing. She is still my mother and I need to do something."

I could hold it in no longer, tears began to slowly fall down my face. They fell faster and harder as I felt my nerves begin to unravel.

"Do you not find this maddening?" I yelled, "That our loved ones suffer and we can do nothing? We must sit and watch like lambs waiting to be slaughtered!"

"We are only human, child...."

"But we are not even that!" I said loudly. "I should have gone to the Holy Roman Emperor when we were in Prague and pled for my Grandmother's...."

He began to laugh loudly. "Now *I know* you have gone mad! Speaking to that Hapsburg puppet would have cost Erzsebet her head, I guarantee you that! You are being irrational Katrine."

"You have no idea of the guilt...."

"The guilt of what?" Gabriel snapped. "How quick you have forgotten that *I was the only person close enough and powerful enough to help her!*"

"Would you not do something more now if you could? If you had any chance would you not try?"

He sighed loudly, putting his head in his hands. His hair shone with some gold, his hands seemed thin and his nails looked ragged and broken.

"I can do nothing while we are on the move," he said from between his hands. "That will give you time to consider how to approach the situation, and decide whether you had a true vision or something else entirely. I do not advise communicating with the Order but if you insist."

I sat on the floor in front of him, unfolding his hands and taking them in mine. I smiled at him but he was not responsive.

"Thank you," I said.

"What for? I have done nothing," he replied.

"You accepted me. That is enough," I said, kissing his hands.

"I know a Bathory when I see one."

"And though we may be helpless in many ways, we have each other and that is what matters," I replied.

"Of course, cousin," he said. "It least we have that much."

Katrine

SWELTERING HEAT.

Several weeks later the summer weather finally came in the form of a sweltering heat. I had never experienced anything like it and was not fairing well, so I was pleased to hear we were finally moving on.

It had also caused me to rethink my vision, I could not imagine snow anywhere while we suffered like this. I knew deep inside myself that it had been real and I could not get past it, regardless of the circumstances.

As we began to pack up my concern grew for those in the covered wagons.

"I had thought much about it when building," Charles said as we stood in the shade watching the carriages being loaded. "There is plenty of ventilation and when moving it picks up a breeze. They will be fine, I assure you."

"Are you nervous about Russia?" I asked.

"Not exactly. This Lappish witch thing is a bit disconcerting. I am not sure how to deal with the situation, I am sure William is powerful enough...."

"What about Morgana?" I asked.

"What about her?"

"She also knows magic, I am sure she can help. You should ask her, I am sure she would be quite honoured," I replied.

He seemed to contemplate what I had said, I assumed weighing Morgana's potential strength against the threat of the Lappish Witches.

"Charles, I know this may sound foolish but where do they come from?" I asked.

"The north of many countries, like Russia and Sweden. Northern Europe, to the best of my knowledge, is their origin, for they are in fact their own race of people," he began. "But I am quite uneducated in the matter of spell casters. I wish we had more around, sadly I think the reputation of William of Naples has frightened many away."

I could not help myself from chuckling, Charles gave me a very serious look and I quickly stopped.

"I wish I was kidding. I hoped that your relationship would improve his mood, but it does not seem so," he replied. "Gigi asked to have blood canisters put in your carriage. Is something wrong?"

"Not that I am aware of. The heat has been an issue, but that is the only one I am aware of," I said.

"Good," he said, and he took my stiff, sticky arm from under my cloak and we walked together out to the carriages.

Luckily the sun was to go down soon, so we would not set out in the sweltering heat. Vincenzo stood with Hannah next to our carriage, both supervising the loading of the canisters.

Vincenzo handed me a small fan that appeared to be made of well-polished wood. "I thought you might be in need of this."

"Thank you, mon ami," I said happily. "I am most grateful."

I took the fan in my hand, running my fingers over its smooth surfaces. I felt Charles tense beside me, and saw a hint of jealousy in his expression.

"Is it time?" I asked. "I would have liked the chance to speak to my cousin before we set out."

"Then you will. Shall we return to the shade until the sun has gone for the day?" Charles asked. I held out my other arm to Vincenzo and the three of us returned to the safety of the inn.

Almost as soon as the sun set the others appeared, my cousin arm and arm with Mathilde and Victorie not far behind. They seemed fresh and happy, as if they had rose at dawn as opposed to dusk.

Gabriel smiled happily when he saw me. "Good evening to you, cousin. Are you ready for this last part of our journey? I cannot believe we are so close to reaching Russia, I must admit I am quite excited."

"So am I, but I am not fairing well in this heat," I said, showing him the fan. "Luckily I have friends who think of me when I am not quite with myself."

"It helps that you are a beautiful young woman with a pleasing disposition," he replied. "I am lucky to have wonderful women to share this journey with since we must be separated."

I smiled at Mathilde, who had crossed the room to speak with Gigi. "I am pleased for them also, cousin. I only want joy in your life."

"And I in yours," he said, his eyes examining my face. "Something is troubling you, Child. I can see it in your eyes."

I glanced briefly at Gigi and our eyes met, I could see that she was exhausted but also extremely tense. She had been reciting Morgana's chants almost constantly when she was alone, I worried she was not sleeping. Being the toast of the Russian court could be her greatest triumph but she needed to have her wits about her, and that would not happen if she remained in constant fear.

"It will be good when we finally arrive. There has been too much anticipation," I replied.

"Have you reconsidered?" he asked.

"No, but I cannot imagine there being snow anywhere in this heat," I replied. "I am unsure, but have not thought much about it. I have other pressing matters that take priority."

"You shall have your joy, I promise," he said, taking my hands and kissing them.

"I hope so. The way things have been going I have been wondering if things will ever be settled and if happiness is even possible."

He smiled again, the action stretching up to his eyes and causing them to sparkle.

"You will have happiness and joy and all the good things in this world if I have any say in the matter."

KLARA

PROPER BEHAVIOUR.

They rode through the night, always on the lookout for a place to stop. But there was nothing, only endless desert that blended into the heavy darkness. The horse seemed to know the way so Klara allowed it to guide them, the fear and tension a hard knot in her throat.

Olivia clung so tightly to her back she could feel her heart pounding through her chest. Klara could not tell if the other girl was sleeping, and it did not matter. She could not speak to her anyhow.

"But which way do we go?" Klara mumbled to herself. Olivia tapped her shoulder and pointed straight ahead.

"Are you sure? It seems as if we have been going this way all night and there is nothing! Not even a shack! And where are all the trees? Why is there no grass?" Klara began, then gasped. "What sort of hell are we in that grass does not grow?"

Olivia only poked harder and pointed in the direction they were already headed.

"That is where we are going but it still does not answer my question. Do you think we are still in France?" Klara asked, and Olivia shook her head no. "Where on earth are we? Never in my life have I seen a place like this."

Just then the sun started to come up, casting an orange glow out over the horizon. The path in front of them slowly became clearer and buildings were visible off in the distance.

"Thank the Heavens!" Klara exclaimed. "Do you think I'll be able to find a bath? I am starting to feel like I have an outer crust of sand on my skin! I probably look like a flame haired Arab, can you imagine?"

She could not see Olivia rolling her eyes but she felt the heavy sigh.

"Perhaps we should write my parents," Klara mused. "If they heard what had happened, surely they would send for us? And then I could laugh while I drain their blood and take what is rightfully mine!"

She couldn't see Olivia's face perk up and the smile growing larger as she continued.

"And then. Then! We will have the means to go after that Little Rat and I will make Lord Charles Westwick watch as I torture her. He will regret turning *me* away! I will destroy everything he has!" Klara continued, pleased to be able to express her thoughts to someone else, even if they could not say anything in return.

They reached the outskirts of the small village just as the sun reached full height. Both women were glad to be off the horse and find some shade. It was agonisingly hot, the sun reflecting off the white stone buildings causing such a glare that they both had to shield their eyes.

Walking through the stone streets, pulling the horse along, they searched for water and a place to get some information.

Finally they found a watering hole where many other horses had gathered, they let the horse drink then took in their surroundings.

Klara listened to the people who were out in the streets, trying to decipher what language they were speaking. They got plenty of stares and whispers. After a few minutes Klara got frustrated and got in the path of a woman with a cart of produce.

"Pardon me, Mademoiselle," she began in French. "But my friend and I are quite lost. Could you tell us where we are and perhaps direct us to the closest inn?"

"You are in Monaco, girl. It is a separate country from France you know. And you passed the inn on your way in to town," she snapped, pushing Klara aside and continuing on. The woman even spat on the ground as she walked past, Olivia grabbed Klara's arm before she was able to lunge.

But Klara was beyond disgusted. She was of noble blood, such treatment was unheard of by common peasants. Olivia kept a tight grip on Klara's wrist as they collected their horse and headed back the way they had come, the peasant woman turned down a narrow alley. Klara seriously considered killing her, simply because she could and so she could see the look of horror on her face when she realised she should not be so rude to a stranger in need.

Olivia pinched Klara's upper arm and scowled at her as she yelped in pain.

"What was that for?" Klara asked as they continued on. But Olivia only continued to scowl and they went the rest of the way in silence.

It wasn't surprising that they had not seen the inn, the only identifier nailed to the wood door in the form of a small sign with a red house pained on it. There was a small path along the side that led to a stable, and the two women were relieved to be able to tend to the horse, if it was only for a short while.

The main floor of the inn was oddly quiet when they walked inside, and the patrons stared long and hard at the two young women. Klara could not help but wonder if they did not get many visitors, or perhaps their overall appearance was worse then what she had thought. Klara crossed the room and headed into the path of a short, very round woman who was serving food.

"Excuse me, Mademoiselle, but we are in need of some assistance," Klara asked.

The woman didn't even look up from the bowls she was serving. "Take a seat."

"But Madam..."

"Take a seat and wait your turn!" she spat. Klara recoiled back, her mouth turning up into a sneer.

"Do you have any idea who I am?" Klara began.

The woman chuckled. "You could be the bloody Queen of France but you still have to sit and wait your turn!"

Klara's fangs withdrew but before she could pounce Olivia grabbed her upper arm.

"Oh, her majesty does not understand the term 'wait'? It means you sit quietly *over there* until I have some time to speak to you. And at the rate you're going it'll take a while," the woman continued, laughing loudly.

But Olivia could not pull her away fast enough, and within seconds Klara had the woman by the throat. She showed the woman her fangs before biting down and drinking her blood.

The woman screamed and the shocked patrons of the inn tried to scramble away and run. Klara quickly snapped the woman's neck then grabbed the closest person and did the same. Olivia soon followed suit, tearing skin and flesh and spitting it on the ground as she discarded the bodies.

Silence fell over the room, and when Klara stopped and looked around all she could hear was Olivia's deep breathing as she held a young man by the hair.

"Wait!" Klara exclaimed, rushing over before Olivia could finish. The man was still breathing; the two women sat him on a bench, pushing a body aside so they would be face to face.

"Where are we?" Klara asked him. The man's eyes were big and round, he stayed silent in fear.

"You saw what happened to the last person who did not answer my questions in a timely fashion," Klara continued, her eyes scanning the man's flood stained clothes. "And, I apologise for that. Things have not been going my way lately, and as you can see I am not pleased about it."

"Monaco," the man said, his voice barely a whisper.

"That's what I was told but, to be honest, it's not very much help."

"We're...the south..."

"South of what exactly?"

"South of France. By the Mediterranean. Very small."

"Fantastic! Now we are making progress. I am almost finished, and if you help me I will let you survive. Can you tell me which way to Vienna?"

The man took a shallow breath. "Italy."

"Vienna is not in Italy, sir," Klara said. She smiled, and the man recoiled in terror.

"No, no," he continued, panic rising in his body. "East, through Italy, then North to Vienna."

"Wonderful! Thank you for all your help. You have given us a wonderful impression of your fair city. Now, we will let you go, but you must swear that you will speak nothing of this until tomorrow, and we will be gone by sunrise," Klara took his chin and cupped it between her thumb and two fingers. "But if you tell anyone before then, we will come to your house and burn it down with you and your family inside. Do we have an understanding?"

The man nodded hard enough it looked as if his eyes were rattling around his head. Klara pulled away from him and Olivia stepped out of the way, the man paused just to make sure they were serious then ran out the door.

Klara sighed, rolling her head from side to side and cracking her neck.

"We'll see what they have, clean up, and be on our way. Do you want your own horse?" Klara asked. Olivia shrugged her shoulders, then began working her way around the room picking up the purses and money off the dead bodies. Klara went back to the kitchen and found some water and rags they could use to clean up.

They kept the hose they'd had originally and took another beautiful white horse that looked like something from a fairy tale. With saddle bags evenly distributed the two women set out again under the cover of darkness.

The young man had kept his word and no one noticed them leave, or so it appeared.

Several figures stepped out of the darkness that surrounded the town walls, examining the two women who, in an instant, had disrupted their fragile existence.

It was rude and unnecessary, and would not go unpunished.

KATRINE

BEAUTY OF THE LAND

MOSCOW, RUSSIA.

I saw the great top of a tower made of gold first as we rode into the city.

"They call them onion domes," Vincenzo said to me. He had decided to ride into Moscow with us.

"Why?" I asked.

"Because of their shape. If it is the top of the Cathedral of the Intercession, the building has several more domes," he began. "There is a legend that the Tsar Ivan, the one many refer to as Ivan the Terrible, had the architect killed so no other building could be built like it."

"You know something of Russia, Vincenzo?" Gigi said, slapping him on the knee with her fan. "Ma petite, our Italian friend has been holding out on us."

"No, no. It's not so. I only have the stories told among tradesmen, nothing of consequence," he replied.

"Is this Ivan the Terrible still in power?" I asked.

"No, he died in 1584....before you were born. I suppose before you were born as well, Morgana," Vincenzo said.

Morgana smiled. "I am much older than I look, Monsieur."

Vincenzo rolled his eyes. "I am not going to debate with you. I am pleased to finally be here, I am hoping to acquire some furs while we are here, Russia is known for their furs, Grisela."

"That I do know, mon ami. I hope you shall give us priority when you are selling," she replied.

"Of course," he said, smiling at me as I fanned myself. "I am so pleased you are enjoying my gift, Katrine. I know a woman in Minsk who makes lovely things out of wood."

"Once again, I thank you kindly for thinking of me," I replied.

"I think of you often, my dear," he said. I did not add my thoughts on how pleased I was that it irritated Charles, I assumed he was aware.

"Unfortunately Katrine cannot join you on your fur hunt, I will need her close by at all times," Gigi said.

"You should inform Charles when you can," I told her. "He wishes me to join him on his hunt for the skinwalker. I think he may even ask Morgana, something about Lappish witches."

"It is the reason why we are here, Grisela," Vincenzo said, shrugging his shoulders.

"Yes, I am well aware we are spending the summer out of France to chase some creature we are unsure even exists," Gigi said, her tone frustrated and impatient. "And he is trying to take mes filles with him. Crétin."

Something in Morgana's face lit up when Gigi referred to us as her girls; it had taken some time for the two of them to warm to each other and I was glad it had finally come.

"You know he has a fondness for Katrine," Vincenzo replied.

"He appeared quite frightened of her for a while, I was enjoying that," Gigi continued. "And Lappish witches, Vincenzo? I think Charles has finally lost his mind."

I tried to keep my eyes focused on the landscape as it rolled past, the colours were bright and the smells fresh and crisp.

We rode over a large river, the carriage rattling as it moved over each wood plank. It reminded me a little of Vienna, I wondered why we did not take a ship.

The buildings seemed to be made of wood and they were quite grand. As we continued everything seemed to stop as we reached a grand red brick wall; we passed beyond it and I felt stones under our wheels. A market seemed to emerge around us as if from nothing, one like I had never seen before.

Quite suddenly we stopped and my stomach lurched forward, my anxiety tugging at my insides.

"Did....did....did we finish the b...b...blood?" I asked, suddenly feeling quite thirsty. My throat started getting a little tight.

"Yes, petite, but do not worry. You are just nervous," Gigi said. She patted her face with a handkerchief, preparing herself for our first moments on Russian soil. I tried my best to do the same; luckily Hannah had pulled my hair off my face, we both thought it would allow me not to worry too much about my appearance on exiting. The heat actually gave Morgana some colour, even though it was red.

Gigi took a deep breath and squeezed my hand, the door to the carriage suddenly opened and the noise of the market invaded the small space.

They all got out before me, Morgana looked back for a moment before stepping out into the sunlight.

I tried my best to breathe and pulled myself out, shading my eyes from direct sun. The market was bustling with activity, wood booths set every few feet selling more things then I could decipher at first glance.

The tower with the great gold top, what Vincenzo called an 'onion dome', and the building it sprung out of were now within walking distance. I grabbed his hand and pointed him in that direction, we both stared in awe at the great gold and coloured domes of Ivan's stunning cathedral.

"I can see why he would never want it duplicated," I said quietly to him.

He chuckled and said, smiling happily. "It is fantastic, isn't it? I wonder about the inside, the decoration of the Orthodox is quite marvellous. You will see lots of things decorated in gold that you did not think would take it."

On the edge of a passing breeze I caught the scent of something as two figures came through the crowd towards us.

One was a large man, tall with wide shoulders, draped in pieces of fabric that covered his body, the lower half of his dark skinned face showing from under his head covering. There was a slight bump poking out from his side that I assumed was a sword hilt.

The smaller person moved within the great drapes of fabric with presence, the great strides had purpose. I could tell by the smell that the smaller was a woman, and there was something else I was unsure of. Fresh blood was overwhelming as they got closer and passed us without consequence.

"Dhampir," the word passed my lips before I could think, I felt Vincenzo's body tense as he looked around.

"What? What is it?" he asked quietly.

"I don't know," I said. "My senses are off from the long journey. But our eyes should always be open."

"Isn't it glorious?" I heard Charles exclaim as he came towards us. "I have sent word of our arrival. Someone should come to help us soon."

"Perhaps we should have arrived at night," I said, looking back at the string of wagons behind us.

"The rest of our company will arrive at night, Katrine. Do not worry," he said, taking my free hand. "I have thought of everything."

He began to scratch his arms and moved his neck from side to side, I could sense his tension.

"Is something wrong, Charles?" I asked.

He shifted his head again. "I think I need to go for a run. Perhaps I should plan for one later with the others."

"I don't understand....," I began.

"An opportunity for those of us who can to shift," he whispered in my ear. "Perhaps you should come along, to gain some understanding before we start looking for the skinwalker."

"Will Gigi approve? She has certain expectations of me while we are here, as her protégée I...."

"Don't worry. It will not disturb Gigi's plans," he said sharply.

"Then I would be happy to. Perhaps it will erase some of the frightening images of what happened to my mother," I replied.

"Do not get confused, my dear. The process is not pleasant. It is not like what happened to her, but it is still not a pretty sight. I agree that it might be good for you," he said, turning his eyes to the cathedral. "I wonder if all of Russia is as impressive as this place."

I heard the man long before I ever saw him, his big voice switching from French to Russian so rapidly I couldn't understand a word. I heard Tolone and Hannah trying to communicate with him and appeared to be failing, his thunderous laughter made me wonder what was going on in the man's head.

He wore a long coat, even in the oppressive heat, with big leather boots that seemed better suited for snow. He had fair hair that reminded me of my father, and a beard that seemed to stretch to his waist. Tolone and Hannah followed close at his heels.

The man exclaimed loudly in Russian, squeezing Charles' shoulder in greeting, then doing the same to Vincenzo. He nodded to me, I assumed it was his way of greeting me.

He started speaking French to Charles, who asked the man what languages he spoke. I thought I heard him list five languages and when he said English Charles explained himself.

"Wonderful, Lord Westwick," the man said, "for my English is much better than my French. I am Alexi Mikhailavitch, your escort while in Russia."

"A pleasure, sir. May I introduce Signor Vincenzo Amori, my associate," Charles said, pulling Gigi and I forward. "This is Madmoiselle Grisela Delphine, one of our lead dancers and her protégée, Katrine Bathory."

Gigi and I swept into low bows usually meant for royalty. He seemed surprisingly uninterested in us, perhaps women were not exceptionally important in Russian culture.

"It is an honour to meet you all. Our Tsar is much looking forward to your entertainments," Alexi said. His eyes turned to us again only briefly, and I wondered if he thought dancers and whores were one in the same.

"We have a house a short distance away ready for you, and Nikoli Osomov asked me to inform you that he will come to call on you soon. I believe it is his house where you will be staying," Alexi continued on to Charles. "He is your contact in Russia, yes?"

"Yes, we met in England many years ago and he has stayed at my chateau in Paris," Charles said, and I wondered why I had never heard of this Nikoli before. "He is an old friend, I look forward to seeing him. Now, I hate to be pushy but my people are very tired from their long journey...."

"Of course! Of course! I shall get my horse," he said, walking away from us. Gigi rolled her eyes and we headed back to our carriage.

"I should have known Nikoli Osomov had a hand in this," Gigi said as we started moving.

"You did not know he was Russian?" I asked.

"I did not know he spent any time in this country, let alone at the court," she continued. "He is always trying to get Charles to participate in these grand schemes. If he is involved in this skinwalker business you two will most certainly not be involved. I do not trust him."

"Grisela, please. You make him sound like the boogyman," Vincenzo replied. "He is not someone that I suggest you befriend, girls, but he is by no means frightening."

"I do not like it one bit, Vincenzo. The very idea that Charles has dragged us halfway across the world because of Nikoli Osomov does not sit well with me," Gigi said sharply.

"We do not know where Charles is getting his information from. He could just be using Nikoli's house, every other shifter he mentions skinwalkers to thinks he's mad," Vincenzo replied.

Grisela sighed, opening up her fan and softly fanning her face. "I hope you are right, mon ami. This place is already nerve racking enough."

KATRINE

WHITE WOLF

The house, located just outside the city centre, was on the other side of the river close to a heavily wooded area. The building itself was made of brick with a large set of gates at the front.

"We have many fires here in Moscow," Alexi Mikhailavitch said in his heavily accented English. "Some of the boyars with much money and land began to build houses from stone and brick. They still burn, cooking whatever is inside like pot in a hearth."

I stared up at the house as we stood outside in the shade, watching as Hannah and Tolone ran the unloading of our household. The great covered wagons sat parked and quiet by the stables.

"Tomorrow we shall formally present you to the Tsar, when the rest of your company arrives. You must pay respects to the ikons of our church each time you enter the room that is of the utmost importance," Alexi said, pounding his fist into his palm. "You must tell all your people. It is a grievous insult not to."

I thought to ask him for a list of these ikons, descriptions perhaps, for we knew nothing and could insult quickly and easily, but I did not. Asking Charles' man, whose house we would be living in, was perhaps a better way to approach the situation.

Alexi took his leave promising to collect us outside the palace tomorrow at sunset. Charles seemed relieved when the dust finally settled after the man's departure, he began making arrangements for a run later that evening.

"Do you suppose I could run with them?" I asked no one in particular as we were being shown to our rooms.

Gigi chuckled. "You would look quite peculiar running with a pack of wolves, ma petite."

"But it sounds so relaxing," I said. Hannah directed Morgana and I to two smaller rooms that surrounded Gigi's, a door into Gigi's room from each of ours connecting us together.

"There will be plenty of time for us to relax later! Now we need to prepare for our official presentation," Gigi said, going into her room followed by two servants.

"I will be back to help you change for this evening," Hannah said quietly to me, "and take direction from her regarding dress for the court. I am sure she has everything planned so you do not need to trouble yourself."

"And it should give you some time to rest," I replied.

"If you are to take a maidservant to court....," she began.

"You will be requested, of course. There is no question," I said, and she smiled widely.

"You could trade places with me if you like," Morgana said to Hannah as she turned to leave us.

Hannah snorted, mumbling, "Not in this life," under her breath as she walked away.

The joy of being able to close the door behind me and know this was my personal space for an extended period of time was indescribable, it was a great relief to know we would not be leaving for some time.

I had travelled more in four years than most do in a lifetime. I was growing quite tired of it.

I stripped off my dirty travelling clothes and a maidservant came to collect me to be washed. The bath would come tomorrow and I longed for it, the hot water wash only giving me some of the relief I craved that only came from being submerged up to your chin.

Hannah came afterwards and helped me dress in one of my simple gray dresses and plaited my hair down my back.

"I must admit I like pretty dresses but they are bloody uncomfortable," I said. "I am so pleased to have some time out of the fancy clothes."

"Enjoy it while you can for you know Madmoiselle Delphine will have you in full dress at every opportunity. I am wondering how the Scots girl will fare in such a state," Hannah replied as she began unpacking my things.

"To the best of my knowledge she intends on staying in the background with Josephine. She will not have herself as the focus in any way, at any point. That I know for sure," I said. Hannah went and lit the candle beside my bed, the sky was beginning to get dark.

"Are you sure you are ready for this? After all that happened to you, Katrine, do you think watching the shifters is a good idea?"

I smiled. "I will not know unless I try. I am wondering if it would help me conquer some of my fears."

"As long as it does not add to your nightmares I suppose it cannot hurt," Hannah said, kissing my forehead. "If you need me I will come running."

Gabriel was standing on the great stone porch at the back of the house, staring out into the wooded area at the end of the great lawn.

"The air here is different," he said, taking my arm in his. "It seems so clean and crisp even though it's terribly hot."

"Are you here for the shift?" I asked.

"Mathilde wants me to see, she wants me to know every part of her," he said.

"She seems to care quite deeply for you, Cousin."

He sighed. "She does not seem to understand how hard all of this is to process. She does not seem to remember what it was like for all of this to be new."

"I am not sure how she came about her condition, or how long she has been this way. If she was born this way she may have no idea at all," I began. "But this is part of our world, we must accept our need for blood. I am hoping this will help me move past some of what happened to my mother."

"You are very brave, Cousin. Braver than myself, and I have been involved in armed combat," he said and he squeezed my hand.

People came out the back doors. Mathilde, Charles, a tall red haired woman, a very handsome fair haired man and a scruffy man who looked like he belonged in the stables. I only had memory of the woman, her stunning head of flame coloured hair was bright even in the darkness.

Mathilde came towards us, her blonde curls bounced as she pranced over in her cloak, holding her hand out to Gabriel.

He kissed the top of her hand as she smiled happily. "Be well, my darling."

"I will be much better when it's done, mi amore," Mathilde replied, walking down on to the grass.

Charles came to me and held out his arm, his smile made me a bit nervous.

"Come along, Katrine. I cannot do this in full view of the house," he said.

I felt my body tense. "I did not think I would be so....close by."

"Don't be afraid you are perfectly safe," he replied. I took one quick look at Gabriel before taking Charles's arm and following him into the night.

We walked until we reached a small clearing just inside the woods where he handed me the long cloak he was wearing.

"I thought you would prefer this to nudity," Charles said as he bowed to me in his shift. Seeing his form under his light clothes brought colour to my cheeks.

"I am pleased to see you still have some attraction to me," he said, chuckling to himself. He crouched down in the dirt and I caught the strong scent of wolf, followed by what sounded like the snapping of tree branches.

Charles's spine bowed, a sound almost like a moan escaping his mouth. My hand went over my own lips before they fell open in shock and I went to walk away when his eyes turned to me and I couldn't leave, I got down on the ground and sat beside him as his body began to change.

His skin began to split and fur sprouted, his hands and feet stretching and cracking as they retracted and the claws sprung forth.

My heart began to hurt and I was filled with a deep sadness, I crawled closer to him and began stroking his back as tears fell from my eyes.

I felt a deep loneliness as I watched his body continued to shift, his face protruding forward as it formed into a snout. I wanted to hold him close to my body, cradle him like a child as he went through this. I could not even begin to understand this experience, the world blurring as my tears flowed faster.

I felt something wet nudge my cheek as I tried to wipe my eyes, when they could focus again a large black wolf was standing before me, pushing his nose on my face and rubbing up against me. I ran my fingers through the coarse fur and he rumbled happily.

"Thank you, Charles. You've changed everything for me," I said, scratching his head and saying into his ear. "I'm not afraid anymore."

He licked my cheek then took off, running full speed into the forest.

I saw the white wolf as she stepped away from the back stairs and trotted off into the forest, leaving Gabriel looking quite stunned.

I hurried my pace to catch him before he went inside. "Are you well, Cousin?"

He smiled, reaching out and taking my hand.

"She is a beautiful creature, is she not?" he said. He led me back up to the porch where we stood and stared out into the night.

"You have said nothing of how you are fairing, my dear. And your eyes are red as if you have been crying," he continued. "Are you well? Did Charles frighten you?"

"No, not at all. I actually feel quite different about the whole situation, I am not sure what the feeling is but it is not the same as it was. And now I wish to know more about what happened to my mother, and if the Bathory have any connections to shapeshifting," I replied. "I wonder if what happened to her would have happened anyway, as someone mentioned in regards to me."

"I do not understand."

"They say I am dhampir, born of a human and vampire. I believed that the mark my mother gave me in beast form made me this way, but it was pointed out to me that because of my birth this would have come regardless. Perhaps it was also the case with my mother, somehow," I said.

"Do you know how one goes about becoming a beast?" he asked.

"No," I said, we stopped speaking for several minutes after hearing a wolf howl. "Maybe I should ask some questions."

He sighed. "You have too many worries, Cousin. Perhaps you should focus on tomorrow's presentation."

"That is what I have Gigi for, all I need to do is be present and mind my manners, all the other details have been decided for me."

"And I suppose Grisela enjoys doing such things, most women are naturally inclined towards mothering..."

I could not stop my giggle. "I am not sure I would refer to what she does as mothering."

"It may not be in the traditional sense but it is a form of mothering, the only way she knows how," he said, and I heard some people come outside. I turned to find Vincenzo, Hannah and Tolone leading a stable boy out by the hand. The young man's eyes were glazed over and he looked a bit giddy.

"What's this about?" I asked them.

"Our supplies are low and you both need to feed," Vincenzo said.

"I would prefer to wait," I replied.

"That is not an option," he said. The boy nodded off, falling softly into Tolone's arms, who eased him to the ground.

Vincenzo took the boy's arm and opened the vein at his wrist, the smell of fresh blood so strong it took everything I had to stop myself from attacking.

Vincenzo pulled me to him, holding me close to his body as we sat, and I took the boys arm and began to feed. A smooth, steady hand rubbed my back and stroked my hair as I drank the boy's blood, the warm liquid flowing in my mouth and surging my body to life. I lost myself so completely I did not feel Vincenzo pull me off and back into him.

I sensed being pulled back so Gabriel could take my place, and I lay safely cradled in Vincenzo's arms. I felt so at peace that I forgot about the rest of the world, except this man whose stunning green eyes stared down at me.

He kissed me softly on the lips, licking the sides of my mouth gently with the tip of his tongue. The close howl of a wolf pulled me back to reality and I sat up, only to see that Gabriel was still feeding and that no one had paid any attention to us.

I looked at Vincenzo, his eyes sparkled with something I did not understand, something I had never seen from him before.

"They are returning," Vincenzo finally said. I looked at my cousin again, it was as if we had disappeared.

"It is a trick I inherited from the one who turned me," he whispered in my ear. "The world goes on, but whoever stands close to me exists with me for a short time."

"It is quite wonderful. I am happy to share such space with you," I replied.

"The pleasure is mine, Katrine," he said, pulling me to my feet. Gabriel had pulled away from the boy, who was being carried away by Hannah and Tolone.

"We cannot feed from humans often," Gabriel said, panting. "I will not be able to maintain control if we keep going back and forth."

"I agree, Cousin," I said to Vincenzo. "This is not good for anyone."

Something in Vincenzo's face seemed to shift, as if I had said something that offended his honour.

A piercing scream came from somewhere in the woods, a sound mixed heavily with a wolf howl.

Vincenzo grabbed my arm before I could move towards the stairs. "You cannot go, mon ami."

"Why? What is going on? It sounds as if someone is hurt," I said.

"If you go out there, especially when they are preparing to shift back and they smell fresh blood you are as good as dead," he replied sharply. "I will not have you maimed in a wooded area like common folk."

"But what if something goes wrong?"

"They have been shifting since before you were born. You do not need to worry. The only thing you should concern yourself with is totally nude people emerging from the woods, though I am sure Osomov has the area well secured."

"Gigi does not like him."

He snorted. "I am surprised you have not learned by now that Grisela genuinely likes very few people."

"What are your feelings about him?"

"As I said, it would be unwise to befriend him but he is no monster. Only an ambitious man looking for ways to boost his position in life," he replied. "The curse of well borne men in most countries, my dear."

"Does that make him a bad person?" I asked.

"No, just potentially quite dangerous," he said, and we stood to watch when we heard rustling in the trees.

Mathilde and the other woman came out first, both wearing their cloaks and looking quite happy and glowing. The two other men came next, moving quickly passed us and into the house. Charles came last, his cloak pulled tightly around his body, his hair dripping wet. When he got closer I could see he was shivering.

"That river is extremely cold," Charles said. I could not help but smile, holding my arm out to him.

"Let us find something to warm you up," I replied, leading him back into the house. I was surprised to find the dining room completely laid out with a wide variety of foods, it seemed the absolute best of what the house cook had to offer.

"It appears your contact has his staff well trained," I said.

Charles chuckled. "Most shifters do, my dear. It is a testament to the loyalty of humans."

"Will you really eat all this food?" I asked.

"Shifters have an enormous appetite, we do a fantastic job of hiding it," Mathilde said as she came into the room, the other shifters trailing behind her.

They were all fully clothed and appeared as if nothing had happened. I wondered why Charles did not do the same, but then I noticed he, in fact, had hose and some sort of bottoms on with no footwear.

A young maidservant came in, one that belonged to the house, with a pair of fur slippers for Charles.

"Will you join us, Katrine?" Charles asked.

"Non, elle doit dormir maintenant," Gigi's impatient voice said from behind me. "We have a busy day tomorrow and I insist petite be well rested."

"Until tomorrow, then," Charles said. I smiled and said goodnight as Gigi grabbed my arm and pulled me away.

"Tomorrow will seem like the longest day of your young life," Gigi said as we ascended the stairs. "And that is not including when we actually arrive at court. It will be a true test in what you have learned from me these past few years."

"I will not let you down," I replied. She turned her eyes to me when we reached the top of the stairs; her normally sparkling gaze was dark and seemed full of anger. I stepped back, startled.

"I never thought you would," she said coldly, turning and heading into her own room.

I would do more than not let her down. I would make her proud.

Anastasia

ESCAPE

They came in the night under the cover of darkness. The magic had only been in place for a few days and when the wards were penetrated it jolted Anastasia out of her sleep and sent her running for Iren.

But she wasn't fast enough.
Something shot quickly past her head and landed with a *thunk* in a nearby tree. She did not stop, all she could do was try to dodge the arrows as she ran.
The royal tent was in flames, the burning smell causing her to choke. Lynde grabbed her and pulled her back before she ran in head first.
"Find the others and gather them up and head for the mountains," Lynde said quickly.
"But I was...," Anastasia began.
"If they survived we will find them. Now go!" Lynde yelled. She quickly took off, shifting as she ran.
Anastasia shifted also, then began searching.

Horrors began unfolding in front of her; a sword cutting a wolf in half, bodies skewered with arrows, charred burning bodies. Those still standing began to run with her but she lost some as they tried to dodge their attackers. The wolf to her left made a sickening sound when an arrow penetrated its eyeball and stuck in its head, she could not even stop to look or think about it as others fell around her.

When they reached a hidden path she sent the others off, turning to see the village now completely engulfed in flames. She could hear screams mixed with howls of agony, and she could not decide whether to run or go back in and try to help. If they were attacked because of her and she left them to die what kind of person did that make her?

From where she sat she could hear them coming, the thumping of someone running and the slashing of swords. Anastasia thought about running then was reminded of what Iren told her. She needed to use what she had to help them.

So she shifted back, then stood tall in the bushes. She lifted her hands and cast her first spell so she could see how many attackers there were. It looked like more than a dozen they were moving so quickly.

She used her magic to push the fires on them, and she was able to put some of the larger fires out at the same time. Snapping the bows in half and knocking the swords from their hands was simple.

Then something pushed her off her feet, something with much stronger magic then hers, and sent her flying, slamming her back on a tree. She heard a loud crack and when she fell to the ground she prayed her spine was not broken.

But she stood with ease, using what power she had left to start the wind spinning. She could hear the trees bending and snapping in the force of the wind. Whatever had pushed her sent her flying straight up in the air, and soon she was above the tree tops. She knew if she landed wrong she could die so she had to think quickly.

She cast a spell to try to slow her down and when she landed it still hurt but no bones were broken. When she was safely under the cover of the bush again she shifted back, Lynde had told her some time ago that the process would help her heal.

A mother wolf protecting her pups flashed in her mind and it sent her running. She found them not far away from another secret path, Lynde was badly hurt and the twins cowered behind their mother in fear. Anastasia ran up and stood beside her and the two women made eye contact.

Before Anastasia could decide her next move Lynde lunged, a sword tearing her body in half with one stroke.

Shock did not have the opportunity to set in, Anastasia put one twin on her back and grabbed the other by her scruff with her teeth and ran.

The pounding of footsteps of their pursuers was like thunder in her ears. She tried not to follow the scent of the others directly, she did not want to lead them to any survivors. She kept running until she found a large tree with a cavern in the bottom big enough for the three of them to fit. She pushed the twins in, then laid her body overtop of theirs to try to conceal them.

It was a decent hiding spot and they sat back and watched as they were frantically looked for, whoever it was gave up when they heard something else in the bushes.

Anastasia thought to get up, thought to take the twins and go find the others, then decided against it. She owed it to Lynde to protect her children, the others could wait until first light.

Anastasia watched as the slaughter continued, and their home was burned to dust. She did not know how many had survived, or how many had stayed behind to try to protect their home, like Lynde.

The twins curled up together, pushing their small bodies as close to Anastasia as they could. When silence finally fell cold came with it, the forest seemed empty and deserted.

Anastasia did not sleep, could not sleep because of what she saw when she closed her eyes.

As soon as the sun rose she woke the twins and they carefully followed the scent of the others towards the mountains. If there was no one left the three of them would move on.

She prayed there was someone left.

KATRINE

PRESENTATION

Some find the simple act of having their hair brushed quite soothing. I remembered as a child one of my greatest joys being when my father would brush out my hair, my mother being busy with the baby and my father taking great pride in the task.

As we prepared for our first official appearance at the Russian court I found no joy, and missed my father so deeply I thought I might cry.

I hoped he thought of that time with some happiness, remembered my smiling little face and the silence as I sat perfectly still while he worked. I hoped he remembered the praise he gave his perfect little daughter who never complained, even when he worked through the knots.

The bath hadn't calmed my nerves; my skin having been scrubbed until it was pink, my hair so thoroughly washed and scented I thought I might be mistaken for a rose. I was put into a pale blue dress trimmed with the finest examples of French lace and raised blue embroidery on the bodice. To me I looked very French, I did not know if it was an entirely calculated move by Gigi but it would seem odd if it was not as planned as everything else.

Hannah brushed my hair until it shone, looking like a piece of fine silk falling around my shoulders. It was to remain loose, against my protests, as a sign of my maidenhood. I was not sure if the Russians would perceive it was inappropriate but that did not seem to matter, what Gigi wanted Gigi had.

"I am sorry it took so long," Hannah said to me, holding out my father's cross on a silver chain. "But I figured now was a good time to give it to you, even if you cannot wear it."

I took it in my hand, and I was brought back to my father's workshop. I could see his kind eyes, and smell his musky scent, his light hair and scruffy beard. My vision began to blur as my eyes welled with tears.

"Thank you, Hannah. You are a gift," I said, wrapping the chain around my wrist and putting the cross in my sleeve. I looked at myself in the mirror, I had no resemblance to him in any way. I wondered if I would someday forget his face because I saw nothing of him in me.

"Are you nervous?" Hannah asked.

"Is it obvious?" I replied.

She smiled warmly. "No. Only someone who knew you well might see it."

"Will Gigi know?"

"She may, but she is probably nervous herself. It is entirely natural," she said. "If you were quite calm I would be concerned."

She stepped back to examine her handiwork, I noticed I was breathing slowly and rather deliberate.

"If I don't do well she may send me away, or leave me here," I began. "Or perhaps she'll make me her personal servant. Not that it isn't an honourable position, but you would be out of work."

She snorted. "Don't be foolish. Mlle Delphine looks to you as if you were her own. She would never cast you aside. Besides, you will do better than fine. You will be remarkable."

A halo of gold curls circled her head, secured with a row of small pearls. Her dark blue dress sparkled in the light as if covered with diamonds, but I knew it was the intricate hand of the dressmaker with a spool of silver thread. Her skin was flawless, her cheeks elegantly flushed.

"You look like a Queen," I said proudly.

"And you my perfect Princess," she replied. I could hear a slight bit of fear in her tone.

I followed her down the stairs to where the others were gathered, preparing to leave. I was surprised, with all the activity, that everyone was silent.

"Where is Vincenzo?" I asked quietly.

"Men have their own preparations, ma petite," she replied, and she motioned for me to put on my gloves. It was warm for gloves but it was part of proper decorum; I had my fan on a chain at my waist and that was the best I could do.

"But I thought he would ride with us," I said quietly. We stepped out into the night and quickly into our waiting carriage, falling in line behind the string that had gone before us. Somehow we had managed to have the carriage to ourselves, I was surprised with all the extra people we had once it was dark.

She looked at my face when we got seated and moving, a strange little smirk on her face.

"You have grown accustomed to his presence," she began. "I understand, but it needs to stop. He is a man with no ties, he will not always be around. He will be present tonight, but you must pay no man any special attention. And, because I am sure you are completely unaware, an ikon is a painting on a piece of wood of a saint, a prophet, or Jesus Christ himself. The Russian people take them to be a close likeness to the subject."

"Our first useful piece of information! Where did you learn that?" I asked.

"I saw one of the housemaid's kiss a painting and I asked what on earth she was doing, she was quite happy to explain herself to the ignorant French woman," Gigi replied. "Now, that does not mean we have to kiss every painting in the room, but we must show respect as if it is a person. Other things can be forgiven but that cannot."

"Are you nervous at all? I mean, we are about to meet a King."

"Tsar, ma petite. In Russia they call their ruler Tsar."

I smiled. "What a lovely word. It is wonderful that the first royal person I meet is called something as fantastic as Tsar."

"I do not know if the man himself is in any way fantastic, so please do not get your hopes up. He could be a drooling, malformed, inbred monster, as I have heard some other nobles in Europe are."

The carriage rattled on, I had thought to look out the window but I could not, I was too unsettled.

I did not think about the second Gigi until that moment, wondering if I would meet Beatrix tonight. I knew in my heart the woman in my vision was Gigi's sister, and that name was the only one mentioned.

I said nothing, I did not want her to think of it if she wasn't already.

The carriage stopped and the door flung open, Gigi turned her eyes to me and it was as if something had turned her light back on and her glow returned stronger than ever. The force of nature, the great Grisela Delphine had returned.

"Take a breath, ma petite," she said proudly, "for your life is about to truly begin."

I heard Alexi Mikhailavitch, again, long before I saw him, speaking a mix of broken English and Russian to Charles as they led us inside. My cousin winked at me as Gigi and I moved up in the crowd, her position in the company giving her prominence in the introductions, and I being her protégée went right along behind her. It felt strange leaving a Prince behind, but that was no longer his station and I had to remember that.

I could not give the entire situation much thought for I was being led inside and through the lavishly decorated halls. I wanted to stop and look around but had no time, a great set of wood doors was opened and we entered a great hall.

Immediately I ignored the part of my brain that wanted to stand open mouthed and stare. I followed Gigi as we went round the room and paid respect to each painting of a religious figure we could see, not knowing if it was an ikon or not. I was surprised at the quantity of gold on each picture.

We fell into a grouping as the astonished court stared at us. Men with exceptionally long beards and women with high neck gowns and headdresses that covered their hair. All I could think was they must be very hot.

There was a sharp bang on the floor and the entire room fell into low bows. Everyone was silent, all that could be heard was a strange thump and slight drag that I assumed was someone walking with a limp.

IKON

It took an eternity for this man to cross the room, and it sounded as if he was alone. I was surprised I had assumed any entrance that warranted such a bow would involve a large procession.

But perhaps a man called a word like Tsar had no need, his lone figure a symbol of his supreme rule. His and his alone.

We finally stood and I quickly glanced at the man, the Tsar, who sat on a great wood throne on a raised platform.

The Tsar was a boy.

Not a young boy, perhaps the same age as me, but a boy none the less.

Alexi Mikhailavitch stepped forward to introduce us and we bowed again, this time only for a few moments. The Tsar and Alexi exchanged a few words in Russian, and I caught something about Nikoli Osomov. It sounded as if they said something rude.

Charles seemed to catch it, too, and he stepped forward to say something but was not given the opportunity. His body became quite tense, Vincenzo and William stepped forward to stand behind and support him.

Gigi began to curse under her breath in rapid French, about Charles's stupidity and something about Osomov I did not catch.

The Tsar stood and proclaimed to the room, he could have told them all we were the Devil's army for all we knew, then sat back down. He and I made eye contact for a brief moment.

I saw something in his eyes that made me want to turn and run back to France. I could not explain what it was, perhaps a brief window into the mind of a young man who had absolute power over a very large country and its people, but whatever it was frightened me to my very core.

Alexi turned his eyes back to us, said something to Charles, and led us back out of the hall.

"That's it?" I whispered sharply to Gigi.

"It was only a presentation, petite. And the Tsar did not sound impressed," Gigi replied, stomping forward and grabbing Charles by the elbow. She whispered something sharply to him, her eyes quickly turning to me as I hurried to catch up. We separated from the group when we got outside and got into our waiting carriage.

"Have you lost your mind?" Gigi yelled at Charles, throwing a vase at him that he caught easily. "Did you not think to consider your precious contact might be disgraced at this court? That this man you hold to such high esteem could have led us to the slaughter?"

Charles sighed. "Gigi, please...."

"He brought us here under false pretences, Charles, any idiot can see that. Did you see the look on the Tsar's face? That was not a look of interest or excitement in any way....I don't speak the language but they are clearly, and quite openly not fond of Nikoli Osomov," Gigi continued.

Charles turned to me and I raised both hands as a sign to leave me out of it.

"I am sorry but I agree with her, Charles. I would be more than happy to go home right now, that was quite unnerving," I said.

"No," he snapped.

"There is no skinwalker, Charles. Accept that you have been tricked and allow us to move on. We could go back to Prague, we could dance in Prague to a packed house, Charles," she replied. "Don't you find it odd that Nikoli is not here? Should *he* not have presented us to the Tsar? Where is he, Charles?"

He sighed again but said nothing.

"Where is Osomov, Charles?" William asked from his place beside the fireplace. Several of us had gathered upon returning to the house, Gigi had held her anger for as long as she could. Vincenzo sat in one of the large carved wooden chairs and stared uncomfortably at the ground.

"You are hiding something," I said as I watched Vincenzo, then turned my eyes to Charles. "Both of you are hiding something."

Gigi snorted. "Our dear Lord Westwick is *often* hiding something, ma petite, but I am quite surprised that you have a hand in this, Vincenzo."

"You are overreacting," Charles said. "My Russian is not fantastic but what I did understand was nice towards us but...."

"But not towards Osomov," Vincenzo added. Gigi began cursing them both in French, words polite women did not often say in public. She picked up everything she could manage and threw it at Charles, some he caught and others, like a large candlestick, struck him painfully. William started to curse at Vincenzo in Italian, I understood things like stupid, naive, and underhanded but little else.

I sighed and began to massage my forehead, a headache starting to grow somewhere behind my eyes. I wished for my bed, either here or in Paris I did not care. I would do what Gigi wanted in this case, and wait for her to dismiss me.

"I could get you something for the pain," Morgana said quietly in my ear. I was startled by her sudden presence.

"Where did you run off to?" I asked her.

"I told you I would be with Josephine," she replied. "Grisela has good reason to be angry."

"Why do you say that?"

"While you were at the front those of us at the back got to experience the rest of the room, and believe me when I say it was no better. I do not speak Russian but it was obvious the French are not well liked."

"Oh dear," I said, continuing to massage my head. "This will not do at all."

Morgana leaned in closer to my ear and whispered. "There is also someone in that market we must find, it is very important."

"I do not understand," I replied.

"I saw something, only a brief glimpse. Whatever you sensed in the market that first day is something important and we need to figure it out," she said. I looked into her eyes to try to gauge what she was thinking, something mischievous was going on inside her mind.

Charles stumbled back and fell when he failed to catch a brass candlestick. Gigi stood and watched until she was satisfied he was injured, I wondered if she would laugh but that would be beneath her. She turned her eyes to Vincenzo, William continued on his tirade.

"How long shall you watch?" Morgana asked quietly.

"Until Gigi gives me leave," I replied. "Besides, it's refreshing to witness an argument that has nothing to do with me. And that man, the Tsar, I looked in his eyes and saw something frightening. He's quite young to be so.... corrupted."

"He is absolute ruler of all Russia and has not yet spent twenty years on this earth, Katrine."

"I did not think he was so close in age to myself....but you think he is?"

She chuckled. "And could you imagine having to rule and govern a country of this size and its people? Not knowing if you can truly trust anyone, or if they're using you for personal gain. Surrounded by people, but lonely."

"No, I cannot. I am not entirely comfortable giving orders to servants, I cannot imagine giving instructions to an entire country," I replied.

Gigi pointed at Charles and Vincenzo, the injured having returned to his feet.

"You will tell me everything," she began in French. "Every plan, comment, plot, arrangement, anything that could effect petite and I, and the Scots girl for that matter. If I even so much as get a hint that you are not totally being honest with me I will pack up the entire company and go back to France with or without you. Do you understand me or shall I say it again?"

Neither man said a word, but Vincenzo's eyes followed us as she stormed out with me close behind.

She continued a string of profanity as we walked up the stairs, grabbing my arm when we reached the doorway.

"If either of those men asks you for anything you tell me immediately," she said sharply.

"Of course," I replied.

She smiled. "You did beautifully under the circumstances, ma petite. I am very proud."

I smiled, blinking back tears.

"Now, get some rest. We have a rough road ahead and we will be perfect, regardless of the foolishness these men are involved in," she replied, kissing me on both cheeks before retiring to her room.

KATRINE

ROSES

I woke the next morning to total silence. I lay in bed and stared at the ceiling, wondering how long I would have this peace before the world needed something from me. I wanted to return to Paris, but after last night I knew Charles would do everything he could to keep her happy and keep us here so we could be staying for some time. I could not ask to return alone, so I would do as I was taught and make the best out of an uncomfortable situation.

I stood and went to the window, which looked out over the wooded area. The sky was a clear blue and seemed to go on for miles, it made me think about what Morgana had said and how big this country actually was. It was overwhelming. I could not imagine trying to rule even this house.

A soft knock at the door took me from my thoughts, Hannah came in with a tray of food.

I sighed. "Thank Heaven it's you, I am to be dressed immediately?"

"No. I have no orders for you yet today. I thought we could break fast together," she said.

"I assume you want to hear about what happened?" I asked, smiling.

"We all heard Mlle. Delphine's fury last night, there is very little to explain," she said, setting down the tray and sitting in a chair. "Was the reception that bad?"

"It was awful! I am not sure if it is related to Osomov or if the court just does not like the French, but whatever it was they were not exactly warm. But I did not know what to expect in any way so I am not the best judge," I said. "I would not be the slightest bit bothered if we turned around and went home right now."

"You think of Paris as home?" she asked.

"Of course. It's the only home I have now, if I tried to go back to my father he would surely send me away."

"Why would you say that?"

"Without my mother I am a burden," I began, interrupted by a sharp knock at the door. I couldn't help but sigh, we had just begun the meal.

Hannah answered and had a quick exchange.

"I won't be a moment," Hannah said, leaving the room and closing the door behind her.

So our moment of peace was short lived. The day was about to begin.

We had been invited to a social function at court, a time to mingle with the Russian nobility, so we had to begin the long process of getting ready. Luckily I could finish eating while my bath was being prepared.

The rose water was particularly fragrant, I wondered if in this country the blooms were larger and that created this overwhelming scent. When I stepped out of the bath I felt like I was a flower.

I was in a dress of rose coloured silk trimmed with lave and embroidered with flowers on the bodice, decorated with tiny rosettes in a lighter colour.

I wondered if it was too much as Hannah plaited my hair and pinned it to my head, covering the whole thing in a silver net. But, I understood very little of this life and trusted Gigi, this was what she knew best.

We finally finished as the sun began to go down. No one at the court seemed to question that we only came at night, or perhaps they did and Charles had answers to all possible questions that might cause people to suspect us.

Vincenzo was in the sitting room when I came downstairs, I was about to turn back around when he noticed me.

"Did she tell you not to speak to me?" he asked.

"Do you think I would listen?" I replied, sitting in one of the wooden chairs.

"You are angry," he said, a statement not a question.

"Of course. I believed you would do what you could to protect us, lying about the situation does not do that."

"It is not what you think."

I sighed. "What I think is not a factor, I do not make the decisions."

"But you are afraid, enough so that you would happily return to Paris immediately, if given the opportunity," he said. I said nothing, only nodded and smiled, trying to show him that even though I was angry my opinion of him had not changed.

I would not, could not believe that he would be involved in some great act of deception that could cause us harm in any way.

"As soon as Charles sees there is no skinwalker he will have fully embarrassed himself and we can go home," he said, pacing back and forth across the room.

"That could take long," I replied.

"Let's hope the Russian's warm to us in the meantime, and Nikoli Osomov does not return from wherever he is."

"And Beatrix?"

He paused when I said her name, this name caused such disturbance in my life since I'd first heard it I was no longer phased.

"We will cross that bridge if we come to it," he said, turning away from me and staring out the window.

"Do you mean 'if' or 'when'? You have openly admitted you are hiding things, how do we know you aren't sure of exactly where that woman is?" I replied.

"You have to trust me that I do not."

I stood and went to him, standing close behind as he looked out the window.

"If she appears and Grisela thinks you know beforehand it will destroy her," I said quietly. "So whatever it is, please think before you act."

I heard Gigi call my name before she came in the room, I quickly turned and moved forward just before she stepped in the doorway. She was a vision in shining blue that reminded me of William's eyes, the bodice heavily embroidered with gold and silver thread in a filigree pattern similar to my father's cross. I had decided to keep it in my sleeve until it was an appropriate time to wear it. I had not realised how much I had missed it.

"Is he corrupting you, ma petite?" she asked.

"Of course not," I replied. "You look wonderful, by the way."

"Oui Gigi, you are a vision," Vincenzo added.

She rolled her eyes. "Flattery will get you nowhere at this point, Vincenzo. The possibility, after all this time and all the years we travelled together, that you are not the man I believed you to be make me physically ill."

"Grisela please," he began, and she raised a gloved hand to stop him. I went to move past her, realising I had forgot my own when she stopped me and passed them over.

"Your maid tried to sneak past me as well to get them to you," she began, stopping me from interrupting. "Proper decorum does not relate to the weather, petite. We wear gloves, especially when coming or going."

I put the small white gloves on, a large bump showing where my ring sat on my right hand.

"That looks terrible. You should take that ring off," she said.

"No," I snapped, and she appeared startled. "My father's cross I understand, but I will not take off my Grandmother's ring."

She watched me, wide eyed, for several moments before saying, "Of course, I apologise. But please, try not to attract too much attention to it, for it does slightly resemble a deformity."

"Those who wear gloves will recognise a ring, Grisela," Vincenzo said.

"But is it proper for women to wear gloves in Russia? Since you seem to know so many things about this country that we do not, perhaps you would like to enlighten us," she replied, sitting in one of the cushioned chairs. Vincenzo sighed loudly, throwing his hands in the air before turning back to the window. She smiled, apparently quite pleased with herself for frustrating him, then turned her blue eyes back to me. She examined me as closely as she could without touching.

"Bon," she finally said. "You look splendid. Your Hannah is a marvel, the best decision we ever made. Don't you agree, Vincenzo?"

"Yes, yes, of course. We must give Kardoska some credit also, she did push the matter," he replied, the first part barely a mumble.

"Do not start with that now, petite," she said. "You cannot mourn the woman constantly, you have to get on with your life."

"I am trying my best, Gigi. I have stopped wearing white and...what was the word? Did you say moping?" I replied.

She wrinkled her nose. "I was not criticising, I only wanted to be sure the mention of her did not send you into a tailspin."

"I am quite alright, I assure you," I said sharply. "But I will begin to become unsettled if we do not leave soon. This is entirely too nerve racking, unsure if we are walking into a lions den."

Gigi turned to Vincenzo and said in Italian. "Are you pleased? Our girl is afraid?"

I pretended like I did not understand and sat in one of the wood chairs. There were too many things going on for me to become absorbed in arguments.

William came in, oblivious to the tension in the room, and went directly to Vincenzo. Gigi looked annoyed and I could not help but laugh.

I assumed she would be used to William's general lack of proper decorum.

The men spoke quietly to each other with their backs to us, it looked like William had spent much time getting prepared and he was wearing new clothes. They did not turn when Charles came in, his usual glittering self. He smiled at Gigi and I before going to the men.

It was obvious to me that things had changed. While they were in the wrong with their behaviour it seemed that Gigi's outburst had caused them to look at us differently. I did not quite understand how this all worked, Gigi deserved more respect then what they were showing her.

"And what are you three chatting about?" Gigi asked. They appeared startled when they heard her voice, as if we had not been there the entire time.

"Shall we leave soon? I am beginning to grow impatient," I said. Charles smiled and held his arm out to me and I stood, letting him lead me out of the room.

In a matter of moments we were loaded into our carriage and on our way.

We did not speak as we rode, Gigi clearly caught in her thoughts and I tried to calm my nerves. In these sorts of situations I was pleased we rode alone, I could not bear the chatter of women when I was nervous.

Moscow rolled by rather quickly, the farther we went into the city the more houses I saw made of wood. The people seemed to be covered completely in clothes, the only visible skin on their faces, which were round with pink cheeks and sad eyes. It looked as if they were preparing for the cold to return quite suddenly, I was glad we had not come in winter I had experienced harsh weather at my village, but I had never seen any who looked visibly afraid of the cold.

The palace seemed different this time, perhaps because my excitement had fully transitioned over into full blown fear by the time we walked through the grand doors of the great hall.

All activity in the room stopped for only a matter of seconds as the Russian court paused to look at us then returned to what they were doing. We paid our respects to the ikons then crossed the room and bowed to the Tsar in this throne, I made sure not to look directly at him. We then tried to blend with the crowd, Gigi and I taking a position at the edge to examine the crowd.

The women were dressed in high necked gowns with large headdresses, some of their outfits were covered with highly detailed embroidery in gold thread the likes of which I had never seen before.

"Close your mouth, petite," Gigi whispered to me sharply. "Don't worry, we shall get you something with Russian embroidery, if you wish."

"Would you not like something? It is quite exceptional," I replied.

She tilted her head slightly, watching a particular woman as she walked passed. "I suppose. I *am* happy that head dresses have gone out of fashion."

I heard some music playing but could see no musicians.

"I thought there was dancing at these sorts of functions," I said to Gigi. Victorie joined us, she looked radiant in dark green and appeared quite board.

"At most courts I have been to there is dancing, but it appears we are farther from home then I thought. Damn Charles for bringing us into this.... what if they don't enjoy dancing?" Gigi replied. "When I get my hands on that blasted Osomov...."

"I heard he is on his way, so you will get to him soon enough," Victorie said in French, along with, "and trust me when I say you are not the only person who wants a shot at Nikoli Osomov."

Gigi cursed in French after sighing loudly. I continued to watch the room, and our people stuck out amongst the Russian nobility in such a bizarre way I could not find a word to explain it.

And then, like a single star in a dark sky Gabriel and Mathilde came out of the crowd. My cousin was majestic in navy and gold, every inch the Prince he was clearly born to be. While Mathilde looked lovely in plum, her dress perfectly accenting the curves of her body, she every inch outshined by the beauty of Gabriel in that moment.

All eyes turned to them, and I noticed something on a few of the men's faces that made me extremely nervous.

Recognition.

I had not thought he could be known here, the 'dead' Prince of Transylvania who'd been killed, according to rumour, by his own men. By the way he looked he was not thinking about either.

"Do you think they recognise him?" I whispered to Gigi.

"Who?" she asked.

"Don't you see the way they look at him?"

"Who, petite?"

"Gabriel," I said sharply, as quiet as I could manage. "Could they know him?"

She paused, then said. "Only he could tell you that, petite. I do not know if he held court as Prince, but you would assume he would have considered such possibilities."

I went to go to him and she grabbed my arm.

"Attracting unwanted attention will not help anyone, petite. Now is a perfect occasion too for you to understand the importance of timing," Gigi began.

"But what if he is in danger?" I asked.

"Then we would surely be able to tell by now, don't you think?"

"No. We are not sure if we are in danger. We are not sure of anything here."

She snorted, then said quickly in French, "When you are saying something negative please speak our language, God forbid someone should overhear we are having problems. And if you have any grievances you can take them up with Charles and Vincenzo."

Continuing on in our language, as Gigi put it, Victorie said, "I heard you will leave if Charles continues to be dishonest. You should start packing, and I would very much like a seat in your carriage."

"I am thinking that would be wise, I would also like to leave," I added, the Russians began to look at us strangely as we carried on in French.

"And you did not want to attract unwanted attention," I said.

"Speaking our language does not count," Gigi replied. Servants came in and began serving some sort of fowl smelling warm drink.

"Do you suppose there are some of them amongst us?" I asked them both. "Blood drinkers or shifters? I cannot imagine there would not be, they seem to be everywhere else. Perhaps we should seek them out."

"Predators seeking predators is not a wise idea, unless it is to claim territory," Victorie said, smiling when she saw the expression on my face. "Did you not realise we are predators, Katrine? Grisela, have you taught this girl nothing of the blood sucker's nature?"

"I thought I would teach her to be a lady before I taught her about being a vampire," Gigi said angrily.

Victorie laughed softly and said, "Whatever you choose, my dear, she is your protégée after all."

I stopped listening, though they continued to argue, and tried to observe the room. The Russians seemed to love the drink being served, and the entire function was spent socialising, though none of them spoke to us.

The women seemed to stand behind the men, speaking to each other but rarely to anyone else and only looking directly at us when they had no other choice.

I was starting to feel like I had some infectious disease with boils growing on my face from how they looked at us, then the men appeared and seemed in good spirits.

"Are we at the same place?" I asked as they approached us. "Because we are clearly missing something."

"No, il mio amore, you are missing nothing," William said quietly to me. "We are not well liked, the women more so then the men. We have been wondering if it is something as simple as wardrobe."

I grabbed Charles by the sleeve and said quietly in his ear. "How long do you intend to subject us to this, Charles?"

"Is she angry again?" he asked.

"Not yet, but the night is still young," I replied.

"We have not been here long, Katrine."

"Is that supposed to make me feel better?"

"Some would take your forward manner as rude."

I smiled. "Those are the same people who think we should not speak at all, and they should crawl back under whatever rock they came out from."

"Tell that to the Tsar. It seems the Russian noblewomen have very few liberties," he said, then whispered in my ear. "I see now why he frightened you so. He is very intimidating."

"He's a child, similar in age to myself. I think," I whispered.

"I know, and that makes it much worse," he replied, squeezing my hand. "It won't be much longer tonight, I promise. Please entertain Grisela until it's time to go."

"I will try my best," I said, readying to leave then remembering, asking him in French, "Do you believe there is a chance Gabriel could be recognised?"

"I am not sure, but it is something to consider. I did notice the way he was being looked at, it did not seem right," he replied.

I smiled again, bowing to him slightly as I prepared to walk away. "Merci, mon seigneur. I am pleased to hear you are so highly observant."

He laughed as I went back to Gigi and Victorie, calling to me in French. "I promise tomorrow we will have a grand adventure."

Katrine

THE MARKET

Charles's idea of a grand adventure was taking us to the market in the square outside the palace.

"It will give you the chance to learn about the regular people of Moscow," he said as we got out of the carriage. Gigi had stayed home, feeling such a task was beneath her, but she had still insisted that my appearance was *just so*, which meant I had to wear a fancy cloak and hat and gloves even in the scorching heat. Morgana thought it was hilarious, but I understood I was representing Gigi also when I went out in public.

"The only person you would embarrass is yourself," I said to Morgana while I began to fan myself. "I have to think about Grisela also."

Morgana chuckled. "She has you trained well, young pup."

"If it was not for that 'training' you would still be in a cage in the basement of the chateau in Paris," I replied. We began to walk through the market, Charles and William not far behind. Vincenzo has separated from us early on, claiming he needed to find something and would catch up with us later.

"Remember what I told you, Katrine. Whatever you sensed before here is significant. We need to find it...or them," Morgana said, her eyes scanning back and forth as if she was on the hunt.

"Stop that, you are not an animal," I said quietly.

"Then use your senses so we can figure this out," she replied. "And get a bloody move on, its boiling out here."

I couldn't see much more than a few feet ahead of us, the market was so crowded with people. I tried to use my senses, as Charles has begun to teach me what seemed like an eternity ago, and pick up on anything around us. I was overwhelmed by the heavy smells of fish, different foods, and dirty bodies and it took some time to push through all these layers and actually reach that particular note that one would have to know to identify.

And when it came it felt like I was surrounded by it.

"What's happening?" Morgana asked.

"They're everywhere," I replied.

"What?"

"Others, like us. There are so many I cannot count. But something is not right."

"I don't understand."

"It's like someone has put the scent out, but those creatures are not really here. There is no way there are that many blood drinkers out right now."

Morgana paused, then said. "It's a cover spell of some sort. Think of what you sensed that day and search for that."

She whispered something to William, his eyes lowered and he looked angry.

"Are you sure it's a cover spell?" he asked.

I nodded in agreement, and Morgana said, "She can smell it, you bloody moron. I think Lord Westwick needs to give us all the information he has on these particular Lappish witches."

I continued on as they spoke, trying to set myself to that exact thing I had picked up before. I visualised those two people who had appeared to be wrapped in rags and all I could remember of them, what I had thought to be a dhampir.

Then it hit me again, this time like a slap in the mouth. Now, the 'it' became a 'she' and her energy was vibrating through the market like wind creating waves on an otherwise calm lake.

"Something is wrong," I said to Morgana.

"I am aware of that....," she began.

"No. The girl. We have to go," I said and I started in the direction of the vibrations.

Two men had her arms, trying to hold her down as she thrashed violently. The rags had fallen away into a strange sort of outfit, her brown skin and dark hair fully exposed. She turned her golden eyes to me and began to curse loudly, the four of us standing at one end of a pathway between booths watching the events play out. Her companion stood on the sidelines as if he was attempting to blend with the wall, only a soldier stood pointing a weapon I did not recognise at his chest.

"What is that?" I asked no one in particular as I assessed the situation.

"A pistol. Have you never seen a pistol before?" Morgana asked.

"Not exactly," I replied. Someone held my shoulders as I went to step forward. The girl kept her eyes on us, yelling at us as if we somehow understood what she was saying.

"We can do nothing at this moment, Katrine," Charles said to me.

"We have to help her Charles. Morgana saw it, it's important," I replied.

"Jumping in at this moment will help no one, and make our situation worse," he continued. "We will find out where they are holding her and go from there. Those are the Tsar's guards, Katrine."

"She won't be killed outright?" I asked.

We stopped and listened, Charles could understand the Russian being spoken. William looked frustrated and very, very angry.

"She's being arrested for stealing," Charles told me. "And taken to some prison to await trial, but they appear to know her well. They are calling her 'the Turk' and saying she's had too many chances already."

"She's a Turk? Did someone not mention a Turkish Princess being held captive," I asked. The guards began pulling her away, leaving her companion standing alone.

He turned his eyes to us, I could now see he was an enormous man dressed in a similar fashion to the girl.

"But he's human," I said. "Why would she keep a human?"

I pulled Charles along with me as I started towards the man, he stood and waited for us as if we had been expected.

"Do you speak his language? Do we have anyone who speaks the language?" I asked Charles.

He shrugged. "I speak some, so does Vincenzo I believe. Gabriel also, if I am not mistaken."

When we finally got to him he smiled at us, I poked Charles in the ribs. He began to try to converse with him, awkwardly at first, but when the other man started talking it started to move more smoothly.

"Tell him we will help the girl," I said to Charles.

"Sybilla," he said to be after several moments.

"What?"

"Her name. Sybilla. And my large friend says if we do not she will be executed."

"Will he come with us? Please ask him to come with us. Tell him we can help him. Tell him, Charles."

Charles sighed. "He's a doctor, he calls himself human. And he calls her 'vampir' bit I think he's saying 'day vampire'. It could be dhampir."

The man looked excited and relieved when he heard the word 'dhampir', and told Charles so.

"That is what he meant. And he called her 'amiirah'. I will have to ask Vincenzo. But he has agreed to come along until we can free Sybilla," Charles said. "It sounds as if he has freed her the other times she has been captured, and he thinks that's why she will be executed."

"Tell him we will get her back, and I am of her kind," I replied.

"He knows. Says it's his 'gift', and he was charged with Sybilla's care because of it. She did something and they had to leave Constantinople.... her father was a vampire, and a Prince," Charles continued. "We should go. It's really not safe here."

Charles said something to the man and they continued to talk as we began walking back towards the carriages.

"What could someone want to hide so badly that they would cast such an immense cover spell?" Morgana asked. I turned to William, who was still scowling.

"What do you make of this?" I asked him.

"Charles has not been forthcoming with us, or Osomov conveniently did not tell him everything. There is more power here than just some simple country witchcraft," he said.

"You're angry."

"Unbelievably so. I think Grisela had the right idea in wanting to go back to Paris."

"There is only one reason I can think of why they would go to such lengths to confuse us."

He chuckled. "I'm amazed they know we are here."

"They know someone is here and the only reason they would cast such a spell is if they have something to hide."

"Meaning?"

I turned and smiled at him. "Meaning there is a skinwalker somewhere in Moscow, I'm thinking close by, and these witches want to keep it for themselves."

The man's name was Aseem, and Sybilla was a Turkish princess of some sort. The details of how they ended up in rags in a Moscow market were not explained, and Aseem made it clear that he would allow us to help him free Sybilla but then we would part ways. Charles offered safe passage to wherever they wanted to go, as long as Aseem swore they would leave Moscow for good.

Vincenzo had stepped in at this point, his Arabic much better than Charles's, but this did not seem to comfort Aseem. We had brought him back to the house, fed him and tried to make him comfortable but that seemed to do no good. The man was visibly uncomfortable and wanted to go get Sybilla immediately, regardless of our reassurances.

"You go out on your own and return with an Arab doctor and problem that could bury us all," Gigi said, sighing loudly. "Vincenzo should keep a closer eye on you."

"As I said before, Morgana had a vision. We need to help," I replied.

"Did anyone die in the vision?" she asked.

"Not that I am aware of. Perhaps I should ask," I said, her eyes grew wide with horror.

"You're all mad!" she yelled in French as she left the room. I went back to where the others were trying to talk with Aseem, Morgana and William were standing together talking quietly.

"What's going on?" I asked Morgana.

"It seems your man and I have been volunteered to lead the rescue mission," she replied.

"Why?"

"Apparently sending the spellcasters in to do the job is the smartest idea," she said.

"So then I will come along also," I proclaimed, the two of them about to turn on me. "What? I have some spells. I could be helpful."

She smiled at me and said, "That is all well and good, but...."

"No," William cut in sharply.

Morgana sighed. "Exactly."

"I will not allow the two of you to go into the prison alone," I said.

"We would not be alone, we would just be in front," Morgana replied. "And a blooddrinker and shifter, along with the Turk. Won't do much good, regardless."

"But I am coming," I said to them, then repeated it loudly to the room. I walked over to Vincenzo and tapped him on the shoulder.

"Tell the man, mon ami," I said, gesturing to Aseem and smiling proudly. "Tell Aseem I will go with them to rescue Sybilla."

"No," Vincenzo said angrily.

I sighed. "This is not a discussion. Tell the man."

Vincenzo told Aseem what I said, and he seemed overjoyed, making a show of bowing to me.

"He said thank you, Princess," Vincenzo told me. "He seems to think you are, well, a Princess."

"We will iron out the details but in a few days we will return to the court to perform, it will act as a distraction while we free Sybilla," Charles said, turning back to Aseem. "Perhaps he can draw us a map beforehand."

"So then it's settled," I replied, sitting down and motioning for one of the maids to bring in some tea.

William's face finally brightened. "Yes, until Grisela finds out what you intend to do."

Klara

THE OPEN ROAD.

The landscape quickly turned from desert to trees and greenery, and the roads from dirt to the paved ones created by the Romans. Klara knew that those roads meant they were close to Italy, if they had not passed into it already.

Olivia rode silently beside her, her eyes focused intently on the road. Occasionally she would turn and smile at Klara, facial expressions and hand gestures their only form of communication. Sometimes Klara missed being able to really speak to someone, but the quiet gave her the chance to be alone with her thoughts and try to make a plan.

She was not sure they could just ride into Vienna and up to her parent's house. Could it possibly be that simple?

They needed to put as much distance between themselves and Monaco as they could before they stopped again. Leaving a trail would be a very bad idea.

But the horses would get tired, and they could not ride them into the ground.

After many days, and many small towns, they came to a stone wall of a larger city. When they passed through a set of gates they easily found an inn, where they brought the horses around back.

Klara recognised Italian being spoken when they went in the main room of the inn, and she breathed a sigh of relief. They were headed in the right direction.

Once they were seated at a small table food came quickly, their server probably no more than fourteen and with a big happy smile on her face. Klara was amazed at the difference in the hospitality of these people, perhaps they recognised their betters on sight.

They ate well, and Klara's mind began to wander to their diminishing supplies. After Monaco they had a decent amount of money, but Klara was unsure that was the best way to spend it.

"I think we are going to have to take some supplies when we decide to move on," Klara whispered, and Olivia gave her a confused look. "I do not like it either but I am wondering if our money is better spent elsewhere. I mean, we have plans, and we may need..."

Olivia reached across the table and touched Klara's arm, smiling at her with encouragement.

"I am pleased we are thinking the same way," Klara told her. They finished up in the main room then purchased a room for the night.

With the door finally closed behind them the two women seemed to relax, Olivia immediately headed for the window.

"Where are you going?" Klara's voice was heavy with panic as she grabbed Olivia's arm, as she leaned forward to look out the open window. Olivia scowled at her, putting hands on the other woman's shoulders and sitting her down on the bed.

"You cannot just leap out a window," Klara began, but was stopped by Olivia's determined stare. The two women stayed with their eyes locked for some time.

"I am *not* leaping out a window," Klara told her, and Olivia simply shrugged her shoulders. She smiled, and Klara could only roll her eyes as Olivia turned and went out the window.

The night dragged on, and eventually the bed began calling to Klara. She had tried to wait for Olivia to return, but when she began having trouble keeping her eyes open she knew she could not. As she got into bed she reminded herself that Olivia may not come back, it was something she really needed to prepare herself for.

Meanwhile, Olivia moved smoothly through the shadows of the sleeping city. She was able to smell out where the food carts had been and follow them back to the sheds where they were stored for the night. The magic she could use without being able to speak the words of a spell opened the lock quickly, something it had come in handy for. Grabbing a sack in the first shed she took only enough that the owners would not notice until the cart was basically empty and locked the door behind her, moving on through as many sheds as she could until the sack was full.

It would be enough to sustain them for some time, if they were conscious of it.

Olivia continued to explore the city, she had not been alone and free in quite some time and was really enjoying it. With no shackles or whips her body could finally relax, and she did not need to be so cautious.

But even before being a slave she'd had to be careful. Cutting out her tongue would not keep her silent forever.

Climbing up to the second storey window she had leapt from was easy, even while holding the sack. Klara was fast asleep, Olivia could not help but smile. She watched the other woman, who looked so peaceful, her orange hair spread around her like a halo. Something stirred inside her, she put the sack down in the corner then crawled into the bed.

She reached out and ran her finger gently over Klara's lips, something she had wanted to do since that first night in the barn. Klara stirred only slightly, leaning into the warmth of Olivia's hand as she slept. She continued to run her finger along her body, gently tracing, spending extra time as she carefully touched her nipples through her dress.

Olivia hadn't noticed Klara open her eyes, and seemed surprised when she pulled her close and kissed her. Olivia's shock was evident on her face, as if she had expected Klara to have an entirely different reaction.

What began as an innocent kiss soon turned into a passion filled embrace, with hands exploring as their mouths combined with a deep hunger. Soon Olivia's body began to react, the feel of Klara's fingertips sending electricity through her body. She moaned into the other woman's mouth as the hand moved between her legs.

Then suddenly Klara let go, backing away and leaving Olivia very confused.

"I apologise. It has been some time since I've known pleasure," Klara said. "But we can go no further, for a woman cannot satisfy as a man can. We do not have the proper parts."

Olivia laughed, taking that as a challenge, then moved back on top of Klara. She kissed her hard, kneading her breasts and playing with her nipples until her body reacted, then she moved her hand between her legs.

With a steady rhythm Olivia used her fingers, gently inserting and rubbing as she kissed Klara.

In mere moments Klara was moaning in ecstasy, clawing at the bedsheets as her body moved in climax.

Olivia pulled away, first her fingers then her mouth and body.

Klara sighed loudly, then said, "I guess I was mistaken, or perhaps you are very talented."

Klara then rolled over and cuddled up to Olivia, who watched her until she fell asleep.

The next morning when Klara opened her eyes she was alone, Olivia's smell lingered on the sheets. Her initial shock passed quickly to anger, the pile of rations in the corner of the room not helping her foul mood.

She could not understand, how could Olivia not be there when she woke? Did she not know how that made her feel?

There was a small basin of water set aside that she did not remember being there yesterday. Perhaps she has gone to get my breakfast, Klara thought as she started cleaning herself up. The water felt good on her skin, she hoped it hadn't burnt and damaged her appearance. She could not look common if she ever expected to marry.

The doorknob quietly turned and Olivia crept inside, as if she thought Klara would still be sleeping. They made eye contact, Olivia smiled proudly as she held up a sack full of goods.

"Where have you been?" Klara snapped, Olivia held the sack higher with a look of confusion. "It could not wait until I was awake, so I would not think you abandoned me?"

Olivia frowned, staring at Klara as she went back to washing herself. She put her sack down with the other things she had gathered. A wave of anger flashed through her, and she picked up and launched an apple at the back of Klara's head, missing by mere inches, the fruit exploded on the wall sending bits flying everywhere.

Klara slowly turned around, Olivia pointed and shook her fist wildly. She gestured to the pile of provisions she had spent the night gathering and growled angrily at Klara.

"Alright, I get it. I am sorry!" Klara exclaimed. "Thank you for getting all of those things."

Olivia continued to scowl at Klara as she went to another basin that she had set aside for herself and started washing up.

They packed up their things and headed out, riding out into the blazing sun. Klara silently wished they had stayed inside, the sweltering heart turning her stomach.

But Olivia was forceful and determined to get moving. The amount of things she had stolen could get her hanged, or her hand cut off depending on what region they were in, and she was not willing to risk it because of Klara's attitude.

As they continued on more riders began to appear on the road, some alone and others with carts and big caravans. Klara thought that must be a sign that they were approaching a major city. She tried to listen to any voices she heard, any signs as to where they were headed. It must be a market town, she thought as she looked at some of the contents of the carts.

Then she heard an older man say 'Genoa' and she could not help but smile. Her father had spoken at great length about the city and she knew it was large and wondrous. She would have to rack her brain to remember any names he may have mentioned.

They followed along with the other riders into Genoa and stayed with them as they went deeper into the city, only stopping as they reached the outskirts of a large market.

Klara looked at every sign they went past, hoping that something would spark her memory. She carefully watched every person who passed them, looking for any clues that they were more than mere humans.

But there was nothing, and she began to grow more frustrated.

Olivia gestured to an inn that was close to the market and Klara obeyed without a second thought, the expression on Olivia's face was angry and sour, a clear sign not to argue with her.

Once they were able to bring their things into their room, they returned to the main area to have some food.

"My father spoke often of this city," Klara said quietly. "Perhaps if I can find one of his contacts I can secure us better passage to Vienna."

Olivia ignored Klara completely and dug right into the food that was brought to them.

"It would be nice to have a proper carriage to ride in. Not that I do not enjoy riding, but it is exhausting and we have such a long way to go," Klara continued, her eyes wandering around the room. They eventually fell on a couple who sat across the room, staring intently at them.

Klara boldly stared back, unconcerned with the consequences. Who would sit and stare at a young woman in an inn in such a way?

The only thing she could think was that they must be others, whether they were blood drinkers or shapeshifters it did not matter. They could sense what she was, and perhaps they knew who she was as well.

Olivia turned her head only briefly then went back to her food. She could care less about anyone else, and if they involved others in their journey it could prove problematic.

She heard the chair legs scrape the floor then two people were standing by their table, she did not even bother to look up.

"Hello, and welcome to Genoa," the male voice said, his accent was very thick.

"Thank you. We have not seen much but it appears to be a lovely city," Klara replied.

"Are you here on business?"

"We are on our way to Vienna."

The woman shifted her weight, as if she leaned over to whisper something to the man, and he said, "What is your family name? Your face looks familiar."

"My family name is Von Dores."

"You are related to the Baron?"

"I am his only child and heir," Klara proclaimed.

"Well then, it is an honour to meet you. Begging your pardon but I must ask, you two women are travelling without an escort?"

"I prefer it that way," Klara snapped. "Sometimes I tire of all the pomp and circumstance."

"And you allow your servant to eat with you? That is quite remarkable," he continued, Olivia's body tensed as she waited for Klara's response.

"This woman is my personal guard, sit, and she deserves respect."

"I apologise, for I am but the same to the woman who stands beside me. May I introduce my employer Amelia de Loncrey, and you may call me Xavier."

Klara held out her hand. "Klara Von Dores, and this is Olivia."

"It is not often that a noble has a woman as a personal guard, you must be quite skilled," Xavier said to Olivia who simply shrugged her shoulders.

"Perhaps you could help us with a map to Vienna. Ours was stolen from us in Monaco..," Klara chuckled. "I am surprised we made it this far with no map. Thank the Heavens the Roman roads are still so beautifully intact. What marvels they were!"

"Maps do not come cheap," Amelia said.

Klara chuckled. "Of course. We will send the bill to my father, who I am sure will pay handsomely to ensure his only daughter's safe return home."

"Of course. I will see what I can do," Amelia replied, her voice was flat and without emotion. "Now, I must ask, if you wish to feed your other appetites that you do so through me. We cannot have any sort of scandal."

"Of course. We have a room at this establishment, so whatever arrangements are convenient for you," Klara said casually. Amelia's eyebrows lowered, her blank expression starting to sour.

"I am assuming you have coin to cover your expenses?" Amelia asked.

"As I said, the bill can be sent to my..."

"That may be acceptable to procure a map but is not for other expenses. I am afraid if a deal cannot be reached I will have to escort you both out of Genoa immediately," Amelia's voice was sharp as she began to lose her patience.

Klara smiled. She knew she had to be careful, this woman could have heard her story and believe all the terrible lies. She had to be on her best behaviour.

"Of course. Please pardon my error. I am not quite used to such independence, no matter how much I enjoy it," Klara purred at her. "We will happily pay, within reason, of course."

"I will make the arrangements then send word," Xavier said, then he and Amelia turned and left.

"Well that was odd," Klara said to Olivia, who had not looked up from her food. "But I suppose it is all well and good, we can just get more coin from somewhere else."

Olivia growled and slammed her fist on the table, startling Klara.

"Do you not wish to feed?" Klara continued. "I thought it a wise way to spend our..."

Before she could continue Olivia slammed her fist on Klara's hand that lay flat on the table, she shrieked in pain.

"I do not understand what your problem is," Klara's voice squeaked as she cradled her sore hand. Olivia let out a loud sigh, stood and left, heading to their room and leaving Klara alone in the dining hall.

Amelia de Loncrey returned immediately to her small home to check her correspondence. She knew she had heard something from somewhere about these two; the arrogant, disgraced daughter of a courtier with bright orange hair and her flaxen haired companion who did not speak. The blood drinkers in Monaco were angry, the scandal that the two young woman had created had almost made them evacuate the city.

Amelia would not allow such things to happen in Genoa. And if there was a price out for these two she wanted to know that as well. The first time she had done such a thing she felt terrible, like she had committed some sort of sin, but now she knew she was doing what was right bringing criminals to justice. It was an honourable job for a woman interested in law and order.

With Olivia gone, Klara thought it was high time she amused herself.

She brushed her hair from her face and smiled at the first man who caught her eye. It felt good to have some male attention again, it seemed like an eternity since she had felt a man's touch.

He quickly came and sat with her, buying her a fine mug of mulled wine and gently stroking her hand. He asked her name in Italian, but she decided to play coy and pretend she did not understand, adding to the romantic tension.

They drank, she giggled, he smiled and said moderately nice things, she knew immediately he was working his way to an intimate encounter.

She considered it, and she stared deep into his pretty green eyes that were accentuated by his tanned skin.

She could not take him to her room, so when he asked her to come for a walk she decided to take her chances.

Klara and the young man stepped out into the night, she leaned on him and played into the idea that she was drunk. He coaxed her along, leading her into a dark alley a safe distance from the inn.

He kissed her hungrily, pushing her against the wall as his lips seemed to bite into her. His hand went straight to her breast and in frustration he untied the front of her tunic so he could touch her skin. He pinched her nipple and she grabbed for him, the two motions sending waves of pleasure through their bodies.

Within moments he lifted her skirt and he was inside her, the motion of him slamming her body against the wall quickly causing her to climax.

Then, without thinking, she turned his head and bit his neck. She did not realise it had become a reflex until his blood was in her mouth and he was screaming in climax.

But she only took a little, and when she released him and saw the look in his pretty green eyes she felt almost back to normal. This man's life was hers now, he would worship her like a God.

Katrine

A Rescue

The plan was set, the maps drawn, every possible scenario played out so there would be no surprises. Victorie and I were dressed similar so I could seamlessly slip in and out of the room, we hoped, with minimal problems. All in our company with long dark hair were dressed the same, for that matter; Charles was slightly concerned that because of my status my absence would stick out.

"I don't like this," Hannah said as she helped me dress that night. "I don't like this one bit."

"You do not have to. The girl needs my help, and I will not allow my Will…," I began, stopping myself.

"Trust me when I say to you, Child, that William of Naples can take care of himself."

I sighed, I had not realised that I still thought of William that way. "That is not the point, Hannah."

"But you are going because of William, are you not?" she asked.

"I am going to help a dhampir in need," I snapped.

"And you are directly disobeying Mademoiselle Delphine by doing so. I thought you were deeply concerned with pleasing her," she continued.

"She is aware that I feel responsible, having found the two in the market. I could not, in good conscience, not be involved in fixing something I helped create."

"Because the Scots girl had a vision?"

"Partially."

"Following all the Scots girl's visions will not bring Kardoska back, Katrine."

"I am not a fool, Hannah," I said through gritted teeth. "Please don't take me for one."

"I am quite surprised William would even allow it."

"He does not command me. Now, can we speak of something else?" I asked. She secured my hair to my head in a net of silver which matched the pattern on my stomacher. I was impressed that Josephine could pull together several similar outfits with such short notice.

"Fine. Are you nervous about tonight?" she asked.

"More about the court than the rescue. This has not been the most inviting and friendly experience; I am not sure how they will react to our dancing, considering we are barely acknowledged when we enter the room," I began. "I am also worried some of the Russian nobles recognise my cousin."

"There is no need, my darling girl," Gabriel said, stepping into the room and closing the door behind him. "Any chance they knew my face it would be from a portrait or in battle, I rarely held a court large enough to have envoys or ambassadors from foreign courts."

"But you could see why I would worry, they looked at you as if you had stepped into the room with a crown on your head," I replied.

He laughed. "Perhaps I give off the impression I am royal."

"But you are."

"Not anymore."

I smiled at him. "You were bred to behave in such a manner since birth, cousin. I don't believe it is something that would leave you, regardless of the change of circumstances. A royal is always a royal, even if they have fallen."

"Thank you for the lovely compliment, but that will not soften me to your plans. You are potentially putting yourself in great danger," he said.

"I will have William and Morgana with me which is more than enough protection," I replied. He was about to say something but silenced himself when he remembered Hannah was in the room. But his expression I thought I had a clear idea of what he wished to say, there was very little he could not speak freely of.

"I would ask no favours from those I am not interested in," I said quietly to him.

He shifted around uncomfortably then excused himself quite suddenly. I wanted to chase after him, I had no interest in involving the Order in something so small, if any part of my life at all. I did not want to owe them any favours.

"You will not listen to Gabriel either?" Hannah asked.

"No," I replied. "And I hope you will pray for success, whether you agree with what I am doing or not."

Victorie rode with Gigi and I, the two made polite conversation as we went. Gigi was not speaking to me and I was fine with it, I would fix things after the night was finished.

They stayed together as we walked with the group into the palace, I kept close to Gigi but remained on my own as planned so I could step away at a moment's notice without attracting attention.

We entered the great hall and paid the necessary respects to the room before getting in position for the dance. At that point I drifted close to the back of the room, waiting for William to cast a spell to cover us as we left the room.

"We heard you needed help," a familiar female voice said behind me, my body began to tense. "We are prepared to extend our services to keep you safe."

I sighed loudly. Gabriel had done what I had sincerely hoped he wouldn't, the member of the Order of the Dragon who had approached me in Paris was standing behind me.

"Your help is not needed," I replied sharply.

"This is a dangerous task, Katrine...," she began.

"You will address me as Mademoiselle Bathory," I said angrily. "And perhaps you should aid those in true need. My mother is out there alive somewhere and my grandmother is being kept captive and humiliated so men can steal her lands. Help them, it's much more important. Do something good with your great powers."

The signal came and I walked away, without even turning my head to look at that black hooded figure and scowl. I was so angry I was having difficulty catching my breath. But I did not have time to think, the spell would not last long and I had to get out of the room before it wore off, which would be the moment the dance started. I hoped the spell worked on whatever members of the Order were in the room, I pushed any thoughts of the situation from my mind as I caught sight of William and made my way down the hallway.

I caught up with him and Morgana as we got closer to the end, Don Tommas and one of the male shifters were not far behind us.

"Is there a problem?" William asked me. We passed some groups of people as we headed for a large flight of stairs where Aseem was supposed to be hiding.

"Not right now, but there will be when I find Gabriel later," I replied. He examined my face for only a moment before turning to watch what was going on around us. Aseem came from the shadows close to the staircase and began to guide us down.

The first set of guards was positioned half way to the bottom. William and Morgana cast as we walked, I heard the bodies lean against the wall and slide to the floor before we saw them, they looked quite peaceful curled up on the floor. I wondered how a large, dark skinned man like Aseem had got past the guards on multiple occasions, suddenly becoming suspicious.

But, I really only had one focus. It was a long way down to the prison, longer than I had thought, and it was my job to act as backup if magical help was needed. So the amount of guards that lay peacefully on the floor was irrelevant, as long as they stayed down.

A large wood door stood between us and the prison when we got to the bottom, William prepared to cast a spell to blow the lock.

"Should we not look for a key?" I asked, and I began looking around at the sleeping guards belts.

"No time," he replied, I grabbed his hands and held up the keyring.

"Remember you must knock out the prisoners as well," I continued as I found the right key. "It must be seamless."

William rolled his eyes. "Yes, boss. I am aware."

It took both Aseem and William to push the large door open. I was surprised at how many prisoners were there, I only looked briefly at the shapes in the cages as we walked down the narrow hall. Aseem, in a state of panic, moved to the front as he scrambled around looking for Sybilla. When I heard a woman cursing in a strange language I knew we were close.

Another voice began to call out to us from one of the cells as we walked past, we all paused.

"I thought you knocked everyone out?" I whispered to William.

"I did!" he replied. "But it only works on humans."

The voice continued but we did nothing, William took my arm and pulled me along. I handed him the key and they freed Sybilla.

I said one of the spells William taught me, "Vado turpis," so we would go unseen by whatever was still awake in the cell as we walked out.

The rest was like a blur. I locked the large door to the prison behind us and left the keys where I found them, running to catch up with the others as we went up the stairs. We moved together as one unit until we were met by Vincenzo, and he, Tommas and the shifter took Aseem and Sybilla out and we continued on to the main hall.

The dance was just finishing and I moved back into the group, joining the bow that was followed by a thunderous applause.

I came up beside Gabriel, getting as close behind him as I could.

"You crossed the line," I said quietly to him. He turned his head only slightly, acknowledging me but saying nothing.

"If it happens again I will tell them about the Order, and that I believe them to be dangerous. And, to the best of my knowledge, you are one of them," I said, my voice flat and emotionless. Before he could say a word I caught sight of Gigi and followed her and Victorie as we left the hall.

"Est-ce fait?" Gigi asked me as we walked.

"Oui. It is done," I replied. We stepped out into the warm night, she slowed as we approached the carriage so I could walk beside her.

"I hope this is the end of you putting us in danger, but I feel it is not. You are inclined to help people when you can," she continued in French. "A less favourable trait in a woman but I cannot fault you for it."

We got into the carriage, Gigi's eyes remained on my face.

She said quite flatly. "Something is wrong."

"I am beginning to think my trust has been misplaced in Gabriel," I replied.

"Should I ask?"

"Not yet. I must speak with Vincenzo, perhaps we could speak together."

Gigi snorted. "Things are not as they were. He has secrets."

"It seems we all have secrets."

Katrine

SPREAD HER WINGS AND FLEW AWAY

Vincenzo sat across from me with his eyes turned down as he stirred his tea. I had sent Hannah as soon as I'd woke to tell him I wished to speak with him, they had both arranged breakfast for us in his room.

"You will be pleased to hear Sybilla is resting comfortably," he said. He would not look directly at me.

"I am, thank you for that," I replied. "Is something wrong? You seem troubled?"

He sighed. "It is too complicated, la mia colomba."

"Are you very overwhelmed, mon ami? Because I am in need of advice."

"Please tell me, it is a welcome distraction."

"I think I may have been wrong to so easily trust Gabriel, and my heart is breaking over it," I said.

"What has he done?" he asked.

"He tried to involve the Order of the Dragon in our plans to free Sybilla."

"And why does that trouble you?"

"Because he came to see me, then within a short time I was approached," I began. "It was maybe two hours at the most. Which, to me, means they are close by. Perhaps even following us. They are a danger to us and he does not seem to understand I do not want their help."

"Have you considered the possibility that this Order has something on him, or they are threatening him in some way and that is why he is involving them?"

"No, I had not. I had only thought of what he has done to me, and the danger he put us all in," I replied.

"Gabriel is a good man...."

"How do you know? What makes you so sure?"

"Mind your tone, Katrine."

"The Order of the Dragon's sole purpose is to rid the earth of evil, Vincenzo, and *we* are that evil. He is one of them and he is not being entirely honest about it. They could kill us all."

"It does not mean they will."

"But they could wipe us all out in an instant and there is nothing we could do to stop it. My God, why are you so calm about this?"

He finally made eye contact with me, and he was noticeably angry. "I do not believe he would sell us out so easily."

"Neither did I, until someone came up to me last night within an hour, maybe two. I am frightened, I would not have mentioned it if I wasn't," I said, and he continued with his tea in silence. After a few moments of watching him not look at me I realised something.

"What are you not telling me?" I asked.

He chuckled. "You spend too much time with Grisela."

"And you are doing nothing to aid your cause, Sir. Keeping things from me scares me."

"You have no reason to be afraid. We have things under control," he replied.

"How can I believe you?" I asked.

He smiled, then, looking up at me and saying, "Did you really think you could tell me about something as serious as the Order of the Dragon and I wouldn't look into it?"

"Why didn't you tell me?"

"Because they need to think we are unaware and unprepared."

"Are they holding something over Gabriel?"

"That I do not know, and that is the truth. Be angry, but be careful. We are not sure of anything with him, but I strongly believe he would not do a thing to harm you purposefully."

I sighed, taking a sip of my own tea, then said, "I hope you are right, mon ami. No good can come from keeping secrets."

A large commotion came from downstairs and I heard Gigi yelling in French. Vincenzo and I carried on for several moments, ignoring the noise.

"I suppose we should go and see," Vincenzo said, putting down his tea cup and reaching his hand out to me.

"I suppose," I replied, taking his hand and allowing him to lead me downstairs.

She was in the sitting room, her voice now a high pitched scream as she raged on at Charles and a blonde man who closely resembled him but with a beard.

"It appears the infamous Nikoli Osomov has returned," Vincenzo said quietly to me. I could not help but stare at him, he was not in any way what I had visualised.

"I was thinking he would me taller, more menacing," I replied, Vincenzo chuckled softly. "I know you said he's no monster, but I was expecting him to it least be mildly frightening."

"Sorry to disappoint you," he said. Gigi realised we were present and began going on to Vincenzo about how 'they' could not allow it, and I should not be subjected to such dangers.

"Katrine," Charles called me over to him, Gigi tried to intervene but Vincenzo stopped her. "Katrine, this is Nikoli Osomov."

"You are not half as menacing as I expected," I said as I held out my hand to him.

"It is still early in the day, my dear," he replied, his voice heavily accented. He softly kissed my knuckles, his eyes staying on my face. He was a bit creepy, but not enough that I would be bothered by him.

"So why have you finally decided to join us?" I asked him.

"I had intended on being here when you arrived but unfortunately I was delayed. But now I am here and Charles and I can proceed with our plans," he replied. There was a loud thud behind me and Gigi came flying across the room, knocking Osomov onto his back. She crouched on top of him like some sort of wild animal, grabbing his throat with one hand. I only caught a brief glimpse of her mouth and I thought I saw fangs. Vincenzo lay in a heap on the floor beside me, she clearly had tossed him out of the way.

I could not hear what she was saying, her voice sounding more like a low angry growl. I stood and watched her in complete shock, Charles went to pull her off but backed away when she turned her eyes to him.

Osomov looked panicked and began to plead with her, his eyes and become big and round, his pupils were completely dilated and the whites seemed larger than normal.

"If you force him to shift it's on your head, Gigi," Charles snapped. She stared silently at Osomov for a few minutes then stood, moving to sit in one of the chairs as if nothing had happened. I sensed William come in, he attended to Vincenzo.

"I assure you, Grisela....," Osomov began.

"Mademoiselle Delphine," she sharply corrected him.

He bowed to her in defeat. "I assure you, Mademoiselle Delphine, these Lappish witches are only simple forest witches. They are of no concern."

I felt myself chuckle and I heard William snort behind me.

"Is there a problem, Mademoiselle Bathory?" Osomov asked.

"Only that I believe you are wrong, sir," I began. "They cast a cover spell over the entire market to hide from us. I don't think that's the work of some simple forest witches."

"It is not," William added. "It takes skill and an enormous wealth of power."

"But they would be no match for the great William of Naples," Osomov replied, laughing uncomfortably.

"Who says I am involved or even willing to help?" William asked, and he smiled. I knew that look well, the contempt in his eyes, and I could not help smiling myself. Osomov's face sank, he looked to Charles for help.

Gigi began to laugh. "And what would you do if William refused? Eh Charles? Could you hunt for your precious skinwalker without him?"

"He won't refuse. Katrine has agreed to help me, and I cannot imagine either of you would allow her to do it alone," Charles replied, an evil smirk spreading across his face.

I was about to say something in protest but stopped myself, I had completely forgotten about our deal. I had agreed to help him in exchange for his silence, and I could not afford him telling anyone about the slave trader now.

"You agreed to this, Katrine?" William asked me quietly.

"Yes, but that does not mean you need to. Contrary to popular opinion I can take care of myself," I replied.

"And I will be joining you on this hunt," Gigi began, standing and preparing to leave. "And should anything happen to my protégée, Nikoli, I will kill you myself."

"Not if I get to him first," William added as Gigi left the room. He had pulled Vincenzo up and put him in a chair.

"Are you alright, mon ami?" I asked. Vincenzo nodded, his eyes looked dreamily around the room.

"We, we...we must prepare," Osomov said, his face had gone totally white. He stumbled lazily out of the room as if someone had kicked him, he was clearly in shock.

"I hope all this trouble is worth it, Charles," I said to him.

"It will be in the end," he replied. "Perhaps, while preparations are being made, we should go and check on our guests."

We had decided to keep Aseem and Sybilla in the basement with the others, there had been some concern about the servants reacting to a fugitive in the house.

Charles and I went down and knocked on the small wooden door.

Aseem answered, he brightened up when he saw my face and bowed. Sybilla stood from her place on a small bed pushed against the wall. She and Aseem conversed in Arabic, I supposed he was explaining my part in the situation.

"He believes you are the sole reason that we helped them," Charles began. "She seems to think you two have some sort of magical connection."

Sybilla stepped forward and said, in perfectly elegant French. "Thank you for what you have done. You will not regret it, I swear to you."

"I felt compelled. I knew I had to help you. Perhaps you will tell us how you ended up in a market in Moscow," I replied. "If you are not in too much of a rush to move on."

"Move on?" she asked. "I was hoping we could stay with you for a while."

"That would be wonderful. Your companion gave us the impression that you wished to leave as soon as possible, so we thought...."

She smiled widely. "If it is no trouble we have decided to continue on with you."

"No, no! No trouble at all!" Charles said.

"This is your husband?" she asked.

"No, this is the leader of our faction, Lord Charles Westwick," I said. "My name is Katrine Bathory. I am being mentored by Mademoiselle Grisela Delphine, the lead dancer of the Danse Macabre."

"And I am Sybilla, daughter of Crown Prince Mahmud and his second wife, Ralmolunda. You have met Aseem," she began, motioning to the man who was clearly cursing in Arabic, "royal doctor and my guardian."

"A pleasure," I said, Charles kissed her hand. "I am deeply curious now as to why a woman of your status would be in such a state in a market in Moscow."

She smiled coyly at me. "I am sure we have plenty of time to speak on such matters. Now, I must ask, are we confined to the basement?"

"No, but I must ask that you do not leave the house. I am not sure if you are being hunted and we cannot afford the scandal," Charles replied. "Once we go back to the court and hear if there is any news regarding your escape you can go out and walk the grounds if you wish."

"We are quite alright, so please do not be overly concerned. I have been well taken care of by those who also reside in the basement. We are happy and content," she began, and a large commotion began above our heads.

Charles stared at the ceiling, listening to the bumps and crashes before saying. "If you will excuse us, Sybilla, it sounds as if we have some matters upstairs that demand our immediate attention."

Before I could say anything more he grabbed my arm, clamping on tightly as he pulled me back upstairs.

We found Osomov and Vincenzo deep in conversation in the sitting room with no signs of any issue or where the noise came from.

"Ah! Good!" Osomov exclaimed. "Are you ready? We should go to the market before it gets dark."

Charles turned to me, as if I was leading the entire expedition. My stomach tightened and my face felt flush.

"Morgana," I said to him. "I must find Morgana. I cannot go without her."

"I will collect your things. Please sit," Charles replied, trying to direct me to a chair.

"No. It would be best if I found her and Gigi. I cannot guarantee you would be well received," I said and I left him waiting while I went and gathered my women.

I found them together in Gigi's room, practicing the enchantments Morgana had taught her to protect us from what we had seen in the visions. I sincerely hoped that she was overreacting, but I could not help but wonder what this person, or persons, who frightened Gigi was like.

They were both reluctant to go, and did not move without protest.

"At the very least if this proves in any way difficult we will get to watch Gigi hurt Osomov, and potentially Charles as well," I whispered to Morgana, her face lit up at the very idea.

She froze when we reached the bottom of the stairs, her eyes locked on Osomov as he spoke to Charles.

"What is it?" I asked her quietly.

"He has blood on his hands. He smells of the fires," Morgana replied.

"I don't understand. What fires?" I said.

She turned her eyes to me and I shuttered. "The killing fires. He smells as if he has been close to where people have burned. The same way my family died."

I looked at him then, and tried to smell what she did. My senses were strong, there was little reason why I would not be able to.

The smell of blood hit me hard, like a slap in the face, with an under lying hint of something I did not recognise at first. When that smell fully hit me, I got a flash of Roza's face, and of Bytca.

"What does it mean?" I asked her.

"Keep one eye on him. Always," she said. We followed the others out and quietly got into the carriage.

"Mon dieu," Gigi said as we stepped out into the market and began walking. She stared at all the things around her; the vendors and their wares, the shoppers, the sights and smells of the great Moscow market. She was like a curious child, but managed to keep herself restrained.

I cast out to try to see if I could sense anything, I caught the residuals of the original cover spell and another large wealth of power being pushed out into the world.

"I think they are in the middle of redoing their cover spell," I said to Morgana.

"Quite possibly. Perhaps we should find the source of that spell and get a look at what we are dealing with," she replied and we continued on into the crowd. The men were not far behind with William on his own behind them.

As we got closer my body felt like it was vibrating, the power was emitting so much energy it seemed like it was rattling my insides.

It appeared that Morgana felt it too and she began to walk with great caution. Gigi seemed oblivious along with the men, except William who had pushed his way forward to walk with us.

"How can they not feel it?" I asked.

Morgana sighed. "Most block out any magical influence, it is easier on their day to day life."

"But that is so strong, I do not understand," I replied. "I can feel it inside me."

William took my hand, lacing my fingers with his, and I suddenly felt more secure and my body relaxed.

We continued on in silence, and it seemed like the world began to slow around us as we walked. I did not quite understand what was going on so I took William's lead, my thoughts began to swim and I became quite confused.

Morgana kept close behind, I only knew because I could hear her breathing. I had lost track of the others, and when I tried to sense them my mind became more clouded.

A child appeared in our path, a girl no more than eight years old. She was dressed plainly with her hair covered with some sort of bonnet. She smiled.

William's eyes locked with this child and they stood and stared at each other like two animals waiting for the other to do something. I felt like a shackle on his wrist and I tried to pull away but he only held tighter. I waited for one of them to move but it didn't come.

"They are coming," Morgana said. "We need to keep moving."

"No," William replied sharply. "She is the power source. We need to stand our ground."

The girl giggled, and she sounded much younger than she looked. She raised her hands and William instantly tensed, moving into a defensive stance. She flicked her fingers and the world came to a halt.

"She froze time. Only the very powerful can do such things, it takes a lot of energy. I am amazed such a small child is still standing after that," William said.

Morgana came forward, I did not see what she did but time started up again. The child flicked her fingers, causing Morgana to stumble back only slightly as she began to advance on her.

I saw something out of the corner of my eye, a quick flash at the far end of the path. The child saw our attention shift and tried to distract us. An older woman moved behind the child and the two began using magic to try to push Morgana back.

"I saw something," I said to William. "The cover spell must not have worked."

"Where?" he asked, pulling me along after I showed him. He cast a spell and we began moving quickly through the path and crowds of people, his hand gripped tightly around mine. I could sense something moving around us that gave off the strangest scent, an odd mix of animal, forest, and something raw and filthy.

"Come along now. We don't have time to doddle," Charles' voice came booming behind us. He, Osomov, and Vincenzo came walking up, carrying large pistols like they were soldiers. Gigi wandered behind them looking rather confused.

"Did you see it, Katrine?" Charles exclaimed. "I knew you would!

We've got the upper hand, I tell you!"

"Why on earth do you have guns? I thought you wanted to catch it not kill it," I replied. Our small group began weaving through the wood stalls with Charles leading the way.

"Thank goodness for the Scots girl, I am so pleased we kept her around Vincenzo," Charles said. "Show some initiative, William, we're on a bloody hunt here."

"He has completely lost his mind!" Gigi began. "We are chasing some phantom around the market like a bunch of lunatics! So much for being inconspicuous! He's going to get us all killed!"

William said nothing and we continued marching on. Leaving Morgana behind was causing me some worry.

"She will be fine," William said as if he read my thoughts.

People began coming out of the crowd, standing in a line as we walked past as if they were watching some grand procession. They all had the same covering over their heads as the child.

"Perhaps we could have planned this better," I said. William chuckled, he was quite obviously annoyed.

Gigi rolled her eyes. "Perhaps we should stop pursuing things at the encouragement of a man who is clearly insane."

I smiled at her and asked, "Which one?"

She laughed, and though he did not relax so did William. I smiled at him, looking at his face in his annoyed state reminded me that I truly loved this man, even with his faults. I could not escape that.

We stopped when we were up against a brick wall, a girl was cowering in the corner. She looked up at us through a sheet of yellow hair, her eyes full of fear and hatred. Feathers were tied into her hair and she wore different coloured pieces of fur on her body.

Osomov pointed the gun at the girl and I grabbed his arms.

"What are you doing? You *are* mad!" I yelled at him. I turned my eyes away from the girl for only an instant, and in that short amount of time she started to shift. Quickly, and what looked like pain free, the girl began to sprout feathers, the tips easily pushing out of her skin until beautiful brown and gray wings began to form, with speckles of white on the ends. In what seemed like minutes, almost nothing compared to the wolf, the girl had shifted into a hawk. We stood back in awe as she spread her wings and flew away.

"Magnificent!" Charles exclaimed. "A true and perfect skinwalker."

I looked to William, who answered my thought by saying. "There is no known species of shifter that can change to bird."

"So it could only be. I must say I did not quite believe," I said.

Gigi sighed. "And now that we have proof, we will not leave this god forsaken place until she is coming with us."

KATRINE

SEEING DOUBLE

Osomov stayed in the shadows as we prepared for our next court appearance. It would be our first with him, and after the earlier reactions with simply the mention of his name I was quite nervous.

It had been several days since the incident in the market, Morgana had caught up with us on the way back to the carriage. She had said very little, only that we needed to continue to watch out for that child. The incident seemed to have only affected her mood.

William sat with me as I dressed for the evening, we had spent some time together since the market just sitting silently and enjoying each other's company. I had missed him.

"You really saw it? The skinwalker?" Hannah asked as she put pearls in my hair.

"Turned into a bird and flew away," I said. I was beginning to tire of telling the story.

"I apologise, Katrine, but I just cannot believe it! We are all totally flabbergasted," she replied, stopping herself mid-sentence. She glanced at William, she would not freely speak her mind to anyone other than me and I already knew what she would say.

It was the same thing we had all said at some point or another on this journey; Charles had lost his mind, and we were chasing a lie concocted by a madman with a more sinister motive.

"If I had not seen it for myself I would not believe it either," I said. "I have seen some things that would baffle the mind in my young life, but nothing quite as spectacular as that."

William snorted. "Someone has been keeping things from us. Those are no mere forest witches."

"And I must thank you again, sir, for protecting our girl. I am so happy knowing you are keeping her safe," Hannah said. He smiled at me and touched my hand where it sat on my knee.

"I would do anything for her, Hannah. She is my girl, too," he replied, then whispered to me, "if you'll still have me, of course."

I squeezed his hand and smiled at him. "Was there ever any doubt?"

"Katrine, I...it will never happen again," he stated, I could feel Hannah smiling. There was a sharp knock at the door and a command through the wood that it was time to go.

I stood, smoothing down the front of my forest green dress and standing out so the two could examine my appearance.

"A vision, as always," Hannah said proudly. "We must give a bonus to the dressmaker when we return to Paris, he is a genius."

"And you are quite talented, I must say, but you did have such a lovely starting point," William added, he finally had a genuine smile on his face. I took his arm and he lead me downstairs to where the others waited.

Gabriel stayed close to the back and as out of sight as he could manage, I had not spoken to him since the night we freed Sybilla and he was trying his best to hide from me.

"He's a coward," William whispered to me when he noticed my eyes had turned.

"With good reason. He's probably never been in a position where he could be cast out," I replied.

"Would you?"

"If I believed he was putting us in danger I would do it without a second thought."

"How do you know he isn't?"

I sighed, he helped me into the carriage and came in after me. Our conversation stopped when we started moving. Gigi was dressed in silver with her hair pulled up. She looked tired and rather troubled.

"Damn him," she snapped. "And damn that girl for being real! I want to go home!"

"We could go without them," I said.

"We cannot without Vincenzo and he won't budge! Believe me, petite, I had begged and pleaded. The man is like a mountain," she began. "Perhaps you should try. And tell him you have William's support, and Morgana will go where you do. He has no chance of catching this thing without the three of you."

"Did you think that maybe we should try? To catch her, I mean? It cannot possibly be good to leave her with those witches. Who knows what they will do to her," I replied.

Gigi stared at me as if an extra eye had grown in the middle of my forehead.

"You're just as mad as they are! What is *wrong* with you, girl? The Arab girl is enough," she said, then turned on William. "What say you, William of Naples? Are you the only sensible man left in this company?"

"You are both right," he replied casually. "She cannot be left to the witches but we should not stick our necks out for this."

Gigi's face wrinkled as she scrunched her nose. "And what do you think we should do?"

"We need a plan. And I am not talking about a Westwick plan," he said, gesturing to us. "I am talking about a plan amongst us. A real plan."

"Anything in mind?" I asked.

He smiled coyly at me. "Of course, but now is not the time."

Osomov lead the way as we entered the great hall. I was so nervous I thought I would vomit, the evil stares and ugly smirks of the Russian court as we walked past were unfriendly and absolutely terrifying.

He presented himself to the Tsar, who laughed as soon as he saw him. A long conversation in Russian began and we drifted off into the crowd.

They looked on us with pity, and it seemed like they were warming to us.

"Are we not to dance?" I asked Gigi.

"From what I knew. Perhaps it is to be more impromptu," she replied. I wondered if the court sympathised with us women for being connected to such a man, I could not imagine he did not develop a reputation everywhere he went.

Gigi and I found a place to stand and I watched Mathilde and Gabriel on the other side of the room, they appeared to be bickering. She kept looking our way, it looked as if she wanted to come and stand with us but he was resisting. It was annoying, I wanted to yell across the room for her to leave him there but bit my tongue.

After Osomov finished with the Tsar, and Charles had come forward to join the conversation, we were signalled and we stepped out to begin the dance. It was similar to what we had done when we had freed Sybilla, a simple group dance that the Russians could join if they wished.

Before Gigi was to step into her first move Vincenzo appeared and tried to pull her out. He went to tell her something, it looked important, but she stepped away and ignored him. I was too far away and had to begin myself, he gave me a worried look as I stepped into my first position.

Vincenzo stayed close to the edge of the crowd, trying desperately to get Gigi's attention but she ignored him. She was stunning, her silver dress catching the light as she moved so she shimmered like an evening star. She glided smoothly across the floor with such elegance that all eyes turned to her, everyone could see why she was the star of the show. Even the Tsar watched her, his predatory stare made him look much older.

Vincenzo grew impatient, locking his green eyes on me and trying to pull me aside but not succeeding. I tried to read his expression but could not, and when he brought Morgana out beside him I knew something was wrong.

The dance finally ended and the room erupted in applause, I actually saw what appeared to be genuine smiles. I connected back with Gigi and took my place beside her. We went to go back to where we were previously standing and Vincenzo finally caught us, but he paused and his eyes grew wide as dinner plates as someone stood behind us.

"Bonjour ma chére soeur," a female voice said and Gigi froze. I could feel her heart skip a beat and her breathing speed up as she started to turn around. I moved to my place behind her, and beside a large well-groomed man stood the second Gigi I had seen in my vision.

She had sharper angles than what I remembered seeing, her body was quite slim and her hair almost white. She smiled, and instead of just seeming beautiful she was also a little frightening.

"Beatrix, I did not know you were here. Why did you not show yourself before?" Gigi said smoothly. She had flipped from being tense to quite calm rather quickly.

"Because we only just arrived, as soon as I recognised you we did. I am so pleased to see you," Beatrix replied, Gigi moved in front of me as they went and kissed on both cheeks. I felt the hair on the back of my neck stand up when she got close to me, and Vincenzo moved closer to me also.

"Ah! Signor Amori, it has been a long time. How very lovely to see you," Beatrix continued. "I see that the whole company has come to Russia, that must have been quite a journey. And who is this young lady?"

They both moved to into protective stances beside me as Gigi said. "This is Mademoiselle Katrine Bathory, my protégée."

"Protégée? Really?" Beatrix exclaimed. "You must be quite a young woman for my sister to take you on. I look forward to getting better acquainted with you."

"It is wonderful to meet a member of Mademoiselle Delphine's family," I managed to say, I could think of nothing else. I saw Morgana peek out from behind Vincenzo than she came to stand with me. I grabbed on to her hand and silently wished for William to appear.

Beatrix brought the man forward, motioning towards Gigi. "Sister, this is my husband, the explorer Luka Toronovitch. Luka, this is one of my older sisters, Grisela Delphine, retired courtesan and lead dancer of Paris's Danse Macabre. Her associate, Signor Vincenzo Amori and her protégée, Mademoiselle Katrine Bathory."

"Are you from Hungary, child?" he asked me.

"My maternal side, yes. My paternal side is from Wallachia," I replied.

"Lovely. I know some Bathory from Upper Hungary. Kings among men," Luka said, my heart jumped into my throat.

"Thank you, sir. That is a great compliment," I replied, trying to sound calm. I wondered if he knew Gabriel. But, if he knew of his wife's condition then there should be no problem.

"We should dine together. Then we will have a better chance to speak, it has been many years since we've seen each other," Beatrix said. "You and your protégée."

"Of course," Gigi began.

"Do not worry, Osomov knows how to find us," Beatrix said, she and her husband bowed only slightly then turned and walked back into the crowd.

"I was trying to tell you," Vincenzo said.

"We are going to dinner?" I asked.

"My sister is married," Gigi said flatly.

"And Osomov knew she was here," Vincenzo added. Gigi's shoulders rose and fell as she took a deep breath in and out, with a slight flick of her hand she motioned for me and I followed her out of the hall with Morgana.

"Did you see him too?" Gigi asked to no one in particular.

"No," we replied in unison.

"Do you think he would know Gabriel?" I asked.

"I care nothing for your precious *Gabriel*, petite!" she snapped. "Something so silly as that man recognising him is nothing compared to the danger we are in."

"Then why did you agree to dinner?"

"I *will not* be terrorised by my baby sister! I've had quite enough of this fear mongering about Beatrix.....I will not be intimidated, and if she attacks I will remind her of her place," Gigi yelled. "And when we get back to the house I will remind Nikoli Osomov of *his* place, the bastard will be lucky if I decide not to kill him on the spot."

"Killing him won't solve anything," Morgana said. "Killing him won't send us home."

"No, but killing him will make me feel much better, and that is the most important thing as far as I'm concerned," Gigi replied. All I could think was that if Vincenzo had been a bit more forceful some of this may have been avoided, but perhaps it would have made it worse. I hoped for his sake he had not known for too long beforehand.

"We will not go there unprepared," Gigi began. "In two days time we shall go, I will send word. That will give us time to plan. You shall wear the finest gown you have, and we shall show Beatrix who holds the power."

Katrine

BLOOD ON THE CARPET

"Do you know anything about Beatrix Delphine?" I asked William the next day as we walked through the gardens.

"Very little. She is supposed to be a little bit insane, all of Grisela's siblings born after her are said to be, more so the younger they get," he replied. "But I have taught you enough magic that I feel confident you both will be safe."

"She wants to kill Osomov," I said. He had disappeared since the performance.

"Most of us do," William replied.

"You are not worried I will kill him and hide it from you?"

He stopped me, taking my hand in his. "I am so sorry, Katrine. I realise my error now, I don't care if you killed the slave trader. You did what you thought was right for your family, I would do the same. I was not thinking."

"Thank you William. That means a lot to me."

"So you forgive me?"

"Yes, I do."

He sighed. "Thank goodness!"

"So what do we do now?" I asked as we continued to walk hand in hand.

"We talk of love and the future, and of our plans to leave here safely with everyone still intact," he said.

"Did you have any ideas?" I asked.

"Perhaps it would be wise for us to not try to charge in like a hunting party and only a select few should try to approach the girl," he began. "And we make a deal with Charles. We bring her back, he takes us home. Then I will ask Grisela about a formal betrothal."

I could feel myself beginning to smile.

"Would that please you?" he asked.

"Very much," I said. "I am not sure if she will agree, but we will cross that bridge when it comes. And you have no need to ask Gabriel. I am a bit concerned Beatrix's husband will recognise him, he said he knew some of the family."

"And if he does? He is her husband, he must be keeping her secret if he does not have one of his own."

"Do you think I will ever meet your family, William?"

He shrugged his shoulders. "Maybe someday, but I will not actively search them out. I know you may not believe it but it is really not important."

"It's your family."

"That means very little."

"But if you are to be married? Would your mother not wish to know? What about our children?"

He squeezed tightly on my hand. "You wish us to have children?"

"Of course. It may be a while off but I love you and carrying your child, I believe, is an ultimate expression of that."

"And I love you, Katrine. One day we will have our future, I promise."

"What shall we do in the meantime, with the present?" I asked. He began to speak but was startled by shouts from the house.

"Sounds like Grisela has found Osomov," he said as we took off for the door.

Gigi had him by the throat and he was bleeding all over the fancy carpet on the sitting room floor. His eyes were wide as he squirmed like a fish on a hook.

She was saying something but it was so quiet all I could see was her lips moving. Vincenzo and Charles stood back near the wall watching and Morgana stood close to the door.

I tried to go to her when William grabbed my arm.

"Not yet, my love. The man needs to understand he does not want to face the wrath of Grisela Delphine," he said quietly. I nodded in agreement as the smell of blood began to overwhelm me. Gigi finally released him, there was a gash on his neck that was bleeding profusely.

I could hear the man apologising, saying he was innocent because he assumed Gigi knew where her sister was living. She went to grab him again but he pulled away, then in a flash she had him again and she bit back down into his neck and began to feed.

He opened his mouth to scream and nothing came out. After what seemed like an eternity she flung him away and he fell into a pile on the floor. I waited to see if he was breathing before I approached her. She turned to me, her eyes radiated with fury.

"We go tonight. I will inform Hannah so she can prepare you," Gigi said, then she strode from the room.

I grabbed William's arm and pulled him to where Charles and Vincenzo were talking.

"Charles, we need to talk," I said, before he could say anything I continued. "I have a proposition for you. William and I will go into the market alone and bring back the skinwalker."

He chuckled. "No, no. I do not think so. I will be on any mission to get the skinwalker."

"Fine. The three of us will go into the market, just us three, and bring back the skinwalker."

"What is the other half of this proposition?"

"When we do, you take us home. Immediately, no questions asked. And, we go into the square alone. No hunting party."

He smiled, looking at William, then back at me. "You two have spent some time thinking this out, I see. Okay, we will try your idea. And if it works not only will I take you home I will reward you handsomely."

"Good, so its settled. Now if you'll excuse me I have to dress for dinner,"

I said, leaving William behind as I left the room.

"I am pleased you did not want to include me," Morgana said as I went past.

"Are you being sarcastic? I thought you did not want to come," I replied.

"I do not. I am not needed. There was no sarcasm involved," she said, smiling. "Do you really think you can catch her?"

I shrugged my shoulders and called back to her. "We won't know if we don't try."

I was dressed in a gown of black silk that shone brilliant colours of red, purple and pink with my hair brushed out and worn long so it fell around my shoulders. I wore my father's cross around my neck, once it was back on it felt as if I had been reunited with a missing part of my body.

I looked at myself in the mirror and for the first time I saw Erzsebet Bathory in my face. I smiled to myself, I still found it odd that I missed someone who I had only seen twice in real life as much as I did.

There was a sharp knock at the door and I turned to Hannah.

She placed a hand on my shoulder. "I want you to remember, my dear, if you are afraid at any point tonight that you *must* take care of Mademoiselle Delphine. That is the most important thing."

"I will, Hannah. You have no need to worry," I replied, heading out the door.

ANASTASIA

RETURN TO SAFETY

"Here! Mother, I found someone!" a young woman's voice called out. Anastasia opened her eyes to see a girl about fifteen years old crouched down and peering into the hole. Anastasia took a quick sniff, it seemed that the others had found her first.

She pulled herself out of the hole and changed, taking the twins in her arms as she stood. They stayed in wolf form, their warm bodies pushed tight against her.

Iren came out of the brush, her body crusted with dirt, ash and dried blood.

"Anastasia, thank Heaven!" Iren exclaimed. "And are those Lynde's girls?"

"Yes," Anastasia began. "She..."

Iren raised her hand. "No need. We buried her this morning with her mate. This is my daughter Gisli."

"How many...?" Anastasia began as she followed the two of them into the forest.

"Including you there are thirteen of us," Iren began. "Only thirteen, when our numbers had swelled to over one hundred at the time of your arrival.

And we are mostly women."

"What of Gavril?"

"He died trying to save our two eldest children. He was not successful. According to our laws I am Király now."

Anastasia followed as they went back to the others, who were busy gathering what was left of their supplies and giving the dead a proper burial.

She tried to set down the twins so she could help but they clung to her.

"Stay with them. That is the best thing you can do right now," Gisli said, softly touching her arm. "We have things under control."

She sat down next to the pile of supplies, others would come and say hello and pay their respects to the twins, who remained curled together and ignored the rest of the world.

When they were ready to move on Anastasia took some fabric and, with a little help from Gisli she tied it around her body in such a way that the twins were securely strapped to her front and her hands were free.

She walked with Iren, who led the way with her son, Knute.

"He is an excellent hunter," Iren said of her twelve year old boy. "He has good instincts and well-tuned senses. He will find a safe place for us."

Anastasia thought the scenery looked familiar. They were going back in the direction Lynde had found her, back towards the mountains.

"I am sorry about Gavril. He was a good man," Anastasia finally said to Iren.

Iren chuckled. "No, he wasn't. But you hardly knew him so I understand. He did the honourable thing by trying to protect our children and will be remembered for his sacrifice."

Anastasia said nothing, touching the bundle on her stomach to see if the twins were still breathing.

"They are yours now, I hope you know that. You saved them, you are all they have left," Iren's voice was flat and empty.

Anastasia nodded. "I know. I hope I can do right by them."

"You will."

"Iren, I do not mean to question your judgment but...the way we left the camp. Is that safe for us?"

Anastasia's mind immediately flashed back to the line of graves, the burned out tents, the arrows still stuck in trees.

"It will look as if a camp was slaughtered, perhaps one would think we were gypsies. Only those who could identify us by smell could tell otherwise."

Knute stopped in his place a few feet ahead of them. When Anastasia and Iren stood beside him they noticed he was staring at the mountain in the distance.

"What is it, son?" Iren asked him.

The boy stood silent for several moments before quietly saying, "We will be safe there."

"Where?" his mother asked.

He pointed. "The mountain. He says we will be safe there."

"Who says that?"

"Father," he told her, then started forward. Iren paused only briefly, considering what he had said, then followed.

"Should we stop to rest? Or for some food?" Anastasia asked.

"No," Knute snapped. "We do not stop until we are safe. We cannot rest until we are safe."

Katrine

THE PRINCE

Gigi sat in the corner of the carriage in silence. She was wearing a dress similar to mine, but the effect of the black silk shining blues and greens was stunning against her skin, which seemed translucent in the moonlight. Her golden curls were piled on top of her head with a few loose tendrils framing her face and falling down her neck. Black pearls the size of grapes hung around her neck.

She was perfect. I would have expected nothing less.

"William has a plan, and if it works we will be going home soon," I said.

She continued to stare blankly at nothing. "Oh?"

"No need to worry. We have it under control. Your only concern should be the task at hand," I replied.

She chuckled. "I must warn you, ma petite, my sister may do some strange and disturbing things. Do not let it faze you. Pretend it is all commonplace. She will take any signs of any emotion and exploit it."

"I don't understand," I said.

"Do you remember when Victorie said I should be teaching you about being a vampire? Well, this will be your first lesson," she began. "Beatrix is everything horrible you have ever heard about vampires, but much worse because she is civilised and very much a proper lady. My mother would have nothing less, of course. She suffered greatly because she was unfortunately born after me, and the comparisons were constant. It was not her fault, all that were born after me were not quite right."

"So she's crazy?"

Gigi smiled to herself. "That is a polite word, I suppose. We are very, very different. I just wanted you to be aware."

"And what of this man? Is he a man? Or is he something else altogether?" I asked.

"I could not get a read off of him, could you?" she sighed after I said no. "So he is either hiding what he is very well, or he is a seriously warped man and we should be very careful of him."

"Why?"

"Because those who involve themselves romantically with vampires are usually not quite right," she said, and the carriage rattled to a stop.

She sighed, and we stared intently at each other for a few moments in silence before the door was opened.

The house was large and stone with a flight of stairs leading to the front door. It reminded me of Paris, what would be a stately chateau at home seemed odd and out of place in Russia.

A grand staircase was in the entry way almost immediately when you stepped inside, the dark wood banister was overwhelming to look at as it wound its way upwards.

Beatrix stood at the top, dressed boldly in red, the cut of the dress in the French fashion. She descended the stairs as if she was royalty, looking down on us like we were mere insects.

"Sister!" Beatrix exclaimed. "I am so pleased you have come, and brought your young protégée. Please follow me into the sitting room."

"Your husband's house is quite grand," Gigi began as we followed her deeper into the house. "What does he do with himself?"

"He is an explorer, an adventurer," Beatrix said, gesturing for us to sit. The room was filled with different style tapestries from the Orient and other lush decorations, the furniture was covered in dark green velvet.

"When were you married?" Gigi asked as we sat down.

Beatrix chuckled. "Do not fret, you would have been notified had there been a legal wedding."

"When did you leave Constantinople?" Gigi asked.

"Some time ago. Luka and I spent several years on a ship in the Orient. We took Mother and the children to Egypt," she said, and she sighed loudly. "Mother still cries for you. It is so pathetic."

"So you are pretending to be married?"

"Is the Danse Macabre not pretending to be a dance troupe? Come now, Grisela, you should know better than anyone that we do what we have to to survive. Everyone has their secrets. And Luka is a lovely man and I adore him."

Gigi smiled. "So why not marry him?"

"Because we Delphine women do not believe in marriage, remember? Our mother taught us well," she replied.

"That is not entirely true, our older sister was married. It was that Mama had no room in her life for marriage."

"Enough of that," Beatrix said, waving her hand in the air. "Tell me how the two of you met."

"I, well actually, Vincenzo found Katrine in Vienna when we went to collect Klara Von Dores...," Gigi began.

"I heard about that disaster. Luckily the Baron is such a lovely man. I heard Klara is slaughtering her way through Egypt, I'm surprised Charles set her free," Beatrix replied.

"He didn't, and to the best of our knowledge she was dead," I said. Gigi's body tensed and she opened and closed a fist.

Beatrix giggled softly. "Perhaps I am mistaken. Now, shall we have a snack before we eat?"

She snapped her fingers and a servant came in, pulling a young man behind her. He was so pale his skin looked gray and his eyes were sinking back into his head.

"We don't feed directly from the living," Gigi snapped.

Beatrix frowned. "I thought that now that we are face to face we could spend some time as we once had, reunite as sisters."

"It was your choice to leave Paris, not mine," Gigi replied.

"Why does everything have to be so difficult with you?" Beatrix said, sighing. "I have a few humans I acquired for blood, they are willing and well provided for until their life ends. You make it sound like I am some sort of barbarian, this does not make me a savage because I choose a different path than yours. The path that I have chosen leads to greatness beyond anything you can imagine."

Beatrix looked at me, her blue eyes full of intensity. "The shadow of the great Grisela Delphine is a dark place, very hard to escape from. But, I am on my way."

She waved the servant and the young man away and I was relieved, I did not want to feed in such a way.

"So it was quite a blessing you were found in Vienna....I am sorry, I have forgotten your name already! Tell me something about your life," Beatrix said. "You said you are a Bathory?"

"My name is Katrine, and Countess Erzsebet Bathory is my Grandmother," I began, and I saw some acknowledgement in her eyes. "I left my village in Wallachia in search of something more, and while working for a baker in Vienna, Signor Amori found me."

"I am surprised the Bathory would let one of their own do something as common as bake. Who are your parents?" she asked.

"My mother was born to Countess Bathory before her marriage, and my father is an enameller by trade," I said.

Her eyebrows raised. "Bastard child of royalty? You and my sister are well matched."

"Most don't believe her," I replied.

Beatrix laughed. "Of course not, but I was there and I saw him with my own eyes. He was a King's son and a King's brother, but never a King himself. My mother always said he would have been a great King. To this day he is one of the most handsome men I have ever seen, and one of the only men my mother ever truly cared for."

"You remember him? I barely do, and you were so young....," Gigi began.

"He was not an easy man to forget," Beatrix said.

"What about your father?" I asked Beatrix.

"My father?" she paused for a moment, than said. "I....I do not remember him. He was unimportant compared to the Spanish ambassador my mother had children with before she was turned, and the Valois who helped create Grisela."

"Perhaps he was too important and his identity kept secret," I replied.

Beatrix laughed again, smiling with genuine pride. "You are very charming, Katrine. My sister has chosen well."

"Thank you, Mademoiselle Delphine," I said.

"Please! Please call me Beatrix. I believe we will come to know each other quite well," Beatrix replied. "Now, let us eat!"

"Where is your husband?" Gigi asked as we were seated. The dining room was all dark wood with an enormous table that looked like it seated sixty people comfortably. Large gold candelabra's held a half dozen burning candles that gave a warm glow to the vases of fresh roses and the stunning gold plate settings.

"He is at a court function, and I thought it more appropriate if we met in private," Beatrix replied.

"What are you hiding? If he has met Mother and the children it cannot be much," Gigi said.

"He does not know the extent of it," Beatrix said dismissively. She began to play with a charm on a necklace that I could not see clearly.

Gigi chuckled. "You are carrying on the pretence of being married to this man and he does not know your true nature? Tsk, tsk, dear sister. That cannot end well. And how do you manage to have live food around? It's not as if they are cows or chickens."

"Do not worry. I have taken care of everything," Beatrix replied. Gigi watched her sister's face as the food came in and was served to us.

"Mon dieu, please tell me you have not enchanted this man, Beatrix," Gigi said, her voice fading into a whisper.

"Do not be silly! You are not the only person in this family who can attract a man, Grisela. Any feelings he has towards me are all his own," she replied. "Now, will either of you tell me the real reason you are in Russia? I have known your Charles for many years, Grisela, and he does not go to such lengths without good reason. It was quite an expensive trip to bring you all here, was it not?"

"He's a fool," Gigi said between bites. "Nikoli Osomov told him some ridiculous story about a skinwalker and he dragged us across Europe for a myth."

"Really? Because there is this wild story that a skinwalker running loose in the market in the Red Square with a horde of Lappish witches chasing it. There is no truth to this?" she asked.

"Not that we are aware of," I replied.

Beatrix smiled, scanning my face to try to read my expression.

"So, Grisela, now that we are face to face tell me the truth. Are you happy in this life, as opposed to the life our mother had planned for you? Do you not miss having power?" Beatrix asked.

"I am, There was much too little freedom, where now I can, for the most part, do I as I please. As much as a woman can at this time in the world," she began. "And I grew tired of court politics. I began my life in an age when there were few courtesans, then old King Henri had a mistress who was of mother's time, I believe, and then every girl who could not be bothered to be married decided to make herself a courtesan. Many of us, who were true born and bred, tired of the nonsense."

Beatrix sighed. "Some people would be content with just being at court. Many would never in their lives be privy to such extravagance. And the power, power like some only dream of."

She tapped her hand on the table and the same servant came in, leading the same man that resembled a walking corpse.

Beatrix grabbed the man's arm, and with a small cap on her one finger that came to a sharp point she split open the vein at his wrist and began to pour the blood into a wine goblet. She said something to the servant who proceeded to fill two more goblets.

"Now! We should have a toast to our fantastic lives!" Beatrix exclaimed. I took the glass and stared at it, waiting for something to happen. Waiting for the blood to take on some bizarre form and attack me, I smelled it to see if I noticed anything peculiar.

"Katrine, what are you doing?" Beatrix asked. "Raise your glass and let us toast!"

"She's suspicious, with good reason," Gigi replied, smelling the blood herself.

Beatrix sighed loudly. "There is nothing to fear from me, child. I have no want or reason to harm either of you at this time."

"My apologies, Mademoiselle Delphine," I said to Beatrix.

"Come now, Katrine. While on one hand it is always wise to question on the other I am your mentor's sister. I would like it very much if you'd think of me like family, and please call me Beatrix. We will only address each other formally when necessary," Beatrix continued. "So please raise your glass with me, then tell me what you think of Russia."

We raised our glasses in a toast, than drank, I tried to sip the blood slowly as if it were wine.

"Now, Katrine. How are you enjoying Russia?" Beatrix said.

"Can I ask you a question?" I asked.

"Of course. Anything."

"Where are the Russian vampires? Are there none at court? It seems very odd to me that there are just none anywhere," I began. "And what about the Tsar? Is he as frightening as he looks?"

"Tsar Mikhail came into power quite young after the country had gone through a long period of political strife, some call it the 'Time of Troubles', so you can understand why he needs to come off as quite ruthless," she said. "And the Russian vampires are not as evolved as others and are extremely guarded. They will show themselves when they feel comfortable, but do not be surprised if they remain hidden. The Russian people, by nature, are not accepting of foreigners."

I did not reply but continued to eat and sipped casually on the blood, even though my body was surging with new energy. Nothing seemed abnormal and I did not feel as if their blood or food had been tampered with.

Perhaps Gigi's paranoia had rubbed off on me.

"So what is next for you two? When you leave here, I mean," Beatrix asked.

"We go home, and return to our life as we know it," Gigi replied. "And you, sister? What are your plans for the future?"

"I must say, after seeing the two of you I am wondering if I should have a child of my own," she said, smiling. "With the way my world is becoming...."

"There is an enormous difference between carrying and birthing a child and taking on a grown girl as a protégée. Look at the difficulties our mother had birthing children once she was turned? The twins almost killed her, only to die before they reached maturity....and the children, Beatrix, they've had so many troubles! I am not sure it is wise to bring a child into this world," Gigi replied.

"I believe much of that was related to mother and her behaviours and attitude."

"She did the best she could."

"By you, Grisela. She did her best by you and left the rest of us adrift. Perhaps if she had put some work into all of us things would have been different. And the children needed guidance and discipline to help mould their weak minds. We all came to seek personal power because of what we weren't given," Beatrix replied angrily.

Gigi sighed, then said. "The bond between a mother and the child they bring into this world is the strongest connection one can have in this life. I don't blame you for wanting to experience it."

"Where is your mother, Katrine?" Beatrix asked me.

I took a minute to think before saying, "I don't know exactly."

She studied my face, I could feel her watching me while I stayed focused on my food.

"I do not understand," Beatrix said. Silence came, I supposed she was waiting for one of us to explain. I glanced briefly at her, then looked again when I saw something in her expression that made the hair on the back of my neck stand up.

"It's a very complicated story, perhaps another time I will explain," I replied. She smiled and nodded and I returned to my food. I tried my best to contain myself, to give no signs of what I'd thought I'd seen.

The meal went on, Gigi and Beatrix spoke at great lengths about people and things I knew nothing of so I remained silent. My mind was swimming with the unexplained; the possibility that Klara was on a rampage somewhere made me want to vomit. I did not know if Beatrix would outwardly lie and I would be speaking to Charles as soon as I saw him.

And then there was the other thing, that hint of something I saw in her eyes when my mother was mentioned. As if she knew everything about me, even more than I did.

Beatrix suggested we retire to the sitting room for tea once the meal was finished but Gigi refused.

"We have an early rehearsal tomorrow for our next performance and Katrine has a full day of lessons," Gigi said. "Our world does not change because we left Paris."

"Of course, of course. Perhaps I will come to the house for a visit, I would love to torment your Charles for going to such lengths for a fairy tale," Beatrix said. Her servants brought us our cloaks while we waited in the doorway.

The sisters kissed each other on both cheeks, linking their hands together and squeezing for a moment.

"We should do more to keep in touch," Beatrix said. "But I am sure we will see each other again before you return to Paris."

"Of course. Thank you for your hospitality," Gigi replied, stepping out the door and leaving me alone.

"Yes, thank you Beatrix. It was an honour to meet you," I said, bowing to her.

"Wait one minute, I have something for you," she said, turning to a bureau that sat in the hallway and pulling an object from the top drawer. She handed me a slim leather bound volume that appeared old and well worn.

"I thought it appropriate that you have this. It belonged to Grisela, who gave it to me. I am pleased to have someone special to pass it on to," Beatrix said.

I examined the book, the leather was soft in my hands. "What is it?"

"Grisela can explain better than I, but some may believe it to be an important part of a young lady's education," she replied.

"Thank you," I said, and she kissed me on both cheeks before sending me out into the night.

"What is that?" Gigi said, snatching the book from my hand as I stepped into the carriage. She opened the cover and her eyes widened in shock.

"Beatrix just gave you this?" she asked.

"Yes, she said you would explain. What is it?" I said.

"My mother gave it to me when I was learning to be a courtesan, she said my father gave it to her," she began. "I remember, it is the only real memory I have of him, I could not have been more than seven years old. I gave it to Beatrix, and she was never very good at her lessons but she studied this book like it was the gospels. I never thought I would see it again."

"You still haven't told me what it is, Gigi."

She smiled. "It's called 'The Prince' and it's by an Italian man named Niccolo Machiavelli. It's a manual for acquiring and keeping political power, is the clearest way to explain it. My mother believed its principles could be used for living, especially as a courtesan. It's ironic that the book would return to me at a time when we may really need it."

"Do you think what she said is true?"

"Which part?"

"About Klara? Charles received a letter that she was dead....her jailer had killed her...."

"Oh ma fille chérie," Gigi said, patting my knee. "Of course we shall look into it. But once we leave Russia there is little chance you will see my sister again so take what she says, in most cases, with a grain of salt. Now, we must focus on the task at hand."

"Yes, of course," I replied, easing back into my seat. She was right, we needed to focus on catching the skinwalker. But before we went home I would find out what exactly, if anything, Beatrix Delphine knew about what happened to my mother.

Katrine

TASK AT HAND

The following day in the early afternoon we set out for the market.

William watched me from across the carriage, his blue eyes examining me as I stared out the window.

"What?" I asked without turning my head.

"How was dinner? The two of you came in last night and went straight to your rooms as if everything was business as usual," William said.

"Can we focus on the task at hand? Any concern about Beatrix can be dealt with later, it's not urgent," I replied.

"That's right! I'd forgotten you had dinner with Beatrix....," Charles began.

"Is Klara really dead?" I said flatly without moving.

"What? We received a letter weeks ago...."

I sighed. "And you trust that information? Because I have heard something contradictory and I am not comfortable with the idea that she is on a bloody rampage through Egypt."

Charles paused for a moment, staring at me while I continued to look out the window. "I will look into it."

The carriage stopped and I took a few calming breaths to try to ready myself.

"So what's the plan?" Charles asked, at this point I finally looked at William.

"We find her, ask if she wants our help, we leave," William said.

"It's that simple?" Charles asked, a hint of confusion in his voice.

"Anyone who tells you it should be more complex is trying too hard to complicate the matter," William replied. "And has something to gain from your failure."

Charles sighed loudly and was about to continue until I rushed them both out of the carriage and into the hot sun.

The market was a buzz with activity even in the sweltering heat, a bizarre stench was in the air that almost made me gag.

"Is she here?" Charles questioned me like a small child after its mother.

I turned to him and he stepped back, I pushed out my awareness and began trying to pick up on the skinwalker. After a few moments I felt her presence, and several of the Lappish witches.

"She's here. This way," I said, and I began leading the men through the market.

I could not get the expression on Beatrix's face out of my mind. It was a look of recognition, but I could not figure out how she could possibly know anything about my mother even if she did hear lots of rumours and stories. This did not fall into either category, only a select few knew the true story except for....

I stopped and stumbled as the answer hit me like a smack in the face.

"What? What's the matter?" William asked as I regained my footing and continued walking.

Beatrix was one of them. She was of the Order of the Dragon. It made perfect sense, she knew things. Gigi had sent letters everywhere, there was no way that none of her contacts would not be able to locate her even if she was on a ship, especially if she had such precious cargo as the head of the Delphine family and her younger children.

She was not found because she wanted to stay hidden until it suited her, and only the Order of the Dragon had that kind of power.

"Later," I said. I tried to put the thought from my mind and kept focused on the image of the skinwalker while she was in human form. I could not sense the witches but at that point I did not care. I just wanted to get the girl and leave this country before things got any more complicated.

William took my hand and we continued on with Charles close behind. Something about holding William's hand caused a power surge between us, he made me feel safe.

We turned a corner and the air grew thick, seeming to vibrate off a blonde girl who walked in front of us in dirty bare feet. She turned her head to the side as if she heard us, the feathers in her hair flowing with the movement as if they were an extension of her body.

I gestured towards her and we sped up our pace.

Charles moved ahead, calling out to the girl in Russian. She turned only for a moment then stopped and smelt the air. She looked at Charles and something seemed to register in her eyes. She held out her wrist to him, he took it and gently sniffed the inside of her wrist, then she did the same to Charles.

"What on earth are they doing?" I asked William quietly.

"It's shifter etiquette. You'll have to ask Charles later," he replied.

The two of them began to speak, Charles was clearly struggling but even I could hear that her Russian sounded different than what we'd heard at court.

"She must be speaking a country dialect. I hope he's not struggling too much," I said. The girl turned and looked at us, her eyes widened and she backed up in fear.

"She's scared of us," William said flatly, a statement instead of a question.

I sensed something strong come up behind us and the girl spoke quickly to Charles, trying to pull him away with her.

"She's not afraid of us, it's whatever is standing behind us," I whispered. He and I began to turn around slowly, until we were facing the little girl, an old woman, and a young man.

I told Charles in French to get the girl back to the carriage and did not check to see if he listened. William tensed as he prepared to cast.

I used a spell to push the little girl back while William sent a ball of energy at the other two. The girl was knocked back off her feet and flung through several wood stalls, sending fruits and other things flying through the air. The old woman tried to send her own energy ball at us but William stopped it midway, sending it flying back in their direction.

This time he hit the old woman in the chest and she crumpled in a heap on the ground. He grabbed my hand and we started running, not looking back to see if we were followed.

With the carriage finally in sight something hit me in the back, hard, leaving a sharp pain. I stumbled forward and William pulled me roughly by the arm to keep me moving, fear began to overwhelm my body as the pain started to spread through me.

William continued to pull me when all I wanted to do was drop. He shoved me in the carriage door and as soon as I stopped I started gasping for air.

"Did they stab me?" I asked, trying to turn my head so I could see my back. The carriage started rolling, the jostling was painful.

"What? No! Why?" William asked.

"Because something hit me hard. And. It. Hurts!" I said, gasping after each breath. Tears started streaming hot down my face.

William put his hands on me, trying to see if he could feel the spot on my back. I tried not to scream but I could not stop myself from crying.

"I can't....Katrine, I don't....," William stuttered, barely coherent.

And that's when she started, the steady Russian babble from the skinwalker as she leaned over where I had hunched over. She put her stiff, cold hands on me and William pulled away, she did not stop talking even though I am sure no one understood most of what she was saying.

The pain began to grow sharp, like a quick stab every time I took a breath. I had to get back to Morgana, and I could not figure out why William could do nothing for me.

I could hear Charles talking but did not understand a word, I hoped he was translating for the girl. William stroked my hair as I curled up as small as I could, the cold hands continued to poke and prod me as she clearly looked for something.

When the carriage stopped everything moved like a blur; William lifted me out of the carriage and there was much yelling and rushing around until he placed me softly down. Not until I could feel Morgana's presence did I start to relax.

I could hear her cursing around me, her accent became thicker when she was angry. The less I moved the better so I lay perfectly still while she and

William worked.

Except for this setback, the plan had worked. I hoped Charles would live up to his end of the bargain, I was sure that this was mild compared to what the Lappish witches would do if they caught us.

"What is wrong with you? She is the weakest, of course they would attack her!" Morgana yelled. "You know better. You should have taken care of her!"

"I thought I did!" William screamed back. "They were stronger than I thought. I used a protection spell, I guess it did not work...."

"Or perhaps it is why she is alive," Morgana replied, leaning over my body. "Katrine? Katrine, can you hear me?"

I took a breath in and the pain slowly began to ease. I opened my eyes and looked up into her pale face.

"I want to go home," I said softly. "Tell Charles we are going home."

Klara

UNWANTED GUESTS

Olivia leaned over the edge of the bed and eyed the strange man who slept on the floor. Klara was gone, *again*, the fourth night in a row. Each night she went out the next day there were three or four men hanging around the inn waiting for her to come down from their room.

But this man from the first night just stayed, like a pup who was clinging to its mother. Olivia wished she could have told Klara to take him along, instead she got stuck with him. She prayed they did not decide to come along when they left Genoa, if there was a way to break whatever Klara had done so the men could continue on with their lives.

She had waited for Klara long enough, and with the man sound asleep she decided it was time she did the same.

Out on the streets of Genoa Klara walked arm and arm with a new man, she thought he was a soldier but could not remember. And the fact of the matter was that she did not really care about the details, he was a man and she had needs. She had thought briefly about contacting Amelia de Loncrey then decided against it. She was a grown woman and could handle her own business. She would prove to the ones who knew her father that she was a worthy heir, and they would tell him and make him regret all the things he had put her through.

She sighed. She could not believe it had been years already.

A man stepped in her path, saying something that caused the other man to release her arm and walk away.

"Excuse me," Klara began.

"You are so entertaining," the man said. "Every time I think I know how you will react you continue to surprise me. And you must know I have experienced many things so I am not easily surprised."

"Pardon me, sir, but have we met before?" Klara asked. She eyed him curiously as he adjusted the hood of his cloak, which covered most of his face.

"Yes, well, I would not expect you to remember, but we met in the wagon on your way to your new life," he said casually. "Then I was present at your triumph over the slave trader."

She paused. "Balcor? What are you doing here?"

In a blink he disappeared then reappeared by her side, taking her arm and linking it with his.

"I am here to speak with you, young lady, about your future," he began as they started to walk.

"We could return to my room and you could meet Olivia," she said.

"I know your companion rather well," he snapped.

"I do not understand."

He sighed. "I would not expect you to. Have you not wondered what happened to the girl's tongue?"

Klara actually had to stop and think, she had not considered the reason only its appeal.

"Her tongue was cut out so she could not speak of her life, so she could not repeat to another what she knows," he told her. "She is very important, that is why she is with you. Your destinies are aligned...but I would not want to bore you with prophecies. What you did in Monaco was remarkable."

"Thank you. I have tried to move quietly here in Genoa at the request of..."

"Amelia de Loncrey. I saw. You should not concern yourself with such women when you are on a very important path. You are just starting to make your mark on this world."

"She asked me to go through her to feed..."

"Ha! Foolish creatures are trying to make the act of blood drinking very civilised, which is preposterous! You are predators...and you, Klara, with your special talents are of the most skilled and deadly of your kind. Why they would try to give you such restrictions is beyond me. You should be allowed to move freely and as you so please."

Klara smiled proudly. "Perhaps if I travelled with you..."

"My kind does not move well with others. We are only here to inspire, it was decided when we were cast out of Heaven that was could only meddle."

"Cast out of...so that would make you..."

He waved her off. "Labels are so unnecessary. And besides, we are here to talk about you..."

He stopped, noticing something on the road in front of him. Klara turned her gaze to find Olivia watching them.

"Oh, hello Olivia!" Balcor said. "Lovely to see you again. You seem to be fairing well."

Olivia stalked over to them until she was mere inches from Balcor, staring angrily at him.

"Would you two like some time alone?" Klara asked after this stare down went on for several minutes.

"No, no. We are quite alright. Aren't we, Olivia?" Balcor replied. Olivia finally turned that anger towards Klara, gesturing in the direction she had come from.

"It looks as if your paramours are keeping Olivia awake," Balcor said. "Perhaps you should keep them in the stable with the horses."

Klara chuckled and Olivia did not look impressed. She turned and stormed off, quickly fading into the darkness.

"Just because your paths are intertwined does not mean she will ever understand you. Olivia has had a very hard and complicated life, one day I will explain. But now we must focus on your current path," Balcor continued. "You need to return to Vienna to reclaim what is rightfully yours, and destroy whatever stands in your way."

"What about the Danse Macabre and those who sent me to slavery?" she asked.

"One thing at a time, my dear. And you are only one woman. You will need your family's wealth and influence if you hope to challenge them successfully."

"Amelia de Loncrey said she would provide me with a map."

"Before you leave Genoa you will have to kill her, and her guard Xavier as well."

"Why?"

"Don't you understand? For you to be successful on this path, you will have to kill them all."

Klara paused, a small smile beginning to grow larger.

Balcor pat her hand. "Yes, my dear. Now you are starting to fully understand. You must kill them all."

Katrine

IMPROVISE

I slept for days, waking only when Hannah force fed me, after which I fell back into a heavy, dreamless sleep. I thought maybe I could sleep until we were packed and ready to go to Paris but apparently it wasn't so.

On the third day the arguing began outside my door, I could hear Hannah trying to force people away but could not identify who they were.

I sat up and tried to right myself, I was surprised to find myself bundled in the bed in a nightgown I did not think belonged to me. I tried to use my senses to see who was in the hall with Hannah but it made my head ache. My body felt drained and I desperately craved blood.

"Hannah!" I called out. There was a shuffling in the hallway and she came bursting in the door.

"Good! You're awake!" she said.

"Are we going home?"

"No, not that I am aware of," she replied.

I sighed loudly, swinging my feet over the side of the bed. "I want to get dressed, I need to go outside. And can you send for some blood? I'm having a craving."

"Of course. Of course. I won't be a moment," she said. "And I am supposed to dress you for court, Mademoiselle Delphine has insisted but I tried to tell her you were not able...."

"I cannot stay in bed forever. I will be alright, but I need blood," I said. She paused only for a moment then began preparing my outfit.

"Your cousin has come several times to see you but Mlle Delphine forbade him entrance. She said that is what you would have wanted," Hannah replied. "No one has been allowed in without her permission, which has only been the Scots girl."

"And the girl who we brought from the market?" I asked.

"Oh! Lord Westwick's new little pet? Her name is Natalia, we found a maid who speaks her country language. Why is she here?"

"You do not know? You mustn't tell anyone other than Tolone, who I'm sure already knows."

"What is it?"

I sighed. "Natalia is the skinwalker."

I heard something clatter to the ground.

"Are you sure of that?" she asked.

"I would not be in this state if I wasn't," I replied.

She picked up whatever she had dropped and began to giggle. "We thought she was a whore, she is so enamoured with Lord Westwick. But it makes a world of sense if she believes he rescued her. Is she going to stay with us?"

"How would I know? I've been asleep. How is Sybilla doing?"

"The Arab girl? She is lovely. She has been doing what she can to try to help around the house, she is sweet and charming and an absolute pleasure, doing her best to try to earn her keep. Her companion is not as wonderful but not worth complaining about," Hannah said as she began organising my things. "The language barrier may be the problem. He has been spending much time with Signor Amori, they seem to be getting on quite well."

"Good to hear," I said, pulling myself up on wobbly legs. She rushed to try to help me and I pushed her away, after walking back and forth a few times I'd regained my footing.

"Are you alright, Katrine? If you need to rest I will tell Mlle Delphine....," she began.

"I told you I am fine. Just please get me some blood!" I replied. She nodded and left the room for a brief moment.

"It's on its way," she said, putting me in a stool and brushing out my hair from the plait. "And the bath is being prepared, it shouldn't be long."

I sighed, trying not to slouch on the stool as she pulled a comb through my hair. I could feel my shoulders slump as I focused on my breathing, I was anticipating pain that never came. Whatever it was had been cleared out of my system but I could still feel something, like a bruise or a scar from a wound.

The blood I continually asked for did not come until after my bath and by that point I was irritable and cranky. After quite an argument Hannah put me in one of my white dresses trimmed with French lace, hanging beads in plaited hair so it appeared to be dripping with pearls.

"Mademoiselle Delphine will not be pleased," Hannah kept mumbling.

"She'll survive," I snapped.

"But she has these plans...."

"And she must learn to work around them," I said, rising from the stool. "I am not a doll or some plaything. I can make my own decisions."

Hannah sighed. "You can take it up with her, my dear. I have no problem with it."

I tried my best to smile and was about to apologise when there was a sharp knock at the door.

"I guess that means it's my time to shine. I will be beyond relieved when we can return home and all this is behind us," I replied.

"You do not enjoy this? The beautiful gowns, court life....," Hannah began.

"No. Well, that is not entirely true, I enjoy dressing up. I do not enjoy the pressure of a social life and being at court," I replied. "But there are many factors here, I suppose the French court would be different."

Hannah smiled. "I suppose. Now, a mark of a true lady is that she can make the best of a bad situation. So go and try to enjoy what you can."

William smiled proudly as I walked down the stairs, he looked as if he was doing everything he could not to run and hug me. I smiled back and nodded in acknowledgment, nothing would have made me happier then to run to him.

"That is not the outfit I picked for you," Gigi said quietly to me when I took my place beside her.

"I thought I would improvise. I hope you don't mind," I replied. Her face moved like she was trying to smile and I followed her out to the carriage.

"Are you alright?" William asked. He had joined us in the carriage and Gigi appeared rather annoyed.

"Yes, William. I appreciate your concern, but I am fine. If not you'll be the first to know, after Gigi of course," I said.

He smiled at Gigi and she softened a little. "Yes, it appears that the amount of people who have your true interest at heart is quite small."

"What do you mean?" I asked.

He looked at Gigi again and she said. "Your cousin was insistent that he wanted to bring in some outsiders to heal you. I think he's mad, personally."

"Outsiders? What outsiders?" I asked.

"Apparently he has a network of some sort," Gigi replied "What do you know about this?"

"Now is not the time," I said.

"Are we in danger?" she asked.

I sighed. "Quite possibly. It is all quite complicated, I am not sure I could...."

"Try," she said sharply.

"Gabriel is a member of an organization called the Order of the Dragon...."

"And?"

"You know of them?"

She snorted. "Petite, please. I was not born yesterday."

"Very well, then. They first approached me in Paris, wanting me to join them. They know things, and they keep offering me temptations, such as aid in freeing Sybilla. Gabriel swore to me he was not in close contact but he is, and I have some to believe Beatrix is one of them."

Gigi stared blankly at me for several moments before saying. "You were right, it is complicated. But you should be concerned with Gabriel's deceptive nature, not with the Order."

"Why?" I asked as the carriage rolled to a stop.

"Do you really believe this is the first time we have encountered the Order, ma petite?" she replied, giggling. "They have been in operation for over two hundred years."

The conversation stopped when we stepped out of the carriage, the new night sky was stunning in a deep shade of blue.

Gabriel got out of one of the carriages behind us and started towards me, William immediately stepped into his path. I heard them talking but I ignored them, turning and following Gigi towards the palace. I caught William telling him that now was not the time and was out of range for the rest.

Something seemed different when we stepped into the hall, paying our respects to the ikons around the room and the Tsar, who turned his angry eyes to Gigi and I as we bowed to him. He said something to one of his people as we stood and walked away, following us with his gaze. I tried my best to ignore it, the feeling of someone watching me made my stomach turn.

Gigi and I took a position near the wall and began watching the room, her eyes scanned the crowd as, I assumed, she looked for Beatrix.

A Russian man was deep in conversation with Vincenzo and Charles across the room, and they seemed overjoyed. I was quite confused until I saw a well-dressed Russian woman approaching us.

"Good evening to you," the woman said in Russian, then continuing in French. "My name is Xenya Poplova, and I thought it high time we introduced ourselves."

I smiled up at the woman; she was tall, with a wide face and small, wide set eyes. Her head dress covered her hair and made her seem impossibly tall.

Her gown was heavily embroidered with gold thread. I could not help but stare in complete awe.

"Pardon my protégée, Madam. She has been marvelling at the stunning quality of Russian embroidery since we arrived," Gigi said. "I am Mademoiselle Grisela Delphine, and my young friend is Katrine Bathory."

"I deeply apologise, Madam Poplova," I said quickly. "I just adore your dress. I am quite pleased to meet you."

She smiled down at me and I caught her scent, and when the warm scent of lavender mixed with fresh blood surrounded me I knew that something marvellous had happened.

"Lovely to meet you both and again, I apologise we did not present ourselves sooner, I am sure you can understand apprehension in regards to outsiders," Xenya began, "especially those associated with Nikoli Osomov."

Gigi chuckled. "I understand, and trust me when I say the association begins and ends with Lord Westwick. Unfortunately, as he is our benefactor we have to on occasion indulge him."

"Ah! No need to worry. The life of an unmarried female in this world can be a complex one, regardless of the circumstances. Perhaps it would do some good for your group to make new contacts," she said. "May I ask, Mlle Delphine, are you any relation to Beatrix, Lord Tornovitch's wife? I know her unmarried name is something French and it sounded...."

"Yes, Madam Tornovitch is my sister. I was quite surprised to see her, we had lost contact some years ago," Gigi replied.

"Come, let us walk. We can talk of our worlds, I also have a sister I have not seen in many years," Xenya said, motioning for us to follow her.

We walked the room and Gigi and Xenya spoke of many things. It reminded me of Vienna and the night I met Klara, I had not thought of the city I'd loved so much in some time and I felt a pang of guilt. It felt strange that everything else in my world had changed but this simple act remained.

The two women talked and laughed while I walked with them in silence, they had much in common and seemed to enjoy each other's company. The tone of the room seemed to have changed now that we were conversing, the men had now turned into quite the group.

"You have done an impressive job of concealing yourselves," Gigi said.

"You have encountered our little problem out in the market, you can see we have little choice," Xenya replied. "The Lap witches are trouble from a variety of angles and we do our best to avoid conflict."

I felt myself tense at the mention of the market. I had not thought of how others would react to our invasion of their territory and trying to take the skinwalker away.

"So I suppose it is silly of me to ask you about skinwalkers," Gigi said, I was surprised by her boldness.

Xenya said a word in the language Roza has spoken, koźe choditko, something that was familiar to me but I had not heard for many years.

"You know koźe choditko, Katrine?" Xenya asked.

"Only as a cautionary tale I was told as a small child," I replied. "My father's mother had an odd approach to dealing with children."

Xenya smiled. "Perhaps there was some truth to the stories. We know of them, you must know Russia is a big place and there are many creatures roaming our lands that are like nothing you could ever imagine. If one wishes to return to Paris with you then so be it. But, there are some details you should be aware of."

"Such as?" Gigi asked.

"By nature koźe choditko is feral and hard to control. Also, because of the multiple shift it causes," Xenya said, gesturing to her head, "insanity."

"Well, thank you kindly for the warning," Gigi replied, and they continued on with their walk.

I was genuinely surprised at how candid and honest my mentor was with this new person. I wondered how deeply the meeting with Beatrix had affected her; if she kept Xenya as a contact she would be able to keep a closer watch on Beatrix's movements.

Xenya walked with us out to our carriage when the night finally ended.

"May I introduce my associate Liev Rolmonov," Xenya said, gesturing to the man who stood with our companions. "Liev, this is Mademoiselle Grisela Delphine and her protégée Katrine Bathory."

His large face lit up as he smiled at us, he looked warm and friendly.

"Thank you for your company this evening, Xenya," Gigi said. "I hope that we have an opportunity to become better acquainted before we return to France."

"As do I," she replied. We bowed to each other, Gigi and I got in the carriage while Xenya went back inside the palace.

"So what would you call that?" I asked Gigi as the carriage got moving.

"What?" she said, closely examining her gloves as she adjusted them.

"When we finally have the skinwalker the Russian vampires decide to come out and they are perfectly fine with us taking her? Does this not seem slightly odd to you?" I said.

"When were you planning on telling me you had been approached by the Order?" Gigi began, her voice becoming shaky as her anger rose. "How am I supposed to trust and support you if you keep things from me, petite? I am your mentor! You are making me look and feel like a fool!"

My breath caught in my throat. "I....I...."

"And something so serious as Bea....why do you think my sister is involved?"

"Something in her eyes, she knew about my mother. It was as if she knew more of my story than I do," I replied. "They said in Paris they had followed my mother since birth, and me as well. Beatrix knows something, I wonder if they know where my mother is now."

I looked at Gigi's face, I could only see her tears faintly in the dark.

"I took you in, a little urchin on the streets of Vienna because I saw something more in you. I saw something shining in your eyes. And you treat me as if I am a second rate person. I put myself out for you," she said.

"Gigi, I am so sorry. I thought I was protecting you. If something happened to you I could not live with myself," I replied, biting back tears. "I am so sorry I have disappointed you and I will do everything I can to make it up to you."

She sighed. "I should be your greatest confidant. And I am the one who should be protecting you. I had hoped we would develop a bond similar to mother and child."

"And we have!" I began to sob. "I am so sorry I have made you doubt me. I promise I will tell you everything."

I moved so I was sitting beside her and began to sob on her shoulder. She put an arm around me and used her other hand to gently stroke my hair.

"I know you did not behave that way on purpose, ma petite. Everything will be fine, please keep nothing else from me, especially when it comes to the Order," Gigi said softly.

"I swear I will! I will come to you first in all things," I managed to blurt out.

"Merci," she said. "And no, I do not find the Russian vampire's behaviour odd. If they have strange creatures running loose around the country, as Xenya claims, it would be easier to get rid of them than try to control them and they cannot kill them all. But, could you imagine? If Russia has the fabled skinwalker what other creatures they have in uncharted territories? Fantastic, mythical things of dreams like dragons and the like....and what about rural areas in other countries? Perhaps we are missing so many things!"

I pulled a handkerchief from my sleeve and wiped my face.

"And we must go to work, petite. Charles cannot fornicate with the skinwalker, he cannot add that poor country girl to his list of conquests, it would destroy her," Gigi said.

"I love you, Gigi," I said quietly to her.

"And I you, Katrine. And I you."

Charles ran to us the second we stepped out of the carriage, grinning like a proud child.

"She will come! She will return with us! Can you believe it?" Charles exclaimed.

I grabbed his forearm and pulled him to me. "You cannot fornicate with the girl, Charles."

"Her name is Natalia, Katrine. And am I sensing some jealousy?" he asked, his childish smile turned to a predatory leer. I pushed him back as I released him.

"You are not so lucky. My concern is for another young girl becoming a conquest of yours and you not thinking of the consequences for her. Please think before you act," I said. His face had not completely soured but I did not wait for a reply or try to make it worse, I followed Gigi into the house without a second thought.

We went straight to our rooms without speaking to or seeing anyone else. I followed Gigi to her door, she turned to speak to me.

"Perhaps tomorrow we should speak about the book my sister gave you," she said. "I have been reading it, I had forgotten how powerful it is."

"Could we talk about my mother?" I asked. "And if, by any chance...."

She placed a finger on my lips. "Shhh, not here. Yes, we can discuss your concerns. Hopefully I can do something to ease them."

She turned and went into her room before I could say more. She was right, now was not the time and I did not know who was listening.

Katrine

DISPLAY OF POWER

First they came to the gate. Luckily they were locked and the guard, believing they were gypsies, refused to let them in and abruptly sent them away.

But, this was a distraction, a diversion of sorts, so they could get into the forest unnoticed.

Gigi and I were having tea in the sitting room when Sybilla came running.

"Pardon me, ladies, but there is something that urgently needs your attention," she said quickly in her perfect French, Gigi appeared quite shocked.

I smiled proudly. "Sybilla's French is fantastic."

"I can see that," Gigi said. We stood and followed Sybilla from the room, Gigi watched the girl closely as we walked through the house.

"I thought I saw something out in the woods," Sybilla continued. "But I ignored it, it could be an animal or a bird of any variety of thing. Then she came in."

We walked into the kitchen and found the skinwalker staring intently out the back windows, mumbling incoherently.

"Any idea what she's saying?" Gigi asked.

"I caught a few things, Madama, but one of the other girls understood it all. Though I am not sure what to make of it," Sybilla replied, then asked quietly.

"What could she mean by 'there are witches in the forest'?"

"Most likely exactly that, quite literally," Gigi replied. "Ma petite, could you please go get William? And Morgana? And Vincenzo for that matter?"

I ran back in the other direction and began calling out names, getting louder as I stood at the bottom of the stairs.

William came charging down first, pulling on his jacket. "What is it? What is happening?"

"Apparently there are witches in the forest," I said. Morgana, Vincenzo and Charles paused as they heard me from the top of the stairs.

"How do you know?" Morgana asked when she reached me.

"Sybilla and Natalia have both seen, Natalia will not leave the back window," I replied.

She raised an eyebrow. "Who?"

I could not help but sigh. "The Arab girl from the market and the skinwalker."

William was already gone and Morgana quickly raced after him, I took Vincenzo's arm and we walked to the kitchen together.

As soon as Natalia saw Charles she started talking, gesturing wildly to the windows. He tried to calm her in his broken Russian but had no success.

"Where is Osomov?" Gigi said angrily.

"I do not know," Charles said in between talking to Natalia.

"You don't know? The man's house is going to be sieged and he is nowhere to be found? That's awfully convenient," Gigi replied. "Perhaps he's why they would have the sense to attack us in the daylight."

"Gigi, please. They are clearly not stupid and have sensed us all along, they could have figured out we have a limited number of daywalkers all on their own," Vincenzo said.

"We did go to the market, Gigi," I added.

"I know that but there is no clear explanation of where he is and it all seems odd," Gigi replied.

"Can you sense him, Katrine?" Vincenzo asked. I closed my eyes and concentrated on Osomov, trying not to be frightened by the considerable amount of witches that were scattered throughout the forest.

Something strange scratched at the back of my neck and I picked up the vibration of him but it was somehow different.

"He's here. Well, he's out there but he somehow feels different," I said.

"He must have shifted," Vincenzo said, then he turned to Gigi. "Perhaps he sensed them and went out to defend his property."

Gigi stuck her tongue out at him, I was about to laugh when I caught William trying to go outside.

"What on earth are you doing?" I asked, grabbing his sleeve.

"Do not worry, my love. I will handle everything." he said politely.

"Have you lost your mind? Do you want me to tell you how many of them I can sense?" I tried to calm my voice and hide my panic.

He took my hand and smiled. "Please, Katrine. Will you trust me?"

I said nothing as I backed away from him, he told Vincenzo in Italian to keep everyone away from the windows then turned and walked outside.

Vincenzo took my arm and said, "Relax, mon ami. He can handle this on his own."

Gigi rolled her eyes. "He *is* William of Naples."

I watched in horror as my William walked out to the edge of the terrace, staring out into the forest. He called out something loudly and we could not hear it. I wondered if it was a warning. He stood with his hands at his sides and I saw his face moving as his mouth did, casting repeatedly. He began to float, his body rising slowly off the ground until he was in the air. I could see energy swirling around him like he was caught in a gust of wind.

Then the energy shot out like a cannon, knocking things off the walls and bending back some of the trees surrounding the terrace. A loud, strange thump made us drop to the floor from fear that the windows would explode but luckily they didn't. My ears were ringing, I went to try to speak to Vincenzo but could not hear my own voice. I clung to his arm and shook my head several times to try to release the sound.

Sybilla sat with her mouth hanging open, completely shocked, while Natalia continued to babble on to Charles and he desperately tried to calm her. I watched out the window as William stayed in the air, trying to prepare myself in case he did it again.

The ringing finally stopped and I pushed out my senses; the witches were still out there in the forest but there was a rising tension, something that felt like a mix between anger and fear.

"They're not leaving," I said to no one in particular, hearing the door quietly shut as Morgana crept outside.

"Either they are very powerful or William is losing his touch," Vincenzo said.

"He does that often?" I asked, gesturing outside.

"Only when he needs to show his strength. Consider it like a flexing of his magical muscles," Vincenzo replied.

"It usually sends people screaming for the hills," Gigi added.

I chuckled. "I am surprised it doesn't cause a head to explode."

Vincenzo sighed. "I am afraid he was being controlled because you are too close, my dear. Because I believe, without a doubt, he could if he really wanted to."

I shuddered at the thought. It was hard for me to imagine him in such a way.

Morgana appeared beside William, raising her hands to the sky. A low rumbling began, like the thump of a coming cavalry, and with a loud thunderclap a torrential downpour started over the forest. The wind picked up and the trees began to violently sway back and forth.

Then, as quickly as it had started, the rain turned into balls of ice the size of my fist.

A fireball rose out of the trees and came flying towards the house as if it had been launched by a catapult. It crashed into us in a mess of sparks and smoke but no damage, the smoke getting caught in the swirl of energy as William prepared to strike.

I plugged my ears, the shot rang out again, this time causing the windows to crack. I could hear the ice as it thumped on the ground, it reminded me of being in Csejthe and hearing the soldiers riding for my Grandmother's castle.

The forest had become a weapon itself, I was sure that the angry movements of the trees had done some kind of damage to whoever stood near them. The kitchen maids had begun to panic, either running away screaming or rushing to try to cover the splintering windows.

A strange heavy darkness fell over us, so thick I thought I might choke. Before it had time to set in it was pulled out through the cracks in the windows, forming into a large swirling ball that William shot out into the forest.

Natalia started to shake, tiny pieces of her skin began to split where feathers tried to push through but got stuck where fur through it would try to grow instead. She screamed in agony, Charles pulled her into his arms to try to comfort her but she angrily pushed him away.

"This has to end now!" I yelled, hoping William and Morgana heard.

Apparently they did because everything stopped for several minutes, then a giant fireball erupted and the forest burst into flames. It was the biggest fire I had ever seen, then it was gone, as if nothing had ever happened.

I lay on the floor with my hands over my ears, paralysed by shock and confusion. Natalia had stopped screaming and the world fell into an eerie dead silence.

I watched as William returned to the ground, that deep calm that I felt was suddenly overrun by a strange sense of panic and the need to run away.

"They're leaving," I said. "But I do not get the feeling that they are scared enough never to come back."

"We'll cross that bridge when we get to it," Vincenzo replied. He stood and began giving orders to what was left of the kitchen servants.

"Should we be concerned about the servants? What just happened was quite bizarre," I asked Gigi quietly.

"They would not work here if they could not be discreet, ma petite. Osomov knows that much," she replied. "And besides, no one would believe them anyway."

The door quietly opened and William and Morgana came in, I ran to try to help them both.

"I am fine, thank you," Morgana said as she shooed me away. William, on the other hand, leaned his full weight on me as I helped him into the sitting room.

We sat together on one of the small couches were William put his head in my lap and immediately fell asleep.

"Will he be alright?" I asked Vincenzo as he came in with the others and multiple servants carrying food.

"Yes, but it will take time for him to regain his strength. Power use is physically taxing," Vincenzo replied. "He will be vulnerable so we must do our best to protect him. Let us hope they do not attack again until he is healed."

I gently stroked William's close cropped hair; I would protect him until he was healed, as he had done and would do for me. I loved him so entirely that the gravity of what had just happened, the display of the power that coursed through this man's veins was unimportant.

We took tea and our meals in the sitting room, carried on our daily business while I sat with William. No one questioned me, no one raised an eyebrow or bat an eyelash at what could be perceived as my inappropriate behaviour. Gigi understood and stayed in the sitting room with me, she seemed almost relieved for the opportunity to relax.

And, with her staying in the room my tending to William did not seem improper.

He slept in a deep, heavy sleep until the sun set, finally stirring when the maids came to light the candles.

He looked up into my face, his blue eyes felt warm and happy.

"You're here?" he said quietly.

"Of course I am. Where else would I be?" I replied.

"I did not think she would allow you to stay with me," he said.

I smiled. "I think your preconceived notions of her are incorrect. And she is aware of how I feel about you."

"How do you feel about me, Katrine?" he asked.

I leaned over and whispered to him, "I love you with every fibre of my being, William. Something I must come to accept."

He took my tiny gloved hand and squeezed it tightly to his chest.

"And I love you, Katrine. I will do everything in my power to make sure you do not regret your feelings for me."

Katrine

STANDING GROUND

Another court function came up two days later, and despite my protests Gigi insisted we go, mostly to establish more of a connection with Xenya.

William rode with us to the palace, I insisted he remain where I could see him when he was awake, ignoring any reassurances from others who had seem him perform such feats of magic before and could tell me, most definitely, that he was just fine.

"Do you think the witches would attack us at the palace?" I asked as we rode.

"Maybe while travelling to and from, but not while inside. They could not risk such exposure, even though I am sure all Russians know something about the Lapps," William replied.

"And, petite, please do not spend the night worrying about an attack. After what happened, *if* they attack again, and I strongly use the world *if*, it would have to be quite major. Don't you agree, William?" Gigi said.

"Telling her the attack would have to be something major may not calm her, Grisela," William said to her.

Gigi sighed. "She understands what I mean, William. I mean, really."

"Of course. Now, just try to relax and enjoy the evening," William replied.

He helped me from the carriage when we arrived and we walked together into the main hall at a close pace behind Gigi.

She and I continued on while he separated from us to go speak to the men, walking the room as we did most nights we spent here, looking for an optimal place to stand.

"What do you suppose has become of Beatrix?" I asked Gigi. "It seems quite odd that she is here one day and gone the next."

"Good question," Gigi replied, drifting off as her mind began to wander.

Xenya appeared and fell into step with us, I stayed close but did not involve myself in the conversation.

Out of the corner of my eye I saw the first dark cloaked figure near a far corner as we walked past, when I turned back to check it was gone. But as we continued there was more, they were dark, shadow like spots that I only saw in the corner of my eye. I wondered if I was just worried and imagining things, until we stopped and I saw a figure coming towards us.

"We are no threat to you, Katrine," the female voice from Paris said behind me.

"What hold do you have on my cousin?" I snapped.

"That is not your concern," she said.

"And my mother? What do you know about my mother?" I asked, turning around and staring into the dark space under the hood. "What does Beatrix Delphine know of my mother?"

She paused, clearly considering how to respond. "Who?"

"Liar!" I said angrily, reaching out to grab her cloak but she stepped back. "Maybe, *just maybe*, I would consider trusting you if you thought enough of me to tell me the truth! What kind of people, especially those who are supposed to fight for the good in the world, won't tell a young woman the truth about what happened to her mother?"

"They shot her. Your friends shot her," she said, her voice lowering to an angry growl.

"She tried to kill us! And *she survived*! I know she did, why will you not tell me the truth?"

"Perhaps if you were more accepting of our help...."

"I cannot accept something I know nothing about, and the web of lies and secrets that is around you makes me very nervous," I said. "I am going to ask you now to stay out of my life unless I invite you in, regardless of what my cousin or anyone else would tell you. Is that clear or do I need to repeat myself?"

She paused, and I decided this was the time to really make a statement.

"You and your people need to leave. I will not tolerate this for another moment. You have already driven a wedge between Gabriel and I and that is the end of your involvement," I said. She chuckled, without a second thought I cast one of the spells William had taught me.

Two simple words, *permoveo mulier*, and she went flying back and hit the wall. I was surprised that no one seemed to notice, perhaps they had cast some sort of enchantment on the room.

I cast the power binding spell, just in case, and watched as the black figures seemed to fade into the walls. I went straight to Gigi, who was deep in conversation with Xenya.

"We should leave," I said quietly to her in French.

"Pourquoi?" she asked casually.

"The Order decided to pay me another visit, and I had to make it clear to them I wasn't interested so I used William's magic he taught me," I replied.

She sighed. "And you want to run? Tsk, tsk, ma petite. You must stand your ground. Show them you are not to be toyed with. Chasse."

"Are you sure that is wise?"

"I am. And I know for a fact it works," she said, flashing me a devilish smile before we continued on.

I did my best for the rest of the evening to act as if I was not afraid. To not seem like I was watching every corner, every shadow, every cloaked figure in the room, bracing for an attack.

But it never came, and by the end of the night I was feeling quite confident and was proud of how brave I'd acted. I told William what happened on the carriage ride back to the house.

"I saw nothing. I did not even sense magic in the room," he said.

"Could it be because you are still regaining your strength?" I asked.

He started straight at me, and said in a sharp and dismissive voice. "No."

"So what does that mean?"

"They have their own magic," he replied. "Very, very strong magic."

"But you stood your ground, ma petite. They will back off.. I am not sure about the situation with Gabriel, but that is not your problem," Gigi said.

"He is my cousin," I said.

"He is your Grandmother's cousin," she snapped. "Just because he shares some blood does not make him true family. Perhaps accepting him at face value is not a wise decision."

"It is what she would want," I replied.

"I understand that and I know how important the Countess is to you but if *he* is not respecting you or how you choose to live. One cannot be expected to constantly give to someone who only takes," Gigi said, and William nodded in agreement.

I sighed. "Perhaps I am too naive."

"No, il mio amore. You try to see the good in people, which is admirable in a world where most only see bad things," he said, gently patting my hand.

I fell into my bed completely exhausted, but before I drifted into sleep a vision began to overtake me.

I was frightened at first when the cold began to surround me and all I could sense was immense stone walls in the darkness.

Then I heard a voice, felt a presence as someone rose and went to light a candle.

"God is calling me home, my darling," my Grandmother's voice came strong from within the darkness, the light from the candle blanketed the room in a warm glow.

"Why would you say that?" I asked, crossing the room and sitting on the edge of her small bed. I was in her prison cell, the same room in the castle I had seen her in all those years ago.

"I can feel it in my bones, my time in this world is ending," she said, her eyes turned towards the floor. "How I wish I could stand in the sunshine one last time."

"Perhaps God will finally reunite you with my mother," I replied.

"Perhaps," she said. I could not remember what I had told her, and it did not matter. She knew something had happened.

"I feared I would be leaving you alone, but I am not am I? You have my darling Gabor, and Mademoiselle Delphine shall take fantastic care of you," she continued. "Unfortunately there is very little I can give you once I am gone, the fight for my things is something I do not wish you involved in, but do not think I have forgotten you. If there is something you shall have it."

"There is nothing I need. Your presence in my life is more than enough," I said.

"You are always refreshing, my dear. My shining star in a world of greedy, soulless vultures. I hope you can live free of such tortures."

My eyes began to tear up. "I have so many questions, so many things I want to know...."

She ran her thumb along my jawline, her skin was dry and cracked with fingernails that looked chewed down almost to nothing.

"Gabor knows it all. He can tell you everything about the Bathory, and I sincerely hope he has some kind words for me after all this time," she replied. I felt her look at me as I looked away. "What is it? What's wrong? What has he done?"

"I can't....I do not trust him. He did not tell me about the Order of....," I began.

"Katrine, the Order of the Dragon is part of the Bathory lineage. Why are you so concerned about them? They are warriors of the church and nothing more. Their sole purpose is to fight the Turks, what could they possibly want with you?"

I sighed. "It is unnecessarily complicated, Grandmother. Please don't trouble yourself. I do not know when I will see you again."

Our eyes met, the sparkle she once had was gone and her eyes hung heavy with tears, surrounded by darkness where they had begun to sink back into her head.

"You are well? And how are your studies coming?" Grandmother asked, her face brightening up a tiny bit.

"I am, we've been travelling. We did not have much time so Gabor and I plan to return to Poland one day to learn about King Istvan," I said. "We have been at the Russian court for some time now, and I've met a lovely girl named Sybilla who says she's a Turkish Princess and a girl who can shift into different forms....do you know koźe choditko?"

"Really?" she exclaimed. "How fantastic! Oh, how I wish I could join you."

"We could still come get you, we're not far away. You could see the sun again," I replied.

She cradled my cheek in her hand and said, "I so wish I could. But if I was to disappear the King would steal all I have and my poor son would have nothing. He is only 14 years old. And it is already bad enough that....that *man* is his guardian."

"So this is it? You will just die alone in this cold stone room with no light?" I asked. She pointed at a small hole in the stones, not even big enough for a fist. I glanced around the room, except for the writing on the walls all I could see was stones.

"If I stand on a chair I can see clouds through the hole," she said softly.

"Do you ever get visitors?" I asked.

"Kata has come, on occasion. She was closest to me, this has been hard on her. I have tried my best to ensure she inherits what I give in her own right," she began. "My oldest, Anna, I think she is disgusted by what has happened. I do not believe she will ever speak of me once I am gone. I did the very best I could, but for reasons I am unsure of it was not enough. Nothing was ever enough. First my brother, then my husband. Then the nobility turn against me along with my children. But Anna....we never bonded and were never close. She was very attached to Jo Ilona, perhaps she will mourn for her. I am not sure anyone else still on this earth will, and the poor woman deserves that much. She was good to my children."

She lowered her eyes, staring down at her tattered skirt, the smell of the place finally hit me. A woman of such power, grace, and beauty who had truly been reduced to living in filth.

I supposed those horrible men who had done this to the Countess were proud and happy, but I knew they would answer for what they had done in the end, when the time came for them to explain themselves.

"I wish I could do something for you, Grandmother. I hate that you have suffered so," I said, my voice stronger than I felt.

"God will reward me, my dear. I am quite sure of it. Why else would I have suffered so? It must be part of some divine plan," she replied. "You want to know what you can do for me. Katrine? Think of me, pray for me, keep my memory alive for I fear all thought of me will be lost if you do not. Wear the Bathory name with pride, and regardless of whether you trust Gabor or not, listen to the tales he tells you of the family so you can repeat them when the time comes. You may still have questions, I am sure they will be answered someday. And love, my darling, love with a force beyond all measure and do not settle for any less that someone who feels the same for you."

"I will, I swear to you."

"Also, be good to those who have taken you in for you are lucky to have such an opportunity. Mademoiselle Delphine is a fantastic woman and you can learn a lot from her. But above all things, do not compromise your integrity because that is truly all we have as women," she said, a tear fell off her face and on to her skirt. "Your mother and I are always with you, don't ever forget that."

I took her hands and kissed her chapped, dry skin repeatedly, trying to remember every finger, every inch of her hands so I could commit her to memory, moving down her arms to her body and her perfect face that watched me with such joy.

"I will miss you always," I said to her face. Within an instant she was gone and I was alone in my room.

I got out of bed, pulling on a dressing gown and heading downstairs.

I found Hannah awake in the kitchen, she was startled when I came behind where she sat and touched her arm.

"Are you alright, Katrine? What do you need?" she asked.

"Could you find me some paper and something to draw with?" I said, stopping her as she stood to move. "Not now, tomorrow is fine. Try to get some sleep."

"What on earth do you need that for?"

I turned and headed back upstairs, calling back to her, "I just have something on my mind."

KATRINE

UNANNOUNCED

Later that night I was woken by loud, horrible screams. I fell out of bed and frantically fumbled to my feet, running out into the hallway as the terror filled screams continued.

Tolone ran past me as I opened the door, the panicked commotion confused me even more. I pushed my way past the scrambling, petrified servants and found Morgana pushed up against the wall outside Gigi's door.

"Something is attacking us," Morgana said flatly. "And it is not those witches, I am sure of it. It is some kind of monster."

I heard Tolone yelling for help from inside Vincenzo's room. I went to run but Morgana grabbed my arm.

"We need to be with Gigi," Morgana demanded. She kept one hand on me and used the other to bang on Gigi's door.

"But what about the others?" I asked.

"The men can defend themselves, now come on," she replied, banging again on the door till Gigi quickly pulled us inside.

"What on earth is happening?" Gigi asked as Morgana and I leaned our backs against the door to keep it closed.

"Something is attacking," Morgana said. "Use your senses, Katrine. See if you can figure this out."

I nodded and let my senses go, trying to see how far outside the house I could manage.

"Dead," I said, and I gasped. "My God, so many dead servants I cannot even count. Vincenzo is hurt, but alive, So is Charles, and....no, no! I have to go to William!"

"You cannot!" Gigi exclaimed.

"But he is hurt and alone....," I began.

"We need to know what's doing this, Katrine! Focus!" Morgana hollered. I began to breathe heavily and tried my best not to cry.

A feeling washed over me, and the word "Vampire" fell out of my mouth without any thought. A strange feeling crept up my spine when I focused on this creature, a feeling that I did not quite understand. It only left more questions at a time I could not think about them.

"One or many?" Morgana asked, grabbing my arm and shaking me. "Katrine! One or many?"

"One. One, there is only one," I said.

Morgana turned to Gigi. "Is that even possible?"

"Unfortunately, it is," Gigi replied.

"It's coming towards us," I said, my breath caught in my throat as that thing got closer.

Something hit the door with a bang, shoving us back only slightly as it tried to open the door. But we quickly regained our footing and leaned our body weight against the wood, fighting to try to keep the door shut.

With a loud crack that resembled thunder the wood door split down the middle, knocking us both to the ground.

A large, black hooded figure loomed over us as it pushed its way through the doorway, stepping over us like stones on a path. Gigi started screaming and it was as if something in my mind split, I jumped on the attacker's back as it advanced on Gigi. I tried to pull the hood of the cloak back but it would not move, I clawed inside where the face should be, trying to find its eyes.

It grabbed my nightshirt and flung me at the wall. I was convinced by the way the pain shot up through my entire body that I had, in fact, gone through to the next room but when I looked up Gigi was close as she tried to throw the figure aside to get to me.

I attempted to stand but the pain got worse, so I did the only thing I could think of which was scream and cast the movement spells William had taught me to try to push the thing away.

But nothing seemed to work and as it kept coming I got more and more frightened when nothing seemed to work.

Morgana rose in front of Gigi and an energy bolt shot from her outstretched hands. The thing flew back and out the door, Morgana stalked after it continually shooting bolts of energy that looked like small snaps of lightening.

Gigi ran to my side and pulled me to my feet. "You're alright. Please be alright."

She continued to mumble, I wasn't sure if she was reassuring me or herself, as we stepped out into the hallway.

Morgana and a wolf bounded down the stairs after the thing, I could sense another wolf waiting downstairs for them to help drive it out.

Gigi half carried me down the hallway towards Vincenzo's room, several servants bodies lay discarded on the floor. Tolone had stopped yelling, the door was open only a crack as we pushed our way in.

Vincenzo's eyes turned towards us from where he lay on the floor being held in a seated position by his man servant. There was blood everywhere.

"I am alright, go check on the others. Go! Now!" He insisted.

Next we went to Charles's room, which was empty. There were no obvious signs of a struggle with the exception of several splashes of blood.

"He must have shifted. He would heal faster in wolf form," Gigi said as we moved on. I stopped in front of William's door and became overwhelmed by fear. I had not seen inside his room since we arrived in Russia, as we stepped in the doorway I immediately began to cry.

I let go of Gigi as I stepped into the room from my vision, running to his bloody body where it lay on the floor beside the bed. He gasped for air as I sat down beside him and pulled his body into my arms. I called for Gigi to go get help.

"Please don't die," I began to repeat over and over again as I watched his blood soak into my nightshirt, causing it to stick to my skin. He shook his head at me in protest, letting me know he had no plans on dying.

He clung tightly to me as I felt his energy surge, causing his body to vibrate. This continued on for some time then eased off until it was gone, and he breathed steadier. The blood seemed to slow and he looked as if he was improving.

I checked him for bite marks before asking, "Did it bite you?"

"No, not for lack of trying," he said, his voice a whisper. "Are you hurt?"

"A little, but I fear the wall I landed on is not going to survive," I replied, he winced in pain when he tried to laugh.

"It was a vampire, but it wasn't at the same time. It was some sort of monster," William stated plainly, his voice becoming clearer.

"Yes, I believe so," I said, sincerely hoping I had no clue who or what it really was.

The language barrier became irrelevant as Aseem went to work, doing his best to tend to the injured. He was completely in his element, a truly gifted doctor, but even someone so skilled cannot perform miracles.

Eight servants died, most were ones we had brought from Paris. Hannah, who suffered a broken arm, believed our people had tried to fight because they were trained to deal with such occurrences. They were brave and would be remembered as such, Charles had said, and he would pay to have the bodies transported back to Paris.

He had been injured but was recovering well because he had shifted so soon afterwards. Vincenzo had several broken bones, William had flesh wounds and my ribs were badly bruised. Victorie, who had apparently been on the front lines when the attacker tried to go into the basement, was badly hurt and still unconscious. Mathilde was one of the wolves who had helped drive the thing from the house, all the others had come out unscathed.

And they had all come to a consensus as to why.

"Whatever it was, it wanted upstairs," Mathilde said.

"It tossed most of us out of the way," Vincenzo said.

"It only tried to rip apart one room to get to one of us," Morgana said. "It only split apart one door."

"But it threw Katrine aside like a rag," Gigi said. I put my hand on her knee, we were sitting together on a small couch in the sitting from where those who were able gathered.

"It threw me aside to get to you, Gigi. Whatever it was, it was looking for you," I said softly.

"Do you all agree?" she asked the room. Most reluctantly nodded, Mathilde was the only one to openly proclaim her agreement.

"Does anyone believe they know who or what may have done this?" I asked, staring directly at Gabriel where he sat across the room. He blinked, his eyes showing recognition to what I meant.

"No," he proclaimed, and I actually believed him.

"Could someone be looking for the skinwalker? And be very angry that we have her?" Mathilde asked no one in particular.

"That does not explain their interest in Gigi," Morgana said. I watched Gigi's face as she thought, and allowed the thought I was also having into her mind.

"Could she?" I asked her quietly.

"Not could she, petite. *Would* she," Gigi replied. "It is a bit excessive, but it is a possibility. How she could have concocted such a monster is beyond me."

"So what do we do now?" I asked.

"We start asking questions," Nikoli Osomov said, appearing quite suddenly from a far corner of the room.

"Where were you?" Gigi asked.

He chuckled. "I meant of your new contacts, but just to ease your mind Mademoiselle, I tried to catch it as it climbed the staircase and was tossed down after it. Hence the broken arm and injured shoulder."

He stood so we could see his bandaged body well, then sat back down.

"Should we send a letter or go directly to them?" Gigi asked, going to stand but I pulled her back down.

"You will go nowhere without proper protection," I said sharply.

She laughed. "And who do you suppose shall do that, when the thing tossed most of you aside like rags? There is an impression in the wall from where your body hit it, ma petite, I will not allow you to be in such danger again if it can be avoided."

"You have little choice in the matter, Mademoiselle. Katrine and I will travel with you at all times," Morgana said. "William will need time to heal, which makes me the only substantial spellcaster in the house."

"I tried, but it did nothing," I told Morgana.

"Exactly my point," Morgana replied.

"So you two better prepare because I am going to find Xenya," Gigi said, standing again and pacing. I pulled the dressing gown Hannah had found me around my blood stained nightshirt.

"I will not be as quick as you would like," I told her.

"Why?" she asked.

"To be quite blunt, I am only wearing a blood stained nightshirt under my dressing gown and I refuse to leave until I bathe. It will take time for us to be properly dressed, and considering Hannah must now care of us both...," I began.

"Fine, I understand. But in the morning we shall go," Gigi said. "And I want Morgana and I moved into your room immediately."

I nodded to Hannah, who left the room to begin making arrangements. Things would be complicated but we would make due. I did not question Gigi's decision, I knew she was frightened.

Things were put together quickly so we could all try to sleep. I checked on William, who was sleeping soundly in his bed. One of the few people we had left was cleaning his room, she reassured me she would keep a close eye on him and alert me if anything changed, as well as making sure Aseem checked on him regularly.

I watched Tolone help Vincenzo into bed then make himself a space close to the end. I was worried for my friend, I had been so wrapped up in William I did not know the extent of his injuries. I knew enough to know that if Tolone was in bed with him it was serious to the point that he needed to be watched and I thanked God that his manservant had not been hurt.

Hannah and I were silent as she washed me and helped me change. It would take too long to fill a full bath so she just cleaned me up and put me in a clean nightshirt, which felt warm and comforting against my skin.

Morgana and Gigi appeared to be sleeping when I finally got back into the room. I quietly crawled into my bed and pulled the blankets up to my chin, breathing deeply to try to calm my body enough so I could sleep.

As the quiet began to surround me and I started to drift to sleep, I heard someone stirring. My bed sank down as the person crawled in, a soft hint of lavender and rose passed over me as Gigi got comfortable. I curled my body around her and squeezed myself up to her back. I thought I heard her crying, her body moving up and down as she quietly sobbed.

I so badly wanted to comfort her but I knew there was nothing I could do or say that would make it better so I just lay with her, holding her tightly to me as we both fell asleep.

Anastasia

GUIDANCE

They walked for many days, Knute would only allow them to stop for a short period of time and he never slept. Anastasia even began to wonder when the last time the boy sat down was, he was constantly on alert and watching.

The twins remained in wolf form and as close to Anastasia as they could. They were quiet and kept to themselves. Soon Anastasia could even tell the difference between Astrid, whose fur was more golden in colour and Amalie, who stayed as close to Anastasia's heels as she could without climbing up on her leg.

They wanted to be carried but after a few days strapped to her front her back was aching so she insisted they walk.

As they approached the mountains the weather grew colder, especially at night. They all needed a decent sleep in a warm place but Knute was determined and could not be swayed.

Finally after a fortnight Knute stopped at the entrance to a cave that was well hidden by some trees and fragrant flower bushes. It was at the very base of a mountain.

"Here," Knute told his mother.

"He says we will be safe here."

Iren nodded and she, Gisli and Anatasia headed inside. When they stepped in the cave opened up, and running water could be heard in the distance. It was not warm but not cold either.

"It is not what I expected," Gisli said. "Why would Father tell him to come here?"

Anastasia could not help but wonder if the boy was actually speaking to Gavril's ghost, and why no one seemed to question him.

"Well protected. Easily defended. Almost as good as a castle," Iren replied, she walked further into the cave while Gisli helped the others come inside.

Quickly the others began setting up beds, lighting a fire and Knute gathered a few together to go hunt for some food.

Astrid and Amalie set off by themselves. Anastasia followed and sat down beside them.

"You heard what Knute said, girls. You are safe now. I will protect you, you both should know that," she began. "You can change now."

Astrid just stared at her, Amalie kept her eyes lowered.

"You cannot spend the rest of your days as wolves. I thought for a time that I wanted to do the same. But it will not save you from the pain, or take away the memories."

Amalie's fur was the first that started to ripple, she changed quickly and pulled herself into Anastasia's lap, soon her small body began to shudder as she quietly cried. Astrid came over and licked the tears from her sisters cheeks, but made no move to change herself.

"One day I will tell you what happened to me, how I came to this life. I have not suffered in the same manner you have, but I have suffered in my own right," Anastasia began. "And while you may have lost so much you are not alone. I promise you both that I will take care of you as best I can. That is how I will honour your mother's memory. I believe you must mourn but I will not allow you to stop living, do you understand me?"

Amalie nodded, Astrid looked at her sharply before laying down beside them.

"Do you think they were in a lot of pain, Ana...stasia?" a tiny voice asked, and Anastasia realised she had never heard Amalie's voice.

"No," Anastasia replied without thinking. "No, Amalie. I don't."

Gisli came over to them, leaning down and saying. "There is a bed for you, if you wish, girls."

Anastasia nodded, picking up Amalie and taking the girls over to the small sleeping area Gisli directed them to. Once the girls were down and comfortable Anastasia went to the fire.

She tried her best to warm the cold that felt as if it was radiating out of her bones. The massacre played over and over again in her mind and she wondered how she got so lucky. Why did she get to live when so many others did not? And Lynde, so strong and brave, such a proud woman and mother. *So much better than me,* Anastasia thought. *I would trade my life for hers, purely because of those two little girls.*

"What about us, Mother?" Katrine's voice rung through her head like a sharp bell. "What about your children? You would leave us behind so easily?"

"I am no good to you now," she answered in her mind. "I am not sure I ever was."

Katrine laughed, a sinister angry laugh. "You blame yourself for something you could not control! Your blood did this to us! If anyone is to blame it is the Countess and the man who fathered you! Who was that man?"

Anastasia massaged her forehead, a headache coming on quickly. Katrine's voice repeating the taunt, "Who was that man", only making it progressively worse.

She left the fire and went to lay with the girls, who were sleeping soundly, wolf curled together with little girl. As soon as she put her head down she quickly fell asleep, thoughts of her father swimming around in her mind.

She should have asked about him.

Katrine

CHARLES'S PROMISE

"No one has claimed responsibility for the attack on your people," Xenya began. "But we have some ideas. As I'm sure it is in Paris, when such things happen it can be quite obvious as to whom it is. I will gladly tell you what we suspect but I do not wish to upset you or ruin our new friendship."

Gigi sighed loudly. "Your cautious behaviour only confirms my own suspicions."

"So you believe Beatrix Tornovitch could be responsible?" Xenya asked. "Because I hate to admit it but we also do. She is involved in some dark and terrible things that I do not have proper words for. But I am sure you know of this, she is your sister. We are embarrassed such a thing could happen, we hope you do not judge the Russian people harshly."

"Xenya, you have no need to worry. I would not judge because of the actions of one, who is only married to a Russian. I hope you will not judge me because of my sister's actions," Gigi replied.

Xenya smiled. "Of course not. I had sister who was also mad, but she did not live long."

"What do you advise we do?" Gigi asked. Xenya's eyes drifted as she gathered her thoughts.

"You are a guest in our country, we would be honoured if you would allow us to deal with the matter," she said. I stayed silent as I walked behind the two women, my eyes constantly searching the great hall for any signs of Beatrix.

"That seems appropriate, and we are also not equipped to do anything in regards to dealing with the situation," Gigi said. "Do you agree, Katrine?"

"Yes, of course. Because even when we leave she will still be here," I replied.

"And we welcome your involvement, of course. So I must ask, when do you plan to return to Paris?" Xenya asked.

"I do not know, but the sooner the better. Not that we are not enjoying Russia, I am sure you understand our discomfort," Gigi said.

Xenya laughed. "Only thing I do not understand is why you did not leave immediately. I would have! The comforts of home are unquestionable."

"I agree, Xenya. But it is unfortunately not my decision to make, and it would be unwise for Katrine and I to travel alone so I have very little options," Gigi replied.

"Yes, it is unfortunate we must be so reliant on men. The world would be a much different place if the tables were turned, don't you agree?"

"I sincerely hope we shall see that world one day, my friend. It would be an amazing thing," Gigi replied dreamily, the two women fell silent as they thought of their shared dream.

Then, out of the corner of my eye I saw the back of a red dress, shimmering light hair pulled up off her face, which I only glimpsed in profile.

Beatrix was deep in conversation with Gabriel, they walked the room trying to keep out of our eye line. At first I was in shock that she was even here, then I immediately switched to feeling angry and protective. I desperately tried to separate my thoughts from Gabriel and this ultimate act of betrayal, choking on my rage.

"Katrine? Katrine, are you listening to me?" Gigi said sharply, following my eye line. "Xenya, I apologise, but I think it is time for us to leave."

Xenya caught on quickly then began to usher us out of the hall. I caught William's attention and signalled him to follow us as Xenya rushed us outside.

"Please don't be overly concerned, Grisela. We will do what we can to deal with this situation," Xenya said.

"Thank you," Gigi replied, stepping in the open door of our carriage. William stood behind Xenya awaiting an explanation.

"Beatrix is in the hall," I said quickly, "speaking with Gabriel. Please quietly let the others know we have left. Xenya and her people are dealing with the situation."

He nodded and helped me into the carriage, turning his head when he heard someone calling.

"You forgot Morgana," he said.

Before I could reply she pushed him out of the way and climbed into the carriage.

"Where on earth have you been?" Gigi snapped at her as the door closed and we started moving.

"Keeping an eye on her. Next time you two plan on leaving quickly please send me a signal somehow," Morgana replied. "She was talking to Gabriel. I am sorry Katrine."

"Don't be. He is a man and can take care of himself, my obligations are to Gigi," I said angrily. "If he cares more about the Order of the Dragon than living a somewhat normal existence, that is his problem, not mine."

Gigi placed a hand on my knee, patting it gently. "Do not worry, ma petite. His behaviour will not be overlooked."

"Could he have been involved?" I asked.

"Heaven's no!" Gigi replied, giggling. "I am sure my sister acted alone, and the Order would not approve of such frenzied behaviour. If they wanted you dead it would be clean, quiet and neat and no one would ever suspect them, a practice that can be respected. They do nothing without great thought and calculation, and what happened to us was fuelled on anger and the need for complete destruction. The objective was my death and crushing anything that stood in its path."

"So what should I do about Gabriel?" I asked.

Gigi smiled. "Do not worry, and allow the men to deal with the situation. Charles is not *completely* useless."

We enjoyed the silence of the house and took our time alone as an opportunity to catch up on our reading. It was like the calm before the storm, knowing what was coming when the others arrived home.

The three of us were in the sitting room, taking a break while Hannah served us tea when the other servants began to rush to the front door, signalling an arrival.

With a loud crash the doors flung open and Mathilde came storming in, cursing loudly as she flew past the doorway in a flash of pale purple and headed straight for the basement. William and Charles came in shortly after, pulling Gabriel behind them by a rope that tied his hands together. Vincenzo followed slowly behind them.

They shoved Gabriel into a chair, I quietly closed my book and put it in my lap as if I was quite undisturbed.

"We thought you may wish to speak to him before he is imprisoned," Charles said coldly.

"About what?" I asked Charles.

"Katrine, please....," Gabriel began.

"Don't you dare," I said angrily. "I told you your allegiance to the Order would get you in trouble and you would not listen! And you lied to me!"

"Katrine, I...."

"*She* tried to kill us, Gabor. *Last night.* What were you thinking?"

"She's dead, Katrine."

I paused, rethinking what I was going to say before replying, "Do not change the subject."

"Katrine, listen to me. I had sent them away, told them they were destroying my happiness. They wanted me to give you a letter and Beatrix was the only person who could get close enough. I put them out of my life, but they wanted you to hear it from someone who cares for you because they knew you would not believe them. She's dead, Katrine. Erzsebet is...."

"*No!*" I screamed, throwing my book at him. I began to pace the room, picking up anything I could and throwing it at him, yelling obscenities in every language I knew.

"Katrine, they gave me a letter they intercepted from a priest in Csejthe to the King. She died on the 21st day on this month," he continued, and my world began to spin. I had no idea what the specific day was, how long ago the 21st was or how any of it correlated.

But it could have only been a day or less if my vision meant anything.

"I have the letter, it's in my pocket," he said, motioning towards William with his neck. I nodded and William reached into Gabriel's pocket, pulling a neatly folded letter out with a broken seal.

My vision went blurry as my eyes filled with tears. William handed me the letter, all I could do was stare.

"I wish to return to Paris," I said with as much force as I could muster.

"Katrine, it's not that simple," Charles replied.

"Then make it, Charles! I am sad and I am scared and I want to go home! Why can't we just go home?" I started to sob. "I just want to go home. Please take me home!"

William grabbed me as I fell to the floor, sobbing. I tried to speak but the words just would not come.

"Charles, stop doddling and make the arrangements. We must leave by the end of the week and I will not take no for an answer," Gigi said. "William, please help me take Katrine upstairs."

"I won't go until he swears we are going home," I said angrily.

Charles sighed. "Alright! Alright! By the end of the week we are going home. Please don't worry, Katrine. And Gabriel, you'll be imprisoned until we can decide what to do with you, if Mathilde doesn't kill you first."

With his agreement I allowed my emotions to overwhelm me, I moaned in agony as I cried, William scooped me up into his arms and took me upstairs.

He carefully laid me on my bed, I used my free hand to grab his sleeve before he stood. He sat back down, pulling my head onto his lap and stroking my hair as I sobbed.

The letter remained in my hand, clutched tightly between my fingers, the weight of its contents much heavier than the paper it was written on. I could not bear the thought of even reading it; I had seen her only days ago in my mind, the vision so fresh it was as if I had been with her in person. The idea that I would never see her again made my chest ache.

I had planned on trying to draw her before we were attacked, and when I had a chance I would do so in an attempt to preserve her as I saw her. The closest I had ever come to drawing was making embroidery patterns, people would be a challenge.

At some point I fell asleep, when I opened my eyes again the room was completely silent. William was breathing slowly and rhythmically, I had never known someone who slept so soundly and peacefully.

He stirred as I sat up, examining my face before smiling at me.

"It is alarmingly quiet," I said, standing and smoothing my skirts. I folded the letter in half and stuck it in my sleeve.

"We could stay here, wait for someone to come check on us," he replied.

I sighed. "As much as I would like that it is part of my concern. Gigi would not just let us be, especially now."

He followed behind me as I headed back down to the sitting room, others were around but the house was very quiet.

Gigi sat by a window, staring out into the green while a few of the men chatted on the other side of the room, Morgana stood uneasily on the edge and rushed to me when I stepped through the doorway.

"A message came for her and she has not spoken since. Vincenzo thinks it was from her sister," Morgana said.

"She did not show anyone?" I asked.

"No. She read it, sat down, and nothing," she replied. "We tried to speak to her but she would not acknowledge us."

I pulled at chair over and sat down beside Gigi, joining her examining the blowing trees. The sky was turning an ugly gray, it would rain hard tonight.

Gigi dropped a letter in my lap and I examined the broken seal, an elaborate B D cypher with what appeared to be a dragon.

Written inside in perfect French, with very elegant handwriting, was:

'For now we see through a glass darkly, but then face to face; now I know in part, but then shall I know even as also I am known.'

I had no idea what it meant but by the look on Gigi's face I knew that she did.

"What is this? I do not understand," I said. "It's not even signed. You have to explain this to me, Gigi, because I do not understand."

She turned her blue eyes to me, they were dark and clouded with something sinister, a hint of something truly frightening buried deep inside her soul.

"It's a threat, ma petite. A threat in a bible verse, as only a Delphine would put it," Gigi said flatly, as if receiving such a letter was a common daily occurrence.

"So what should we do?" I asked

Her eyes moved back to the window, a strange smile grew on her face that sent shivers down my spine.

"*She* should be afraid, for I am not to be trifled with," she said angrily. "She seems to have forgotten that I am my mother's daughter."

Katrine

TRUE TALENT

Charles remained true to his word and the next morning we began preparations to return to Paris.

It was like a strange sigh of relief among what was left of our group; the dead had gone on ahead of us for a variety of reasons, mostly because it was impractical to have coffins lying about. Extra space was needed for our three new additions, shifting around so the doctor could ride with the badly injured was an absolute necessity. Victorie was not doing well and needed supervision, which bothered Gigi immensely.

The skinwalker was proving to be quite agreeable and easy to deal with, all she wanted was to be with Charles and he was more than willing to accommodate.

Many things went on in the early days of preparing, but Gigi and I kept it to ourselves. She spent much time pouring over 'The Prince', and when I was not studying I began to try to draw my Grandmother from memory.

Vincenzo found me early one morning in the sitting room facing a window, I felt him watching over my shoulder before he said a word.

Hannah had found me something akin to black chalk that I was using to sketch on a sheet of velum, it had taken several tries to get accustomed to it but now I was beginning to enjoy myself.

"Is that her?" Vincenzo finally asked. "Is that the Countess?"

I stopped and looked at the image, from when I had first seen her. "Yes, but I fear I am not doing her justice."

"No, no, mon ami. It is quite wonderful. You have a true talent," he said.

"I did not want to forget...," I began, choking back tears. "How is Gabriel fairing?"

He chuckled. "Mathilde has not killed him, if that is what you are wondering."

"Well, there is still time for that. Perhaps it would be better for him if he actually died."

"Katrine, you do not mean that."

"I know," I said, sighing. "I am angry, how could I not be?"

"And you have every right to be. Let's hope his captivity has caused him to rethink his position," he replied, turning to walk away.

"Vincenzo, can I ask you something?"

"Of course. Anything."

"Should I be concerned? About this business with Beatrix?"

He laughed this time as if I was a child who'd asked a ridiculous question. "No, not deeply. Please trust me when I say that our Gigi is much more frightening, given the opportunity. She is not so obvious about it, but she is ruthless, and slightly unhinged like you could not imagine."

I sighed again. "That is what I thought, I just needed some reassurance. Thank you, mon ami."

"Glad to be of service," he replied. "Now, we are to have our formal goodbye at court tonight and Gigi has sent me to fetch you, for the process of dressing will be time consuming with so few capable hands."

I rolled up my drawing and put the art supplies away in the small case Hannah had found me.

"Sometimes I wonder if life would be easier if I were a boy," I said, taking the arm he held out to me.

"No, my dear. It would not be."

Even though I had not spoken of it, and the letter Gabriel had given me remained tucked into my sleeve, I insisted on wearing white out of respect for my Grandmother.

"Could I skip tonight's outing?" I asked Gigi.

"What happened to travelling with me at all times?" she answered.

My eyes lowered. "We could both stay behind. There is no harm in that."

"I will not *skip* our final appearance at the Russian court, petite," Gigi snapped. I felt her watching me as Hannah dressed my hair simply.

"I thought you were done with being in mourning," Gigi said sadly. I knew how annoyed she was with my insistence on returning back to my white dresses. Not that they weren't grand, trimmed with silver thread and white French lace at the sleeves and neckline.

"Perhaps I should adopt white as my signature colour," I replied.

She snorted. "At least you have not lost your.spark. I was told you have been drawing."

"Yes, it is quite difficult."

"May I see?" she asked. I handed her the rolled up paper without thinking to deeply or I would become nervous. I tried to seem as if I was not paying attention as she unrolled the sheet, her eyes teared up as she stared at the image.

"She is as beautiful as I remember, and it has been years since I last saw her," Gigi said quietly.

I blinked back my own tears and said, "I did not want to forget what she looks like."

She rolled the paper up and handed it back to me, shaking her head and smiling.

"Perhaps I should wear white for her also?" Gigi asked, looking at her blue dress in confusion.

"Not tonight. I would not want us to match," I replied. "If you insist we should go, it would be best not to have someone question whether we are wearing the same thing."

Morgana came in our shared room, dressed in a simple black gown with the hair pulled back from her face. She was quite striking in the dark colour.

"In Scotland when there is death we wear black," Morgana said after several minutes of us staring at her. "As I am sure they do in your and your grandmother's homeland, Katrine."

"Every country has different customs, Morgana. In my opinion, we are travellers and can wear whatever colours we wish. If you wanted to wear yellow, which is the mourning colour of Spain, you could," Gigi replied.

"I have white mourning clothes, I thought they were appropriate for Roza and they seemed appropriate in this case. Especially since we shall be returning to Paris soon," I said, trying to keep my voice steady. I had forgotten about Roza.

"Charles has said we shall not have as many stops, or stay in one place for an extended time period on the trip home," I continued. "So perhaps it will not take months and we may be back before it really begins to snow."

"I should hope we are because we are in no way equipped for winter travel," Gigi said sharply. She stood and left the room, Morgana and I followed closely at her heels.

The evening at court was much like every other evening at court. I wondered, as we stood by the wall watching the people, if it was like this in every country because it was not exciting at all.

Xenya came and stood with us, Morgana and I silently watched the room for Beatrix while Gigi spoke at great length with our Russian friend.

The rest of the group was circulating throughout the room, the Tsar had not arrived yet and Xenya had agreed to say our official goodbye regardless of what Osomov tried to do. All I was concerned about was keeping safe until we could leave.

The Tsar came in and the room dropped to the floor like falling stones, I was happy this would be the last time I'd hear his shuffled walk across a room, the last time his gaze would frighten me.

I enjoyed many things about Russia, I wish I'd been able to see more of the country.

Xenya stepped forward and spoke boisterously in Russian; whatever she was saying sounded fantastic to me and I was quite excited when she called us into the room.

He actually smiled at us as we bowed before him, letting out a string of what I assumed were compliments that was followed by a thunderous applause. Xenya escorted us away, coming over to me as we went back to the wall.

"I have told Grisela, and I wanted you to know I will be sending some embroidered fabric to Paris, for you both," she said quietly to me. "I am looking forward to the French lace Grisela is sending me."

"Wonderful!" I exclaimed. "It was such a pleasure to meet you, and I sincerely hope you can come to Paris to visit one day."

"That would be lovely. And, please do not worry. The attack on your people will not go unpunished," she replied. We bowed casually to each other, she returned to her conversation with Gigi and I back to my post along the wall.

"This will get worse before it gets better," Morgana said quietly.

"What have you seen?" I asked.

"Do not worry, I know what is coming and I am prepared. I will let you know when it is about to happen. In case I'm wrong."

"Can you give me a clue?"

"You honestly did not believe she would just let us leave, did you?" she asked.

I stared at her, quite stunned.

She rolled her eyes. "I said I am prepared. You have to trust me."

"Will more die?"

She looked at me now, examining my face as if it were a map.

"Not that I saw, I swear," she replied.

I sighed, swallowing hard. "So we wait."

"Yes, all we can do is wait."

Klara

OBEY

As they days continued on Klara's swarm of paramours grew larger, lucky for them they fattened the innkeeper's pockets enough that he did not complain.

Amelia de Loncrey watched from the shadows, her anger bubbling like a pot of boiling water. There was a rumour that Klara was in league with a demon, they had been seen walking the streets together. Amelia thought it was wise to tread carefully; if Klara or her guard were really a demon's spawn it would make an already difficult situation all the more complicated.

But it could not continue on this way. She either had to drive Klara Von Dores out of Genoa as quickly as possible, or remove her from this world.

Klara sat in the room she shared with Olivia and prepared for the night, as she had done so many times since that first night. Her first man in Genoa with the pretty green eyes sat obediently massaging her feet, his eyes glazed over as if he were lost in thought.

"Will you finally come with me tonight, Olivia?" Klara asked the same question she did every night, without turning to look at her.

"If you have any sense in your stupid head you would not go either," a voice said from the window. The two women were shocked to find Amelia de Loncrey sitting in their windowsill.

Amelia turned to Olivia and said, "You are a terrible guard," then continued on to them both. "I asked you to do one very small thing while you were in Genoa. One! And you deliberately do the opposite, and much worse create an army of slaves! Do you have anything to say for your behaviour?"

"What to say?" Klara mused. "Hmmm...well. What can I say? I will do as I please, and if you are wise you will get out of my way!"

Amelia stared at her in shock. She tried to calculate how quickly she could slit ones throat until the other was on her.

"You have insulted me, and gone too far. Are you prepared to suffer the consequences?" Amelia stood, preparing herself for Klara's attack.

Klara rolled her eyes. "You have no knowledge of suffering."

Amelia quickly crossed the room and grabbed Klara by the hair, pulling her around till she had a dagger at her throat. The man began to cry while Olivia went back to brushing her hair.

"You have one hour to leave Genoa," Amelia growled, snapping Klara's wrist as she tried to twist out of her grip. "Or I will show you true suffering."

She tossed Klara into the sobbing man then went back out the window.

Before Klara could say a word Olivia moved to begin gathering their things.

"I will not be treated in such a way!" Klara screamed. Olivia slapped her so hard across the face she stumbled, her cheek stinging.

Olivia mouthed the words 'we go now', ignoring the blubbering man at their feet. She went back to packing up their things while Klara stood and watched.

"You know...," Klara began, and Olivia gestured like she would hit her again. She growled at her, and when Klara's expression remained defiant she grabbed a few things and stormed out.

Klara found Olivia readying her horse, then silently went to do the same. Balcor did not elaborate on their shared fate but Klara knew enough to know it wasn't something to be taken for granted. Olivia briefly acknowledged her with a head nod and the two continued to prepare, Klara forgetting to mention she had left the pretty green eyed man's body under the bed in their room.

An armed escort awaited them as they came out of the stables, Xavier in the lead. The only thing that Klara really saw were the rifles and crossbows they carried.

The group surrounded them as they rode out, Xavier was the only one whose face was visible under the cloak hood. Klara tried not to look at them, tried to bit back her anger. She wondered if Amelia had sent word to her father, if he knew that she was coming.

When they reached the city gates the group stopped. Xavier and the others moved away, only allowing them space to exit.

"It would be wise if you never returned," Xavier said with a crossbow pointed at them. He clearly had orders to kill them if there was any problem.

"After the way I was treated, believe me I will not," Klara snapped. "And this is not the end, I will not allow such disrespect to go unpunished."

Xavier laughed as they rode away, Olivia could not help but wonder when the bullet or arrow would strike their backs.

Klara had been right to wonder if Amelia de Loncrey had been in contact with her father; when they rode out of Genoa the bounty was already set.

Only Klara was not to be returned to her parents but to Lord Westwick of the Danse Macabre, and he would oversee her punishment. That sort of thought did not even penetrate Klara's mind.

She did not even entertain what could happen, only that they were riding for Vienna and perhaps they would not stop again.

"Can you believe that?" Klara said to Olivia after some hours on the road. "Such disrespectful treatment! And even after they knew who I was!"

Olivia kept her eyes focused on the road. She should have left Klara behind the instant she saw Balcor, she should have disappeared like a thief into the night. She should have taken her share of their things and ran, gone to find some quiet peace on her own.

"But that will all change. Balcor showed me the way. I know what I must do and exactly how I must do it," she continued, mumbling *kill them all* under her breath.

Olivia's eyes remained forward, considering what lay ahead, blocking out the sound of Klara's voice.

At the first opportunity she would leave, she wondered if she sprinted ahead for long enough if she could lose Klara now before things got worse.

At full dark, when it seemed like they were riding through a sea of black, Olivia felt something around them. It was creeping around on the edge of her senses, and made the hairs on the back of her neck stand up.

Klara rode closer to her, leaving over and whispering. "I think someone is following us. What should we do? I cannot fight from horseback."

Whatever it was started to get closer, and as it approached there seemed to be several of them.

Olivia pulled up on her horse's reigns and surged forward, Klara close behind her. Whatever it was, it gave chase, and it became clear that they were being actively pursued.

Klara could barely breathe as the rode hard. Whatever it was behind them was like a swarm of bees, a large cloud coming up fast. She kept as close to Olivia as she could manage, she could hear her but not see her clearly. She was having trouble telling the difference between the pounding of horse hooves and the pounding of her heart in her ears. Balcor will come and help them, she kept telling herself. Why would he tell her all those things and let this happen?

Before she could do anything else she was grabbed from behind and pulled from her horse, her screams slicing through the darkness as she flew through the air then fell quickly to the ground.

All she could do was scream.

KATRINE

FINALE

Our final appearance at court was a blessing, for every available hand was needed to pack the household and could not be spent dressing us. Hannah was reduced to giving directions and orders because her arm had not healed. I could see the frustration in her face and it was taking a toll on her.

We spent as much time studying as we could, Gigi was still keeping the book Beatrix had given me to herself and I was growing more and more curious about it every time I saw her reading.

Several days after going to court Morgana was quite tense and easily startled, I knew then that today was the day.

We took tea in the sitting room, Vincenzo joined the three of us at Gigi's insistence. He had recovered well but was still not himself since the attack.

"I must admit I am happy to be leaving," Vincenzo said.

"Have you heard anything about Klara?" I asked him.

Gigi sighed. "Come now, petite, do not trouble yourself so...."

"What about Klara? I thought she was dead," Vincenzo replied.

"Beatrix said otherwise, and I asked Charles to look into it but I think he forgot. Could you?" I asked.

"Of course. But you must know she's just trying to upset you, Katrine,"

Vincenzo said.

"I am sure you are right but I need to know for sure," I replied. A commotion started outside as if someone was arriving in a carriage, Morgana immediately tensed. The servants rushed towards the door to receive the visitor, Hannah's panicked eyes turned to me as she passed by the doorway.

"Bonjour, je suis ici pour voir ma soeur Grisela Delphine," Beatrix's voice cut sharply and I lost my breath for a moment.

One of the servants showed her and Luka into the sitting room, Gigi stopped me from rising as they approached.

"I heard you were returning to Paris. I thought you would have sent word," Beatrix said.

"I assumed it was unnecessary at this stage, considering the circumstances," Gigi replied. "I knew you would appear eventually."

"I believe we have come to an impasse," Beatrix continued. "I cannot allow you to simply walk away. There is too much at stake."

"Don't you think you've done enough? Vous avez essayé de nous tuer, n'est pas. I think it's time to move on."

"If *that*," Beatrix began, gesturing at Morgana, "had not been here I would have succeeded. I almost disposed of the sorcerer."

I went to stand again, my anger rising with my body, but Gigi pulled me down. The knowledge that she had intentionally tried to kill William caused my thoughts to swirl and all I could think was that I really needed to hurt her somehow. The idea that the monster was her had not fully penetrated my thoughts yet.

"Don't you want to know why?" Beatrix asked.

"Non, sans importance," Gigi replied. "Now you have come and said your goodbyes. It is time for us to part ways, perhaps for good."

"And why should I allow you to simply leave? There are things that I need from you that I will get, one way or another. Besides, your protégée is in my debt. I am sorry about your Grandmother, Katrine," Beatrix said.

"You were only delivering on behalf of the Order. Credit will go where credit is due," I snapped.

"One day you will *beg* for my help! And when that day comes I will be so strong you will cower at my feet!" she hollered at me. Gigi rose as Beatrix advanced towards us, pausing mid step and turning her eyes to Morgana. I sensed the others come in and I immediately wanted to run to William. But I could not take my eyes off of Beatrix, whose skin began to move and bubble as if she were being burned.

Luka stood and watched, dumbfounded as to what was happening to his wife.

She began to pull and scratch at her skin which was swelling and bubbling up like she was burning from the inside out. She stared at Morgana, who smiled proudly back at her.

"It's over, Beatrix," Gigi said flatly. Beatrix screamed wildly and dove at her sister, ignoring the fact that her skin was now smoking.

But Gigi seemed to know exactly what she would do and she was ready, tossing Beatrix aside with ease.

The burning began to get worse, flames started to shoot from her skin and she screamed in agony. With one glance from Gigi Morgana stopped, the burning and whatever marks it left disappeared like they had never existed.

Beatrix looked down at her skin. "Well done, Druid."

"It was lovely to meet you, Grisela," Luka said, nervously grabbing his pretend wife and pulling her away. "All of you please have a safe journey back to Paris."

We all stayed silent and remained completely still until we knew for sure they were gone.

"So the bitch tried to kill me on purpose," William finally broke the silence.

"She knew she could not fight you so it was logical to try to kill you if she could. She knew no one could shift fast enough," Gigi said, sitting back down. "I am sorry she tried to use your Grandmother against us, ma petite."

I shrugged, trying to hold back my tears. All I could manage to say was, "I want to go home."

"So do I," Gigi replied softly.

"We shall be ready in two days," Charles said loudly. I had forgotten he had come into the room.

"Are you sure?" I asked him.

"I would not say so if I wasn't," he replied, quickly turning and leaving the room.

Later that night I went down to the basement, past the small rooms until I reached the cell in the back.

"I was hoping you would come," Gabriel said from a dark corner.

"She would have wanted us to be close, to try to behave as a family would," I began. "But I do not trust you. After all that has happened I am not sure how I ever could again."

He sighed, remaining hidden by the darkness. "And I deserve that. I have wronged you without realising I was doing so. There are so many secrets that I don't know where to begin explaining things to you. I guess I thought the world was the same as before but I was so wrong. Everything has changed. I need to find a way to accept it and move on."

"You must adapt or you will not survive," I snapped.

"How did you learn?"

"My circumstances were different. You chose this life, whereas I was ripped into it."

He chuckled. "I suppose you think I am quite mad for wanting this life, for being afraid of death."

"No. My life would have been nothing without these people, and I would have never known my Grandmother. I would not trade what I have for anything."

"You will trust me again, in time," Gabriel called after me as I walked away.

"Perhaps," I replied, not turning back.

Klara

THE RIGHT TIME

Klara screamed as she flew through the air, quickly pulled off the back of her horse as if a rope were tied to her back.

The horse squealed in fear and bolted, Olivia had to hang tightly on her reigns so she wouldn't be thrown off. Klara continued to scream and flail around on the ground but something kept her body pinned; she kicked and struck out hoping she would connect with something, whatever it was that was doing this to her. She could not even think about why Olivia wasn't helping her, she just needed to get free. She would find her once she could stand.

"What do you want?" Klara's hoarse voice cried out. "Leave me alone! I haven't done anything wrong! You can't do this to me! Do you have any idea who I am?"

She heard trampling footsteps, then felt a warm hand grab her arm and start pulling.

"Olivia? Help me! You have to help me!" Klara screamed and the pull got stronger. When it felt like she was getting somewhere Olivia was tossed in the air, her grip quickly flying off Klara's arm.

There were no screams, only her going up and the sickening thud when her body hit the ground.

Klara gagged in horror then began to cry. She was actually relieved to be surrounded by darkness so she could not see what had happened to Olivia.

A dark figure hovered over where she lay, she could only see the outline of where it stood.

"You shall hang when my father hears of this!" Klara yelled in defiance.

The figure made a strange noise, was it a laugh? Then leaned over her and said in a voice that was not quite male or female, "Who do you think sent us, pet?"

Klara did not say another word, did not question it. The figure picked her up but not with its hands, somehow with magic, and carried her along before tossing her into something. As she hit the wood floor it reminded her of when this all began, when Charles sold her to that slave trader and that man put her into a similar wagon.

Only this time she wasn't put in shackles, and the covered wagon was more like a prisoner's box. Something else was thrown in beside her. She did not move or try to see what it was, only stared up at the ceiling and tried to plan her next move.

Katrine

WELL DONE, DRUID

He ran the smooth skin of the underneath of his thumb gently over the top of my thumb as he held tightly on my hand. The movement was oddly comforting, soothing in a way I had never felt from another human being.

He was fully healed now, it had taken longer than expected. I did not know if the intent to kill him had caused a different type of damage, and perhaps I was not told about the extent of his injuries and he was not really better.

All I knew, which was my focus, was that my William was standing here beside me and that we were *finally* going home.

The sun had just gone down and the covered wagons were being loaded. Aseem had carried a thin but alert Victorie up and out from the basement; she smiled proudly at us as she sailed by, her body still bandaged and her tiny feet the only thing visible at they got farther away.

"Will you ride with us, love?" I asked William.

"I hope so, but I am unsure of Charles' and Grisela's seating plans," I replied.

"I have a duty to...."

He gently squeezed my hand. "I understand, il mio amore. Say nothing more."

"I am happy to know that if you are not with me you can watch Vincenzo. He has not been the same since the attack," I said quietly to him.

"She scared us all quite badly, and would have killed us all if things had gone her way," he began. "The others know her and I do not, really. It is hard to accept that she wants us dead and only Grisela knows why and she's not sharing. The connection to Gabriel and the Order of the Dragon is not helping the situation, and I have not even touched on the death of your grandmother. What did the letter say?"

"What letter?"

"The letter Gabriel gave you, the one of the Order claimed to have intercepted. You *have* read the letter, haven't you?"

I looked down at my feet. "I can't. I just can't bare it. Perhaps when we are back in Paris."

He ran his thumb over mine, squeezing my hand as he did so.

"I would be honoured if you would allow me to be with you when you do decide to," he said softly. I smiled up at him, his eyes sparkled while his expression remained stern.

"Thank you," I replied. I stuck my fingers into my sleeve, pushing past the tightly folded piece of paper until I felt the little chain that had warmed so much that it felt like part of my skin. I pulled it out, being careful not to disturb the letter, and my father's cross swung like a pendulum as it fell, my fingers pinched around part of the chain.

I tried to put it on myself but William quickly took over, the warmth of the object seemed to spread through my body when it touched the skin around my neck.

"I have never seen that before. Was it a gift?" he asked as he took my hand in his.

"Yes, from my father," I replied.

I smiled as he rubbed his thumb over mine. " Perhaps that is a story for the ride home."

Anastasia

KEEPING UP APPEARANCES

"There is a village," Saskia told the group while they were gathered around the fire. Transitioning had gone well, but the hunt was not bringing back enough good to sustain them for long.

"We have no coin," Gisli said.

"We do not need coin," Saskia replied.

"We are not thieves," Gisli snapped.

"It's not about thievery, daughter. There are ways we can acquire food. The issue I foresee is lack of human clothing," Iren said. "That we may have to steal. Nudity would attract unwanted attention and wolves would be shot at."

"What do you propose we do?" Anastasia asked.

"We find something to wear, which Danys and Larya are working on as we speak. Then we go in, several of us, and gather some supplies," Saskia answered.

"I want to go," Astrid and Amalie said in unison. Anastasia was about to tell them no, then decided against it. A mother and children may gather some sympathy and people could willingly give.

"So it is decided then," Iren proclaimed. "We will go and gather what we can, later we may try to make a plan about getting coin."

At the entrance to the town they all separated and she and the twins began their walk in together. Anastasia felt strange, it had been so long since she was properly dressed she did not remember how to move. She pushed off her cloak hood and continued forward.

The townspeople paused and stared at her with a strange mix of shock and awe. She tried to ignore them and keep walking but it was hard.

"Why are they looking at us, Anastasia?" Astrid asked.

"I do not know, but let's keep moving," Anastasia replied.

"My lady!" a man called out. "My lady!"

Anastasia kept walking, not realising the man was in fact speaking to her until he tapped her on the shoulder.

"My lady, I did not know you were in town. I would be honoured if you would come to my shop," he began.

"I am sorry, sir, but...," Anastasia began.

"Begging your pardon, Countess Bathory. I apologise if I am disturbing you."

Anastasia's heart jumped into her throat, her voice cracking as she said, "No...no need to apologise. My ward's and I were just coming to collect some food to take back to our waiting carriage. We are going to stay in an old Nadasdy house up the mountain while work is being done."

"How wonderful! I would be honoured to help you load your carriage with supplies..."

"No need. I have servants in the village who will help. Allow me to send my wards to get them and I will come to your shop," Anastasia said.

"Wonderful!" he exclaimed. He started off, and Anastasia bent over to whisper to the girls.

"Go get the others. Tell them they must act as if they are my servants," she whispered.

"Who is Countess Bathory?" Astrid asked.

"I will explain when we are safely back at camp. Now go."

ACKNOWLEDGMENTS

There are a lot of people to thank with this one. It was an absolute labour of love and I hope you love it as much as I do.

Any errors are my own and I take full blame for them.

A double thanks to RM Gilmore and RMGraphX not only for Ikon's amazing cover but Rebirth's – and for being the coolest chick I know. You're awesome. Thanks for everything.

Thank you to my father Lawrence Maurice for the history discussions, for indulging my ramblings, and for being one of my early readers. I appreciate everything you have done to help make this book great. I hope you enjoy it. Any historical errors I take full blame for.

Another big thank you to Sheila Carmichael, my personal cheering section. Thank you for your constant encouragement and kind words. I hope you enjoy this one as much as you enjoyed the first.

Thank you to my husband and partner Michael for not letting me give up and kicking my butt when I need it, and for always finding me some space to write. For stimulating my creativity and not thinking I'm totally weird, and for just being my friend. It's rare to find a partner who is also your best friend, and I'm lucky to have you.

And, as always, I dedicate this book in part to my daughter Khaleesi. Her face reminds me every day why I continue to do everything.

I cannot forget about my Mother, Janet Ravin, who died shortly after the first version of Rebirth was released. It's bittersweet that she's not here to see the second one, but she is always on my mind. Writing about Anastasia helps be feel closer to her and keeps her memory alive for me. May she rest in peace.

CPSIA information can be obtained
at www.ICGtesting.com
Printed in the USA
LVHW030052130519
617576LV00006B/35/P

9 781775 169345